# ∽ THE ∾
# EXECUTIONER'S HEART

A Newbury *and* Hobbes
*Investigation*

Also by George Mann and available from Titan Books

*Encounters of Sherlock Holmes*

## Coming soon

*The Casebook of Newbury & Hobbes* (September 2013)
*Sherlock Holmes: The Will of the Dead* (November 2013)
*The Revenant Express: A Newbury & Hobbes Investigation* (July 2014)
*Further Encounters of Sherlock Holmes* (February 2014)

# ~ THE ~
# EXECUTIONER'S HEART

## GEORGE MANN

TITAN BOOKS

THE EXECUTIONER'S HEART: A NEWBURY & HOBBES INVESTIGATION

Print edition ISBN: 9781781160053
E-book edition ISBN: 9781781166444
Limited edition ISBN: 9781783290123

Published by
Titan Books
A division of Titan Publishing Group Ltd
144 Southwark Street
London
SE1 0UP

First edition: July 2013
10 9 8 7 6 5 4 3 2 1

Visit our website:
www.titanbooks.com

What did you think of this book? We love to hear from our readers. Please email us at: readerfeedback@titanemail.com, or write to us at the above address.

To receive advance information, news, competitions, and exclusive offers online, please sign up for the Titan newsletter on our website: www.titanbooks.com

A CIP catalogue record for this title is available from the British Library.

Printed and bound in Great Britain by CPI Group (UK) Ltd, Croydon, CR0 4YY

FOR LIZ

# CHAPTER 1

### LONDON, MARCH 1903

The ticking was all she could hear.

Like the ominous beating of a hundred mechanised hearts—syncopated, chaotic—it filled the small room, counting away the seconds, measuring her every breath. A carnival of clockwork, a riot of cogs.

She realised she was holding her breath and let it out. She peered further into the dim room from the doorway, clutching the wooden frame. The paintwork was smooth and cold beneath her fingers.

The room was lit only by the flickering light of a gas lamp on a round table in the centre of the space. A warm orange glow seeped from beneath the half-open lamp shutters, casting long shadows that seemed to carouse and dance of their own volition.

The air was thick with a dank, musty odour. She wrinkled her nose in distaste. The room probably hadn't been aired for years, perhaps even decades. Most of the windows had long ago been boarded over or bricked up, hidden away to keep the outside world at bay. Or, she mused, to prevent whoever lived inside from looking out. Clearly, the hotel had fallen on hard times long before the accident had put it out of business.

The décor reflected the fashions of the previous century, an echo of life from fifty or a hundred years earlier. Now the once-elegant sideboard, the gilt-framed mirror, the sumptuous chaise longue, were all covered in a thick layer of powdery dust, which bloomed in little puffs as she crept into the room, particles swirling in the air around her. There was evidence that rodents had nested in the soft furnishings, pulling the downy innards from the cushions and leaving their spoor scattered like seeds across the floorboards. There was a sense of abandonment about the place, as if whoever had once lived here had up and left, leaving everything *in situ* for her to find years later. She could almost believe the place had remained like that, untouched until now, if it hadn't been for the clocks.

All around her the walls were adorned with them. More clocks than she had ever seen, crowding every inch of space, their ivory faces looming down at her from wherever she looked. There were small clocks and large clocks, fine antiques and dirty, broken remnants. Spectacular, gilded creations from the finest workshops of Paris and St. Petersburg, discarded junk from the rubbish tips of London, each of them slowly meting out the seconds like chattering gatekeepers, each in disagreement with the others. To her there was something ominous about them, something wrong.

She crossed to the table in the centre of the room. The sounds of her movements were muffled by the constant, oppressive ticking, which threatened to overwhelm her, making her feel dizzy and unsure of herself. The noise rung in her ears, drowning out everything, even her thoughts. She fought the urge to flee, reaching instead for the gas lamp and flipping up the shutters.

Light erupted from the lamp in a bright halo, flooding the room. Everything became indistinct, hazy, as she waited for her gloom-adjusted eyes to grow accustomed to the light, and at first she had to squint to see. Ghostly shapes and hulking shadows took on new forms now that the darkness was dispelled: a dresser where a lurking presence had been, a chair where previously some nightmarish creature had crouched in wait. The light gave her strength. She absorbed it.

She sensed sudden movement behind her and spun around, but there was only a wide fan of dust drifting in the still air, most likely disturbed by her own frantic movements. Nevertheless, she felt uneasy. Was someone in the room with her? Were they skulking somewhere in the shadows, watching even now?

She hefted the lamp from the table and turned in a slow circle, considering the room. There was evidence that someone had slept there recently: a heap of scarlet cushions on the floorboards in the far left corner, the faint impression of a human body still evident upon them. Beside these lay a number of discarded food wrappers, cast aside and left for the rodents to nose through at their leisure. Whoever it was, they were clearly accustomed to sleeping rough, although how anyone could sleep at all with the constant chattering of the clocks, she did not know.

She was beginning to wish that she hadn't come alone. This was not, she told herself, an admission of weakness, but simply a matter of practicality. If anything happened to her here, no one would come looking. Or rather, they would have no notion of where to find her. She might end up like one of those missing young women reported with alarming regularity in *The Times*, nothing but a brief description and a desperate plea for information, for witnesses, for hope. Or worse, like one of those artefacts announced in the columns of the lost and found, misplaced and much-lamented, but lost forever to the annals of time. She was adamant that this would not be her fate. She should have left word of her intentions and her whereabouts, but she no longer trusted the men she had once confided in. The men she had once considered incorruptible.

Their duplicity had confounded her, had left her with few options of how to proceed. She no longer understood their motivations. There was an irony to be found in that, but she took no comfort from it.

Movement again. This time she was sure it was more than just the hands of the clocks describing their ceaseless, monotonous circles; there was another presence in the room. She twisted around sharply, the gas lamp still clutched in her left hand so that her sudden movement set it rocking wildly back and forth in her grip. One of the shutters snapped closed. Strobing columns of light flickered to and fro as she searched the room, creating stuttering snatches of light and dark, a series of jaunty stills that flashed before her eyes.

Her heart was in her mouth. She glanced nervously from side to side. And then she saw it. A glimpse of something half-expected, frozen for the briefest of moments as the lamp swung around, framing it, capturing it for a second in its shimmering rays.

There was a face in the darkness. It was ghostly white, stark in the orange lamplight, with terrifying black eyes that seemed to bore directly into her. There was accusation in that stare. Envy, even. As if the woman hated her simply for being alive.

The woman's brown hair had been roughly hacked off, short and unkempt, and every inch of her exposed skin had been tattooed with elaborate whorls and eddies, with runic symbols and arcane pictograms. Thin traceries of precious metals had been inlaid in the soft flesh of her cheeks, glinting with reflected light.

One moment the face was there, the next it had gone, swallowed by the gloom as the lamp continued its pendulous motion, swinging back and forth, back and forth.

She braced herself, fighting panic, and raised the lamp in the vague hope that she might catch another glimpse of her quarry. She had come here in search of answers, but instead she had happened upon this murderess, the woman they had hunted through the mist-shrouded alleyways of London, from crime scene to exhibition hall, from the Revenant-infested slums to the splendour of Buckingham Palace itself. But now, somehow, she felt like she was the prey. It was as if their roles had been reversed, as if by coming here to this half-ruined hotel with its ticking, clockwork heart, she had altered the relationship between hunter and hunted.

She felt the ghost of movement to her left, of disturbed air currents brushing past her cheek. She turned, swinging the lantern around, but there was nothing to see, only darkness and clocks. The woman was toying with her.

A shiver passed unbidden down her spine. She felt for the grip of the pistol tucked in her belt. Her fingers closed around it and she tugged it free. The wooden butt was smooth and worn, the metal cold against her palm. She hated the thing, hated that she'd used it to kill people, harnessed its violence to snuff lives out of existence. No matter that she had done so to protect herself and others; it was still an odious tool for an odious job, a constant reminder of the terrible things she had done. Was she really any better than the woman who was lurking in the darkness? Did the fact that she had acted in pursuit of a just cause make any difference whatsoever?

She heard the scuff of a boot against the dusty floorboards behind her and knew it was time. She would bring an end to this now. She raised the pistol and swung around, launching the lamp in the direction of the sound, then snapping out two brisk shots. The lamp clattered noisily against the wall, missing its target and dislodging a cluster of timepieces, which skittered across the floorboards in a chaotic jumble. The light guttered and blinked out, shrouding the room in a heavy cloak of darkness.

She clutched the pistol, her hand trembling. Had she hit her mark? She didn't think so. She couldn't hear anything other than the strangely symphonic chattering of the clocks and the thumping of her own heartbeat, pounding relentlessly in her ears.

She twisted from side to side, drawing the nose of the pistol through the musty air as if it could somehow cleave a path through the darkness or divine the location of her adversary.

For a moment she did nothing, standing alert and still, waiting to see if the woman would make a move. There was nothing else she *could* do. She'd lost all sense of her bearings in the immaculate darkness. She had no idea of where the doorway might be, or which direction she was facing.

She started as she felt something touch her cheek: the cool, almost gentle caress of a metal blade. Involuntarily her arm came up in defence, knocking the other woman's hand aside. She aimed a kick in the same direction, hoping to take the woman's legs out from beneath her, but her enemy was still toying with her and had already danced off, melting away into the darkness.

She grunted in frustration. She had almost overbalanced with the momentum of her kick, and had to throw her arms out wide to stop herself from falling.

She righted herself a moment later, feeling a strange tightness in her chest. Was she having trouble breathing? It was as if she suddenly had a heavy weight bearing down on her, preventing her from drawing breath.

She gasped for air ineffectually and felt panic beginning to well up inside her. Her left hand went to her chest, exploring, as if drawn there, and she realised with dawning horror that something was protruding from it, right above her heart. With realisation came pain, a sharp, excruciating pain the like of which she had never experienced before. Her head swam, and she thought she was going to swoon. Her world began to close in around her. All she could think about was the blossoming pain and the long metal blade buried deep in her rib cage.

She screamed, a deep, guttural scream of horror and frustration and shock. She screamed so loudly that her throat felt raw and hot and bloody, so loudly that it drowned out even the noise of the clocks and the pain in her chest and the pounding in her head.

She toppled, falling backwards into the darkness, barely aware of the ground coming up to meet her.

There was no sign of the woman, but she imagined those black eyes watching her, boring into her, standing over her.

"Veronica?"

Veronica Hobbes heard her name being called, but the frantic voice sounded distant, and the pain in her chest had bloomed in intensity until it was all she could see; a bright, white light of pain, blotting out everything else.

"Veronica?"

Somehow, Newbury had found her. Somehow, remarkably, he had known she was there. But her last thought before the white light swallowed her was that he was far too late.

Veronica was already dead.

# CHAPTER 2

## LONDON, FEBRUARY 1903

London had always been a place of death. Sir Charles Bainbridge, Chief Inspector of Scotland Yard, mulled this over as he considered his lot in life at six in the morning on a wet, dreary Wednesday.

Ever since the city was birthed on the banks of the Thames, since the Roman interlopers had destroyed the primitive settlements of the early Britons and founded the city proper, its streets had run red with blood. Oppression, suppression, festering rebellion, and bloodshed—each of them was key to understanding London's history. And, some might say, its present, too.

Bainbridge wondered if there was something to the notion that it was the place itself that was rotten, haunted by the spirits of all those millions who had died within its boundaries. Did those spirits somehow exert their influence on the psyche of the modern populace? Was it this that drove people to commit such dreadful acts?

Newbury probably thought so. Bainbridge could imagine the argument now: both of them flushed with brandy, Newbury leaning across the table at his White Friar's club, passionately gesticulating as he outlined his case. "Of course,

Charles! Can't you see it? There's no doubt in my mind that the landscape plays a fundamental role in the development of a killer's mindset. And, in turn, that the history of that place also has a role to play. Spirits or not, the grisly biography of this city has a bearing on how its present populace behaves."

Bainbridge, of course, would argue in favour of self-determinism, that people had a choice to behave however they wished to, but that wouldn't wash with his friend. Newbury saw the world in ways that Bainbridge never could. It was this, Bainbridge believed, that gave Newbury his edge, the remarkable insight that had seen them both through so many scrapes. Bainbridge believed in absolutes—good and evil, right and wrong—but Newbury took a different, more complex view. He often berated the chief inspector for viewing the world in such simplistic terms, in plain black and white, and slowly, inch by painful inch, he was teaching Bainbridge to see in shades of grey.

Bainbridge grinned at the thought of his old friend. There hadn't been many arguments in the White Friar's of late, nor many other opportunities to spend time in each other's company. Bainbridge had been busy—far *too* busy—and, if he was truthful, he'd been avoiding Newbury in recent weeks. It was cowardly to keep away, but it pained him to see his friend so in thrall to the dreadful weed to which he had pledged his allegiance.

The wastrel was intent on delving ever deeper into his addiction, despite assurances to the contrary. No amount of stiff conversation on the matter could dissuade him from his chosen path. As a consequence, he appeared to be growing weaker day by day: paler, drawn, his eyes bruised and sunken. When he wasn't in the city engaged on a case, he spent all of his time locked away in his rooms, brooding.

Whether it marked him out as a coward or not, Bainbridge simply wasn't prepared to watch while his friend slowly frittered away his life. And now even Scarbright—the valet Bainbridge had installed at Newbury's Chelsea home to keep a watchful eye on him—had stopped reporting back.

Bainbridge only wished there was something more he could do, some way he could begin to understand the allure of the drug, the grip it exerted on his friend. Perhaps Newbury, too, was under the sway of malign spirits?

Bainbridge sighed. No, that would be too simple. And nothing was ever simple where Newbury was concerned.

Bainbridge glanced cursorily around the drawing room. Whoever lived here—or, rather, *had* lived here—had ostentatious tastes; the decor was of classical design, all white marble and gilded plasterwork. The walls were duck-egg blue; the ceiling decorated with a large, elaborate rosette over a gaudy crystal chandelier. Ranks of portraits, showing gloomy-looking fellows in frilly shirts and plate armour, lined the walls.

Bainbridge thought it was all terribly gauche and embarrassing, as if the owner was trying desperately to cling to some former aristocratic heritage, a proud dream now long forgotten by the rest of the world. He supposed there were plenty of people who had found themselves in that position in recent years; the former scions of society, now fallen on hard times and replaced by the wash of self-made industrialists and opportunists who had identified their niche in the changing, modern Empire.

So much for the frilly shirts and the glory days of old.

Bainbridge laughed at himself. He was grumpy at having to haul himself from his bed at so unsociable an hour. This, of course, was nothing new to such a seasoned man of the Yard, but he was presently nursing a thick head, the result of a late night spent drinking port and conversing with a government man, Professor Archibald Angelchrist. He and Angelchrist had been meeting regularly over the last six months, ever since the beginning of Bainbridge's association with the Secret Service. Angelchrist worked as an advisor to the government in some capacity, chiefly pertaining, Bainbridge had gathered, to matters of a scientific bent. He was a good man, but—as Bainbridge had discovered, to his detriment—Angelchrist liked his liquor. He hoped, perhaps a little unkindly, that Angelchrist was currently suffering as much as he was, but then he remembered the time and realised the other man would most likely still be tucked up snugly in his bed. Just as, if there was any justice left in the world, Bainbridge himself would have been.

He stood for a moment longer, leaning heavily on his cane and staring blankly into the cold grate of the fire. He was growing impatient. Had the constable failed to inform Foulkes that he was here?

He was just about to set out in search of the man, when he heard the sound of approaching footsteps, and turned to see Foulkes striding briskly across the room towards him. He was wearing a harried expression and looked deathly tired. Well, that made two of them, then.

"Sorry to keep you waiting, sir. I was taking steps to secure the scene, as per your instructions. Nothing has been moved." Foulkes tugged at his dark, bushy beard and stared at Bainbridge expectantly.

Bainbridge had always liked Foulkes. He spoke his mind and wasn't afraid of the consequences. There were few men like that in the force these days, and although his frankness had probably stifled his progress through the ranks in some ways, it made him a better policeman, and far more useful to Bainbridge than the many yes men who typically plagued his days.

"Morning, Foulkes," he said, wearily. He already knew what to expect, but he raised a questioning eyebrow anyway. "Well?" Foulkes nodded. "It's exactly the same, sir. Same as all the others." He pulled a disconcerted face and lowered his voice, as if concerned that someone might overhear his familiarity with the chief inspector. "It's a ruddy great mess in there. There's blood everywhere."

Bainbridge tried to keep his grimace to himself. "They took it again?"

"Yes. It's nowhere to be found. Ripped the chest right ope and tore it out, just like the others. It's bloody disgusting."

"Quite literally," said Bainbridge, drily. "Alright, show me the way."

"She's in the library," said Foulkes, gesturing back the way he had come. "Made a terrible mess of the books."

Bainbridge wasn't sure whether Foulkes was being sarcastic or not, but he let it wash over him regardless. Foulkes was most likely as aggrieved as he was at being dragged from his bed into the cold and dark. And, to add insult to injury, both of them knew there was a long day full of questions ahead.

Resignedly, Bainbridge trudged after Foulkes, deeper into the big house, on towards the grim scene that awaited them in the dusty stacks of the library.


The scene itself was just as Foulkes had described. Worse, in fact. It was as if Bainbridge had suddenly found himself in an abattoir rather than a library. There were spatters of blood *everywhere*, as if the killer had made it their sole purpose to ensure that no surface remained untouched by the crimson rain they had unleashed. The stench was foul, too; cloying and thick, it made the air seem humid, metallic, and uncomfortable to breathe. Bainbridge felt his stomach turn and fought the urge to vomit.

If anything, the scene here was even more atrocious than the previous two. It was somehow more flamboyant, more grotesque, as if the killer was showing off. There was certainly something theatrical in the manner in which the body was positioned behind the desk.

Bainbridge inched into the room, taking care to avoid the puddles of blood on the paisley carpet—more because he didn't wish to get his shoes dirty than because he was concerned with preserving the murder scene. It was already obvious what had happened here, and if the prior murders were anything to go by, no amount of tiptoeing around the spilled blood was going to help shed any light.

The room was exactly how Bainbridge imagined a library in a posh London town house should look. Row after row of towering oak bookcases were crammed into every available space, their innards stuffed with serried ranks of musty, leather-bound tomes. A large globe sat in its mount in one corner, a stag's head glared down at him balefully with its beady glass eyes, and a large, antique writing desk with a burgundy leather surface dominated the centre of the room. Beside it, a captain's chair had been overturned and sheaves of paper spilled across the floor in a stark white avalanche, covered with scratchy black script, as if the pages were home to an army of scurrying ants.

So, the dead woman had put up a fight. That was interesting. That was different.

From the doorway, Bainbridge could see nothing of the dead woman save for one of her hands, jutting out from behind the desk as if beckoning for help that had never arrived. The skin was pale, papery and wizened, the hand of someone who had lived, who had seen life. Bainbridge could see little flecks of blood upon the fingers, like ladybirds on a clutch of white lilies.

He rounded the desk, wrinkling his nose at the foul smell. The woman lay sprawled upon the carpet in a pose that might have been comical if it hadn't been for the expression of sheer terror that contorted her face, and the fact that her rib cage had been cracked and splayed open to reveal her internal organs. She was still wearing her skirt, stockings, and shoes, as well as most of her jewellery, but her top half had been stripped naked, exposing her milky-white breasts and her ample belly.

The killer had made an incision at the base of her throat, cutting deeply into bone, gristle, and cartilage, as well as severing a line of pearls, the constituents of which now lay scattered around the body like miniature planets in orbit around a floundering giant. Many of them now nestled in congealing puddles of blood, dulled and strangely obscene amongst the carnage.

The incision continued down to the belly, where it terminated abruptly above the navel. The rib cage had been pulled open like two halves of a cantilever bridge, or two hands of splayed, skeletal fingers clutching unsuccessfully for one another. This, too, was just like the others, and Bainbridge was still no clearer about what kind of cutting device had been used to hack through the bone.

Around the corpse, dark, glistening blood described two distinct leaf shapes, like crimson wings beneath the woman's out-flung arms. The nearest bookcase had taken the brunt of the arterial spray, and even now some of the spines were still dripping ponderously, their titles obscured, their authors rendered anonymous by the bloodshed.

The woman had been in her late fifties, Bainbridge judged, although he'd have to take steps to confirm that in the coming hours. She looked in good health—putting aside the gaping rent in her chest for a moment—and she had a full, stocky figure, suggesting she was well accustomed to fine dining. It was clear from the property that the woman's family had once been well-to-do: the lavish interior decor, the ancient portraiture, the well-appointed library were all indicators that the family had once rubbed shoulders with the upper classes. There were signs, however, that the woman had recently fallen on harder times. There were no servants, for a start, and anything more than a cursory glance at the furnishings betrayed the fact that they were mostly nothing but threadbare relics of a more affluent time.

Leaning heavily on his cane, Bainbridge dropped to his haunches to examine the body more closely. He could sense Foulkes standing over his shoulder, and for the first time since entering the room he registered the fact there were two uniformed men standing in the corner, trying their best not to look at the corpse. He supposed he could understand that—they were young and this was probably one of the worst things they had ever had the misfortune to see. But they had a job to do, and they needed to get used to it. It wouldn't be the last violent death they'd encounter during the course of their careers, and Bainbridge would be doing them no favour by going easy on them now. They would stay with the body until it was safely removed to the morgue.

"She must have put up quite a fight," he said a moment later, taking the woman's right hand and turning it over to expose her wrist. There were multiple gashes crisscrossing the soft flesh on the underside of her forearm, where she'd clearly raised it to protect her face. "The killer must have come at her with a long-bladed knife. I'd wager he didn't expect her to defend herself so vehemently."

"Not that it did her much good in the long run," replied Foulkes, levelly.

Bainbridge twisted around and glowered at the inspector. "Show a little respect, man."

Foulkes looked momentarily taken aback. Then he nodded, his expression suddenly serious. "I mean to say that the killer was obviously relentless, despite the fact that the woman put up a tremendous struggle."

Bainbridge sighed. He was taking out his frustration on the other man, and Foulkes didn't deserve that. Three unsolved deaths in as many days, however, were starting to take their toll on Bainbridge. Three apparently linked deaths, at that, suggesting there were probably more to come. They'd all been virtually the same: each of the victims had been found in their own homes, their chests cracked open and their hearts removed. The organs themselves were nowhere to be seen, spirited away from the scenes, Bainbridge assumed, by the killer himself. The only differences this time were the fact that the victim was a woman, and that she'd clearly tried to defend herself against her assailant. But once again, there was no obvious motive, no clear links between the victims, and thus—much to Bainbridge's chagrin—no leads.

"Was she married?" he asked, spotting the gold band on the woman's ring finger and frowning. Nothing he'd seen since entering the house suggested a man might have shared her home.

"No. She was a widow. She lived alone. Had done so for the last fifteen years."

Bainbridge nodded. That made sense. She still wore the ring for sentimental reasons. "A housekeeper?" He glanced up at Foulkes, who shook his head dolefully.

"Just a maid who came in once a day to see to the washing and cleaning. Either she was fiercely independent, or she'd run into financial difficulties."

Well, at least that fit with what Bainbridge had already surmised, although he cursed himself for not even considering that the dead woman might simply have been deeply private and independent. It wasn't impossible, especially in this age. After all, Bainbridge had spent a great deal of time in the company of Miss Veronica Hobbes, who, to his mind, was the epitome of a modern, independent woman. He should have at least considered the option before jumping to conclusions. Shades of grey.

Nevertheless, there was hardly a comparison to be made

here. The victim in this instance was older, a widow, and about as far from Veronica Hobbes as one could imagine.

Bainbridge sighed. "The maid. Has she turned up for work yet this morning?"

Foulkes nodded. "She was the one who discovered the body. Her routine was to arrive early and take care of her errands before the victim rose for the day. She'd then move on to another household, where she'd carry out similar chores before lunch."

Bainbridge nodded. "Where is she now?"

"She's rather shaken, as you might imagine. She's in the kitchen with Cartwright. There's very little she can add. The entrance and exit point of the killer is obvious from the broken window at the back, and there's no reason to suspect she played any role in her mistress's death."

"Good work, Foulkes," said Bainbridge, and he meant it. Foulkes had saved him a great deal of legwork, making sure all the basics were taken care of before Bainbridge had even arrived. He grunted as he pulled himself upright again. He turned away from the corpse to face the inspector. "There's one thing you haven't me told me, though."

Foulkes looked perplexed. "What's that, sir?"

"Her name," said Bainbridge, indicating the body with a wave of his cane.

"Ah, yes. Right. Elizabeth Peterson, sir. She has one living relative, a son, who's currently somewhere over the Atlantic Ocean on an airship bound for New York. We've sent word, so there should be a message awaiting him when he arrives there in a few days."

Bainbridge nodded. Poor bastard. That was no way to find out about his mother's death, especially in circumstances such as these.

"There's one thing that's been troubling me, sir," continued Foulkes.

"Only one?" replied Bainbridge, and realised he was now being facetious. "I'm sorry, Foulkes. What is it?"

"The missing hearts, sir. There has to be some significance that we're not seeing. Why does the killer take their hearts? He goes to a great deal of trouble to crack the victims' chests like that. I just can't work out what it's all in aid of. I hesitate to say it… but do you think there might be some sort of ritualistic element to it?"

Bainbridge felt the corners of his lips twitch into a thin smile. Foulkes had been paying attention. "I think you're right about the occult significance, Foulkes. The damn trouble is in working out what it might be."

"And doing it before they strike again," added Foulkes.

"Quite."

"So…?"

"You never were very good at subtlety, Foulkes," said Bainbridge, but there was an edge of levity in his voice.

"So you're going to ask for his help?"

Bainbridge sighed. "Yes. I'm going to send for Newbury. If anyone can shed any light on the matter, he can. And, let's face it: we're not getting very far on our own, are we?"

Foulkes smiled for the first time that day, but he didn't say another word as the two men filed out of the blood-spattered library, leaving the young bobbies to guard the corpse until dawn.

# CHAPTER 3

❦

Sir Maurice Newbury lounged on the sofa like a listless cat, warming himself before the fire.

A smouldering cigarette dripped from his thin, pink lips, smoke twisting in lazy curlicues from its glowing tip. His expensive black suit was rumpled and creased, his shirt open at the collar, the cravat long since discarded. He was unshaven, and his flesh had taken on a deathly pallor, as if it hadn't seen the sun in many days. His eyelids were closed and his breathing was shallow.

The pungent aroma of opium was heavy in the air, mingling with the tobacco smoke to form a thick, sweet fog that clung to the corners of the room as if Newbury's Chelsea home was now a microcosm of the city, choking amidst the tendrils of yet another pea-souper.

The fire spat and crackled noisily in the grate. The only other sounds in the small room were the gentle rasp of Newbury's breath and the clacking of his clockwork owl as it hopped nervously from foot to foot on its wooden perch by the window.

Books lay scattered about him: heaped on the floor, piled on the coffee table, balanced precariously on the arms of the green leather couch. Their gilded spines shone in the soft light of the gas lamps, resplendent with titles such as *A Key to Physic and the Occult Sciences and The Cosmology of the Spirit.* Newbury had surrounded himself with them as if they offered him sustenance, as if the mere presence of the leaning piles was enough to grant him strength, comfort. In some ways, they did.

Newbury's eyes flickered open. His lids felt heavy and tired. He unfurled slowly, stretching his weary limbs. He had no idea what time of day it was. The heavy drapes were closed, shielding him from the sunlight, from all the cares and distractions of the outside world. In this haven, he was cocooned against the chaotic morass of humanity that swarmed through the rain-lashed streets of London. More so, he was distanced from their many designs and desires, their concerns and their problems, their petty squabbles and their crimes. In here, the outside world could not intrude, not unless he wished it to.

Newbury took a long, luxurious draw from his tainted cigarette, allowing the smoke to plume playfully from his nostrils. He felt ash dribble over his chin and brushed it away cursorily with the back of his hand.

He hadn't left the house in days. He'd been holed up in the drawing room, buried in his books and the crimson depths of an opium dream. Scarbright had entered only to bring him meals, most of which had remained untouched. It was to the man's credit that he'd continued to deliver the plates of steaming food, simply removing the uneaten remnants of the previous meal without judgement or comment. If the valet was reporting back to Bainbridge as he was supposed to, he'd clearly not said enough to concern the chief inspector, as Newbury had received no calls or summons from his friend.

That, in itself, was rather refreshing. As much as Newbury cared for his old friend, he could do without having his ear bent again about his "lackadaisical behaviour." Bainbridge was in possession of only half of the facts. He couldn't understand Newbury's use of the Chinese weed because he didn't—couldn't—know of Newbury's reasons. At least, not yet. Not until the situation with Veronica was fully resolved. Not until he had divined what terrors lay in the darkness, waiting.

Whatever the case, Newbury couldn't deny that he was badly in need of a bath and a shave. He would see to them both just as soon as he could muster the energy.

His days had passed like this for some months, ever since the storming of the Grayling Institute and the supposed death of Veronica's sister, Amelia Hobbes, ever since he had sworn to discover a means by which to heal the miraculously clairvoyant young woman, to halt her spiralling descent towards insanity and death. His time since then had been absorbed in ritual and the yellowing pages of ancient books, the hours drifting by in a warm, opium-inspired fugue.

There had, of course, been a number of cases over the course of the last six months that had vied for his attention. Some he had been forced to take on at the behest of the Queen, others simply because Bainbridge had needed his help. He'd been able to devote only a small amount of his time and energy to such matters, however, engaged as he was in his search for Amelia's cure, as well as his own ongoing investigation: tracking the mysterious Lady Arkwell across London.

Arkwell was—apparently—a foreign agent, but Newbury was as yet unable to ascertain her nationality, despite the fact that he had met her in person at least half a dozen times, battled with her on three of those occasions, and formed a temporary alliance with her on another. Nevertheless, Lady Arkwell had continued to outwit him at every stage. It was at once infuriating and exhilarating, and he had vowed to bring the matter to a head.

For now, though, Newbury was content to lounge on his sofa, smoke his opium-tainted cigarettes, and contemplate the universe. And he had to admit that he was in no real hurry to rid himself of such a worthy adversary. He was sure she felt the same, and she would make the next move in their little game when she deemed the time to be right. Newbury, for his part, would bide his time.

There was a firm rap on the drawing room door. Newbury sighed. Scarbright. Time for another meal, no doubt. He glanced at the uneaten remains of his luncheon—a thick beef broth, now cold and congealing on the sideboard—and felt a sharp twinge of guilt. It did seem wrong to let so much food go to waste, particularly as Scarbright was such a superb culinary craftsman. He would make an effort, he decided, to consume at least some of Scarbright's dinner, despite the fact that his appetite was practically non-existent.

"Come," said Newbury, his voice a low drawl.

The door creaked open, and he heard Scarbright's footsteps crossing the room towards him. Newbury felt more than saw the shadow of the valet as it fell upon him.

Scarbright cleared his throat pointedly, waiting for Newbury to acknowledge his presence.

Newbury turned slowly to peer up at the valet through half-open lids. The man looked a little peaky, as if he was feeling unwell or had just had a rather unpleasant surprise. He was not carrying a dinner tray.

Newbury raised one eyebrow and removed the stub of the cigarette from between his lips. "What is it, Scarbright?"

Scarbright took a deep breath before speaking. When he did, his tone was calm and measured, entirely at odds with his suspiciously nervous manner. "You have a visitor, sir."

Newbury frowned. "If it's Charles, tell him to go away." He paused for a moment, considering. "In fact, tell him I'll see him at the White Friar's this evening."

"It's not Sir Charles, sir. It's… well…"

"It's alright, Scarbright. I'll rouse the scoundrel myself!"

The voice was deep, commanding, and terrifyingly familiar.

Newbury struggled to pull himself upright on the sofa. The sound of the man's boots clacking on the floorboards was like an ominous drum roll as he strode purposefully into the room.

"Get up, you damn layabout!" Newbury caught only the briefest glance of Scarbright's apologetic face before the newcomer snapped out another command and sent the valet scuttling away. "Scarbright, open a window. I can barely stand this damnable smoke."

Newbury, head swimming, staggered to his feet and turned to regard his visitor. He groaned inwardly as his fears were confirmed: standing there at the arm of the sofa, resplendent in a smart black suit, was Albert Edward of Saxe-Coburg and Gotha, the Prince of Wales.

The Prince had a stately aspect, and he carried himself with enormous confidence and poise. His balding pate gleamed in the low light and his grey beard and moustache were neatly trimmed. He was watching Newbury from beneath hooded eyes, his disapproving expression so similar to that of his mother—and Newbury's employer, Queen Victoria, herself—that Newbury couldn't help but shudder under its glare.

For a moment the two men stared at one another, neither of them speaking. Finally, Newbury found his voice. "Good… afternoon, your Royal Highness," he said, hoping desperately that he'd at least managed to guess the time of day correctly. "You are most welcome. Although I fear you have me at a disadvantage."

"Quite," said the Prince, glancing around at the state of the drawing room.

Newbury winced, both at the sharpness of the Prince's rebuke and the sudden intensity of the light as Scarbright pulled back the drapes, allowing sunlight to flood in through the tall windows. Disturbed puddles of stale cigarette ash swirled in the afternoon sun, dancing amongst the dust motes.

Newbury was beginning to wish that he'd paid more attention to the Queen's summonses, which had been delivered to his door with increasing frequency in the preceding days, and were currently forming a neat little pile on the occasional table. Perhaps Victoria had sent her son to chase him out of his rooms. Surely not? Surely there was more important business with which the Prince of Wales might concern himself?

Newbury glanced down at his crumpled suit, with its oily streaks of smeared ash on the lapels and innumerable stains from where he'd carelessly sloshed absinthe and red wine. It was not the most salubrious of impressions to make upon a future monarch.

"If your Royal Highness would like to take a seat..." Newbury paused as he realised there probably weren't any seats in the room that weren't piled high with occult grimoires, old newspapers, or full specimen jars, then decided that the best thing in the circumstances was to carry on regardless, "...I might just excuse myself for a moment." He began to edge around the sofa towards the door, hoping he might stall things for a few minutes so that he could at least slip away and change while Scarbright saw to the immediate mess.

"Sit down, Newbury, and stop that infernal flapping. Don't you think I knew what I was letting myself in for, coming here? You are notorious throughout the palace for your fondness for that dreadful weed, and no one has seen you for days. I half expected to hear word that poor Bainbridge had once again been forced to haul your sorry carcass out of an opium den in the East End. It's something of a relief to find you here at all."

Newbury swallowed, but his mouth was dry. There was very little he could offer in response to the Prince's words. After all, he had rather been caught red-handed.

Scarbright busied himself, freeing up two Chesterfields close to the fire by unceremoniously tossing heaps of Newbury's precious books onto the floor in one corner. Both men watched him until he straightened his back, approached them, and—with some dignity, given the circumstances—bade them to their seats.

Newbury watched as the Prince lowered himself into one of the armchairs, filling it utterly with both his physical bulk and his voluminous presence. Scarbright took the Prince's walking cane and hat, then swiftly withdrew with promises of tea.

Newbury eyed the Prince for a moment, attempting to gather himself. His head was still swimming with the effects of the opium he'd consumed, and for a moment he wondered if he were actually hallucinating—if it wasn't simply his mind playing tricks on him, fabricating the encounter as a product of his guilt or fears or anxieties. But then the Prince turned and looked up at him, and Newbury knew the situation was all too real. He swallowed, attempting to relieve his dry mouth. He'd just have to carry on as best he could.

Newbury smiled genially, crossed to the Chesterfield opposite the Prince, and sat down. He was intrigued to discover the reason for the unusual—or, rather, positively unheard of—visitation.

"A relief, your Royal Highness?" he said, his voice low and respectful.

"What?"

"You said, your Royal Highness, that it was something of a relief to find me at home. I take it, therefore, that I am able to assist you in some way?"

The Prince narrowed his eyes for a moment before his face creased into a broad smile. "It's good to see the Newbury I recognise is still in there, somewhere. Judging by the state of you, man, I had cause to doubt it."

"I can only apologise. You find me engaged in more of my ongoing… studies."

The Prince harrumphed at this and fixed Newbury with a

knowing stare. "Occult science and paranormal philosophy. Hallucinogens and absinthe. Ritual and corruption." He leaned back in his chair. "You understand, Newbury, that such things are tolerated only because you are able to deliver the desired results?"

Newbury nodded, but didn't say anything in response. Was this the reason for the Prince's visit? To warn him, to admonish him for his pursuits? It wouldn't surprise him to discover it was. He knew the Queen found his esoteric studies extremely distasteful, but also essential to the well-being and protection of the Empire. She reasoned that she needed to maintain an expert in the field, someone who could understand and combat any threats of an occult nature that may arise. But she also feared the lure of it would prove too much, and that Newbury would be absorbed by the darkness. Recently, he'd begun to wonder if she was right.

"Anyway," the Prince continued, "I didn't come here to discuss your peculiar habits, Newbury. I came because I require your help, if you'll give it."

"I am at your disposal, your Royal Highness."

"Very good. As I hope you are aware, Newbury, I have always had great faith in your abilities, despite your... unusual methods." The Prince narrowed his eyes as he delivered this last, and Newbury couldn't help but cringe. "Ever since that affair with Lord Huntington in Cambridgeshire, during which you did me a great service."

"I fear it was not quite the resolution to the matter that you'd wished for, your Royal Highness."

"Nevertheless, you did what was necessary. What was needed. One can ask for no more." The Prince leaned forward in his chair, his eyes searching Newbury's face. "Would you do it again, Newbury? Whatever was necessary?"

Newbury was momentarily taken aback by the Prince's sudden intensity. "I..." he stammered. "Yes, of course.

Without hesitation." Increasingly, this was becoming Newbury's mantra: that he would do whatever was necessary, whatever he deemed to be *right*, irrespective of the Queen's directives. The Crown, he had discovered, was not beyond egoism, self-absorption, and corruption, just like anyone else. As a consequence, he had learned to apply his own moral standards, to make his own decisions.

That said, Newbury had nothing but the utmost respect for the Prince of Wales. "I take it, then, that there is something I might assist you with, Your Royal Highness?"

The Prince nodded approvingly and leaned back in his chair. His eyes hadn't strayed from Newbury's expectant face. "I believe I can trust you, Newbury. God knows, I need to trust someone…" He trailed off at the sound of Scarbright rapping loudly on the door, before the valet bustled through with a silver tea tray in his arms and an apologetic expression written on his face. He took measured steps as he crossed the room, careful not to slosh the hot water or rattle the saucers. With a brief, panicked glance at Newbury, he set the tray down on the low table between the two men, bowed to the Prince, and got out of the room as swiftly as his legs would carry him.

The Prince smiled indulgently at Newbury. "There are agents abroad in London, Newbury. Foreign agents. The great houses of Europe are intent on bringing the British Empire to her knees. They circle like vultures, waiting impatiently for the Queen to die. They bicker and snipe at one another, pledging their undying support to my mother, even as they plot to pick over her remains. They would see her dead and buried, see the Empire broken up and their own pockets lined with the fruit of our labours. What is more, they have allies. Even here in London—in the Houses of Parliament, no less— our enemies abound."

Newbury frowned. Was it really that bad? Had the dissent spread that far?

"I can see from your expression, Newbury, that you doubt the veracity of my words, that you believe me to be exaggerating. But allow me to assure you, I speak the truth. Even now, the enemies of Britain are at work, sowing seeds of dissent, tirelessly endeavouring to destroy the very fabric of our nation."

Newbury waited until he was sure the Prince had finished. His words of warning hung in the air between them, almost tangible. "Do you anticipate war?"

The Prince smiled sadly. "I fear that I do. My nephew, the Kaiser, is inquisitive and impatient. He is hungry for power, and unsatisfied with what he already has. His greed will bring war to these shores before long, Newbury. Mark my words."

War? In the streets of London? The notion was barely conceivable, and yet here was the Prince of Wales himself, sitting in Newbury's drawing room, delivering an impassioned warning of what was to come.

"So... how may I be of assistance, your Royal Highness? I fear I know very little of war."

The Prince turned, staring at the impish yellow flames that flickered and danced amongst the coals in the grate. "I fear my mother is unwell. Too unwell to continue to rule as she has. Her decisions are... compromised. While she sits in state at the heart of the Empire, unseen by her people, her enemies scheme. I fear if something is not done, her legacy will be eroded. Slowly, the Empire will retract, become inwardly focused, until we can no longer sustain our boundaries. And then the vultures will come, and we will not be strong enough to fend them off."

"Surely, your Royal Highness cannot be considering a pre-emptive strike against the Kaiser?"

"I've considered it, Newbury," he said, gravely. "To instigate a full blown conflict, however, would seem somewhat premature. No, I'm talking about making a stand. About positive action. The enemies of Britain cannot be allowed to consider us weak.

We might divert a war by demonstrating to those nations that their subterfuge and duplicity is known to us, and that it will not be tolerated. Their agents must be found and ejected from London. That would send a clear and definite message."

Newbury nodded slowly as he considered the Prince's words. "And what of the Queen?" he asked, his voice low.

The Prince gave him a hard stare in response. "The Queen has a great deal to worry her already, Newbury, without adding this to her burden. We should act on her behalf, for the benefit of the Empire."

Newbury's head was swimming. He wanted more than anything to return to the warm embrace of his sofa and his opium fugue, to escape this conversation of war, spies, and subterfuge. But he could hardly tell the Prince of Wales to leave him in peace. "And how may I be of assistance in this matter, your Royal Highness?" he said, trying to keep the reluctance out of his voice.

"For now, Newbury, by keeping your eyes and ears open. Seek out those who may not have the Empire's best interests at heart. Help to identify the enemies in our midst. Nothing more." He glanced down at the tea tray as if considering whether he wanted to consume anything on it, but apparently decided not to. "Although I'd urge you very strongly to watch your back," he added.

Newbury suppressed a frown. What was the Prince getting at? A witch hunt? With Newbury as Witchfinder General? And that last comment seemed purposefully loaded. Was Newbury himself somehow at risk? "Because of the foreign agents?" he asked.

The Prince left the question hanging, unanswered, but Newbury could read the response in the man's face. *Because of my mother*, the look in his eyes seemed to suggest. *Because of the Queen*.

A shudder passed unbidden through Newbury's body. It

seemed Albert Edward was aware of his mother's scheming tendencies. The thought left a sour taste in Newbury's mouth. Even the woman's own son—and future heir to the Empire, no less—was not immune from her plotting and politicking.

The Prince caught Newbury's eye. "If you ever need me, Newbury, you need only call." He paused, stroking his beard thoughtfully. "I only hope that I might do the same."

"Of course, your Royal Highness. Consider me at your disposal."

"You're a good man, Newbury. Find a way to rid yourself of this blasted habit. It does you no credit. Your talents are needed, and you owe it to yourself and your country not to fritter them away like some common wastrel." The Prince stood, heaving himself up out of the Chesterfield with a heartfelt groan. "I'll say no more on the subject. You know what you must do."

*If only it were that easy,* thought Newbury as he levered himself up, his limbs protesting, his mind still woozy. If only he could explain that people's lives depended on this blasted habit. But he knew he could not. "Thank you, your Royal Highness."

"Thank *you*, Newbury. I knew that I would be able to rely on you. We will speak again soon." The Prince gave the briefest of smiles before turning towards the door. "Scarbright?" he bellowed, so loud that Newbury was sure he felt the room itself tremble in surprise.

Newbury heard Scarbright's footsteps thundering on the stairs. He appeared in the doorway, red-faced, a moment later. "How might I be of assistance, Your Royal Highness?"

"I'm leaving, Scarbright. My coat and hat."

"Quite so. Please allow me to escort you to your carriage."

And with that, Albert Edward of Saxe-Coburg and Gotha swept out of Newbury's drawing room as swiftly as he had arrived.

Newbury waited until he heard the creak of the carriage's wheels and the clatter of the horse's hooves in the street below before he allowed himself to exhale. He slumped back into his armchair before the fire, his head spinning as he contemplated the gravity of what had just occurred. He was just about to reach for another cigarette when Scarbright came barrelling back into the room.

"There was a message for you, sir, while you were engaged with the Prince of Wales."

Newbury raised an eyebrow. Surely not *another* summons from the palace? "Indeed?"

"It's from Sir Charles, sir. He says he needs your help. He and Miss Hobbes are awaiting you at the morgue." Scarbright winced as he delivered this news, as if in anticipation of Newbury's response.

"Does it never end?" Newbury replied, wearily, slipping his silver cigarette case back into his jacket pocket unopened. His heart sank. The morgue. Once more, he was to surround himself with the death and detritus of other people's sordid lives. Further distractions from the work at hand. Yet he couldn't very well allow their call for help to go unheeded. "Very well. Run me a bath, would you, Scarbright? It's time I made myself presentable. Even the dead deserve that."

"Indeed, sir," replied Scarbright, and for the first time that day, the valet smiled. "Even the dead," he echoed, before dashing off again to make the necessary arrangements.

Newbury leaned back in his chair and closed his eyes. He issued a long, heavy sigh. The real world was once again tugging on his sleeve, and it was time he stopped ignoring it.

# CHAPTER 4

✦

It wasn't that she enjoyed killing.

Indeed, she took no pleasure whatsoever in the act. The sensation of her sword tip sliding into the soft flesh of a target; the spurt of crimson blood as she severed their vital arteries; the expression of terrified anguish on their face as it dawned on them that their final moments would be spent writhing in agony, impotent to prevent their own demise... none of these things elicited even the slightest hint of emotion in her.

Indeed, it was this utter and complete absence of feeling that had led her to the role of murderess, mercenary, executioner. She had long ago lost her heart. Now, she was little more than a cipher, a shadow, a leftover trace of the person she had once been. She was undying and immoveable.

She still remembered the first time she had killed. She expected to be overwhelmed with disgust, horror, remorse. She imagined she would vomit and keen into the long nights in the weeks that followed, that she would vehemently hate herself for what she had done and be unable to reconcile her actions with her understanding of herself.

As she sat in the darkness planning every detail of the momentous act—where it would take place, at what time, with what weapon—she quietly accepted that she would be crossing a line she could never return from. Her motive might have been revenge, but in killing the man who had created her—who had turned her into a monster—she would also be killing something inside of herself. By carrying out this act of violence she would inadvertently be continuing his work, and finally giving up the last of her humanity.

She came to this realization as she lay in wait for the man, two curved blades clutched in her fists. The room was silent other than the incessant ticking of the clock on the mantel, measuring the seconds until he would arrive home and the deed could be done.

Everything had unfolded as she'd anticipated. The man stumbled in drunk at close to eleven o'clock. He fumbled to light a candle to guide his way. As the flame took hold of the wick and cast his face in sharp relief, she stepped out from behind the open door and slid the first blade through his belly.

Even now, she could see the look of absolute confusion on his face, how it slowly transformed to an expression of horror and desperation as he realised what was happening, and how the sorrowful realisation finally dawned in his eyes as the second blade bit home, piercing his heart and causing his body to convulse and fall limp to the floor.

She knelt over him as he faded, her breath coming in short, quick gasps. She waited for the welling feeling of loss, for the panic, for the burning shame. Perhaps even for the relief or the exhilaration that she had finally taken her revenge. But none of this came.

At first she rationalised this absence as shock; that the immediacy of what had occurred had rendered her numb, that everything else would follow later. Yet the only thing she felt as she crouched over the corpse of the man who had created her, watching his blood seep from the horrific gashes in his torso, was an acute sense of curiosity.

She had lived a lifetime since that day in Montmartre in 1826. Almost eighty years. Yet it was still vivid in her memory, like an old, stubborn stain that refused to be scrubbed away.

The next death followed a week later, driven by that same intense sense of curiosity: a need to discover whether there was any part of her that could still feel. This time it was a stranger, and she discovered that the fact that she did not know the person, did not understand their hopes, fears, and desires, made no difference to her whatsoever.

*A string of murders throughout the streets of Paris had followed, but nothing she did—no matter the means of death, the condition in which she left the bodies, the manner in which she allowed them to beg or scream—could touch her.*

*She understood that this was not normal, that the people who found the corpses she'd left strewn across the cobbled streets in her wake were disgusted by what they saw. She read the newspaper reports about the hunt to find the killer, who the reporters had dubbed "the Scourge of Paris" or "the Executioner," how the city's populace cowered in fear that this shadowy killer might come for them in the night. She recognised the impact of her actions, but found herself entirely unable to care.*

*For a while after her murderous spree, she joined a travelling troupe of acrobats (for she had always been athletic), quitting Paris and touring from city to city across the continent. This had proved to be a distraction, for a time, but it did not last. She grew tired of being dragged from one unfamiliar town to another, and the initial lustre of a life on the road was soon eroded by the weariness in her bones and the emptiness where her heart had once been. She longed to have her pulse quicken with excitement, to feel alive.*

*One night after a show, she happened across one of the acrobats cursing and thrashing about her caravan in a blind rage. Earlier that day, the acrobat had discovered her lover rutting with another of the girls from the troupe. When confronted, he had simply laughed and carried on.*

*The girl begged her to help, and together they plotted vengeance through the night. The next day, the acrobat woke to find her lover's heart on the pillow beside her. The girl never spoke a word about it to anyone.*

*The Executioner—a name she had embraced by this time—fled to evade discovery. But still she felt no sense of triumph, of fulfilment. There was nothing but a void in her soul, a deep sense of emptiness at the core of her being.*

*She had not sought this strange, nomadic existence, but it found her regardless, drawing her in—out of necessity, perhaps, and as a result of her dispassion. She had fallen into this life because she didn't care enough not to, and because, in some ways, she was still searching, still hoping to find that glimmer of a reaction in the empty space where her own heart had been.*

*She held her breath as the door opened. Her next victim had arrived.*

# CHAPTER 5

Sometimes, Veronica caught herself wondering why it was that the majority of her encounters with Sir Charles Bainbridge involved a visit to the morgue.

Was it that she was simply a glutton for punishment? After all, she might simply choose to abstain from such distasteful pursuits and receive a report detailing all of the necessary findings later. Did she really need to force herself to attend these trips to that detestable place, with its thick stench of blood and carbolic and its grisly occupants, most of whom had died violent or miserable deaths, their remains mangled by weapons or disease?

Of course, both Newbury and Charles would have accepted her choice to stay away without comment. She was, after all, a *woman*, and the morgue was certainly no place for one of *those*. Indeed, she knew that both of them, while perhaps more accepting of her independence than many other men might have been, felt a need to protect her from the more gruesome elements of their shared profession. And that, she concluded, was precisely the reason that she *did* force herself to go through with it, despite the fact that it turned her stomach and left her feeling quite unwell.

The current situation was a case in point. There were three

corpses in the chamber, each of them laid out on wooden trestles. The attendants hadn't bothered to cover them with the thin cotton sheets they often used to preserve the dignity of the dead. The bodies had simply been wheeled out and dumped on the trestles like unwanted animal carcasses in a butcher's shop, spoiled and riddled with decay.

Veronica couldn't stop staring at them. She wanted to look away—to focus on anything *except* the grotesque cadavers—but she felt strangely compelled to look on regardless, unable to tear her eyes away. She supposed it was a form of macabre fascination, a reminder of one's own tenuous grip on life. She'd come close to ending up like that herself on more than one occasion. She wondered who might have gathered around her butchered corpse to poke and prod at it in an attempt to tease information from its lifeless lips. Who might yet...?

The nearest of the corpses, a man who had been in his mid-twenties from the look of him, had a terrible fixed grin on his face. Veronica couldn't help feeling he was laughing at her. It was as if—even dead—he knew some secret that she did not, and was lording it over her from beyond the grave, amused that she was so appalled to find herself in the presence of his battered, bloody corpse. She wondered what he'd been thinking when he died, and whether the bodies of the dead ever did retain the memories of the people who had once inhabited them. The thought gave her a chill.

Memories or not, a corpse could nevertheless tell a story. She'd seen Newbury examine them before, and was always amazed how much he could extrapolate from any given injury or mark, from an eviscerated belly to the pinprick of a needle in an upper arm. He could unravel what had happened to a victim simply by reading the direction of their wounds or the objects in their pockets.

Not that it was difficult to see what had happened here. Just like the others—the elderly man and the middle-aged woman with whom he now made uneasy bedfellows—the younger man's chest had been cracked open and his heart ripped viciously from within. Even now his rib cage yawned open, split into a ragged-edged wound. Around the gaping hole the flesh was puckered, waxy, and spattered with gore. His hands were fixed like rigid claws by his sides, as if he'd been raking at something in the moments before he died, either in self-defence, or more likely in abject pain. Perhaps both. His shirt and jacket—now little more than ragged, bloodied strips—still hung loosely from his shoulders. They had clearly been torn open in a hurry to provide access to the flesh and bone beneath. It seemed to Veronica that the makeshift surgery had been performed while the man was still alive.

The smell, of course, was horrendous. The corpses had already begun to decompose, particularly those of the two men. The woman was a more recent addition, a victim from the prior evening, Veronica had been told, although her flesh had already lost its pinkish hue through so much blood loss, leaving the body looking pale and doll-like.

She wondered what Bainbridge had found at the scene. She could only begin to imagine the amount of spilled blood. It must have been everywhere, pooling on the floor, sprayed up the walls, dripping off the furniture. She shuddered as she thought about these pale, violated corpses *in situ* in their homes. Here, as harrowing as they were to look upon, they seemed to belong. Here in the morgue, that was where corpses like these were supposed to reside. But in their own homes, butchered like swine and surrounded by the accoutrements of their lives, they would have been utterly incongruous, somehow even more awful to witness.

She'd seen their like before, of course, more times than she cared to remember, and each and every occasion had left an indelible impression upon her.

Sometimes she wondered if her life would always be steeped in death.

She laughed at herself. Now she was just being maudlin. Although it was difficult not to be while surrounded by the remains of the recently deceased.

She tore her eyes away from the body of the young man, looking for Bainbridge. She needed a distraction.

He was standing beneath the tiled archway at the other end of the antechamber—really nothing more than a screened off section of passageway—deep in conversation with another man, a Professor Archibald Angelchrist.

Veronica wasn't quite sure what the man was doing there at the morgue, but she harboured a growing sense of suspicion. He had never been properly introduced to her, and ever since he'd arrived he'd been speaking with Bainbridge in hushed tones, evidently intent on excluding her from the conversation. She'd gathered he was a government advisor, although she was not yet entirely sure in what capacity. She'd also gleaned that he already knew Newbury, which had come as something of a surprise. Newbury had never mentioned him, not even in passing. Whatever the purpose of his attendance, it was obscure and left her feeling a little uncomfortable. Well, *more* uncomfortable.

Clearly, though, he and Bainbridge were close. Veronica suspected the man had something to do with whatever secretive business Bainbridge had been getting up to with the Home Secretary these last few months. He was always heading off for meetings of an undisclosed nature, waving away her questions on the matter as if they weren't important. This was despite the amount of time they had spent together over the summer while she'd assisted him on a number of unusual cases.

Newbury had been busy with that Lady Arkwell business—which, as far as she knew, remained unresolved—so Veronica had put herself forward to assist Bainbridge on a number of matters in Newbury's stead. There'd been that whole scandal about the vicar who'd been disinterring freshly buried corpses to feed them to his son, who'd contracted the Revenant plague, and the matter of the Gozitan midget and his "spiritualist" automaton, who they'd caught fleecing gullible members of the gentry for hundreds of pounds. Those were just two of the more memorable cases they'd investigated together in the last few months. There were numerous others, besides. Yet, for some reason, Bainbridge was more distant from her now than he had ever been before. She couldn't understand it, and she hated feeling suspicious. She wondered if perhaps she should discuss it with him, but dismissed the idea, at least for the time being. Bainbridge had never been particularly good at discussing such personal matters. He'd probably only take offence.

The two men turned suddenly at the sound of echoing footsteps in the adjoining room, and she turned to follow their gaze. Two figures were striding purposefully towards them: the willowy mortuary attendant—a weasely, odious man at the best of times, who seemed to revel in his disdain for the police—and Newbury, who looked immaculate in his freshly pressed black suit. He was clean-shaven and appeared to be bursting with energy as he hurried along beside the slightly taller man, beaming at Veronica despite the gloomy, funereal air of the place. She felt her spirits lifting.

Bainbridge stepped in to intercept Newbury's path. "You took your time," he said, morosely.

Newbury grinned, clapping a hand on Bainbridge's shoulder as he came to a stop. He caught Veronica's eye with a sly, mischievous look. "My apologies, Charles. I wouldn't have kept you waiting in this miserable place if it hadn't been for the Prince of Wales."

Bainbridge raised an eyebrow. "The Prince of Wales?

Have they finally managed to get you up to the palace?" The incredulity was evident in his voice.

Newbury shook his head. "No. He called on me, just a few hours ago."

Veronica almost laughed out loud at the expression on Bainbridge's face as he received this news. "What? At Chelsea?" he blurted out.

"Indeed so."

"Good God. You've reduced the monarchy to making house calls, Newbury! What the devil did he want?"

Newbury smiled. "We can discuss that later. Let's get this business over and done with first." He turned to Angelchrist. "Good afternoon, Archibald," he said.

"Likewise, Sir Maurice. Always a pleasure."

Newbury glanced over at Veronica. "I take it you've been introduced to Miss Hobbes?"

Both Bainbridge and Angelchrist looked utterly crestfallen. "Oh... how inconsiderate of me," said Bainbridge, taking two strides towards her. "My dear, I'm so sorry. I've rather let myself down. I just got caught up in the conversation..."

"I fear we've neglected you, Miss Hobbes. We've been a little preoccupied, but nevertheless, it's utterly unforgivable." Angelchrist came to join her and Bainbridge, taking her hand. "It's a pleasure to make your acquaintance."

Veronica lowered her handkerchief and smiled. "Indeed, Professor. I've heard a great deal about you," she lied, studying his face to gauge his reaction. He nodded thoughtfully, as if the idea didn't overly concern him.

Now that he was standing before her, she had to admit he didn't seem all that sinister. He was a smart-looking man in his early to mid-fifties, just a little older than Bainbridge. His hair was thinning and grey, and his moustache was neatly trimmed and still mostly black with a few flecks of white. He was shorter than Bainbridge by a few inches, and his face was careworn and friendly and creased easily around the mouth when he smiled. His eyes were a deep, warm brown.

"Right," said Newbury, coming up behind the two men and clapping his hands. The sound ricocheted off the tiled walls. "Tell me about your corpses, Charles."

"You don't have to sound so enthusiastic about it," said Veronica, although she was careful to keep any disapproval out of her voice.

Newbury laughed as he followed Bainbridge over to the three trestle tables and their gruesome occupants. She decided to wait with Professor Angelchrist, who, like her, was content to watch the proceedings from a safe distance. She noted the mortuary attendant had slipped away during their conversation.

"Three victims," Bainbridge began, indicating each of the corpses in turn with a swift chopping motion. "All killed in the same fashion within the space of a week. No obvious links between the victims, although we are continuing to explore that possibility. Each of them has been opened up in the same way, and their hearts removed."

"Hearts removed?" Newbury echoed, leaning over so that he might peer into the open chest cavity of the nearest victim, the young man who had so fascinated Veronica earlier. He wrinkled his nose at the festering scene inside.

"Yes. We're wondering if there's any ritualistic or occult significance," said Bainbridge. There was a tinge of hopefulness—even desperation—in his tone. Veronica felt for him. It was an awful job, and an even more awful responsibility, to be the one accountable for bringing the killer to justice. More so, for explaining to the victims' families exactly why their loved ones had been so brutally executed.

"Where were they found?" asked Newbury, circling the grisly diorama, drinking in the facts. "Indoors, evidently."

"In their own homes," Bainbridge confirmed. "The first one, the young man, here, had been dumped in his bathtub for the servants to find the next morning. The makeshift surgery had clearly been performed in the same bathroom, too; the walls had pretty much been redecorated with the poor bastard's blood." He sighed heavily as he moved round to stand over the corpse of the older man. "This chap, Mr. Geoffrey Evans, was found in his kitchen by his wife, who woke up in the middle of the night, realised he wasn't there beside her, and went downstairs to look for him. He was spread out on the tiles in a sea of his own blood. And this last woman was discovered by her maid this morning on the floor of her expensive library. This one's slightly different, though. The victim clearly put up a fight. There were signs of a struggle at the scene, and you can see the wounds on her forearms where she raised them in self-defence."

Newbury lifted the woman's right arm and studied the criss-cross pattern of gashes. "It looks as if the killer came at her with a long-bladed knife," he said.

Bainbridge nodded.

"You mentioned the occult. Did you find anything at the scenes that might suggest as much? Any symbols marked out in chalk? Icons drawn in the spilt blood? Tatters of paper covered in strange runes and secreted upon the bodies?"

"No," Bainbridge admitted. "No, none of that. I only thought there might be some significance behind the removal of their hearts."

"So you have no motive, and nothing to connect the victims?" Newbury was chewing on his bottom lip, lost in thought.

"Nothing. The only thing I'm sure about is that it's the work of the same killer," replied Bainbridge.

"Well, you're right about that. You can tell from these wounds that the victims were all hacked open with the same implement, cutting through the breastbone in the same direction. But why? Why would the killer take their hearts?"

He tapped his foot in frustration, as if that might be enough to conjure up an answer.

Bainbridge sighed. "I was rather hoping you were going to tell me that," he said, resignedly.

Newbury looked up from the corpse of the woman. "Well, I don't think there's a particular occult ritual being performed here, or at least not one that I'm aware of, but there's definitely something *ritualistic* about the manner in which they all had their hearts removed. It may look like a crude job, but whoever did this took real care over the removal of the organs themselves. Yes, they've hacked open the chest cavities in a rather barbaric fashion, but they've shown a strange sort of respect for the hearts they were stealing."

"Almost as if they wanted them for something else?" said Veronica from behind her handkerchief.

"Absolutely that," replied Newbury, glancing at her. "Although for what, I'm not at all sure."

"Witchcraft?" asked Bainbridge. "Some Godforsaken nonsense involving human sacrifice and dancing in the woods? Isn't that usually the way? I thought it might have something to do with that cabal, the 'horny beasts' or whatever it was they called themselves."

"The Cabal of the Horned Beast," interjected Veronica, trying not to laugh.

The three of them—Veronica, Newbury, and Bainbridge—had encountered members of this strange devil-worshipping cult just a few months earlier. Newbury had liberated a rare book of rituals from them, from which he derived his unusual treatment for Veronica's sister, Amelia. As an act of reprisal, the cultists had taken Newbury and Bainbridge prisoner. Veronica had been forced to mount a rescue, posing as a cultist and battling one of their abysmal half man, half machine creations to gain entry to the manor house in which they'd established their lair.

Newbury sighed. "I only wish the world were that simplistic, Charles," he said, sadly.

"Or perhaps the killer is reusing the organs, like those automatons with the 'affinity bridges' in their craniums. Could the killer be using them to power some sort of infernal machine?" Bainbridge continued, hopefully.

"It's all possible, Charles," said Newbury, "but at present I have no means of even theorising. There's simply not enough information to go on."

"There are three corpses!" protested Bainbridge. "How much information do you need? Have you even examined them properly?"

Newbury shrugged. "Context is everything. I need to see the victims *in situ*. If there was anything more to be gleaned from the manner of their deaths, it was lost the moment they were moved. You know that, Charles. There's nothing else for me to see here. Sometimes a corpse is enough. This time... well, I'm afraid not."

Bainbridge's shoulders dropped as he recognised the truth in Newbury's words. "Then there's very little we can do. We'll have to wait to see if the killer strikes again."

"I fear so," said Newbury. "I can carry out some research, and I can speak to Aldous Renwick in the hope that we can find some significance behind the missing hearts. Otherwise, we're impotent until the killer shows their hand. I wish I could offer you more, but I have nothing. Not yet."

Bainbridge gave a curt nod. He was clearly frustrated, although it was clear he didn't blame Newbury for being unable to offer up a neat solution.

"Would it help if you were to visit the scene of the most recent murder?" offered Angelchrist, who'd otherwise remained silent throughout the proceedings.

"Perhaps," said Newbury. "It really depends on how much has already been disturbed." He glanced at Bainbridge questioningly.

Bainbridge shook his head. "They've already started to clean up. The place was a terrible mess. Abominable. I'd never have imagined so much blood could have been contained in a single human body." He issued a long, heartfelt sigh. "You'll talk to Aldous, then?"

"I will," replied Newbury. "If there's anyone who can find a ritual involving human hearts, it's Aldous. It may take him some time, however. And it may come to nothing. We don't know yet that there is any occult or ritual significance to the theft. It may simply be an obscene fetish that's driving the killer to act as he is, taking trophies from his victims for his own gratification."

"Let us hope you're wrong," said Angelchrist, darkly. "Otherwise we have even less to go on than we thought."

The four of them stood in silence for a moment, as if weighing the implications of Angelchrist's words. A killer with no motives other than simple self-gratification. A murderer who chose his victims at random, leaving no clear pattern behind, no evidence besides a brutalised corpse without a heart. Veronica knew it would be like searching for a needle in a proverbial haystack.

"I'll send word to Aldous as a matter of urgency," said Newbury, coming around from behind the trestle table that bore the corpse of the woman. He looked to Veronica. "First of all, however, I have some business I must attend to with Miss Hobbes."

"My thanks to you, Newbury," said Bainbridge. "I feel as if our chances of success have improved tenfold, simply by virtue of having your assistance. It's been too long." He patted Newbury on the shoulder. "I'll be in touch."

"See that you are, you old fool," replied Newbury, chuckling as Bainbridge affected mock hurt. He turned to Angelchrist. "Until next time, Archibald."

"Indeed, Sir Maurice. I trust we'll speak again soon. And

you, Miss Hobbes. I hope you will forgive me for capitalising so much of Sir Charles's time this afternoon."

"Of course," said Veronica, diplomatically. "I'm sure we'll meet again."

Newbury held out his arm for Veronica and she took it gratefully, keen to put some distance between herself and the cadavers. He led her towards the exit.

"We have business to attend to?" she asked quietly, so that the others would not catch her trailing words as they walked.

"Indeed we do, Miss Hobbes. I believe it's high time we paid another visit to your sister."

Veronica squeezed his arm in grateful acknowledgement. "To Malbury Cross, then. I have a hansom waiting outside. Once you've attended to Amelia, I'll see that you have time to write to Aldous, too."

She leaned a little closer into Newbury, ignoring the imperious look of the mortuary attendant as they bid him good afternoon and stepped out into the drizzly late afternoon.

# CHAPTER 6

The incense was thick and heady, and it lodged in the back of Amelia's throat, making it difficult for her to breathe. She had no idea what the perfume was: lavender, most definitely, but something else, too, something unfamiliar, herbal, sharp. Accompanying this floral bouquet was a cloying tang of iron, which she really hoped wasn't blood, but fully suspected was.

Not that she would have been able to tell. The room was shrouded in darkness. The heavy drapes were pulled across the windows to banish the watery afternoon sunlight, and the only other light source came from the five white candles arranged in a star pattern around her. She was kneeling on bare wooden floorboards at the centre of a strange pattern marked out in chalk: a complex geometric shape encompassing a five-pointed star, with unfamiliar glyphs and runes etched around it in a wide outer circle. She'd been told that she should never break the chalk pattern or step outside of its barriers while the ritual was being performed.

As a result she sat stock-still, despite the fact that the rough floorboards hurt her knees and her back ached terribly. She was worried that, should she make even the slightest of movements or unknowingly break one of the fine chalk lines with her hand or foot, she might disturb the ritual. She hadn't been told what the consequences of such an action might be, but she was anxious not to find out.

Newbury sat opposite her within the chalk pattern, murmuring gently as he read from the pages of an ancient, leather-bound book. Amelia had tried making sense of the incantation, but had so far been unable to understand a word of it. It sounded as if Newbury was speaking in an eastern tongue, all glottal stops and rasping sounds made in the back of his throat. The book's spine read *The Cosmology of the Spirit*, and from what scant glimpses she'd gotten of its contents, she'd ascertained that its pages were covered in an impenetrable scrawl, along with diagrammatic sketches and patterns akin to the one on the floor they now sat on.

Newbury traced his finger across a page, reading from right to left as if working backwards through the text. The concentration on his face was intense, his forehead creased in a deep frown. His head was slightly bowed, meaning she couldn't see his eyes in the candlelight, just deep, pooling shadows. The effect was a little eerie, particularly when combined with the bizarre nature of their situation.

Amelia had to admit that she'd doubted Newbury's motives more than once. Why was he helping her, and at such great cost to himself? Every instance of the ritual left him utterly drained. Diminished, even. It was as if the act— or else some vital preparation for it—left Newbury depleted of all his strength. Veronica had told her he holed up in his rooms for days following each visit, refusing to see anyone, apparently subsisting on very little but absinthe, laudanum, and cigarettes. Then, when he had gathered his strength once again, he would return to Malbury Cross for another round of "treatment" and the cycle would begin anew. It had been like this for months; Newbury repeatedly giving himself over to the ritual, treating her successfully, but putting himself through great torment each time.

Amelia couldn't help but wonder what that meant, what was causing such physical and mental expenditure. Was he somehow sustaining her at his own cost? She'd tackled him on it, tried to draw the truth out of him, but each time he had brushed her off, waving his hand dismissively and informing her that he was tired and did not wish to discuss it.

Truthfully, she was wary of pushing him too far on the matter, partly because she was deeply unsure of the methods he was employing, but mostly because she was scared he would eventually admit the truth. And if things were as she feared—that he really was giving up something of himself to heal her—then it would have to stop. At the moment she had nothing but suspicions—suspicions that both Newbury and Veronica were unwilling to entertain. Having these suspicions confirmed, however, would mean she would have no choice but to demand an end to the treatment.

Amelia feared that more than anything else, because the treatment was the only thing keeping her alive. As unlikely as it seemed, whatever strange ritual Newbury was performing, it was working. She felt better than she had in years. The visions were still plaguing her, but they were becoming controllable, or at least containable. The seizures had become increasingly less violent, and she felt strong, well, alive. For the first time in months, Amelia had begun to think of the future, and, more importantly, a future with herself in it. She dared not put that at risk. But nor could she knowingly condone Newbury harming himself on her behalf.

Perhaps Newbury was right after all—perhaps it was better that she didn't know. All the same, she couldn't help feeling that not knowing made her weak.

Veronica would tell her to stop worrying, that Newbury knew what he was doing. That she should trust him and enjoy the fruits of his labours, no matter how unconventional they might seem. Amelia saw something, however, that her sister did not… or rather, that Veronica was *choosing* not to see: that Newbury would do *anything* for Veronica, even if that meant giving up something of himself to save her sister.

Amelia watched Newbury as he stirred a bowl of pungent fluid with a wooden spatula, all the while continuing to read aloud from the book that was open on the floorboards before him. His lips moved almost silently, his voice just a low, monotonous murmur. Beads of sweat had formed on his brow despite the chill, and he looked pale, even in the warm yellow glow of the candlelight.

The only other sound in the room was the steady ticking of a carriage clock. It seemed to Amelia that time was passing differently in that room, with its fog of incense and ancient pagan rites. There was a sense of peacefulness, of stillness, a disconnection from the real world.

Suddenly, the murmuring stopped. Newbury looked up. "It's time," he said quietly, sliding the little wooden bowl across the floor towards her.

Amelia gave the briefest of nods. This was the moment she dreaded, each and every time: the consummation of the ritual, the acceptance of Newbury's gift to her. This was the culmination of everything he had done in the past hour. She had to drink the foul-smelling contents of the bowl. The ritual would be wasted if she did not.

She stared at the strange concoction for a few moments, bracing herself for what was coming. The first time they had performed the ritual, Amelia had actually vomited the stuff back up, but she'd since learned how to gulp it down swiftly, to fight off the brief wave of nausea that ensued. She was egged on, of course, by the effect she knew it would have on her condition. It was the only thing that had worked since Dr. Fabian had experimented upon her at the Grayling Institute the prior year, and she had no desire to put herself through that sort of business again.

"Go on," said Newbury softly, urging her on.

Amelia nodded and reached for the bowl, cupping both of her palms around it. It was warm to the touch. She lifted it hesitantly to her lips, fighting the urge to reel back as she drew in its scent. It was indescribable and exotic. She had no notion of the actual ingredients, save for a splash of Newbury's own blood, evidenced by the thin gash he'd opened up in his left palm as he'd prepared the mixture.

Closing her eyes and holding her breath, Amelia parted her lips and took a long, gulping draught from the bowl. She swallowed urgently, forcing the coarse, viscous fluid down her gullet. She felt its warmth spreading through her chest like alcohol, and she tipped the bowl further, emptying it completely. With a shudder as its taste hit her palate, she replaced the bowl on the floorboards before her and wiped her mouth with the back of her hand. She raised her eyes to look at Newbury, whose own face was still shrouded in shadow.

"Good," he said, swaying slightly. "Good." He rocked forward as if he might topple over and Amelia leant in to catch him, supporting his weight in her arms for a few seconds while he regained his senses. He righted himself a moment or two later, mumbling an embarrassed "Thank you."

Amelia nodded. "It's the least…" She trailed off as she realised in horror that—in the sudden grab for him—she had accidentally smeared the outline of the chalk pentagram on the floor. "Sir Maurice, the chalk," she gasped as she indicated the floorboards beneath her knees.

Newbury put a reassuring hand on her shoulder. "It's alright, Amelia. It's over for today. We'll draw a new one next time."

"But…?"

Newbury shook his head. "It won't change anything. The ritual was complete. We were lucky. I'll know not to push myself so far in future."

Amelia frowned. Already she could feel the warmth from

the strange elixir spreading throughout her frail body, filling her with a remarkable sense of well-being. Newbury, however, was more weakened than ever by the gruelling process. "Once again, Sir Maurice," she said, her voice quavering slightly, "I must insist that if this ritual in which we are partaking is in some way compromising your own health, you must put an end to it immediately."

Newbury climbed unsteadily to his feet. He reached out a hand for her and she took it, pulling herself up beside him. "Come on," he said, ignoring her statement. "Your sister and Mrs. Leeson are waiting in the kitchen for you." He turned to her, and in the low light she finally caught the shine of his eyes. It suggested a smile that had yet to form on his lips. "And besides, I'm in urgent need of a pot of tea."

Amelia grinned. "Very well. I'll make it fresh myself. Thank you, Sir Maurice."

Newbury nodded as he reached for his candle snuff and set about smothering the still-burning flames.

With a shrug, Amelia crossed to the door. She opened it just enough to slip through, then stepped out into the hallway, shading her eyes against the dappled sunlight streaming in through the glass panel above the front door. She could still taste the foul mixture in the back of her throat as she headed off in the direction of the kitchen in search of Veronica.

Veronica reached for her teacup and turned it around in its saucer, tipping it towards her and peering inside as if expecting to discover that it had miraculously refilled itself while she wasn't looking. As she'd suspected, it was still empty.

"That's the third time you've looked at that empty cup in the last five minutes, Miss Veronica," said the rotund, middle-aged woman who sat across the kitchen table from her. "Would you like me to make you a fresh pot?"

Veronica looked up, a wan smile on her lips. "No, thank you, Mrs. Leeson. Let's wait for the others. They should be finished soon, and I'm sure they'll both welcome a cup."

Mrs. Leeson shrugged. Her eyebrows were raised and she looked somewhat startled, but Veronica knew this was only a symptom of the manner in which she insisted on wearing her platinum-grey hair, scraped back in the severest of buns. She was a kindly woman in her late forties, and had once been independently wealthy, but had fallen on hard times following the unexpected death of her husband a few years earlier. Veronica had come to rely on her enormously in Amelia's care over these last few months.

They both turned at the sound of approaching footsteps from the hall. "Ah, Miss Amelia!" announced Mrs. Leeson happily, pushing her chair back on the tiled floor and standing to welcome her charge with an expansive gesture. "You do look sprightly. Whatever it is that Sir Maurice is treating you with, it's certainly making a difference. I haven't seen so much colour in your cheeks for weeks."

Amelia, hovering in the doorway, smiled warmly in response. "Thank you, Mrs. Leeson. Sir Maurice is a remarkable man." Her arms were folded across her chest and she rubbed them unconsciously, hugging herself as if cold. She glanced at Veronica. "I said I'd make him a pot of tea."

"Oh, don't you be worrying yourself with such things, young lady," said Mrs. Leeson, bustling over to the stove. "I'll see to that. You set yourself down with Miss Veronica here for a minute."

Veronica nodded and beckoned Amelia over to join her while Mrs. Leeson set about filling the kettle. "You'd better leave her to it," whispered Veronica, just loud enough that Mrs. Leeson herself wouldn't hear. "If you start making the tea she'll complain she has nothing left to do!"

Amelia laughed as she lowered herself into the chair

opposite Veronica, placing her palms flat on the tabletop before her. Veronica could tell immediately that something was bothering her. "What is it?" she asked, concerned. "What's wrong?"

Amelia's face creased in concern. "I don't know. It's Sir Maurice. He... well, he collapsed in my arms after he completed the ritual. He's not himself. I'm worried for him."

Veronica put her hand on top of Amelia's and squeezed it in what she hoped was a reassuring gesture. "You shouldn't worry, Amelia. Sir Maurice knows what his limits are. He's probably just tired. He'll be fine in a few hours. You just concentrate on getting better." It didn't sound as convincing as she'd hoped.

Amelia glared at Veronica in warning. "Don't patronise me, sister," she said. "I know how much he's giving up for me, for *you*."

Veronica suppressed a scowl. "Then you also know it's far more complicated than that," she replied, her tone level.

Amelia sighed. "Yes. I rather suppose I do."

"But it's working? Whatever it is he's doing, it's helping?" Veronica asked.

Amelia nodded. "Last year, when you brought me to Malbury Cross, I thought I had come here to die. But now... now I think I might have come here to *live*." She leaned back in her chair. "Yet Sir Maurice is paying a grave toll for his efforts."

Veronica eyed her younger sister. "You cannot be thinking of giving it up?" she said. "You don't know the lengths he went to retrieve that book, Amelia, the enemies he made. It would slight him if you turned away his help. More than that, it would make light of everything he's been through— that we've been through. Not to mention what might happen to you. Don't forget, everyone thinks you're dead. There's nowhere left to turn."

"You don't have to remind me of that," replied Amelia

hotly. Mrs. Leeson coughed politely over by the stove. As if on cue, the kettle began to whistle shrilly. Amelia lowered her voice. "Of course I'm not about to turn him away. I'm concerned for him, that's all. You didn't see him, Veronica. He didn't seem at all well."

Veronica nodded, relieved that she wasn't going to have to persuade Amelia to continue with Newbury's regime. "Look, I'll go and check on him now. I'm sure he's just tidying everything in there." As she said this she felt the cold stirrings of concern in the pit of her stomach. Newbury *never* tidied anything. His life was a perfect merry-go-round of chaos and disorder. Perhaps something *was* wrong. Typically he would have emerged a few seconds behind Amelia to join them in the kitchen. What might have delayed him?

Veronica suppressed the urge to leap from her chair and dash to his side. It wouldn't do to startle Amelia and Mrs. Leeson, and more importantly, to concern Amelia any further by demonstrating her own fear.

She stood, forcing herself to smile. "You stay here and keep Mrs. Leeson company. I'll be back in a moment," she said, coming around from behind the table and crossing the hallway as quickly as possible.

The door to the dining room was ajar. She pushed it open, stepping inside and allowing it to swing closed behind her. The room was still shrouded in darkness, the heavy drapes pulled down over the windows. No candles or lamps burned, and for a moment it reminded her uncomfortably of the Queen's audience chamber, always cast in a murky, impenetrable gloom.

"Maurice? Are you in here?" She remained close to the door while she waited for her eyes to adjust to the darkness. She could make out very little, save for the edge of the drapes and the thin strip of pale light seeping in from behind them. It wasn't enough to illuminate more than a foot or so of the room, in which she could see the silhouetted shapes of the paraphernalia used in the ritual: candlesticks, bowls, sprigs of holly.

Just as she reached for the light, there was a groaning sound from somewhere close to her, on the floor by her feet. "Maurice?" She stooped, reaching out until her outstretched fingers touched the fabric of his jacket. She dropped to her knees, clutching for him with both hands. Her eyes were finally beginning to adjust to the low light and she could just about make out the slumped form of Newbury on the floorboards. He tried to move, and she helped him, supporting him under the arms as he pulled himself upright. She propped him against the wall, his legs splayed out before him. She couldn't see his face clearly enough to read his expression, but his head was lolling in clear exhaustion. He must have collapsed on his way to the door.

"It's alright, Maurice," she said, putting a hand against his forehead. It was clammy and cold. His pulse was slow and steady. Most likely it was exhaustion, then, rather than anything more fiendish. Nevertheless, Amelia was right. This wasn't typical. Not by any means.

"Veronica," said Newbury, the relief evident in his voice. "I'll be fine. Just give me a few moments."

"You need some rest," she said.

"I need to write to Aldous first," he replied, doggedly.

"No," Veronica's tone was firm. "That can wait another hour or so. I'll set you up on the couch in the living room. You can sleep it off, and then write to Aldous later, before we return to London." She cupped her hand on his right cheek. "Don't worry, I'll see the letter on its way myself."

He nodded slowly. His breath was coming in long, laboured gasps. "Alright," he said, quietly. "I'll rest for a while, but you might need to help me up."

"Don't I always," she said, standing and offering her hands

to help lever him up onto his feet. She heaved and took a step backwards, and a moment later he was standing unsteadily beside her, still semi-conscious. She draped his arm around her shoulder and led him to the door, staggering slightly beneath his weight.

"Everything's going to be fine," she said determinedly, but she knew it was more for her own benefit than Newbury's. She waited for his confirmation, for him to assure her that she was right. But he said nothing, simply allowed himself to be led, in a daze, to the couch, where he could rest and attempt to regain his strength.

# CHAPTER 7

❦

Newbury reclined in his chair by the fire, his head lolled to one side, his eyelids drooping heavily. He was tired, more so than he'd been in years, yet the night had passed and he'd proved unable to sleep; the unnatural effects of the ritual left him feeling physically drained and yet still mentally alert, restless. His mind kept on replaying his visit to the morgue from the previous day, running over each of the grisly details in turn, analysing, dwelling, considering. He was surprised to realise he was anxious to press on with the case. Something about the sight of the three corpses, each with their hearts so brutally removed, had caught his attention.

He'd been slumped in the chair for most of the night, staring blankly into the gloom, seeing things that weren't really there. Apparitions and shadows. Ghosts and memories. Lately, he'd found himself haunted by visions of the past, dredged up by his feverish mind and his chemical and occult experiments. At least, he'd reasoned them to be visions once the sunlight had come to banish them along with the darkness. Visions of Templeton Black, his former assistant, now dead and long sunk in the earth; of George Purefoy, the young reporter he had taken under his wing, only to lead him inadvertently to a brutal death at the hands of Aubrey Knox. And of Veronica, too, pleading with him to help her. Was she to be his next victim, killed because of her association with him, because of his failures? Were his visions somehow prophetic, or simply a product of his guilt? He was not entirely sure. Recently, the lines had become blurry.

Newbury shifted uncomfortably in his seat. His body craved more of the Chinese weed, but in his present condition it would do him little good, so he stilled his hand, resisting the temptation to reach for his cigarette case. At least for a while. He knew he'd be unable to resist for long, but he needed to clear his head.

The room was silent save for the fire crackling eagerly in the hearth beside him and the ominous ticking of the carriage clock on the mantel. The sound had become a constant reminder of his own mortality—a mortality that felt closer and more real to him than it ever had before. It seemed that with each shifting of its gears the device was somehow taking account of all that he had done; stealing away his remaining minutes as punishment, claiming them as its own.

He laughed at himself and opened his eyes. *Even the clocks are judging me now.* He knew he was only maudlin because of the ritual, because of the enormous effort it took, how spent it left him feeling. The irony, however, was not lost on him. The clock might in truth be benign, but other things certainly were eroding his existence, slowly and inexorably. The clock served simply as a reminder.

He stirred at the sound of footsteps on the path outside, which were followed by a brisk rap on the front door. It was a distinctive knock—the silver head of a cane striking the painted wooden panel. *Bainbridge.*

Newbury listened for Scarbright's hasty footsteps in the hall, the creaking of the door hinges, the mumbled greetings. He closed his eyes again and leaned back in his chair, making the most of the few moments of peace he had left. Seconds later the door to the drawing room burst open unceremoniously and Bainbridge stalked in, heaving a heavy, melodramatic sigh.

"You do realise how much damage you do to my paintwork with that infernal stick of yours, don't you, Charles?" said Newbury, peeling open his eyes once again. "It's most inconsiderate. Poor Scarbright is forever complaining at having to touch up the dints in the wood."

Bainbridge laughed half-heartedly. "Good morning, Newbury," he replied, his voice strained.

Newbury noted that his friend was looking a little flustered and red about the face, and had not removed his coat in the hallway. "We're going out, then?" he asked, nonchalantly.

Bainbridge frowned. "Yes," he said, clearly refusing to be drawn. He crossed the drawing room, stepping over a heaped pile of papers covered in Newbury's spidery scrawl, and perched on the arm of the chair opposite Newbury's own. He leaned forward on his cane, then reached into his pocket and produced a small white notecard. He waved it at Newbury. "She's sending them to me, now!"

"A summons?" asked Newbury, nodding towards the neat stack of identical cards on the sideboard. "Add it to the pile, Charles."

Bainbridge shook his head. "No. This time she wants to see us both."

Newbury coughed fitfully into his fist and leaned forward, taking the card from Bainbridge. The message, printed in Sandford's neat copperplate, gave little away.

**SIR CHARLES**
**YOUR PRESENCE IS REQUIRED AT THE PALACE**
**FORTHWITH. BRING NEWBURY. VR**

"You're not getting out of it this time, I'm afraid, old man."

Newbury shrugged and handed the card back to Bainbridge.

"I suppose it's time I put in an appearance," he said, smiling, although his heart wasn't in it.

Bainbridge nodded. "You look dreadful," he said.

"Thank you, Charles," Newbury replied smartly.

"I'm only telling you what you already know, Newbury. God knows someone has to." Bainbridge's voice was full of disdain. "Have you seen the black rings beneath your eyes? And you're as white as a sheet. Anyone would think you were anaemic."

"Yes, yes, Charles," said Newbury dismissively. "None of this is new. Besides, I came to the morgue. I'm helping you, aren't I?"

"Yes, I suppose," said Bainbridge, his moustache twitching. "So you'll come, then? To the palace, I mean?"

"Yes," said Newbury. "I'll come."

"Good man," said Bainbridge, straightening his back. He was wearing a satisfied expression. Clearly, he'd been expecting a row. He lifted his cane and opened his mouth as if to continue, but then rocked back in sudden surprise as a large brass object came swooping down from a nearby bookcase, emitting a metallic squawk and eliciting a curse from the chief inspector. It landed neatly upon his shoulder, folded its wings with the clacking of metal plates, and cocked its head in mimicry of the barn owl it was modelled on.

"Good God!" said Bainbridge, loudly. "This ruddy… *creature* of yours just gave me the fright of my life!"

The owl chirruped noisily, as if giving a satisfied laugh at Bainbridge's expense. He waved his hand at it in annoyance, attempting to shoo it away, but it simply shifted its position on his shoulder with an accompanying chirp, its tiny clawed feet gathering up little folds of his overcoat.

"I think he likes you," Newbury said, laughing.

"I don't know why I ever agreed to let you keep this damnable thing," Bainbridge said, although Newbury could tell he wasn't genuinely aggrieved. The clockwork owl was a trophy from a previous investigation, the former property of Lord Carruthers, who'd been poisoned by his estranged sibling at Christmas a couple of years earlier. The owl had been instrumental in helping to solve the case, and Bainbridge had allowed the "evidence"—with the permission of the family, of course—to be rehomed with Newbury. It had been a fixture of his drawing room ever since.

The bird trilled merrily, spread its gleaming wings, and hopped down from Bainbridge's shoulder onto the arm of the chair. It stamped its feet a few times—puncturing the leather covering of the seat with its claws as it did so—then turned to regard Bainbridge, watching him intently. Its eyes blinked as Bainbridge held its gaze for a moment, before shaking his head and offering Newbury an exasperated look.

"I take it there have been no further developments in the case?" asked Newbury, changing the subject.

Bainbridge shook his head. "Nothing," he said. "I'm damned if I can find a link between the suspects, let alone a motive for the killer. I keep coming back to this ritualistic nonsense, hoping that your friend Renwick is going to turn up something useful."

Newbury sat forward, stifling a groan as his tired muscles pulled in protest, threatening to mire him there in his comfortable armchair before the fire. He placed his hands on the arms of the chair, planning to lever himself free. "If there's anything to be found, Charles, Aldous will find it," he said, hauling himself upright. "I sent word yesterday, and Miss Hobbes took charge of delivering the letter." He stood there for a moment, a little unsteady on his feet. "Look," he said, "I need to make myself presentable. Give me half an hour. Scarbright will make tea, if you ask him nicely."

Bainbridge looked up at him, his expression softening. "It's only because I couldn't stand it if you killed yourself, Maurice. You realise that?"

"I do, Charles," replied Newbury, quietly, placing a hand on his friend's shoulder. "I wish you could understand."

"As do I," said Bainbridge, morosely.

Newbury sighed, leaving the chief inspector by the fire so he could make himself look a bit more respectable before heading out to see the monarch. It wasn't going to be a pleasant experience—it rarely was, these days—but he'd been putting it off long enough. It was time to face his demons.

Or one of them, at the very least.

# CHAPTER 8

*The girl never knew her parents.*

*She had been told that her father had been trampled by a horse two months prior to her birth, and that her mother had died in the throes of bringing her into the world, in the dank, underground cell of an asylum somewhere on the outskirts of Paris.*

*She had erupted into the world in an orgy of agony and anguish—or so she'd been told by the crooked-backed old woman in the orphanage, who seemed to delight in describing the young girl's misfortune, cackling mercilessly and exposing the blackened stumps of her teeth.*

*Later, she would understand this for what it was: the old woman's attempt to rationalise the unfathomable ways of the world, and perhaps to remind herself that there existed people whose circumstances were far worse than her own. The old woman consoled herself in this manner, by averting her own face from the looking glass and turning its scrutiny upon the young orphan who had never known anything better. It allowed the woman to focus on something other than her own lowly lot in life, her pauper's existence.*

*At the time, however, the old woman terrified her. She thought her a witch, an avatar of the devil himself. She cowered from that cavernous mouth and its spittle-flecked lips that spewed only poison and fear, trying to shut out the woman's spiteful words. The onslaught was relentless, however, and by the age of seven she found herself* believing what the woman said: that she had killed her own mother upon quitting the womb, that her very soul was inhabited by evil, and that she would never amount to anything in this life. All that awaited her was an eternity in the fiery pits of Hell.

One day the woman described this terrifying place to her, told her of the torture she was likely to endure, of the demons with their silky forked tongues and pitchforks, the way they would force her to live out her worst fears for all eternity. The girl asked the woman if she, too, would go to Hell, since she knew this place so well. The woman reached out and cuffed her brutally across the back of the head for her insolence.

She wished the old woman dead, then, and not for the first time. She balled her fists and could almost see the woman's wizened old face contorting in pain as she collapsed upon the hearth, near where she sat in perpetual, indolent repose. Her hair would catch alight like dry tinder, and with a whoosh of flame she would ignite, blazing suddenly bright in the grainy dimness of the parlour. The chair would catch fire, and the flames would spread, licking at the table legs, engulfing the wooden shelves, and finally spreading throughout the orphanage. The entire building would be razed to the ground in the purifying inferno, and all of the nannies and maids and tutors would burn incandescent like tallow candles.

The girl would be free, then, to escape a diabolical future in the acrid pits of Hell.

It did not happen quite as she'd hoped. When the old woman finally did drop dead, almost a year later, the young girl was peeling potatoes in the kitchen with two other orphans. They heard a wheezing grunt from the adjacent parlour. The girl put down her paring knife and—with some hesitation—tiptoed through to the parlour to investigate what had become of the old woman.

She was thrilled to see the scene from her imagination brought vividly to life.

The old woman lay face down upon the hearth, her jaundiced eyes still open but unseeing, her skin pallid and grey. Her mouth yawned open, slack jawed, and drool pooled upon the slate tiles beneath her. Her arms were outstretched, as if she'd been reaching for something when her heart had suddenly given out. Everything was as the girl had imagined, save for one small detail. The woman's hair had not caught the dancing flames that even now leapt and caroused in the grate, but had fallen just a little short, fanned out like grey bristles upon the hearth.

She was fascinated by the sight of this dead thing that had once been a person. It was unreal to her that the woman had ever actually been alive. She stood over the corpse for a full minute before she was struck by the notion that, if she wished, she could bring about the conflagration she had always dreamed of. One nudge from the edge of her boot and the woman's head would be close enough to the flames for her hair to catch alight. She could encourage the fire to escape, just as she longed to escape. She could feed it the flaccid corpse of this horrid old woman, who would burn—not in Satan's realm, but there on the hearth, roasting like a suckling pig. It was everything the old woman deserved, and more.

It would look like an accident. She would not be held accountable. She would claim she had found the woman that way, that she had attempted desperately to put the flames out with the jug of water from the table, but it had not been enough; the fire was too ravenous, too eager.

She stepped forward, raising her foot, her heart bursting with excitement, when she heard a wheedling scream from behind her. She turned to see the other girls, half-peeled potatoes still clutched in their pale hands, and knew there and then that her escape was not to be.

The old woman was buried in the churchyard, and the girl was forced to stand in attendance with the other children from the orphanage. Some of them wept sorrowfully, for the funeral reminded them of their own losses. The young girl, however, who had never known her parents and did not feel their loss, wept tears of frustration instead. Her dream was over. There would be no escape from the orphanage, and though the decrepit old woman who had tormented her for so many years was now gone, her words continued to ring in the girl's ears. The devil was waiting for her, impatient to reclaim his own.

When escape did finally come, it was from the most unexpected of quarters. An inventor who lived in the city came to the orphanage to claim himself a daughter. His wife had died that very morning of a terrible wasting disease, and he told the matron how the woman had always wanted a child of her own to nurture, a daughter she could shape in her own image. Her disease, however, had prevented her from bearing a child of her own, and in the latter years of her life she had been too weak for them to take in an orphan.

As she had lain on her deathbed, her husband clutching her hand as she faded, she had asked him to grant her one final promise so that she might rest: she made him swear that he would go directly to the orphanage to find a young girl on whom to bestow all of his fatherly affection. His loving wife had not wanted him to be alone in his grief, and wished only that her legacy might be continued through a child.

The matron saw this, of course, as an opportunity to unburden herself of one of her charges, and as the inventor was well-known and well-respected throughout the city, she encouraged him eagerly in this pursuit.

Without further ado, the matron stirred the girls from their chores, rounding them up in the exercise yard for the man to inspect. She told the girls that one of them would be granted the gift of a new father that day, and that they must all be grateful for the opportunity and pleased for the girl who would be saved by this wonderful, benevolent man. The matron spoke of God and His divine will, and how in the eyes of the Lord all men are made equal. Today he would bestow a gift upon one lowly orphan that would raise her up and alter the course of her life. The matron was unable to hide the wavering note of jealousy in her own voice as she explained this.

The girl held her breath as the inventor paced up and down before the line of smiling orphans, twirling the ends of his exuberant moustache as he contemplated his options. He seemed to be a gentle, intelligent man, and she giggled nervously as he pinched her cheek and ruffled the hair of the girl beside her, measuring them up as if they were livestock on display at a butcher's market.

She did not allow herself to feel even the slightest glimmer of hope that she might be selected to become his new daughter, for she already knew that she was bound for a future of eternal damnation, and that no man in his right mind would wish to take her in as his charge. Consequently, when he ceased his pacing in front of her, removed his hat, and placed it gently upon her head, she could not believe that he might represent the means of escape she had so longed for. But when he took her by the hand, and—after a few brief words to the matron—led her out to his waiting carriage, her tiny number of possessions bundled into a small leather satchel, she allowed herself to smile properly for the first time since the old woman had died.

Perhaps, she thought, this kindly man represented her salvation. Perhaps this was finally her escape, her new life. Her chance to begin anew.

For a time all of this was true, and her most precious hopes and desires were fulfilled. Finally, she was blessed with someone to love her, and a life outside the dingy, oppressive walls of the orphanage.

But time is a cruel mistress, and it was not until many years later that she would learn the truth: that there is no such thing as salvation, and escape is only ever an illusion conjured up by the hopeful.

# CHAPTER 9

The Queen, Newbury considered, was looking decidedly unwell.

This in itself should have come as no surprise. Her Majesty was now living a mechanically assisted half-life, confined to a life-preserving wheelchair that wheezed and hissed and groaned as it pumped air into her lungs and fed nutrients and preservative fluids into her bloodstream. Large coils of tubing erupted brazenly from her chest, snaking away to the twin canisters mounted on the rear of the machine. Her now-useless legs were bound together around the calves and ankles, and a metal rod supported her partially collapsed spine. Newbury had even heard talk that Dr. Lucien Fabian, the man responsible for developing the remarkable equipment, had built and installed a clockwork heart in Victoria's breast. He had no way of knowing if this was anything other than idle speculation, but it wouldn't have surprised him to discover that the monarch was, in fact, as heartless as she seemed.

Whatever the case, it could never be said that the Queen looked well. But today, even in the gloom of the audience chamber, Newbury thought her flesh had taken on an even more sickly pallor than usual, and her breathing was sounding progressively more laboured. This, he presumed, was a consequence of Dr. Fabian's recent death, which meant that the physician was no longer on call to tend to his charge or the maintenance of his machine.

Unknown to the Queen, Newbury himself had played a significant role in Fabian's demise. Now, seeing the consequences of his actions, he felt a sharp pang of guilt. He let the emotion pass. The Queen did not deserve his pity. Her own machinations were what had led her to this point: her constant scheming, her emotionless exploitation of others, her unrelenting desire for immortality. She was the architect of her own downfall, and he refused to repent for the choices he had made. Even if they meant that her life-giving machines would fail and she would die.

He stood over her now, both of them caught in a globe of orange lantern light in the midst of an eternal sea of black. She looked up at him from her chair, a sickly smile on her lips. "You took your time, Newbury."

He nodded, but didn't reply. There was a reason he'd been ignoring her summons for weeks: he'd been unsure if he could face her following the events that had led to Fabian's death. Upon arrival at the palace that morning, however, Sandford, the agent's butler, had explained that, while Victoria did wish to speak with both Newbury and Bainbridge regarding the case in hand, she first desired an audience alone with Newbury. Thus he faced her alone, Bainbridge having been ordered to wait outside until he was beckoned.

The Queen spluttered into a handkerchief. "We trust you have finished with your little rebellion?"

Newbury swallowed. "I was… indisposed."

Victoria laughed. "Yes, chasing the dragon at Johnny Chang's. Do not think your movements have gone unnoticed, Newbury. If we had suspected it was anything other than a temporary aberration, we would not have indulged you for so long."

Newbury smiled inwardly. He knew exactly who was

watching him, and precisely what she had reported back to the monarch. Victoria wasn't as informed as she liked to imagine. Clearly, the Queen had no reason to suspect the truth about what had happened at the Grayling Institute, or the fact that Newbury and Veronica had smuggled Amelia out of there alive.

"I am at your service, Your Majesty," he said, diplomatically.

The Queen raised an eyebrow in haughty disapproval. "Do not attempt to dazzle us with platitudes, Newbury. You are an agent of the Crown. It should not be necessary to remind you that we tolerate your indiscretions and excesses only because it serves us to do so. There must be results as well." She paused, choosing her next words carefully. "We fear for your position." Her tone gave little away, but Newbury heard this for what it was: a thinly veiled threat.

"I understand, Your Majesty," he said, cautiously.

"We sincerely hope that you do," she replied, licking her dry lips and narrowing her dark, beady eyes. "Our summons are not to be dismissed lightly. Nor our patronage. It has limits."

Newbury remained silent, listening to the wheezing grind of the breathing apparatus as they forcibly inflated and deflated the monarch's lungs. The moment stretched. Finally, the Queen spoke. "Now, fetch the policeman. We have business to discuss."

"Yes, Your Majesty," he said, his tone level.

*The policeman?* Newbury considered this as he crossed the audience chamber towards the thin strip of light emanating from beneath the door, behind which Bainbridge was waiting. He wondered if the Queen had ever called Bainbridge that to his face. It was appallingly dismissive. But then, those were the games she played. It was her way of maintaining control, of establishing her position. She would undermine her subjects to remind them that, despite the fact that she was strapped immobile into a grotesque life support machine, she was the one who held all of the power in their relationship. It might once have been an effective strategy, even on Newbury, but he knew this woman for what she was, and he, too, understood the rules of the game. As did Veronica–perhaps more than most.

Bainbridge, on the other hand, still struggled to reconcile her behaviour with the innate respect he held for the woman's position. He made allowances for her because she was the monarch, whereas Newbury did not think such allowances should be granted. If anything, he believed the monarch should uphold the values and integrity of the nation even more resolutely than her subjects, to lead them by example.

Bainbridge was waiting in the passageway, a respectful distance from the closed door, so as to make it clear he had not been eavesdropping on the conversation within the audience chamber. He was staring up at a portrait of the Tsar. Newbury was struck once again by the Russian monarch's resemblance to Albert Edward. The royal family had connections all across Europe, forming an intricate web with Victoria at its heart, matriarch and dictator. That was what had struck Newbury about the Prince's words of warning the previous day: if foreign agents were indeed swarming over London, wouldn't it be at the will of the Prince's relatives?

Bainbridge glanced over questioningly as Newbury stepped into the passageway.

Newbury gave the briefest of nods to indicate that all was well–or, at least, as well as could be expected. He beckoned Bainbridge forward.

Silently, Bainbridge joined him, limping a little without the aid of his stick. Newbury had rarely been to the palace alongside his friend, and always found it somewhat ungracious of the monarch to demand that the chief inspector leave his cane with Sandford. She was clearly growing more anxious about having anything in her presence that might be construed as a weapon.

At the sound of their footsteps, Victoria hoisted her lantern to shoulder height. Her sagging, pale face was cast in harsh relief, taking on a ghostly aspect in the gloom.

*"Ghost" is right*, thought Newbury. This once-great woman had been reduced to a shadow, trapped in the interstitial place between life and death. She went about her days in this miserable darkness, refusing to let go, refusing to relinquish her ever-tightening grip on the Empire. The Prince of Wales was right to question her validity as ruler.

"Come closer," she said. Newbury and Bainbridge approached, their footsteps echoing into the black void that surrounded them.

"What progress has there been in your investigation, Sir Charles?" she asked.

"My investigation, Your Majesty?"

"Do not patronise me, *policeman*."

*So*, thought Newbury, *she does call him that to his face*.

"The bodies found with their hearts removed, of course."

"Little progress as yet, I fear, Your Majesty," replied Bainbridge, his tone altering slightly, becoming more clipped, more restrained. "There are few leads, and we have yet to ascertain the significance of the stolen organs. We are concerned there may be some occult significance to the deaths. I have asked Sir Maurice to assist with the investigation for that reason."

The Queen's eyes glittered as she glanced from one of them to the other. They settled on Bainbridge. "Very good. There may be political significance to the deaths. This is a line of inquiry we urge you to explore."

"A political motivation, Your Majesty?" asked Bainbridge, his exasperation barely concealed.

"Indeed so. At first we assumed it was a coincidence, but it has since become clear that a coincidence is unlikely. All four of the victims have been agents of the Crown."

"All four?" echoed Bainbridge. "Your Majesty, there have only been three reported deaths that match the *modus operandi* of the killer."

Victoria emitted a wet, rasping cackle. "Quite so, Sir Charles. The fourth victim was killed while sequestered for an… *operation.* Due to the nature of that operation, it was paramount that the corpse was removed from the scene and swiftly disposed of. We cannot have everyone knowing our private business."

Newbury silently considered the Queen's words. This changed everything. If the victims were all, in fact, agents of the Crown, then a motive had suddenly appeared. It didn't explain the strange manner of the deaths or the significance of their splayed chests or stolen organs, but it was clearly the link that they were looking for. Once again, Newbury found himself astounded by this woman. He'd worked closely with her for a number of years now, but still had no real notion just how extensive her network of agents was. She was a master manipulator, a matriarchal spider at the heart of her vast and intricate web, guiding her myriad operatives throughout the Empire.

"I fear this puts an entirely different complexion on the situation, Your Majesty," said Newbury. "Were the dead agents all engaged in the same operation? Or could their murders have been revenge for past endeavours?"

Victoria turned her head slowly to regard him. Her eyes narrowed. "None of the agents knew each other, if that is what you're asking, Newbury. And no, they had never been engaged against a common foe, simultaneously or otherwise."

"Then they may have been killed simply because of their status as your operatives," said Bainbridge.

"Quite," intoned the Queen, huskily. "You should tread carefully," she continued. "It may be that the two of you are also at risk."

Was this another veiled threat? Newbury didn't think so. The Queen seemed genuinely threatened by this assassin who was intent on relieving her of her agents. For once, she appeared not to be playing games.

"We are not alone in this," said Bainbridge, quietly. "It seems as if *all* of your agents are at risk. Unless you have reason to suspect that we or others may be favoured as targets?" Victoria shook her head, almost imperceptibly. "Then perhaps, Your Majesty, you might have Sandford provide us with a list of possible targets? I can have my men work to safeguard them."

The Queen let out another almighty cackle that threatened to break into a heaving cough. "Sir Charles, you test our patience. We could not trust even you with that. A list of all our agents? If it fell into the wrong hands…"

"With respect, Your Majesty," said Bainbridge, shortly, "it sounds as if it already has."

"Watch your words, policeman. You would do well to remember that you are far from irreplaceable." The bellows on the back of Victoria's chair concertinaed noisily in tandem with her rising anger.

"Then could it perhaps be a rogue such as Aubrey Knox? A former agent who knows the identity of some of our number, and who to target to most effectively get your attention?" Newbury noted the slight crack in Bainbridge's voice as he spoke these words in hushed tones, as if he did not wish to give voice to his fears. The name of Aubrey Knox invoked bad memories for all of them.

The Queen fixed Bainbridge with a stern look. "Doubtful," she proclaimed dismissively. "We have learned to keep a closer eye on our former or more errant agents," she said, glancing pointedly at Newbury as she spoke. "We keep them gainfully employed. We should know if any of them were not fulfilling their obligations."

Newbury felt the words sting like darts.

"Don't forget, it might still be the Cabal of the Horned Beast, or some other such cult," said Bainbridge. "The ritualistic elements seem too pronounced to be ignored. Perhaps they tortured one or more of their victims, eliciting names…?"

"Or perhaps it's foreign agents?" interjected Newbury. The thought suddenly bloomed in his mind. This was what Albert Edward, the Prince of Wales had suggested: that London was swarming with foreigners keen to undermine the Queen's power. If this were true, surely they could be responsible for the recent spate of deaths. "Could this represent clandestine activity by another nation? Are we at peace with the Kaiser?"

"The Kaiser?" barked Victoria, surprised. "We cannot believe that Wilhelm has any interest in this filthy business," she stated, firmly, and Newbury saw her left hand open and close into a fist in frustration or anger. Clearly he had touched a nerve. "Although we accept it is possible that foreign agents representing other factions may be at work, we believe that it is far more likely that the problem is home-grown."

"Home-grown?" asked Bainbridge.

"This so-called 'Secret Service'," said Victoria, with venom. "Upstarts with ideas above their station."

Newbury felt Bainbridge bristle beside him. "Your Majesty, I hardly feel—"

"We care little for what you feel, *policeman*," she interrupted, savagely.

Newbury could imagine Bainbridge growing redder in the face by the second. "It is my understanding, Your Majesty, that this government agency has been established to aid in the protection of the Empire, not to undermine it. Their stated aim is to ensure the peace and prosperity of our nation and her interests abroad."

"But, what if, Newbury," challenged the Queen, "they feel that the interests of the country would be best served by dethroning the monarch, or, at the very least, undermining our power base?" She paused, fixing him with her jaundiced eyes. "What then?"

Bainbridge began to stammer something in response, but wisely bit his tongue. It wouldn't do to become agitated with the monarch in her presence, and Bainbridge knew it.

"Treat those 'spies' as potential enemies of the Crown. Begin your investigations there. We fear they may be plotting a coup. These unfortunate deaths may yet prove to be a symptom of it," said Victoria.

"Your Majesty, some of their agents are known to me. Indeed, a number of them have assisted Scotland Yard in unravelling some particularly high-profile cases. I myself was involved in establishing the bureau," said Bainbridge, the exasperation evident in his voice.

"It has not gone unnoticed," said Victoria, coldly. "But now you will sever all links and treat all of their activity with suspicion. We shall uncover the truth regarding their motives."

Bainbridge took a deep breath, but didn't respond.

The Queen looked to Newbury. "Now go. Bring this matter to a swift resolution. No more deaths."

"Yes, Your Majesty," replied Newbury, his tone neutral. He knew how to play this game. He bowed briefly, putting his hand on Bainbridge's shoulder and urging him to bow as well. He could feel his friend trembling in anger. He gripped his shoulder all the more firmly, reassuring, but cautionary, too.

Without another word, the two men turned and left the audience chamber, leaving the Queen to revel in her solitude in the heart of her slowly receding globe of lantern light.


Bainbridge did not say another word until they were standing in the courtyard of the palace beside their brougham cab, not even a civil word to Sandford as he collected their coats and ushered them out with a strained smile. Sandford had once been an agent himself. He had long since retired from active duty, but Newbury knew that he understood all too well the Queen's temperamental nature and what it was like to be on the receiving end of her wrath.

Bainbridge shot a glance at Newbury, his moustache quivering with barely concealed rage. "I... I..." he stammered loudly, struggling to give shape to his words.

"Contain yourself, Charles. The walls here have ears. Let us repair to Chelsea where we can discuss the matter in private," said Newbury, his voice firm.

"Must we?" said Bainbridge, bristling with frustration. "That damnable opium fog that lingers in your rooms leaves me feeling quite queasy, Newbury. I don't know how you live with it." He banged his cane decidedly on the ground. "No. Let us repair to my house, where at least there's clean air and somewhere to actually sit down."

Newbury raised a single eyebrow in surprise. "Very well," he said, "but we must send for Miss Hobbes when we arrive."

"Quite so, Newbury," replied Bainbridge, yanking open the door of the cab and bustling up the iron steps. "Quite so."

With a sigh, Newbury spoke a few hasty words with the driver and then followed Bainbridge into the conveyance, closing the door behind himself. Bainbridge was glaring out of the window at the palace, his fists clenched on his lap.

It was going to be an interesting afternoon.

# CHAPTER 10

⬥

"God damn it!"

Bainbridge swung his cane viciously at the side table in the hallway of his home, shattering a vase and sending a notebook and a sheaf of papers sprawling across the floor. "God damn it!" he repeated angrily.

He threw his cane on top of the heaped detritus and stormed off into the depths of the house, bellowing loudly for his housekeeper.

Newbury stood for a moment in the hallway, taking stock. He'd never seen his friend in such a foul mood, nor his face that particular shade of cerise, but then, he'd never seen him treated with such terrible disdain, either. Bainbridge's reaction might have been funny if the circumstances were different, but the Queen—for whom Bainbridge had always maintained the utmost respect—had placed him in an impossible position.

Everything he was working for, the links he'd been building with men like Angelchrist for nearly a year, she had questioned. Worse, she had implied that Bainbridge had actively sought to associate with traitors. This left him no room to manoeuvre, since the Queen was not to be proven wrong, whatever the truth of the matter. Bainbridge would have to sever his links with the government agency, or else risk everything: not only his relationship with the Queen, but his career, and possibly even his life. Newbury fully expected Bainbridge to do as the Queen had commanded—he was a loyal man, and she had left him with little choice—but he would do it reluctantly.

He could hear Bainbridge now, barking at his valet, Clarkson, in the kitchen. The poor man wouldn't know what had hit him. Newbury wasn't overly familiar with the valet. In fact, it was rare that he found himself in Bainbridge's home—he could probably count the occasions he had visited on both hands. Typically they met in Chelsea, or the White Friar's, or else the Yard, or a crime scene. He did not know what that said of their relationship.

The house was an austere sort of place—barely lived in, really, since Isobel had died. It existed in a strange state of preservation, as if these past years Bainbridge had maintained it in the way that his late wife might have done. He had refused to change anything or alter the decor in any way.

The drawing room, for example, was entirely the opposite of Newbury's own. Whereas Newbury's was filled with the accoutrements of his profession and his life—everything from the cat skull on the mantelpiece to the leaning piles of books beside the battered old sofa—Bainbridge's was pristine and quiet, devoid of any heart. It was as if the spirit of the place had died along with Isobel. Now the house existed merely as a tribute to her, a place for Bainbridge to eat and sleep, which he did there as little as possible. It wasn't a place that was *lived* in.

Perhaps that was the reason Newbury was rarely invited to visit: Bainbridge wished to retain that sense of stasis, avoid bringing too much life and change into the house lest he disturb the spirit of his late wife, whose presence he had tried so hard to hold on to.

Sighing, Newbury stooped low, collecting Bainbridge's cane and shuffling the scattered papers into a neat pile. He stood and arranged them once again on the side table.

He heard Bainbridge's clomping footsteps echoing back up the hall towards him and glanced up. "Leave that, Newbury. Clarkson will see to it."

"I fear Clarkson may already have his hands full," said Newbury, with a smile.

Bainbridge's shoulders sagged in resignation. "Yes, I did rather give him both barrels, didn't I?" He sighed. "Anyway, he's sent word for Miss Hobbes. She should be here within an hour."

"Excellent," said Newbury. "Then let us sit for a moment and regain our sensibilities. We need to approach this problem with a level head."

"And a large brandy," said Bainbridge, with a heavy sigh.

"This question may seem anathema to you, Sir Charles, but how do we know that the Queen isn't actually right in her assertion?"

Newbury raised his eyebrows in surprise as Bainbridge blustered in response to Veronica's question.

"Because... because... Gah!" He slammed his palm down hard upon the arm of his chair. "That's a damned impertinent question, Miss Hobbes!"

"But nevertheless one that needs to be asked, Sir Charles," said Veronica, firmly. "Like it or not, the question remains: how do we know what this new Secret Service is actually planning?"

"I count myself among their founding members, Miss Hobbes!" said Bainbridge, his voice raising an octave in sheer frustration.

"And do you play an active role in the assignment of each agent's duties?" continued Veronica. "Are you aware of the nature of all of their current investigations or missions? I admit, Sir Charles, to knowing very little of how you've been spending your days of late."

"Of course not!" said Bainbridge, hotly. "But I hardly

think that means they're waging a clandestine war against the agents of Her Majesty behind my back! I put my full trust in those men and women. Men such as Angelchrist are working tirelessly to protect this Empire from harm, in much the same way as you, Newbury, and I are."

"But why?" asked Veronica.

"I should have thought it was obvious," snapped Bainbridge.

"Don't be obtuse, Charles," said Newbury, leaning forward in his chair. Around them the house was shrouded in utter silence, save for the rhythmic ticking of a grandfather clock and the distant cawing of birds outside. "I believe the question Miss Hobbes is getting at is: why did the Home Secretary decide it was necessary to set up his own bureau of operatives when the Queen already has a vast network of agents at her disposal, throughout not only the Empire, but all across the globe?"

Bainbridge sighed heavily. "Well… yes, I see your point, Miss Hobbes, and I apologise for my impassioned outburst." He paused for a moment to regain his composure. "The notion behind the bureau was to create a network of specialist agents who were free from the… the… *constraints* of being sanctioned operatives of the Queen."

"Constraints?" prompted Veronica, pushing for further explanation.

"Well, we all know what she's like!" said Bainbridge, a hint of the former anger edging once more into his voice. "We know she has a very particular way of doing things, and a rather skewed opinion of her own worth."

Newbury sat forward, shocked to hear such utterances from the mouth of his old friend. "Charles! You astound me."

"Oh, don't pretend you're shocked, Newbury. You saw her today." Newbury noticed that Bainbridge was clenching his fists in frustration. "Overall, I believe the Queen still acts in the interest of the Empire, but she has never allowed it to prevent her from acting for her own good. You know that as well as I do.

The most important thing to the Queen is the Queen herself."
He sat back, folding his arms across his chest defensively.

"So you're saying that the men and women working for
the Secret Service are free from such petty concerns?" asked
Veronica, doubtfully.

"Not at all. Simply that all decisions are made by a
committee, so we are able to insulate ourselves against the
singular will of one overriding egoist. Better decisions are
made that way, Miss Hobbes, and the good of the nation is
*always* paramount."

"I'd never have marked you down as a democrat, Charles,"
said Newbury, smirking, "but I applaud you wholeheartedly
for it."

Bainbridge shrugged dismissively. "So there you have it. I
maintain wholeheartedly that the Secret Service is not in any
way responsible for the murder of Her Majesty's agents."

"Even," said Veronica, refusing to let the matter drop, "if the
actions of those agents were, in the opinion of your committee,
considered to be counter to the good of the British people?"

"Well... I... you're asking me an impossible, hypothetical
question!" replied Bainbridge.

"Am I?" ventured Veronica, quietly.

"Charles is not alone in his assertions, Miss Hobbes. I have
not yet elaborated on the reason for the Prince of Wales's
visit to Chelsea yesterday afternoon. At this juncture he very
much echoes the sentiments of the chief inspector here, in
that he believes the Queen is becoming too self-involved
and inward looking, and in so doing is allowing the enemies
of the Empire to grow bolder." Newbury glanced over at
Bainbridge, who appeared to be listening to him intently.
"He fears that operatives allied to hostile foreign agencies
are currently in London, including those of his cousin, the
Kaiser, who he suggests is spoiling for a war. If he can be
believed—and I have no reason to think that he cannot—then

perhaps those same foreign agents might be responsible for the recent deaths? They may be seeking to undermine the Queen's power base so her position is weaker if it comes to war or a political coup."

Veronica was frowning. "It's certainly possible," she said. "But forgive me, Sir Maurice, for asking why the Prince of Wales should come to you with such grave concerns?"

Newbury laughed. "Precisely my thought, Miss Hobbes. I asked him the very same question. He said that ever since the little affair we took care of for him in Cambridge, he's felt he could come to me with his concerns. He asked only that I remain vigilant and report to him any activity that may come to light on the matter."

"And will you report your theory that those foreign agents might be behind this rash of diabolical murders?" asked Veronica.

"Not yet," replied Newbury. "I have nothing substantial to support the claim."

"Angelchrist will have a better idea," said Bainbridge, eyeing them both as he waited for their reaction. When they kept looking at him blankly, he continued. "I can't think of another man who knows more about the political situation abroad. If there are foreign agents involved, he'll be able to point us in the right direction."

"You're forgetting something, Charles," said Newbury. "Her Majesty has forbidden you from speaking with Angelchrist, or any of the others who might be connected with him. Don't think for a minute that she won't be having you watched. If you put even a foot out of line... well, you saw how adamant she was."

"Poppycock to that!" said Bainbridge, brusquely. "She's wrong, Newbury. Plain wrong, and I refuse to sever ties to a good man for obscure reasons, not when the security of the nation is at stake. She also told us to ensure there were no further deaths. We cannot be expected to work miracles!"

"No, but we *will* be expected to obey her wishes. It's too much of a risk even for me or Miss Hobbes to pay him a visit."

"Then we'll arrange to meet with him clandestinely. He deserves to know the truth, Newbury. You must agree with that, at least? He's proved a good friend to us over the last six months, and aside from any insight he may be able to offer into the Prince's concerns, we need to warn him that the Queen is out for his blood." Bainbridge tugged at the corners of his moustache anxiously, as if he was urging Newbury to grant him permission.

"Are you sure that's wise?" said Veronica. "If—and I grant you, you make a good case that it does not—the Secret Service does have some hand in the murders, you'd be tipping them off that we're on to them. Do you truly know we can trust Professor Angelchrist?"

"I would trust him with my life," said Bainbridge.

"And I," said Newbury.

"Good. Because that's exactly what you'll both be doing," said Veronica. She didn't need to add "and mine along with it." The implication was clear.

For a moment the three of them sat in silence, allowing the tension to stretch. Finally, Bainbridge spoke. "I'll have Clarkson make the necessary arrangements. He can get word to Angelchrist without arousing suspicion. We'll meet somewhere out in the open, where there are lots of people."

Newbury nodded. "Yes. Somewhere we can talk without being seen, and with a crowd sufficient to help us cover our tracks."

"Very well. I'll see to it forthwith." Bainbridge was already heaving himself up out of his chair.

"Excellent," said Newbury. "Then I think it's time we were bidding you good day. There is much to consider."

"Indeed. You'll see yourselves out, won't you?" said Bainbridge, reaching for his cane and crossing to the drawing room door.

"Of course," said Veronica.

Newbury waited until Bainbridge's footsteps had receded down the hallway before turning to Veronica. "Of course, there's one other thing to consider, Miss Hobbes."

"About Professor Angelchrist?"

"No, about the murders." He lowered his voice so as not to be overheard. "The possibility that the Queen herself is responsible. That she's clearing out the ranks of her own operation for some reason, perhaps to minimise her risk of exposure to some piece of information that she doesn't want to get out."

"Surely not? I mean, I know what she's capable of, but, really... would she kill her own agents just to protect a secret?" asked Veronica.

"Nothing would surprise me any more, not when it comes to Her Majesty the Queen," replied Newbury solemnly. "And not after what we saw at the Grayling Institute."

Veronica nodded. "You're right, of course. But why not mention this in front of Sir Charles?"

"Because he'd never believe it," said Newbury, "even with his newfound distaste for her methods. He hasn't seen the things we have, and we're not at liberty to explain why we did what we did."

"No, but he seems to be coming to a similar conclusion all on his own," said Veronica.

"And for that we should be grateful," replied Newbury, laughing. "Provided, of course, that he doesn't go and get us all executed for treason."

Veronica grimaced. "That's no laughing matter and you know it. If we're caught fraternising with the professor she won't be lenient on us."

"In that case, my dear Miss Hobbes, we'll simply have to ensure that we don't go and get ourselves caught," he said, still chuckling.

Veronica shook her head in mock exasperation. "Men," she said, sighing, as she got to her feet.

"Shall we share a hansom?" asked Newbury.

"Only if you agree to find one of the traditional, horse-drawn variety," replied Veronica.

"If we must," he said, grinning and getting to his feet. He hooked his arm with Veronica's and led her to the door. "If we must."

# CHAPTER 11

The spoon was solid silver, with a tapered head in the shape of a leaf and three lozenge-shaped slots in its bowl. It was dulled through use and had never been polished; he kept it in a small, velvet-lined box along with other, similar paraphernalia. Both superstition and ingrained routine meant that he never left the strange assortment of implements out for Scarbright to clean—he didn't know what the valet would make of them, and had no desire to find out. The box resided amongst Newbury's personal effects, nestled in a very particular spot amongst the ageing spines of his bookcase.

Newbury balanced the spoon carefully over a glass tumbler and, using a pair of matching silver tongs, placed a brown sugar cube upon it. He reached for the jug of iced water on the table beside him and held it above the spoon, tilting it fractionally so that only the tiniest trickles of liquid splashed upon the sugar cube, eroding it slowly and steadily so that the sugary water blended easily with the rich, green liquor below. As he watched, the liquid in the glass took on an opaque, cloudy aspect.

He allowed the water to continue trickling until the glass was half full and the sugar cube had completely dissolved. Then, removing the spoon, he dried it with a handkerchief and placed it carefully back into the box alongside the tongs.

Sighing to himself in satisfaction, he leaned back in his Chesterfield and drained the drink in one go, shuddering slightly at the sharpness of the alcohol and the sweetness of the anise. He returned the empty glass to the occasional table and collected one of his opium-tainted cigarettes from the silver case in his pocket. He struck a match and played the flame across the tip of the cigarette, enjoying the slight crackle of burning paper and tobacco as it hungrily caught the heat. He took a long, deep draw, filling his lungs with the sweet-scented smoke, and then closed his eyes, shutting out the world and her many distractions.

This was another of Newbury's rituals; the process by which he retreated inside his own mind, withdrawing from the world around him. It was his means of seeking clarity. In this fugue state he would replay the many sights, smells, and conversations of the previous two days, reordering them in his mind, searching for connections amongst the minutiae. This was how he chose his path through a problem, how he fathomed the meaning of the things he had seen and heard.

Newbury's breath became shallow and his shoulders slumped as the alcohol and narcotics took effect. His head lolled against the back of the chair. Snatches of images and broken sentences began to swirl up from the darkness. He encouraged them, urging them forward so that he might tease out the information he required.

The process would take hours, and he would spend them lost in a distant opium dream. He had much to consider.

That afternoon, after seeing Veronica safely to her Kensington abode, he had ordered the cab driver to take him home to Chelsea, where a most mysterious parcel awaited him.

It was wrapped in innocuous brown paper and tied with string. His name and address were printed on the label in neat capitals, although he could tell from the slight smudges around the edges of the label that the writer had been a little heavy-handed with the ink, and the label had still been wet when the package was collected for delivery. It hadn't come far—there was no postmark, meaning it had been delivered by hand, probably by the driver of a hansom cab at the behest of the sender. That led him to believe that the parcel's point of origin was somewhere within the bounds of the city.

Scarbright, regrettably, had not been there to receive it, but had found it waiting upon the doorstep when he had returned from the market earlier that afternoon. Unsuspecting, the valet had carried it in, placing it upon Newbury's desk to await his return. This suggested that either the delivery man had called at a time when Scarbright was out, or that the sender was aware of Scarbright's habit of walking to the market for provisions at the same time every week, and had chosen that time purposefully to ensure the valet was not there to receive the parcel in person. Newbury—having now seen the contents of the box—suspected the latter option. It was most definitely a message, and whoever had sent it had wished to avoid leaving any clues whatsoever as to their identity.

Warily, Newbury had cut the string and sliced into the brown paper, peering at the small wooden box within. He'd received parcels like this before and they had inevitably contained either threatening gifts or booby traps. As he'd soon come to realise, this particular parcel was no exception.

Newbury had placed the plain, lacquered box upon the table and circled it suspiciously, looking for signs of tampering. There had been no outward evidence of any mechanism contained within—a spring-loaded dart, perhaps, or a small bomb—so he had carefully lifted the box's lid with the tip of his letter opener, standing as far back as he was able.

Nothing untoward had occurred in the seconds that followed, so he'd stepped closer to the table to examine the contents of the box. He had to admit, it was a most fascinating assortment. The human skull was perhaps the most disturbing of the three objects, fashioned as it was into a grotesque mask: the lower jaw was missing and the brain cavity removed with a series of neat cuts. The bone appeared to have been boiled or bleached to remove the last remnants of flesh and muscle, and a series of occult runes and symbols had been etched into the surface with a fine blade. Finally, a mixture of blood and ink had been worked into these etchings, staining them a deep, dark red.

The other two objects contained within the box were a curved silver dagger with a jewel-encrusted hilt and a small leather pouch containing the putrid viscera of a small bird, probably a juvenile crow. There was no card or note accompanying them, or within the paper wrapping.

Newbury, of course, had known what it was at once. These were the elements of a ritual suicide, a death rite practised by occultists since the Middle Ages. It was said to ensure prosperity in the afterlife, the trading of one's living soul for the promise of eternal damnation. It could have been sent to him by any number of people or organisations he had crossed over the years, but the message was clear: *we're offering you the opportunity to take your own life, before we come and take it for you.*

Newbury would take his chances with the living. For now, the threat itself meant very little. If anything, by attempting to frighten him, the sender had shown their hand, and Newbury would now be expecting them when they came for him. He'd beaten the Cabal once before, and, if necessary, he could do it again.

The stub of Newbury's extinguished cigarette tumbled from his fingers, dropping onto the rug before the hearth. His eyes flickered open. He had no idea how much time had passed, but the fire in the grate was cold, and the room was chill and dark. The curtains were still open, revealing the fog-shrouded night beyond.

A smile played upon Newbury's lips as he reached for the jug of now tepid water. He knew what he had to do. Bainbridge had told the Queen they needed a list of her agents to look for patterns in the selection of victims and to anticipate any further attacks. The Queen had refused, but Newbury had another potential avenue through which to obtain the information: Albert Edward, the Prince of Wales.

He would visit the Prince in the morning and seek his assistance in the matter. While he was there, he would apprise him of the situation regarding the murders, and his concerns that foreign agents might prove to be behind them. He was sure that the Prince would come to his aid. Then, assuming Bainbridge was successful in arranging a liaison with Angelchrist, they would meet to discuss the matter that afternoon.

Newbury took a swig of water and leaned back in his chair, closing his eyes. It was too late for bed and too early to rise. He would pass the time with another cigarette, waiting for the sun to bring its warming light through the window.

# CHAPTER 12

❧

"I received your note," said Veronica, anxiously, "and came directly. What's wrong?" She was breathless from rushing across the village green, and her clothes stank of engine fumes and soot. Within minutes of receiving the morning post, she'd hailed one of the odious steam-powered carriages and told the driver to take the most direct route to Malbury Cross.

"Calm yourself, sister," said Amelia, standing and crossing the living room to take Veronica in a hearty embrace. She was wearing a concerned expression. "I didn't mean for you to drop everything the moment you received my letter."

"But you said you needed to speak with me as a matter of urgency?" said Veronica, confused. "I thought... well, I thought something was terribly wrong." Her shoulders dropped as the tension she'd been carrying for the last couple of hours finally dissipated. She felt a curious mixture of relief and annoyance at discovering there wasn't, after all, an emergency. She had immediate business to attend to back in London, and she was anxious to maintain a watchful eye on Bainbridge and Angelchrist. Whatever reasons the chief inspector had given the previous day for his involvement with the Secret Service, she was still wary of the intentions of that organisation. Perhaps Bainbridge was ignorant of their schemes, but she couldn't help considering that perhaps he was not.

Veronica had learned to trust Bainbridge during the course of their association, but nevertheless had shied away from being entirely open with him when it came to her sister or her role as an agent of the Crown. She'd feared—and Newbury confirmed—that Bainbridge was too fixed in his beliefs of what constituted right and wrong, that he wouldn't understand the decisions she had made to protect her family. For the last few months, however, he had been behaving suspiciously, attending scores of furtive meetings which he would not speak of or provide any details, and she had begun to wonder if she hadn't got Bainbridge entirely wrong, after all. Now she was intent on discovering just what it was the chief inspector had gone and got himself involved in, and why it was causing the Queen such consternation and concern.

But whatever else was going on in Veronica's life, Amelia came first, so she had come here to the village directly upon receiving her sister's summons, fearful for Amelia's fragile health and well-being. It seemed now that she might have acted in haste.

Amelia helped Veronica shrug out of her coat. "Look, I'll go and tell Mrs. Leeson to put the kettle on. We do need to talk."

Veronica nodded. "I was worried"—she almost choked on her words—"that perhaps there'd been some sort of side effect caused by Sir Maurice's treatment, or that it had stopped working entirely; that you might have suffered another seizure."

Amelia smiled. "No, nothing like that. The treatment is as effective as ever. It's just... you know how I told you my episodes were becoming more controllable, easier to contain?"

"Yes?"

"Well, there are things I've seen, Veronica. Things you need to know." Amelia sounded suddenly serious. She folded Veronica's grey coat neatly over her arm, picking nervously at the bobbles of lint and refusing to meet Veronica's gaze.

"Right. Well, I'm here now, so let's see about that tea and you can tell me all about it," said Veronica, with some trepidation.

A few minutes later, Veronica found herself ensconced by the fire in the living room, welcoming the warmth back into her weary bones. She still felt shaken from both her journey—the steam-powered carriage had jarred her most efficiently as they'd trundled through the cobbled lanes on the outskirts of the city—and the sudden fear for her sister's health.

Mrs. Leeson was busying herself in the kitchen, seeing to the kettle, and Amelia was sitting opposite Veronica, perched upon the edge of a chaise longue. She looked thin and gaunt, but hauntingly pretty, her raven-black hair tied back from her forehead in a neat chignon. Her eyes were wide with concern.

"So, tell me—what's this all about?" asked Veronica, not entirely sure that she wanted to know. It had been some time since Amelia had discussed the contents of her visionary episodes with her, and the last time, she'd warned Veronica that something dreadful was coming.

Veronica had absolute faith in her sister's ability to see… if not into the future, exactly, then *impressions* of what was to come, and often, it terrified her. "I thought the seizures had stopped? That the treatment meant you were getting stronger?" she said.

Amelia nodded. "The seizures *have* stopped. And I'm certainly getting stronger. But the visions still come. They're not as violent as they once were, and I've learned to anticipate when they're coming. There's a smell, a taste on the back of my tongue. It's like the air before a thunderstorm, a prickle of anticipation…" She trailed off, taking a deep breath.

"Go on," said Veronica, both fascinated and appalled.

"When it strikes, it's like a waking dream. Images flickering through my mind, disjointed and fragmentary. Unbidden sounds. It's over in seconds, and then I come to."

"Just like that? It used to take hours for you to regain consciousness," said Veronica, sitting forward in her chair.

Amelia smiled. "There's nothing but a momentary disorientation," she said. "Sir Maurice's treatment is having a profound effect."

"But...?" asked Veronica.

"But, the things I see..." Amelia hesitated. "Do you remember when we first came here, to Malbury Cross?"

"Of course."

"I told you something terrible was coming," said Amelia, quietly.

Veronica swallowed. "Yes."

"I still fear there is truth in that. I'm concerned you're in grave danger, Veronica," said Amelia, her voice cracking.

Veronica stiffened. She'd feared as much. "Back when I first brought you here, you said there was a word, too. A repeated word. 'Executioner,' I think it was?"

Amelia nodded. "Let me show you something." She rose slowly from her perch on the chaise longue, crossing the room to a large writing bureau. She took a small key from a concealed pocket in her dress, inserted it into a matching lock on the face of the bureau, and turned it with a scrape. She allowed the wooden shelf to drop forward, revealing the disarrayed contents within: letters, scraps of paper, tatty quills and jars of ink; all of them shoved untidily—hurriedly, even—within.

Amelia withdrew a sheaf of rolled papers, and, clutching it close to her chest, returned to her seat. She handed the papers to Veronica. "There."

"What is this?" said Veronica, mystified.

"Open it," replied Amelia.

Veronica did as her sister asked, unfurling the curled pages and smoothing them carefully across her knees. As she looked over the hastily scratched letters and smudges of dry, spattered ink within, she felt her heart flutter in her chest. She studied the uppermost page. The word *Executioner* had been scrawled over every inch of its surface, repeatedly, in the same hand. She lifted the first page. Beneath it, the second was near identical. She shuffled through a sheaf of perhaps ten pages. All were the same. The writing was frantic, untidy—as if the writer had been scared or possessed, or possibly both. "You did these?" asked Veronica, her voice level. "Under the influence of one of your episodes?"

Amelia stared at her for a long moment. "No," she said, finally. "Not me."

"Then who?" prompted Veronica, although she felt a horrible suspicion welling up inside of her.

"Sir Maurice," said Amelia, quickly. "Sir Maurice wrote them."

Veronica took a deep breath. What was going on here? "How? Why?"

Amelia shrugged. "He sees things, too, Veronica. Whatever he does, however it happens, he sees the same things as I do."

Veronica shook her head. "No. He's not like you. He doesn't have your... talents."

Amelia indicated the sheaf of papers in Veronica's hands. "I'd argue that these papers suggest that he does."

"But..." Veronica faltered. She shook her head. "No. Perhaps he thinks he does. All those rituals..." She trailed off again. "He must have heard you talking. Did you tell him about this word, this *Executioner*?"

Amelia shook her head. "No. I did not. I've told only you."

Veronica glanced again at the pages in her grasp. Then, as if her hands refused to hold on to them any longer, she dropped them to the floor. They fell in a landslide across the burgundy rug before the hearth. "Tell me what it means," she said, in a whisper.

Amelia looked away, unable to meet her gaze. "In my dreams I hear the same word repeated over and over, in a variety of voices. It's accompanied by a sequence of flickering images, as if everything is taking place in a darkened room, with an inconstant light source. There's a figure in black, the glint of a blade. And then there is you, lying on the floor. Your face is ashen white and you're bleeding from a wound in your chest. In the background a thousand clocks are ticking."

Veronica's mouth was dry. She tried to swallow, but her tongue felt thick and swollen in her mouth. *If this were true...* "So, this Executioner... is coming for *me*?" Was she next on the list? Was this what had happened to the other agents?

Amelia was staring at the heap of spilt papers on the rug. "I think he might be." She looked up, suddenly, imploringly. "You need to get away. Go somewhere safe, away from here, from London. Somewhere where they can't get to you."

"I can't," said Veronica. "I'm needed."

"By the Queen?" said Amelia, barely suppressing a scoff. "Surely you can't continue to harbour any sense of loyalty to that aged harridan?"

Veronica glanced away, searching the flames in the grate as if they might somehow provide her with guidance. "Not the Queen," she said. "Not her. Maurice."

"Sir Maurice can look after himself," said Amelia. "He'd want you to go. To be safe."

"It's not as simple as that, Amelia. He needs me. There's a chance he's mixed up in something terrible, and there's no one else he can turn to."

"He would want you to get to safety," said Amelia, her voice strained.

"He doesn't have to know," said Veronica, pointedly.

"Even if it means you might die?" replied Amelia, evenly.

"It's a chance I'll have to take." She took a deep breath. "What have you told him? About your dreams. About the meaning of this," she asked, pointing to the papers.

Amelia shook her head in dismay. "You must listen to me, sister!"

"What have you told him?" asked Veronica, firmly.

Amelia held her gaze for a moment in silence. All Veronica could hear was the crackle of the fire and the sound of Mrs. Leeson banging pots in the kitchen. "Very little," said Amelia, finally. "I've told him very little. Only that I think you might be in danger. That doesn't mean he won't have formed his own conclusions, however."

Veronica nodded. "Very well. We shall speak no more of this, Amelia. Do not even think of it."

Amelia laughed, bitterly. "I only wish that were possible." She sighed. "I wish you'd reconsider."

Veronica shook her head, resolute. How could she? After everything that Newbury had done for Amelia. After what had passed between them in the cells beneath Packwood House, when he'd kissed her and told her how he truly felt about her. How could she abandon him now, at his lowest point, weakened by the rituals he was performing on her sister's behalf, addicted to the poisonous weed that fed his understanding of the occult, possibly unable even to trust the word of his old friend, Sir Charles? How could she possibly leave him to cope with all of that, alone?

No. She would stay, and she would face whatever was coming. Amelia's visions were not the truth. They were not the future. They were simply a *possible* future. And that meant it could be averted. Now that she was forewarned, she could prevent it from coming true. "You know I can't reconsider," she said, trying to sound confident, unruffled. "And besides, it's my job. I face danger every single day. What's the difference here?" She left the question hanging, knowing that it was inadequate. Both of them were aware of what she was doing—making light of Amelia's revelations, brushing them under the carpet—and both of them knew the truth: that if Amelia had seen something troubling in her dreams, then it was surely lurking just around the corner.

The sound of heavy footsteps echoed in the hallway outside the door. Veronica and Amelia both turned to look as Mrs. Leeson bustled in, opening the door with her hip and causing the contents of her tray to jangle and clink merrily as she crossed the room. She glanced from one of them to the other. "Tea?" she asked, brightly.

Veronica sighed. "Yes, please, Mrs. Leeson."

# CHAPTER 13

Marlborough House, like so many of the grand houses of the eighteenth century, was an imposing, slab-like edifice that stood proud amongst its palatial siblings in the heart of Pall Mall. Flanked by St. James's Palace and Clarence House, one might have been forgiven for dismissing Marlborough House as just another unnecessary Royal household, similar to numerous other properties that had been co-opted by the monarchy over the years.

What set Marlborough House apart was its occupant: Albert Edward, the future King of England.

It was, Newbury reflected, a most suitable abode for a Prince. The building had a grand, monumental air, with a sweeping approach and extensive, well-tended grounds. Serried ranks of tall sash windows looked out across the city, and a small balcony over the front portico provided the Prince with the means to make a formal address, should it be required.

The house was brightly coloured, and its red and white brickwork, particularly when compared to the grey austerity of Buckingham Palace, gave the place a sense of vibrancy and life. A statement, Newbury considered, that might be applied equally well to the palaces' respective occupants.

He glanced at the gated entrance and was struck by a

dawning sense of trepidation. How did one go about calling on the Prince of Wales? Should he simply walk right up to the front door and knock? Should he have sent ahead to enquire about making a formal appointment? He was confident the Prince would be willing to assist him, particularly given his unexpected call at Chelsea, but had the informality of that interview somewhat gone to Newbury's head?

He couldn't help but ponder these matters as he walked along the outer wall of the grounds, searching for a side entrance—perhaps if he made his presence known at the tradesman's entrance it might not be deemed such a liberty—but he found the side gate locked and threaded with a heavy chain, and was forced to resort to his earlier plan.

Steeling himself, he went back the way he had come, then followed the gravelled approach across the grounds, admiring the immaculate front lawns and the neat hedgerows. He was sure someone inside the vast house would have seen his approach and would be there to meet him when he arrived at the portico, but once again, his expectations were dashed. The house was shrouded in silence.

Newbury finally decided that he was there already and had little choice but to continue. He took the bell pull in his right hand and gave it a sharp tug. The resultant clanging from deep inside the house caused his stomach to turn as the gravity of what he was doing dawned on him.

He had, of course, been granted innumerable audiences with the monarch herself over the course of his career as an agent of the Crown, but the rules of engagement had always been clearly delineated. When he visited the palace, it was at the Queen's behest. While he could never say he had grown comfortable in her presence, a certain familiarity with her means and methods had perhaps taken the edge off. On the rare occasions when he had needed to initiate a communication with the Queen, he had arranged it via

Sandford, the agent's butler, who had ensured everything was properly sanctioned, approved, and in order.

This, however, was entirely different. He had only met the Prince of Wales on a handful of occasions, and they had always been at the Prince's instigation. Now, he was there on the steps of Marlborough House, calling without an invitation to beg a favour of the future king. Bainbridge would have said he was mad. For once, Newbury could find no logical way to disagree.

The Prince's butler did not keep Newbury waiting for long. The massive oak door swung inwards with a perceptible sigh, and a finely dressed man—wearing a black suit, starched collar, and white gloves, and with a face as stern as chiselled ice—offered Newbury an appraising look, raised a single eyebrow, and drawled "Yes?" as if it were a word of ten syllables and not one.

Newbury drew himself up. "My name is Sir Maurice Newbury. I'm here to see the Prince of Wales."

The butler was somewhat taken aback. "And do you have an appointment, sir?" he asked, his voice whistling nasally.

"Not as such," said Newbury.

"Ah," came the response. The butler moved as if to close the door.

"I do, however, have an invitation from the Prince himself," interjected Newbury hurriedly, in an effort to prevent himself from being rejected forthwith. "He asked me to call."

The butler offered him a speculative look. "Indeed?" he said, clearly unconvinced. "Sir Maurice Newbury, you say?"

"That's correct," responded Newbury, with as much gravitas as he could muster. He was not about to be intimidated by a servant with a trumped up opinion of his own role.

"Very well," said the butler, inclining his head fractionally and opening the door a little wider. "You may wait here, in the hallway, while I enquire with His Royal Highness."

Newbury glowered at the man as he crossed the threshold

and stepped into the grandiose foyer. It was as impressive as any royal residence he had seen. The floor was a chequerboard of black and white marble tiles, polished until they gleamed like the mirrored surface of a lake. Huge fronds erupted from pots as tall as Newbury himself, and a sparkling glass chandelier hung low and magnificent, refracting the thin light that slanted in from the upper windows.

The staircase was impressive, too, seeming to flow up and around to a wide upper gallery. But what drew Newbury's attention most of all was the scattering of small birds that fluttered, ducked, and wove above his head, darting around the furnishings, twittering noisily, wheeling and dancing in the lofty space. There must have been ten or twenty different varieties in a multitude of vibrant colours: pink, azure, jade, saffron. He watched them for a while as they fluttered from one perch to another, be it the chandelier, the banister, the potted leaves, the picture rail. He wondered why the Prince would keep such a bizarre and impressive collection there in the hallway, free to affect an escape any time the main door to the house was opened. He imagined the birds would turn up in unexpected places all over the house—the kitchens, the bedrooms, the dining room—perhaps even the grounds; sometimes lost and trilling loudly as they begged to be shepherded back to where they belonged, other times discovered only once they had already perished from hunger, exhaustion, or fright, or else the claws of a malign cat.

It was hardly a conventional way to keep animals. This shouldn't, in itself, have surprised Newbury—after all, nothing about the Royal family appeared conventional, not in any sense that he could understand it. Certainly, the matriarch at the heart of the family was as far from decorous as one could imagine, and the relationships between her and her children appeared equally idiosyncratic. Even Albert Edward, publically a staunch supporter of his mother, had suggested to

Newbury in private that relations between he and the Queen were somewhat strained. It hadn't surprised Newbury, who was keenly aware of the Queen's selfishness and conniving nature. If this extended to her relations with her children, then it was only to be expected that some of them might bear something of a grudge.

Newbury was still watching the birds a short while later when the butler returned. Newbury dragged his eyes away from the avian display to regard the man. The butler's expression had not softened, although he did have about him the air of someone a little more contrite, yet still obstinate and unyielding.

"His Royal Highness is only too pleased to grant you an audience, Sir Maurice," said the butler, hastily. "He extends his apologies"—he pursed his lips as he said this, as though the very thought of the Prince of Wales apologising to such a lowly subject as Newbury was utterly distasteful to the man—"but asks if you would kindly wait in the drawing room for a short while. He is currently engaged in the library with another visitor."

Newbury grinned, enjoying the man's discomfort despite himself. "Of course," he said, genially. "I'd be happy to."

He followed the butler as the man led him down a long passageway to the left of the stairs. Portraits loomed down at him from the walls, faces staring out blankly across the ages, unsmilingly offering their judgements to posterity.

The butler's shoes creaked as they followed the passageway into the bowels of the great house, passing various unoccupied rooms. After a few moments, the butler came to a stop, beckoning Newbury towards an open door.

Newbury could hear the murmur of nearby voices—the deep baritone of Albert Edward, accompanied by the husky tones of a woman. He could not make out what they were saying, but as he paused before the entrance to the drawing room, he glanced over his shoulder at another door, which stood slightly ajar.

Inside he could see row upon row of dark mahogany bookcases, each of them lined with leather-bound tomes, and the back of a woman's head. She was sitting in an armchair about halfway into the room, her back to him. Her dark hair was cut in a shabby, uncompromising style that fell loose around the base of her neck, the flesh of which was pale and stark. She was thin, and appeared to be dressed in black, although he could see only the tops of her shoulders and one sleeve, which rested upon the arm of her chair. She was talking in hushed, whispered tones, and the Prince was silent, perhaps intent on listening to her softly spoken words.

"In here, sir," said the butler insistently, stepping forward to block the other room from view. Newbury nodded and proceeded into the drawing room as directed. He couldn't help but wonder about the identity of the mysterious woman and the Prince's business with her. It wouldn't do to ask, of course—that really would be viewed as impertinence—but it intrigued him.

"Would you care for a drink, Sir Maurice?" said the butler in a manner that made it clear he did not wish to go to the trouble of preparing one.

Newbury didn't want one, but for a moment he considered asking for one regardless, just to teach the fellow a lesson. In the end, however, reason won out and he decided against entering into such childish games. "No, thank you," he said, levelly.

"Very good, sir," said the butler, with a contumacious smile. "The Prince knows you are here and will be with you in a short while. Please make yourself comfortable in the meantime." He turned on his heel and left, pulling the door shut behind him.

Newbury waited for the sound of the butler's retreating footsteps, but they did not come. Clearly, the man had chosen to remain in the corridor outside, to keep an eye on Newbury and ensure he didn't attempt to interrupt the Prince and his other visitor. Of course, Newbury had no intention of doing any such thing.

Sighing, he strolled over to the fireplace. It was ostentatious in the extreme, hewn from white Carrara marble, with two darker supporting pillars to either side. Logs were piled in the grate, but were not lit. Above the fireplace was a huge gilt-framed mirror that reflected the sheer splendour of the room with almost dazzling effect. The door frames, too, were gilded, and the black and white chequerboard floor continued through from the hallway, giving Newbury the impression he was standing on a square of an enormous chessboard, a pawn waiting to be moved. Perhaps, he reflected, he was.

This thought gave him pause, and he glanced around, looking for somewhere to sit. He settled on a low chair, upholstered in red velvet and with gilded feet in the shape of lion's paws. It looked impressive, but was not particularly comfortable.

His eyes were drawn to a series of large canvases on the opposite wall. They were landscapes, but the scenes they depicted were unfamiliar to him. The rolling hills were not the lush and verdant green of England, but scrubland and desert. Small groups of figures in peasant's robes toiled in the fields, and in the foreground, characters from biblical myth acted out scenes from the famous stories. They were not very much to Newbury's taste. Nevertheless, the surroundings were much more appealing than the agent's waiting room at Buckingham Palace.

He started a moment later as he heard the door open.

"Newbury! This is unexpected," came the booming, authoritarian voice. Newbury turned around to see the rotund figure stalking into the room. The Prince of Wales looked immaculate in his grey double-breasted suit. He walked with a wooden cane which scuffed against the tiled floor with every step he made. He was smiling, but appeared somewhat flustered, distracted even.

Newbury suddenly felt himself withdrawing beneath the Prince's penetrating gaze. Had he misunderstood? Had he made a terrible social faux pas by coming here to Marlborough House? He jumped to his feet. "My apologies, your Royal Highness. I did not mean to disturb you."

"Nonsense, Newbury," bellowed the Prince, stopping a few feet from him and leaning on his stick. "I told you to call if there was anything you needed. Now, take a seat, will you, and give it up."

Newbury did as he was told, lowering himself into one of the other gilded chairs by the fireplace. Albert Edward did the same, sitting opposite Newbury and propping his cane on the glass-panelled fire screen.

"I fear I cannot give you long, Newbury," said the Prince. "I've some other damnable business to attend to." He inclined his head in the direction of the door. "Most pressing, I'm afraid."

Newbury nodded. "If there's anything I can do to help…?" he led, trying to ensure it didn't come across as if he were digging for information.

"You are doing enough, Newbury. Assuming, that is, that you are here to talk of the situation I outlined for you the other day?"

"Quite so, Your Royal Highness. I've given some serious consideration to your words."

Albert Edward smiled broadly. "I'm glad to hear it, Newbury. There is no one else I would rather have on the job. I'm delighted to know you've decided to occupy yourself with the matter. It's one less thing to have to worry about." He paused, fixing Newbury with his watery gaze. "So, you have news to that end?"

Newbury nodded again. "I believe so. I've been following that line of investigation. Tell me, Your Royal Highness, have you heard of the recent spate of murders taking place throughout the city? The victims have all been found with their hearts removed."

The Prince blanched. "Indeed I have. A despicable business. You think there might be some connection?" he asked, dubious.

"I do. I believe the German agents may be responsible for the deaths. If not the Germans, then foreign agents of some kind," replied Newbury. He was feeling a little hot around the collar, and he rubbed a hand self-consciously over his face.

"What makes you say that, Newbury?" prompted the Prince, evidently failing to see the connection.

"The fact that all of the victims so far have been agents of Her Majesty the Queen," said Newbury, quietly.

"Indeed?" said the Prince, clearly shocked. "Then it does seem likely that they are being targeted. It wouldn't surprise me to discover my cousin was behind it. If the Kaiser could undermine the Queen's position, erode her power and her network of information, it would make a coup—or even an outright war—far easier to achieve." He shook his head in dismay. "Have you considered, Newbury, that you might also be at risk?"

"Any or all of Her Majesty's agents could be at risk, Your Royal Highness. That's why I'm here," said Newbury.

The Prince frowned. "Go on."

"I'm hoping to obtain a list of the Queen's agents, to look for patterns and potential victims." He sighed. "At present we have very little to go on. I'm working closely with Sir Charles Bainbridge of Scotland Yard, and we're attempting to identify, if not a motive, then at least a pattern in the deaths, so that we might act to prevent further incidents. I fear there must be a double agent in our ranks, someone who is able to identify targets for the Kaiser. I wish to weed them out."

"Have you spoken to the Queen?" asked Albert Edward, his brow creased in thought.

"Yes," said Newbury, wondering precisely how he might broach the subject of the Queen's reluctance to provide the necessary information. The Prince might have spoken honestly to Newbury about his mother back at Chelsea, but that was his prerogative, as her son and the future monarch. Newbury had to avoid causing insult. "I rather fear… well, I fear that Her Majesty does not trust me enough to grant me access to that list of names."

Albert Edward threw back his head with a deep, rumbling bellow of laughter. "Ah, it's like that, is it?" he said, shaking his head in disbelief. "Of course, she doesn't trust me much, either. Thankfully there are others at the palace who do." He nodded, as if weighing his options. His composure returned. "I can get you what you require, Newbury. And if it helps bring an end to the constant threat of war with the Germans, well, then you'll be doing us all a great service. It'll take some time," he said, glancing absently at the grandfather clock in the far corner of the room. "Can you return tomorrow evening? I'm sure I can have it for you by then."

"Of course," said Newbury. "I'm most grateful to you, Your Royal Highness."

"Good to have an ally, eh?" said the Prince, jovially. "Well, I feel the same, Newbury. Let's just say Her Majesty has been a little… confused, of late. She sees enemies where there are none, and doesn't see the assassins that are already lurking in plain sight."

"She believes the Secret Service is out to undermine her," said Newbury.

"Well, she might yet have a point there," replied the Prince. "But it remains to be seen. I'd tread carefully where the Secret Service is concerned, Newbury. I advise you to let that little drama play itself out without your involvement."

Newbury wasn't sure how to respond to this particular revelation. So the Prince, too, had concerns about the legitimacy of the Secret Service. Perhaps there was more to the Queen's comments than irrational fear, after all? But then, everything Newbury had said to Veronica about Angelchrist was true. He had no reason to doubt the man, and every reason to trust Bainbridge with his life. Surely they wouldn't be mixed up in something so nefarious.

Nevertheless... Newbury himself had allowed the Bastion Society's attack on the Grayling Institute to go ahead. He'd allowed everyone to think that the renegades were targeting the palace, when, in fact, they were out to kill the Queen's physician, Dr. Fabian, and destroy his work. Newbury was acutely aware that this might have been a death warrant for the Queen, but he did it anyway, knowing what part she played in the foul, depraved experiments being carried out at that facility, and the impact they had on Amelia–and, by extension, Veronica. Perhaps it wasn't so outlandish a claim as he'd first thought– perhaps the Secret Services, and by extension Angelchrist and Bainbridge, had aligned themselves against the Queen.

"I must say, Newbury," said the Prince, mercifully changing the subject. "It's good to see you looking more... yourself."

"Thank you, Your Royal Highness," replied Newbury, unsure what else to say. He couldn't very well admit that he'd soon be returning to Chelsea to mix a draught of laudanum, or that within the week he'd be back at Malbury Cross, conducting occult healing rituals on a woman everyone thought was dead.

"Very good. Well, I'm afraid I have urgent business to attend to, Newbury," said Albert Edward, reclaiming his cane and levering himself up from his chair. "Trying to rescue an abandoned hotel. Historic interest and all that. Barclay will show you out."

Newbury heard the door creak open on its hinges, and looked up to see the butler waiting in the passageway outside. Clearly, he'd had his ear to the door throughout the whole of the conversation. What was more, it appeared the Prince himself had given the man leave to do so.

"My thanks to you, Your Royal Highness," said Newbury. "I shall return tomorrow evening as you suggest." He flicked a quick glance at Barclay, whose expression gave nothing away. "Your assistance in this matter is very much appreciated."

"Likewise, Newbury," said the Prince, distracted again, as if his mind had already returned to the subject of his prior conversation. "Likewise." He turned his back on Newbury, crossed the room, and once again disappeared into the library. This time, the door clicked decidedly shut behind him.

"I'll show you out, Sir Maurice," said Barclay, pointedly holding open the door.

With a sigh, Newbury nodded in affirmation. He had a great deal to consider before his meeting with the others that afternoon.

# CHAPTER 14

❦

*The girl—now a young woman—and her father were both taken aback by the sudden, crippling onset of her illness.*

*It struck suddenly one night in July, a terrible, excruciating pain in her chest. It felt as if someone were stabbing her repeatedly in the breast with a dagger. She howled and screamed, thrashing about violently beneath her bed sheets.*

*The inventor rushed into her room, panic etched on his face, and held her tightly while an ashen-faced neighbour sent for the doctor. He whispered reassuring words into her ear, promises that she would be safe, that he would protect her from whatever it was that was harming her.*

*Eventually, the pain abated and she was left panting raggedly for breath, covered in a thin sheen of sweat. The inventor laid her head softly upon the pillow, brushing her long, dark hair from her face, and held her hand while the doctor—an overweight, sour-breathed man close to his dotage—asked her a series of short, pointed questions. He put his head to her back and listened to the beating of her heart, examined her complexion, the whites of her eyes.*

*Then, muttering beneath his breath as if he cared not one jot about the girl, her father, or her likely prognosis, he declared that she had a weak heart, giving her no more than a few months to live. The inventor begged him to help her, to offer a means by which his* adoptive daughter could be saved, but the doctor simply shrugged and explained that the condition was terminal and close to its end, and that there was nothing anyone could do. He took his payment and left, and with him went all hope of her salvation. The devil was close at hand, and was laughing at her as he waited to claim his prize.

The inventor wept through the night, and in the morning he sat her down and swore to her that he would find a means to vanquish her disease.

The only outward sign that there had been anything wrong was the fact that she had begun growing paler a few weeks before the attack. Nevertheless, once the doctor had offered up his diagnosis of a weakling heart, the inventor had blamed himself for not seeing it sooner. He told her he had thought the paleness nothing more than a sign of her burgeoning womanhood—she was now approaching nineteen years of age and becoming more beautiful with every passing day—but his experience with his wife should have enabled him to draw the right conclusion much earlier.

How unlucky it was that one man's wife and adoptive daughter should both suffer in this way. He asked her one night if she thought he was cursed, and she smiled and offered him platitudes, all the while believing that perhaps, in truth, he was. What other explanation could there be?

Up until this point, her life with the inventor had been joyful and free of woe. He had lavished beautiful things upon her and had welcomed her wholeheartedly into his life. He had talked to her of his late wife, of her desire that she should grow to become just like her: a calm, joyful woman who thought of others before herself, who was deeply affronted by the injustices of the world, and who had been as beautiful in her heart as she had in the flesh.

The girl liked to think of the inventor and his wife sitting together in the drawing room of his great house. As a small child she imagined herself snuggling amongst the folds of her adoptive mother's elaborate dresses (which still hung in a wardrobe upstairs at the house, and which she sometimes tried on when the inventor went out). She knew, though, that she could never be like this wonderful woman. She did not have it in her to be so selfless, so kind. She tried, of course, for his sake, but all the while she was aware of the evil in her heart, and reminded of the words of the old woman from the orphanage.

He told her how he had tried to save his dying wife, how he had worked tirelessly to find a means of sustaining her, of halting the progress of the sickness that consumed her, but had failed. He had run out of time and had not been able to complete his research. But that research would stand them both in good stead, now that she, too, was ill. He would return to his notebooks and journals, and in their still-crisp pages he would find the means to save her life.

She knew he kept these prized belongings in his study at the very centre of the house, but she was barely aware of the arcane things that went on in there. Indeed, she had rarely been allowed to enter the room, which bristled with the spines of leather-bound books, with vials and jars and silver candlesticks and things that even her wide-ranging imagination could barely conceive of. Animal skulls hung from threads attached to the ceiling, and the walls were daubed with strange, elaborate symbols. Clockwork machines ticked constantly, ominously, their tiny innards whirring. A marble slab filled the centre of the room, and the place had an unusual smell of incense, oil, musty books, and sweat about it.

In the days and weeks that followed her diagnosis, he locked himself away in that room for hours at a time, slaving over what he hoped would be a cure for her condition, a solution to all of their problems. When she pressed her ear to the door, she heard only the ticking of the clockwork machines, the occasional turn of a screw, and his laboured breath. She could not begin to imagine what form this cure might take.

The inventor would emerge from these long sessions with a red face and dripping brow, and she would go to him and hold him and thank him for all of his efforts on her behalf. She could see how tired he was, but also how driven. She rarely saw him at all during those strange, wild days and nights. Yet he appeared to appreciate these moments *of kindness and affection, reminding her that whatever happened, whatever he had to sacrifice, he would not give up on his daughter.*

*And so when the attacks came with increasing regularity she tried her best to be strong, and not to think of those fork-tongued demons awaiting her with their tridents and lascivious eyes.*

*Almost two months passed. The girl became weaker still, and took to her bed, no longer able to manage even the small activities of daily life. The stairs were now a mountain to her, the walk to the privy a mile-long excursion.*

*That was when the inventor finally emerged, triumphant, from his study. He burst into her room unannounced, his eyes wild with success. She remembered feeling not joy, but fear at his wild, frenetic manner. He was trembling as he took her hand, squeezed it, and told her how he had finally found the answer to their prayers. He would mend her broken heart, and she would never have to leave him.*

*Her relief was palpable. She thanked him profusely for everything he had done and told him that, had he not come to the orphanage that day over ten years earlier and whisked her away from that dreadful place, she would already be dead. He had given her life simply by offering her a place in the world.*

*He wept tears of relief. Then, anxious not to risk even a moment longer to the vagaries of the damaged organ in her breast, he scooped her up and carried her down the stairs to his study.*

*She remembered how the smoke stung her eyes, how the marble slab was cold and harsh beneath her shoulders as he laid her out before him. Books were propped open on wooden lecterns all around him, and a gleaming object, forged from brass, rested upon his workbench.*

*She told him she was scared. He smiled warmly and assured her that she need not fear anything. The procedure would take some time. In the meantime, he would help her sleep. That way, her pretty face would not have to be blemished by any pain she might suffer as he carried out his operation.*

She trusted him without question, so she willingly acceded to his wishes, deeply inhaling the fumes of the foul-smelling chemical he presented to her on a rag. Her mind swirled, and soon the dizziness overcame her, sending her spiralling into a deep slumber.

She dreamed of devils and demons, of searing flames and eternal damnation. It was five days before she woke.

She recalled how she struggled to sit up in her bed, the curious sense that her body felt somehow different, awkward and ungainly. She felt the weight of something pressing on her left shoulder. In the darkened room, she imagined it to be a bandage strapped tightly across her chest.

Whatever her father had done for her had worked. She could sense her body was already stronger, flushed with vibrancy and life. He had fulfilled his promises and saved her from the demons that were slowly eroding her heart.

Hesitantly, she swung her legs out over the side of the bed and climbed unsteadily to her feet. She fumbled for a candle and lit it from the dying embers of the fire that still glowed faintly in the grate. She carried the candle to the looking glass so that she might examine his work; see how the colour had returned to her cheeks.

At first the sight of the stranger that confronted her baffled her. Had she been confused and inadvertently gone to the window instead? Who was this demonic woman who glowered at her in confusion?

Then realisation had dawned on her and she screamed. The sound that erupted from her throat was like none she had heard before. What had he done?

The woman staring back at her from the looking glass was covered in the same elaborate symbols as the walls in the inventor's study: circles and whorls, pentagrams and stars, runes and words. They covered her entirely from head to toe. Not an inch of her still-pale flesh remained untouched.

She tried rubbing at the strange marks, wiping them away, but they refused to be scrubbed clean. They were etched deep into her flesh, as much a part of her now as the tiny blemishes and imperfections that she'd noted as a child. Furthermore, nestled amongst the ink-black tattoos were traceries of precious metals: silver, platinum, and gold. They shimmered in the reflected candlelight, highlighting particular symbols or runes like accents on particular words.

Worst of all, the tightness she had felt across her shoulder was not, as she had thought, a tightly bound bandage, but the brass instrument she had seen on the workbench in the inventor's study. It was a brace that fit over her shoulder like a sword guard. She could feel the mechanisms inside it slowly turning, hear the gurgling rush of fluid as her blood passed through the metal chambers inside. A tiny key jutted from a hole in its surface—a winding mechanism, she realised, with which to operate it. This was her new heart, the clockwork engine that would beat in place of her own.

On the front of the device, filling the space where her left breast had once been, was a glass panel like the porthole on a ship. Inside she could see the shrivelled remains of her own damaged organ, now black and necrotic and fused to her new, unnatural components.

She wanted to turn and run from her horrific image, to pretend that she was still dreaming, that the living hell she had glimpsed in the mirror was just another trial, another imaginary torment placed before her by the demons and the old woman. But she now knew the true nature of her damnation. She had been saved from the clutches of the devil by the ministrations of the inventor, but the devil had found a means to punish her regardless: The fallen one had worked through her father, imbuing him with dark intent and the occult powers with which to afflict her.

Something broke inside of her, then. A cold numbness seemed to spread outwards from the void in her chest until it utterly engulfed her. She had lost her heart, and from that day onwards, she would never feel anything again.

# CHAPTER 15

✦

"Are you sure this is where Sir Charles suggested we meet?" said Veronica, shielding her eyes from the dazzling afternoon sun.

"Do you doubt me?" asked Newbury, chuckling.

"No. But I do *know* you," she said, playfully.

Newbury smiled impishly. "I protest! I am quite innocent, Miss Hobbes. I understand from Charles that Professor Angelchrist proposed the location of our little get-together. Although, I admit, I have been rather anxious to pay a visit since the exhibition opened last week."

"Yes, I thought you might be," said Veronica, grinning. "Well, come along, then. Let's take a look." She hooked her arm through his and led him across the lawn towards the entrance.

It was a pleasant afternoon, and the sun was streaming down upon the pleasure grounds that surrounded the immense, impressive edifice of the Crystal Palace. Veronica had never seen the famous structure before, and the sheer scale of it took her breath away. It looked like an enormous summerhouse or orangery: pane upon pane of plate glass mounted in a towering framework of cast iron. It gleamed in the sunlight like a beacon upon Sydenham Hill.

As they approached, she could see that the once-great

building had grown a little tired; not all of the panes sparkled as they once might have. Green stains had begun to encroach on the curved glass panels over the atrium, and creeping moss peeked inquisitively from the gutters. Nevertheless, it was one of the more impressive structures she had seen, rivalling even the grandeur of Buckingham Palace. She found it hard to believe that the structure had originally resided across town at Hyde Park, and had been rebuilt here following the closure of the Great Exhibition, moved piece by piece like the fragments of a jigsaw puzzle.

Banners streamed above the entrance, billowing and rippling in the wind and proclaiming the myriad spectacles to be found within. She had read of the show in the newspapers, of course—Urquart's Monstrous Menagerie and Mechanical Wonders was a travelling exhibition that had toured the great cities of Europe: Paris, Berlin, Vienna, and now London. She had anticipated that Newbury, ever fascinated with progress and the modern arts, would wish to pay a visit while the exhibition was in town, but she had to admit she hadn't anticipated it would be under circumstances like this.

The grounds around the palace were swarming with people. Hundreds, if not thousands of them were strolling in the sunshine, or disgorging from the station of the atmospheric railway that ferried them here from Central London, all wide-eyed and ready to be astounded by the wondrous sights within.

An airship berthing post had even been installed on the pleasure grounds, and was presently occupied by a fat, silver-skinned vessel that cast a broad shadow across the palace as it rocked and buffeted in the wind. Looking up at it was like seeing the underside of an enormous, glittering fish hovering right above their heads. Flights of steps buttressed the passenger gondola, and people descended them in droves. They were mostly the wealthy cognoscenti of the Empire, adorned in fine dresses and tailored suits from Savile Row.

The exhibition was open to anyone, from any walk of life—provided, of course, that they could muster the small entrance fee. For every well-to-do lady or gentleman she spotted, Veronica noted scores of working-class families on outings with their children, there for the once in a lifetime opportunity to glimpse technological and zoological marvels and treasures from other lands.

Newbury led on into the vast atrium, where they were jostled by milling people. He produced two tickets from inside his jacket pocket and handed them to an attendant, who waved them straight through.

"Sir Charles?" asked Veronica, wondering how Newbury had managed to procure the tickets in advance.

He laughed and shook his head. "No. Scarbright picked these up for me earlier in the week. As I explained, I'd been anxious to pay a visit, and I had thought to invite you along. I simply hadn't found the right occasion."

Veronica smiled and tightened her grip on his arm. "Or the right excuse," she said, laughing.

The first things that struck her upon entering the main hall were the clamour of sights and smells, and the almost deafening background chatter of a thousand or more people as they exclaimed in shock and delight at the wondrous exhibits within. The next was the gargantuan brass elephant that was nearly on top of them as soon as they emerged from the atrium. It was immense—at least the size of a real Indian elephant—but it was constructed from a series of interlocking brass plates and rivets. It had been built with intricate care, each of the plates engraved with delicate filigrees of silver and gold.

Its trunk was a snake of segmented copper pieces that curled and whipped through the air in perfect mimicry of its biological counterpart. Steam hissed and vented through ducts behind the machine's enormous ears, which were vast vanes of hammered metal, almost paper thin, that flapped back and forth like fans, as if the elephant were attempting to cool itself. Veronica noted the trickling rivulets of condensation running across the metal plating as the steam cooled.

Atop the beast, in something reminiscent of a dickey box from a hansom cab, sat the driver. He was a short, balding fellow in a brown suit, with wire-rimmed spectacles and a green bow tie. He looked utterly out of place on the back of his immense, ungainly creation.

He appeared to be controlling the elephant via a series of wires and pulleys, not unlike a huge steam-powered puppet. It responded to each of his commands, raising one foot after another, ponderously stomping across the exhibition hall. A crowd of admirers clapped in glee as the creature raised its trunk in the air and bellowed with a loud trumpeting sound that would not have been out of place at London Zoo.

"Marvellous, isn't it?" said Newbury, nudging her. He had a broad grin on his face. "Just look at this place!"

Veronica couldn't help but laugh at his childlike glee. It was nice to see him smile, for once, to seem genuinely happy or inspired. There hadn't been much of that recently, and she felt somewhat responsible. She knew he was helping her sister for reasons beyond pure altruism. He was doing it, even at the expense of his own health, because Veronica had asked him to.

They moved on, pushing their way through the crowd and leaving the elephant and its beaming driver to solicit further rapturous applause from the audience as it performed yet more tricks.

Nearby, a large arena was fenced off. Veronica could see little of what was taking place inside due to the gathered crowd of people. Newbury dragged her towards it. She rolled her eyes in mock exasperation, but truthfully, she was as intrigued as he was to see what all the fuss was about.

As they inched their way closer through the press of people, Veronica became aware of a familiar sound over the din of the crowd: the clashing of sword blades. Clearly then, this was some sort of demonstration of swordsmanship or the like. She glanced at Newbury, who was standing on his tiptoes to see over the heads of the people in front.

"Most impressive," he said. "Can you see?"

Veronica shook her head.

"Hold on." He led her on a circuitous route through the crowd until, a moment later, she found herself standing beside one of the corner posts of the makeshift arena. The ground inside was covered with sand, and–as she had imagined–two men were deep in the midst of an impressive display of sword fighting. They were bedecked in what looked to be mediaeval plate armour.

She turned to Newbury, a question in her eyes, but then stopped as one of the fighting men fell back to avoid a swipe of his opponent's blade, turning the manoeuvre into an athletic back flip and landing once again upon his feet.

"They're not human," said Veronica, astonished.

"Indeed not," replied Newbury. "They're automatons."

"Automatons!" echoed Veronica, with a shudder.

"Oriental, I believe," mused Newbury. "If I'm not mistaken they're soldiers from the army of the Chinese Emperor. It's claimed he ordered thousands of them to be constructed in the workshops of his magus, and that he keeps them stored in the vaults beneath his palace in Beijing, oiled and ready for use. One day, it's feared he may unleash them upon the world."

Veronica could barely imagine the damage that could be wrought by an army of such things. Like the elephant, they were fashioned from interlocking plates of brass, designed in every way to resemble a human being dressed in plate armour. Now that she could see more closely, their faces looked keenly human, and each of their mechanical eyes swivelled on a twisting axis as they each took measure of their opponent.

"Where are we meeting Sir Charles?" she asked suddenly, as if she was really saying: "Can we leave this place?"

Understanding her hidden meaning, Newbury took her arm again and led her away from the scene of the fight. "He said he'd find us."

"What, amongst all of these people?"

"He'll find us." Newbury shrugged. "He is, after all, a chief inspector."

Veronica couldn't help but smile. She was sure he was only searching for an excuse to continue wandering around the exhibits for a while. She didn't want to spoil his mood. Nevertheless, she had to air her concerns. "I remain... unconvinced about all of this, you know," she said, squeezing his arm a little tighter to let him know she was searching for reassurance, as opposed to simply questioning his judgement outright.

"The exhibition?" asked Newbury.

"No. Professor Angelchrist," she replied. "Meeting him here. What if we're seen?"

"We shall have to be exceedingly careful," said Newbury, acknowledging her concerns. "We shall talk as we tour the exhibits, being careful not to be heard or seen together. I have no doubt that more of Her Majesty's agents will be here at the exhibition, perhaps even unknown to us. We should remain cognisant of that."

"Hmmm," said Veronica. However impressive Newbury's stealth skills might be, remaining unseen was not going to prove easy. "Are you sure we can trust him?"

Newbury met her gaze. He looked serious, all the playfulness suddenly gone. "Charles or Angelchrist?" he asked. His jaw was set.

"Angelchrist," she said, quietly.

Newbury inclined his head. "As far as we can trust anyone," he said, his tone level, unreadable.

Veronica nodded absently. What was he getting at? Was that a reference to her, their history together, the fact that it had taken so long for her to admit the truth about her role as an agent of the Queen? Or perhaps even a remark about her feelings towards Newbury, and the time they had shared in a cell, where they had talked about their mutual attraction? Could he even be making an obscure reference to Bainbridge? Was he, too, feeling that his friend had somehow got in over his head, mixed up in affairs that he shouldn't have? Was this his way of advising caution?

Now, she decided, was not the time to press him on the matter. She would do that later, once they had heard what the Professor and Bainbridge had to say, when they could find a moment alone.

She was woken from her reverie by the insistent pinging of a bell and looked up to see she was standing directly in the path of a hurtling bicycle. Newbury was looking in the other direction at a strange dome-like machine. She tugged them both out of the way as the bicycle rushed by, its rider grinning and doffing his hat politely in acknowledgement. She realised, surprised, that the man was not actually pedalling, but that the bicycle—not unlike a penny farthing, with a large front and smaller back wheel—was self-propelled via a handle beneath the seat. She realised that the device must be a part of the exhibition and grinned. Now that was a progressive invention she could appreciate: no smelly fumes, no dusty coal. She wondered whether they'd ever actually take off.

Newbury, intent on other things, dragged her on towards the exhibit he had admired from afar. "Look at this," he said, reading the small plaque beside the strange device. "The 'Tempest Prognosticator.'"

"The what?" Veronica asked, perplexed.

"It's a machine that predicts rain," said Newbury, pressing his face to the glass dome and peering at the contents inside.

Veronica could see over his shoulder that the centre of the machine was comprised of a large bell, a series of strings emerging from its heart. These strings terminated inside a circle of jars, each of which contained the squirming, bloated bodies of leeches.

Veronica took a step back, slightly repulsed.

"Apparently, when it is about to rain, the leeches–sensitive to this change in clemency–climb out of their jars, which causes the strings to pull taut and sound the bell in alarm," said Newbury, grinning. "Quite ingenious."

"Would it work?" asked Veronica.

"Who knows," replied Newbury, with a shrug. "But it's a fine-looking machine, all the same." He glanced around, as if trying to get his bearings. A wide grin spread across his lips. "Look, over there!"

He was pointing to a bright yellow banner hanging between two posts. Painted on it in garish red letters were the words: THE MENAGERIE.

"Must we?" said Veronica, knowing full well what the answer would be.

"Oh yes," said Newbury, laughing. "We absolutely must."

"Very well," she said, with a playful sigh. She allowed herself to be led across the floor of the exhibition hall once again, jostled by the over-enthusiastic crowd at every step.

They stopped before what appeared to be an artificially constructed passageway: a cave system of sorts, formed from elaborate plasterwork designed and painted to represent coral. Embedded in these walls were a series of large glass tanks, each of them filled with burbling water. The lighting inside the cave system was diffuse and dim.

"We're going in there?" she asked.

"Come on, Veronica!" he chided. "Where's your sense of adventure?"

"I rather fear I left it in Kensington," she replied, wryly.

There were only a handful of other people meandering through the unusual exhibit as they stepped into the first of the darkened passageways. Newbury, releasing his hold on Veronica's arm, went directly to the wooden sign beside the nearest of the glass tanks. She heard him chuckle and then turn away from the brief description of the tank's contents, cupping his hands to the glass and peering inside.

"What is it?" she asked.

"Come and have a look."

She crossed over to join him.

"There," he said, pointing to something in the water. At first it was indistinct, a dark shape about a foot long, suspended in the gloom. She moved to get a better view. As the nature of the tank's inhabitant became clear, she must have pulled a face, because she heard Newbury laughing beside her.

"It's… it's…" She was lost for words to describe it.

"A merman," interjected Newbury.

"Grotesque," she finished.

The creature in the water was a sort of twisted hybrid of a monkey and a fish. Its lower half comprised a fish's tail, glistening with silvery scales, but above the waist it had the torso, arms, and head of a small mammal. In its hand it held a tiny spear. It appeared to be unmoving.

"I've seen these before," said Newbury. "It's not alive."

"It's not?" she asked.

"No. It's a fake, an example of creative taxidermy. Someone very skilled dissected the two animals and attached their remains together to form the illusion of a new 'undiscovered' beast. It…" he trailed off.

"What is it?" she prompted.

Newbury's face had taken on an ashen appearance. He was staring at the thing in the tank. She turned to look and saw it move. Its head turned towards her, glossy black eyes peering right through her. Its lips curled back, baring its sharpened fangs, and then its tail flicked once, twice, and it was swimming towards the surface of the water, breaking for air. It moved with a lack of grace born of compromise—as if this creature, whatever it actually was, had been forced to learn its movements anew and was not yet entirely comfortable with them.

"Good Lord," said Newbury, uncharacteristically invoking the deity's name. "Someone's actually done it."

"But you said it wasn't alive?" said Veronica, confused.

"I was mistaken," replied Newbury, "although it certainly isn't natural. This is the result of some diabolical experiment, a creature constructed in a laboratory. Two animals welded together in a bizarre biological alliance. The knowledge and the skill to create such a thing…"

"Look," said Veronica. "There's more." She pointed towards a small rocky shore on the far side of the tank, where the tentacles of an octopus were curling slowly out of the water and onto the rocks. They watched in horrified fascination as the beast ponderously dragged itself from the murky depths. As before, the creature that emerged from the water was an elaborate hybrid, a surgical construction that bore the torso of a monkey with the eight puckered arms of an octopus in place of its legs.

It slid across the rocks, its appendages curling and wriggling as it propelled itself along, its downy fur flattened and dripping. It scuttled towards a crevice in the rocks, squeezing into what Veronica assumed to be a small, artificial cave system or habitat.

"It's unnatural," said Veronica. "Repellent."

"It's a remarkable achievement," said Newbury.

"But those poor creatures…" said Veronica. "It's monstrous. Think of how they must have suffered."

Newbury was quiet for a moment. "Come on," he said, after a while. "There's more to see."

"If it's more of the same, I'm unsure I want to see it," she said as he led her out of the darkened passageway.

A moment later they re-emerged into the bustle and clamour of the main exhibition hall. It took a moment for Veronica's eyes to readjust to the light.

Close by, a large crowd had gathered around what appeared to be a huge glass enclosure. She couldn't see what was within, other than the fronds of a few small trees peeking above people's bobbing heads. There was an insistent tapping sound, too, as if something was repeatedly striking the glass. It reminded her of the noise made by Bainbridge when he rapped on Newbury's front door with the end of his cane.

As she approached the exhibit, Newbury in her wake, whatever was inside the enclosure emitted a shrill, primal screech that caused the skin of her forearms to prickle with gooseflesh. She felt the bass rumble of it in the pit of her stomach, and her every instinct told her to flee. Instead, she pressed on, manoeuvring through the jostling crowd. They parted easily enough as she pushed towards the front.

What became apparent in the first instance was that there were not one but two creatures inside the enclosure. It took her a moment to come to terms with exactly what she was seeing. They were like something drawn from a nightmare of a deranged fantasist: two enormous birds, each at least ten feet tall, with plumages in all the gaudy colours of the rainbow, indigos, yellows, reds, and blues. They stalked about on two legs, splayed, taloned feet reminiscent of huge lizards. Their beaks were large enough that she imagined they could take off a person's head in a single, snapping motion, and their beady eyes were darting and urgent, eyeing the crowd through the plate glass.

One of them opened its immense jaws and emitted another shriek, its pink tongue wriggling inside its mouth like a captive snake. It hissed and darted forward, its small, useless wings twitching as it thundered across the enclosure, butting against the glass and causing the crowd to fall back with a collective intake of breath. The barrier flexed in its housing but held firm. The creature shook its head in frustration, stepped back, and began rapping its curved beak against the glass pane once again, as if was attempting to chip away the glass in an effort to get at the gathered people outside.

To Veronica they might as well have been prehistoric beasts somehow resurrected in the here and now, excavated from the archives of history and renewed through some dark art or technology. She glanced at Newbury, who was reading the information plaque beside the enclosure.

"They were found in the Congo," he said, when he noticed her looking. "A whole colony of them, living amongst the ruins of an ancient civilisation. It says here they can swallow a creature the size of a small dog."

Veronica's eyes flicked back to the twin beasts, which had now returned to stalking around the perimeter of their enclosure, heads bobbing nervously. One of them began pecking at something on the ground, its long neck snaking round as its razor sharp beak tore at the object, gouging chunks from it. She realised with disgust that it was the remains of a goat.

"Vicious brutes, aren't they?" came a familiar voice from behind Veronica. "I certainly wouldn't wish to encounter one in a dark alleyway."

She turned to see Bainbridge standing behind her, a smile on his lips. "It's good to see you, Miss Hobbes." He watched the beasts for a moment with what appeared to be equal parts horror and admiration. "Dreadful things," he said.

"Beautiful, though, in their own way," said Newbury, joining them. "Good afternoon, Charles." Bainbridge inclined his head. "I must say, I'm delighted with the rather impressive venue that you and Archibald selected for our little rendezvous."

Bainbridge laughed. "Yes, I thought you'd like it. Although

I fear I cannot take any credit. Archibald picked the place. Something about killing two birds with one stone." He glanced at the two birds in the glass pen with a grin. "He said it was the perfect place for him to clear up a little misunderstanding."

Veronica raised a sardonic eyebrow. "A little misunderstanding?"

Bainbridge shrugged. "You know as much as I do, Miss Hobbes." He glanced at Newbury. "Any word?"

"From Aldous?" He shook his head. "No, not yet. I did, however, pay a short visit to the Prince of Wales this morning."

"You did *what*?" said Bainbridge, aghast.

"It occurred to me," said Newbury, "that in the Prince we might find an ally. The other day when he visited Chelsea, he expressed his concerns for his mother's... health. He said that I should call if there was ever anything he could do to help."

"And?" prompted Veronica. She was as surprised as Bainbridge to hear Newbury's announcement.

"So I asked about that list of agents we needed. If Her Majesty was not prepared to let us see it, it struck me that perhaps there was another way." He grinned to himself as their expressions changed.

"Let me get this straight, Newbury," said Bainbridge, apparently flabbergasted. "You called on the Prince of Wales to ask for his assistance in obtaining sensitive materials behind the back of the Queen herself?"

"Yes, well. I suppose it does sound rather sensational when you put it like that," said Newbury, laughing.

Bainbridge grinned and clapped him on the shoulder. "The sheer audacity of it! Well, man, what did he say? Did he throw you out on your ear?"

"He said there were people at the palace he could trust, and that I should return to Marlborough House tomorrow evening to collect the information we needed. He's very much on our side in this matter, Charles."

Bainbridge chuckled. "At last, some good luck. Well done, Newbury." He glanced down at his pocket watch. "Right, well, we're meeting Archibald by a particular exhibit. Some sort of search lamp, designed to be mounted on the belly of an airship, I believe."

Newbury nodded. "Similar, I'm guessing, to that one just over there?" he said, chuckling as he pointed across the hall. Veronica followed his gaze. About twenty feet away, through the milling crowds, she could see a large silver lamp mounted on a swivel housing. A man in overalls was demonstrating the device, throwing a brilliant beam of light up and out through the transparent ceiling of the Crystal Palace. A small crowd of onlookers were marvelling.

"Come on," said Newbury, brightly. "Let's see if we can't find the professor." He led Bainbridge away towards the search lamp exhibit.

Veronica took one final look over her shoulder at the two massive birds in their enclosure, shuddering as they continued to rend flesh from the now barely distinguishable remains of the goat. Then, with some trepidation, she followed Newbury and Bainbridge as they started off in search of their somewhat dubious friend.

# CHAPTER 16

♛

Bainbridge had a concerned look etched on his face. In fact, thought Veronica, he was looking decidedly uncomfortable.

"What is it, Charles?" said Newbury quietly, so as not to draw attention to their small group as they stood on the sidelines of the search lamp exhibit, watchful for the arrival of Professor Angelchrist.

"It's just… these faces, Newbury," he replied, quietly. "There are men in the crowd that I recognise."

"How so?" asked Newbury.

Bainbridge frowned, but didn't answer.

"From the Yard?" said Veronica.

"No. They're Service men. Archibald's men," he replied, after a moment, as if lost in thought.

"You mean to say that we're presently surrounded by agents of the Secret Service?" said Newbury. His expression was a little strained, and Veronica wondered again what was going through his head. Was he having second thoughts? Doubts about Angelchrist's motives?

Bainbridge nodded slightly. "In a manner of speaking," he replied, glancing from side to side. "Yes. I'd say we're pretty much surrounded."

Veronica swallowed. "A trap? Is that why Angelchrist

picked this place?"

"Don't be ridiculous," snapped Bainbridge, a bit too hastily. He shook his head, adjusted his tone. "That's not it at all. There must be something else going on here. Something that we're not aware of."

"Well, it's hardly surreptitious," said Veronica. She glanced round, searching the faces in the crowd. She couldn't help imagining that any one of them might be watching her with malicious intent.

Directly behind them was the giant bird exhibit. To the left was a singing and dancing automaton of a woman, clothed in a fine red dress, its hips swaying provocatively as it mimed to the recording of an opera singer. To the right, a skeleton that looked like it came from a prehistoric giant was mounted on a large stone plinth, the fossilised bones dark and roughly hewn from the bedrock. It towered above the people below, posed as if reaching out a hand in supplication. Each of the exhibits were surrounded by thronging masses of people. Any or all of them might have been Secret Service agents, as far as Veronica knew.

"How many?" asked Newbury.

"At least a dozen," said Bainbridge. "There may be more that I'm unaware of, but that's half the men we have in London, concentrated around this exhibit."

"Concentrated around the exhibit where Professor Angelchrist suggested we meet," said Veronica, sceptically.

"Something's certainly going on," continued Bainbridge, ignoring her remark. "An operation, perhaps."

"I'm sure there's a reasonable explanation," said Newbury. "This has to have something to do with that 'misunderstanding' Archibald referred to."

"Look, here he comes," said Bainbridge, visibly relaxing now that he'd caught sight of the professor. "I'm sure he'll set everything straight."

"Remember, Charles," said Newbury, a note of caution in his voice, "we must be careful here. If it gets back to the Queen that we're having this meeting at all…"

"I know, I know," said Bainbridge, irritably. "Although I fear it may already be a little late for that, given that we're presently surrounded by Archibald's associates."

"Yes, well, be that as it may, we mustn't simply throw caution to the wind. Just keep in mind that, as far as any onlookers are concerned, we're here to take in the exhibits. Any conversation we have with Archibald must be conducted with the utmost care," said Newbury, firmly.

Bainbridge nodded.

The professor continued to circle around the perimeter of the exhibit, giving the lamp what appeared to be an appraising look. He was smartly dressed in a brown tweed suit, white shirt, and black cravat, and carried a smouldering briar pipe in his left hand. He was wearing an expression of devout concentration as he slowly edged through the crowd, finally coming to stand beside Newbury a few moments later. He placed the pipe in the corner of his mouth and folded his arms over his chest.

"There's a lot of fuss being made over such an unobtrusive little object," he said, turning to meet Veronica's eye and smiling. "Good afternoon, Miss Hobbes."

"Good afternoon, professor," she said. He offered her an impish grin. Once again, now that she was faced with the man, she felt herself warming to him. He was nothing if not charming, and she could see why Newbury and Bainbridge had been taken in by those charms. But the fact remained: They were currently encircled by a team of agents at least four times their number, possibly more. She couldn't help but feel as if she'd been lured into a trap.

"Gentlemen," said Angelchrist, acknowledging the others.

"A lot of fuss?" asked Newbury.

"Indeed," said Angelchrist. "I'll come to that in a moment. We don't have a great deal of time, however, so I think it's best we get straight to the heart of the matter. I had the gist of it from Clarkson, of course. I gather Her Majesty has rather taken against our little operation."

"To put it somewhat mildly," said Bainbridge. "She's accused the Service of being behind the recent spate of killings, the victims of which, it transpires, all happen to be agents affiliated with the Crown. It's preposterous."

Angelchrist smiled. "I can't blame her, Sir Charles. Of course, she's quite wrong. I'm as baffled about these deaths as you are. But it doesn't surprise me that she feels threatened by the growing strength of the Service, however noble our motives."

"We'll have to tread carefully from now on, Archibald," said Bainbridge, quietly. "She's ordered us to sever all links with you and your men."

Angelchrist nodded. His face looked a little drawn and tired. "So be it," he said, levelly, giving away very little.

"We do, however, have another possible lead in our investigation," said Newbury. "I understand from the Prince of Wales that there are foreign agents abroad in London, and in particular agents of the Kaiser, here with the express intent of undermining the Queen's position. It seems likely that they may be responsible for targeting the Crown agents in an effort to further such aims. Charles thought you may be able to shed further light on the subject...."

"Indeed I can, Sir Maurice, but I fear it may not be the answer you're looking for." He glanced at Bainbridge. "I imagine you've noticed we have company?"

"If you mean that the place is swarming with Service men, then yes," said Bainbridge. "I had rather noticed the fact."

Angelchrist nodded. Again, he met Veronica's eye, as if reading her mind, knowing that his explanation was needed more for her benefit than the others'; that he still had work to do to convince her of his trustworthiness. "You're right about the Germans, in that they do have agents here in London. Their motives, however, are somewhat different from what you've imagined."

"Go on," said Veronica, drawn in to his explanation despite herself.

"The Kaiser fears his grandmother has designs on his throne. It's clear that the Queen wishes to extend the reach of the Empire, but Wilhelm refuses to bend to her will. As a result, the Queen is furious with him, and he's now attempting to arm himself in preparation for her reprisal." Angelchrist glanced back at the search lamp. "Our investigations have suggested that the Kaiser's agents will make an attempt to seize this experimental search lamp today. As you can see, it's designed to be mounted beneath the gondola of an airship, so that the column of light might shine down upon the landscape or city streets below. However, a German hermetist, Gruder, has posited a theory that such a lamp could be focused through a narrow lens, intensifying the beam and turning it into a formidable weapon."

"A focused beam of light and heat," said Newbury, astounded. "The devastation they could wreak from the skies… They could set the entirety of London aflame."

"Quite so," said Angelchrist, lowering his voice. "Which is why we're now surrounded by as many service men and women as I could muster. The creator and his plans have already been secured. We cannot allow them to get away with this prototype."

"But why not simply remove the prototype?" asked Veronica. "Why leave it here in an exhibition hall full of people, at risk?"

"A trap," replied Angelchrist. "An opportunity to send a message to the Kaiser, to put an end to the schemes of his agents here in London, at least for a while. If we can draw out his agents, expose them, perhaps even capture and interrogate some of them—well, then it will be worth the risk."

"Even if innocent people are harmed in the crossfire?" asked Veronica, feeling her impatience swelling.

Angelchrist sighed. "We all have to make difficult decisions, Miss Hobbes. Surely you know that more than most."

Veronica stiffened. What was he getting at? Did he know something about her, about the choices she had been forced to make?

"One thing I *am* sure of, however," Angelchrist continued, "is that the Kaiser's men are not responsible for the murders of the Queen's agents. They've been single-minded as they've planned the execution of their mission. We were able to plant a double agent amongst their ranks, and he has given every indication that they are not even aware of the identity of the Queen's agents, let alone harbouring any desire to murder them and abscond with their hearts. The Kaiser is not, contrary to the beliefs of some of the Court, spoiling for a war. He is simply working to raise his defences, should Her Majesty grow tired of his rebuttals and decide to put matters into the hands of the military. The theft of an experimental electric lamp would not be looked on kindly. The murder of the Queen's prized agents would be quite another thing, tantamount to a declaration of war."

"So you've lured us here under false pretences?" said Veronica, stiffly. "You've dragged us unwittingly into the middle of an operation."

"Not at all," said Angelchrist, his tone conciliatory. "Clarkson said you needed to understand what the Germans were planning." He shrugged. "Since we couldn't meet openly as once we might have, this seemed as good a way as any to demonstrate the veracity of my words. I wanted to demonstrate to both you and Sir Maurice the value of the Service, and to clear up any little misunderstandings regarding its motives." He glanced from Newbury to Bainbridge. "And yes, I suppose I am guilty of wishing to have my friends by my side as we charge headlong into battle."

Bainbridge nodded. He glanced at Veronica, and then back at Angelchrist. "You have my support, Archibald. And thank you. Although it damn well sets us back to the start. We're no further towards discovering who's responsible for these murders than when we found the first corpse."

Newbury clapped Bainbridge on the shoulder. "It's only a matter of time, Charles. We'll get to the bottom of it."

Veronica suppressed her frustration. She decided, for the others' sake, that she would allow events to play out as intended. "So what next?" she asked Angelchrist, moderating her tone. "Do you know what the German agents are planning?"

Angelchrist smiled appreciatively. "There is soon to be a changeover of personnel," he said, indicating the man in overalls operating the lamp, swinging it back and forth on its pivot to the appreciative murmurs of the audience. "The German agents have inveigled their way onto the exhibition staff. Once the changeover has occurred and a new operator has arrived, he'll declare the lamp to be faulty and in need of repair. A crew of engineers will move in and begin dismantling the housing. We'll step in at that point and apprehend the lot of them before they can get away, preferably with minimum disruption to the exhibition." He glanced down at his pocket watch, which he'd extracted from his jacket whilst he talked. The long, golden chain pooled in his palm as he studied the timepiece. "In fact, the changeover is due to occur at any moment."

"Forgive me, Archibald, but it sounds rather optimistic to imagine the German agents are simply going to roll over and give themselves up without a fight," said Newbury, frowning.

"We're ready for any eventuality," said Angelchrist, patting his jacket pocket pointedly. Veronica could see from the bulk of it that he was carrying a pistol. She felt a cold sensation spreading throughout her stomach, something akin to dread. She feared this operation was not going to end well. As soon as they started shooting at one another, things would degenerate. Innocent people were going to end up dead.

She glanced round at the other faces in the audience, but she couldn't tell which of them were Service men, or which might be German agents incognito, waiting for the signal to strike. She felt helpless, impotent.

Newbury gave her a gentle nudge to get her attention. When she looked round, he nodded in the direction of the lamp.

The man in overalls was glowering at his watch, clearly frustrated by the late arrival of his replacement. He sighed visibly, then circled the lamp on its pedestal one last time. Then, as if tired of waiting, he allowed the lamp to swing about in its housing, the beam stuttering briefly and then shutting off. "There will be another demonstration in a short while," he announced to the gathered onlookers, before turning and excusing himself as he pushed through the sea of people. Within a few moments he'd been swallowed entirely by the crowd, disappearing as he waded off into the depths of the exhibition hall.

The gathered audience began to drift slowly away, other nearby exhibits catching their attentions. Veronica was grateful for that, at least—it might mean there was less chance of them being swept up in the coming altercation.

She glanced at Angelchrist, who was looking on intently, his foot tapping nervously as he waited. She felt Newbury's grip on her elbow and allowed herself to be drawn away from the search lamp.

"I thought it best if we removed ourselves from the immediate vicinity," said Newbury, quietly, in her ear. "We can always intervene if the situation demands it."

Veronica nodded. She could feel his warm breath against

the back of her neck as he leaned in. They were standing in the shadow of the giant bird enclosure, and just to her left she could sense the creatures eyeing her through the glass wall. She looked round to see one of them pawing at the ground with its talons, raking furrows into the heaped sand. It was as if the beast could sense the heightened tension in the vicinity and was responding in kind, ready to unleash all of its pent up energy and frustration. It saw her looking at it and stalked forward, craning its neck inquisitively to look her in the eye.

Veronica gave thanks for the plate glass that separated them. The creature, only a few feet away, was one of the most terrifying beasts she had ever seen, and as it bobbed its head, tracking her every movement, she felt the hairs prickle on the back of her neck.

It opened its jaws and she saw a splash of goat's blood make its way down its wriggling tongue and drip from the corner of its beak. She shuddered as she imagined what that beak could do to a human being if it were ever given the chance.

Thankfully, the beast appeared to give up on her then, turning to join its kin on the other side of the enclosure. Then, almost without warning, the bird twisted and lashed out, striking the glass pane violently with its beak. The panel shook in its frame but held.

Veronica started, but was reassured by Newbury's grip on her arm. "Brutish creatures, aren't they?" he said. She could tell from the timbre of his voice that he, too, was startled by the bird's sudden attempt to break free.

"It's more than that," she said, taking a deep breath to regain her composure. "It's the look in their eyes, too. They seem to understand what's going on. It's almost as if they're taunting us."

"They certainly seem to have a keen intelligence," said Newbury. "I imagine it makes them formidable predators. They probably hunt in packs."

"I shouldn't like to find out," said Veronica, flatly. "I'd rather they'd left them in the Congo, where they belong."

"Hmmm," said Newbury. She didn't know whether that meant mild disagreement, or simply that he was distracted by what was occurring beside the search lamp.

The crowds had thinned to almost nothing now that there was little to see, which afforded her a good view of proceedings. Angelchrist and Bainbridge stood shoulder to shoulder, looking on while the replacement operator—a swarthy-looking chap, dressed in similar overalls to his predecessor—fiddled and toyed with the controls of the lamp, feigning frustration as he tried to get them to work.

It was almost as if Angelchrist had choreographed it: within moments the man had thrown up his hands in despair, signalling to others elsewhere in the crowd, who swarmed in a few seconds later to form a small circle around the exhibit. There must have been ten of them, at least, each dressed in matching overalls. They exchanged a few words, then began drawing tools out of leather pouches attached to their belts. A moment later they were busily at work loosening bolts to strip the lamp from its housing.

Newbury took a step forward. "What is he waiting for?" he hissed in frustration. "They'll be away with it in a moment if he doesn't hurry."

Veronica searched the crowd for any signs of the Service men. Where were they?

The birds had begun to rap insistently on the glass barrier beside her again. She turned to glower at them. Her head snapped back round, however, at the report of a pistol being fired from somewhere close by.

She caught a glimpse of one of the German agents folding in half and collapsing to the floor, then she was being jostled as confused people pushed past her as they fled the scene.

More pistols fired. Suddenly, everyone was screaming.

Throughout the exhibition hall, the crowds erupted into a boiling mass of torsos and limbs as people fled, pushing and shoving, sweeping up their children, shouldering each other out of the way as they rushed for the exit.

Newbury grabbed Veronica's hand and dragged her towards where Bainbridge and Angelchrist were taking cover close to the fossilised giant. The battle between the Service men and the German agents had swiftly descended into a firefight, and she watched in horror as a young man no more than three feet from where she was standing took a bullet in the face, blood erupting from the back of his skull in a fine, billowing mist. His body jerked in shock and slumped to the ground, sending his weapon skittering across the tiles.

She heard the crack of broken glass from over her shoulder, and looked back to see the panel on the side of the giant bird enclosure splinter around an impact crater caused by a stray shot. The birds squawked and stamped their feet, raising their beaks to the sky and hissing.

"Get down!" cried Newbury, pushing her to the floor as the firefight intensified around them. She saw another of the German agents slump to the ground beside the search lamp. Around him his cohorts were attempting to retreat, returning fire with wild abandon as they fought for their lives. Bullets pinged off the nearby exhibits, ricocheting into the screaming crowd.

Veronica heard the rapping of the birds again, striking the glass with their beaks. She was about to dismiss it as an unnecessary distraction when she heard the glass begin to fracture beneath their ministrations. She twisted around, glancing back in time to see the entire panel shatter in a shower of glittering fragments. The impact of the bullet had clearly weakened the integrity of the panel, and the birds had taken advantage of this opportunity, exploiting the damaged pane. She watched, dumbstruck, as the first of the beasts burst through the makeshift opening, thundering out into the hall and scattering broken glass. It raised its head to the sky and bellowed in triumph before lurching towards the nearest group of fleeing civilians and snapping at them with its powerful jaws.

They scattered, screaming, as they saw it coming, but the creature moved with surprising speed and grace for its size. Its razor-sharp beak closed on the head of a middle-aged man, ripping it clean off in one sudden motion and tossing the body aside with the momentum. Blood sprayed in a wide arc, coating everything in the vicinity, and the bird, emitting a deep gurgling from its throat, thrust its crown back and swallowed the man's head with a single gulp. Unsatiated, it darted forward, searching for another victim.

Veronica realised that, to the creature, the screaming crowds of people must have looked like a scattering herd of cattle or gazelles. Prey.

"We must stop them!" she shouted to Newbury, who was prone on the floor beside her, his hat long since lost and trampled, his hair mussed, his suit crumpled and out of sorts.

He gave her a pleading look, as if to say 'must we?', but then, with a single nod of agreement, he climbed to his feet, helping her up beside him. The shooting was now confined to the area immediately around them. With a quick glance to ensure that Bainbridge and Angelchrist had not been harmed, Veronica turned, steeled herself, and then rushed directly into the path of the second bird, which was just emerging from the break in the barrier.

She waved her arms frantically to catch the beast's attention. It hissed menacingly and pushed itself out through the ragged hole in the glass, shedding vibrantly coloured feathers as they scraped upon the jagged edges.

Veronica, still waving, inched backwards, leading the bird slowly away from the stream of people on the other side of the enclosure.

The beast tracked her movements, its beady eyes intent, narrowed. It opened its immense jaws and screeched at her, a piercing, guttural croak that left her ears ringing and her heart hammering in her breast.

She felt the wash of its warm breath and balked at the ripe stink of rancid meat, gagging back the bile she felt rising in the back of her throat. This close, she could see the creature's downy feathers were spattered with faeces and spilt blood; viscera, she presumed, from the butchered goat. She swallowed, trying to anticipate its next move.

The bird seemed larger and more terrifying now that there was no glass partition between them, and she fought to suppress the feeling of creeping dread that threatened to overwhelm her. She had no weapon, no way of defending herself if the beast decided to launch an attack. Which, judging by the gleam in its eye and its threatening posture, was a distinct possibility.

Veronica stepped to the left and the bird mirrored her movement, its head dipping. Its splayed talons scratched nervously at the ground and its wings beat furiously. It issued a low, sinister hissing sound. She shifted right and it followed her precisely, as if entranced, never taking its eyes from her. She stepped back and it stepped forward, keeping time, still taut and poised for a sudden strike. As soon as she turned to run it would be upon her, its deadly beak snapping at her, threatening to rip her apart.

She'd lost track of Newbury and she dared not turn around to look for him. Any sudden movement, any attempt to take her eyes off the monster would provide it with the opportunity to attack. She could show no hesitation.

To her left, the crowds were thinning as the civilians bolted for the exit, pursued by the other, squawking bird. She'd managed to distract one, at least, preventing it from feasting on the mass of innocent people, but she had no idea what to do next. She cursed herself for not thinking through her actions. Distracting the creature was one thing; getting herself clear was quite another.

Veronica took another step back, watching the bird creep forward in time with her movements.

"Maurice?" she called, her voice wavering. She didn't take her eyes off the creature in front of her as she spoke.

"Over here!" he called. "Lure it over here!"

She didn't look round, but followed his voice, slowly walking backwards towards where she thought he was. "What are you going to do?" she called, twitching as the bird tentatively snapped its jaws, cleaving the air only inches from her face. As she quickened her pace, still walking backwards, she could tell it was growing nervous, weighing the right time to strike.

The percussive bang of a pistol firing just over her shoulder caused her to start, stumbling backwards. Her feet lost their traction on the tiles and she fell. She thrust out her hands to break her fall, and twisted as she dropped, but still struck the ground hard, catching her chin on her forearm. She called out in shock and pain and rolled, groaning, only to see the beast still looming over her. It was bleeding from a bullet wound in its face, shaking its head in frustration.

She risked a glance round to see Newbury standing a few feet away, his legs planted firm, his arms outstretched and clutching a pistol. He squeezed the trigger again, and then again, emptying the chamber. The bird bucked and screamed as the bullets ripped into its torso, but still it did not stop.

"Veronica! Get out of the way!" he bellowed, but it was too late. She had nowhere to go, no time left in which to run. The massive bird screeched and thrust its beak at her, and she was forced to roll urgently to the left to avoid being impaled.

The beak smashed into the tiles with a force that she felt reverberating in her bones, and the bird reared up, hissing, readying itself for another strike.

Veronica screamed, this time rolling to the right as the beak descended once again, crashing down only inches from her cheek, so that the back of her head bounced painfully against the tiles. She screamed again. Her head was swimming.

Almost as if in slow motion, she saw the monster pull back then whip its neck forward again, its jaws yawning open in readiness.

*This is it*, she thought as she cried out in terror, her throat raw from screaming. *This is how I die.*

The jaws descended... and then the creature emitted a strangled cry and reared back, swinging its head from side to side in confusion. For a moment Veronica had no idea what was happening. It was as if she were being assaulted by a random sequence of images, none of them quite making any sense: the writhing beast, a flashing light, the shadow of her own hand over her face. She could hear nothing but the roar of blood in her ears, drowning out everything else. She breathed and exhaled; blinked.

And then reality rushed in again, and everything snapped into focus. *The lamp!*

She pulled herself up onto her hands and knees. The bird was still thrashing back and forth, stumbling as it tried to get away from the light. She glanced at Newbury, who was clinging to the search lamp amongst a heap of dead German agents, swinging it around so that the brilliant beam flickered in the beast's eyes, dazzling it.

"Quickly!" bellowed Newbury.

"Quickly *what?*" she cried.

"Kill it!" he returned, exasperated.

Veronica stared at the creature for a moment. With what?

She glanced around her in desperation. Nearby, the corpse of a dead Service man lay crumpled, face down. Blood streamed from a wound in his head, pooling on the tiles around him. His hands were splayed to either side of him, and in his right he still clutched the pistol he'd been firing before he took a bullet of his own.

She ran to his side, dropping to her knees and fumbling for the gun. The dead man's fingers were still warm, and his grip on the weapon's handle was still firm. She tried yanking the gun free, but his hold remained steadfast.

"Hurry!" called Newbury.

She looked round. The bird was staggering in her direction, bobbing and ducking its head. It had realised that it took some time to swivel the lamp around in its housing, and was moving quickly, attempting to stay out of the path of the dazzling beam.

Veronica grunted as she tried desperately to prise the weapon free. She heard the thud of the bird's footsteps from behind her, felt its presence over her shoulder, the intake of air as it drew breath to screech. The gun came free in her hands and she twisted. Just as the beast opened its chasm-like jaws, she raised the pistol and fired directly into its mouth.

The bird emitted an agonised wail and took a step back, and Veronica climbed hesitantly to her feet. The creature's mouth was still hanging open, the jaws working slightly, as if unable to close.

She raised her arms and squeezed the trigger again, and then again, loosing shots into the bird's mouth, blowing holes in the back of its throat, the top of its skull. The creature took one final step backwards, and then, with a deep exhalation, crumpled unceremoniously to the floor.

Veronica allowed the pistol to slide out of her grip, clattering noisily upon the tiles.

She heard Newbury's footsteps as he abandoned the lamp and came rushing to her side. "Are you hurt?" he asked, urgent, breathless.

"I'm fine," she said. She glanced around, looking for the others. The entire scene was one of carnage. Bodies were strewn across the ground, scattered around the nearby exhibits. Most of them were dressed in overalls or black suits; agents. At least those men had known what they were getting into. The same could not be said of the civilians who had perished in the botched operation. She cursed Angelchrist for the irresponsible way he had handled the matter. Questions would undoubtedly be asked.

Now, however, neither Bainbridge nor the professor were anywhere to be seen.

She was about to ask Newbury if he knew what had become of them when she saw the look on his face. She followed his gaze. Across the nearly empty exhibition hall, the second bird was still rampaging, snapping indiscriminately at the few remaining people who were trying desperately to find their way to the exit.

Her shoulders dropped. "Again?" she said, with a sigh.

Newbury shrugged. He held up another pistol, which he must have taken from one of the dead German agents. "We can't allow it to get out into the park," he said. "Think of the havoc it would wreak."

She nodded, stooping to reclaim the still-smoking pistol she had dropped. "Very well," she said, with a sigh. "But next time you ask me to accompany you to one of these damnable exhibitions, you can jolly well take it as read that my answer is no."

Newbury chuckled loudly as they set off together in pursuit of the second beast.

# CHAPTER 17

"I'm afraid Sir Maurice is, shall we say... *indisposed.*"

Veronica made a brief appraisal of Scarbright, standing on the doorstep of Newbury's house. He looked impeccable as always in his neatly cut suit, with starched collar and perfectly folded cravat. Nevertheless, the strain was showing somewhat in his expression. His eyes had narrowed, his lips pinched. He'd lost a modicum of his usual confidence. He was clearly embarrassed about the situation, and unsure how to respond.

"Indisposed. Ah, yes. Well, we both know what *that* means," said Veronica, knowingly.

Scarbright gave a shrug, as if to say, What would you have me do?

"Never mind," said Veronica, forcing a smile as she took the last two steps up to the house, gently nudging Scarbright aside with her left arm as she stepped into the hallway. "I'll wait in the drawing room."

Scarbright looked momentarily taken aback, and stammered as if to raise an objection, before sighing graciously in defeat. "Yes... well, quite so, miss." He closed the door behind her. He probably knew already that she had no intention of waiting.

Veronica strolled brazenly down the familiar hallway,

stopping before the panelled door to the drawing room. She rapped loudly. "Sir Maurice, may I come in?"

No answer.

She glanced back at Scarbright, who nodded, gave a strained smile, and motioned for her to enter. She turned the handle and stepped over the threshold, peering around for any sign of Newbury.

She couldn't see him. She stepped further into the room and was assaulted by the cloying odour of stale smoke. She wrinkled her nose in distaste. She had to admit, however, that the place looked tidier than it had in months. Scarbright had obviously managed to get inside long enough to tidy away the spoiled food and crockery, the empty teapots, the overflowing ashtrays and abandoned wine bottles. He'd even managed to run a duster around the mantelpiece and draw back the curtains, allowing natural light to spill into the room for the first time in as long as Veronica could remember.

The room still bore the overbearing mark of its owner, however. Clutter filled every available nook and cranny. Books threatened to burst from the overstuffed shelves, and indeed had spilled out into piles on the armchairs and heaps upon the floor. Weird and wonderful objects lay scattered about the place: the cat skull on the mantel; an idol the size of a small child, with a staring, vacant expression on its stone face, a hole in its chest where its gemstone heart had once been; the clockwork owl he had inherited after one of his cases, silently regarding her from its perch above the dresser.

She moved over to peer at the divan where Newbury could often be found reclining in a state of repose during his opium-saturated episodes. Again, there was no sign of him.

Behind her, Scarbright pointedly cleared his throat. "If you'd like to take a seat, Miss Veronica? Sir Maurice is at work in his study. His instructions are such that he must not be disturbed under *any* circumstances. However, I will take steps to make him aware of your arrival, and I shall warm a pot of tea in the meanwhile."

With a sigh of resignation, Veronica nodded, then dropped into one of the Chesterfields beside the fireplace, being careful not to upset a heap of papers by her feet. Scarbright slipped away, disappearing along the hallway towards the kitchen.

It was cold, and no flame burned in the grate. For a moment Veronica considered starting a fire, but then thought twice. Not because she was incapable—far from it—but because she didn't want to disturb the heaped piles of ash and soot still in the grate and run the risk of covering herself and her dress in oily residue. Besides, with the amount of rare tomes piled up in the vicinity, she was wary of inadvertently destroying a precious relic with a stray ember, or worse, making a bonfire of Newbury's entire collection. Most of them were irreplaceable. Indeed, the book of rituals stolen from the Cabal of the Horned Beast was not the only volume he'd gone to extreme lengths to obtain.

Veronica leaned back in her chair. The only sounds were the ticking of the carriage clock on the mantelpiece and Scarbright's receding footsteps in the hall. She didn't often find herself alone in Newbury's habitat. This room, she thought, gave a measure of the man: intriguing, complicated, unpredictable. One never knew what one was going to discover.

She searched the coffee table for anything of interest. What had Newbury been busying himself with? Days-old newspapers with articles circled in heavy black ink; a notepad covered in his indecipherable scrawl; an ancient grimoire, two hundred years old at least, handwritten on vellum, with woodcuts depicting complex geometric patterns and the aspect of a goat-headed devil.

Close to these was another of Newbury's particularly macabre totems—a human skull, hewn into a mask and covered in elaborate engravings, runes, and glyphs. Some of them were familiar to Veronica, but she had no idea of their actual meaning or purpose. The empty sockets stared back at her, and she felt herself shudder in dismay. Who had it once belonged to? How had Newbury acquired it? She supposed it was best not to know.

She reached for one of the newspapers, opened it, and dropped it across the skull mask so that she wouldn't have to look at it any longer. The thing gave her the creeps.

Clearly Newbury wasn't expecting her—and there was no reason he should be. His note, received earlier that morning, had suggested the three of them—Newbury, Sir Charles, and Veronica—should convene at Chelsea later that afternoon, but she had wanted to catch him early, to talk about Sir Charles and the Secret Service.

Ever since the business at the Crystal Palace the previous afternoon, she'd been mulling things over. The Prince of Wales had evidently been wrong about the Germans, or at least wrong in his suggestion that they were responsible for the gruesome series of killings that Newbury and Sir Charles—and, by extension, Veronica—were charged with investigating.

She'd considered that it was still possible the German agents were behind it, but she doubted they would have shown their hand so openly at the exhibition if this were the case. It was one thing to attempt to seize a search lamp from an exhibition hall. It was quite another to implicate themselves in the murder of four of the monarch's personal agents. The Kaiser would fear the Queen's reprisals and war they might precede. If he truly were waging a clandestine campaign against his grandmother, he would most likely have forgone his attempted acquisition of the weapon to avoid calling attention to his other interests in London.

Who did that leave? Well, they had very little left to go on. Someone who knew the Queen's agents—or at least some of them—and someone who had a vested interest in undermining her power and weakening her grip. A rival organisation, perhaps, making a play for control? Veronica couldn't help thinking that perhaps Newbury had been too hasty in his dismissal of the Queen's assertion that the Secret Service was involved, too trusting of Angelchrist and his followers. What if he was wrong, and the Queen was right? The very thought of that spiteful woman being right made her cringe.

Sir Charles's crime may only have been one of naiveté, but his new associates might not have the same excuse.

She needed to discuss the matter with Newbury, to put her ideas, as well as his assumptions, to the test.

Veronica rubbed unconsciously at her bruised chin. She was aching all over. Her encounter with the giant birds the previous day had left her smarting and sore. They'd been able to despatch the second creature swiftly and efficiently once they'd convinced the driver of the steam-powered elephant to corner it with his machine. Following this, the two of them had made a swift exit from the scene. They might not have been able to disguise their presence at the exhibition, but hopefully they could disassociate themselves from the events that had taken place there for the prying eyes that were even now filing reports to the Queen.

Newbury had insisted that Bainbridge could look after himself, and reported that he'd seen both Bainbridge and Angelchrist making a hasty retreat in the aftermath of the firefight. Of course, it would be down to Bainbridge in his role as chief inspector to attend to the scene and attempt to explain what had occurred. How he planned to extricate himself from the situation if challenged by the Queen was anyone's guess.

Veronica glanced at the clock. It was nearing quarter to twelve. Could she risk disturbing Newbury? Surely, for her, he would make an exception?

She made a decision. While Scarbright was busy making tea in the kitchen, she would make her presence known to

Newbury. She would not stand for being dismissed. Not this time. There were questions that needed answering.

She stood, crossed to the door, and glanced along the hall. There was no sign of Scarbright. She dashed across the hallway and took the stairs two at a time, running on her tiptoes so as not to alert the valet. He would follow his master's word to the letter and attempt to keep her at bay while Newbury finished whatever it was he was up to in the study. *Well, poppycock to that,* she thought.

She turned on the small landing, passed the bathroom, and climbed another, shorter flight of stairs to the second floor. The door to the study was at the far end. It was shut.

She hesitated for a moment. What might he be up to inside? Newbury was weakened by his ministrations to Amelia and might not know his own capabilities. If he was practising more of his rituals, there was no telling what state she might find him in.

With this in mind, she approached the door and rapped gently with her knuckles. There was no response.

She pressed her ear against the wooden panel and heard a shuffling noise from within. "Sir Maurice?" she asked quietly. "Are you there?"

Again, there was no answer.

Veronica tested the handle, and, to her surprise, discovered that the door was unlocked. She pushed it open, the hinges creaking, and stepped inside. "Sir Maurice, I…" She trailed off, lost for words. The sight that greeted her was enough to stop her dead in her tracks.

The room was wreathed in a thick, smoggy cloud of incense. Heavy curtains were closed across the window, and candles flickered in sconces on the walls, or stood in candlesticks peppered around the room, on the floor, desk, and bookshelves.

The room had a funereal air about it. As she moved

forward, the breeze of her passing stirred the candles, causing them to gutter and cast deep, dancing shadows across the bare white walls.

At the centre of all this, on the scarlet rug, lay Newbury. He was naked and was clutching his knees to his chest in a foetal position. He was twitching and shaking violently, and it was immediately clear that the shuffling noise she had heard from outside was the sound of his feet repeatedly striking the floor as he shook. At once she recognised what was happening: he was having a seizure. She had seen Amelia in this position countless times.

Horrified, she ran to Newbury's side.

Never had he looked so vulnerable, so unlike the Newbury she knew. Not even in the depths of his opium trances, or when he'd been wounded and dying in the footwell of a hansom, or the time he'd caught a desperate fever in Switzerland while on the trail of Lady Arkwell and had to be returned to London on a military airship, unconscious and close to death.

She put her hand to his forehead. He was cold and clammy. "Maurice! Maurice!" she shouted, desperately.

His eyes had rolled back in their sockets, and she realised he was babbling quietly to himself, his words barely perceptible. "Tick-tock, tick-tock. Darkness. A throbbing heart, pulsing slowly. Tick-tock, tick-tock." He stopped mumbling for a moment, and then his body shuddered violently again. "Executioner," he said. "Executioner. Executioner. Executioner." He kicked out, thrashing on the rug. His hands clawed at the carpet. His breath was coming in irregular, desperate gulps.

Veronica's heart seemed to stop. Her mouth was dry. She willed herself to move, but she was frozen, rooted to the spot. *Executioner…*

She shook her head. There was no time for that now. She had to make sure he was safe, and deal with that later. "Maurice?

Can you hear me?" His head turned fractionally towards her. "It's me, Veronica. Everything is going to be well." She heard the crack in her own voice, realised she was trembling. How could this be? How could he now be suffering from the very same affliction as her sister, visions and all?

"Maurice?" she said insistently.

He emitted a low moan and his body shifted, his upturned face turning towards her. His eyes were still rolled back in his skull, white and unseeing.

"Can you hear me?" she repeated urgently. She put a hand on his shoulder and shook him gently. "Can you hear me, Maurice? I'm here."

His eyes suddenly flicked around, and his breathing became more regular, his chest once again rising and falling with a constant, reassuring rhythm. He wore a startled, vacant expression.

"Maurice, it's me, Veronica," she said.

His eyes seemed to follow her face, and then slowly focus. His expression hardened. "Get out!" he hissed. "Get out!"

"Maurice… I…" she faltered.

"Get out!" he bellowed for the third time.

For a moment Veronica was unable to act. She remained where she was, crouched over Newbury's naked form, trembling in shock. She had never once, in all the time she had known Newbury, seen such a fierce look in his eyes, such a fearsome glower. She hesitated. She didn't know what to do, how to respond.

Then, a few moments later, something snapped. Reality rushed in, cold and unwelcome. She stood, hurrying from the room, feeling nauseous. She didn't stop to close the door, nor to worry about what Scarbright might think.

She thundered down the stairs, charged across the hall and back to the drawing room, where she stood for a moment, leaning upon the back of a chair, labouring for breath.

What had she seen? The way his body had convulsed, the

muscular spasms, the way his eyes had rolled back in their dark, bruised sockets... and the mumbled word, *Executioner*, as if he were seeing things that no one else could see.

Newbury was suffering a clairvoyant seizure, like the ones Veronica had witnessed her sister have a hundred times before. But why the candles, and the nakedness?

She glanced back at the door. She didn't know what to do. Should she leave? Should she go back to him? She heard a footstep in the hall. Scarbright appeared in the doorway bearing a silver tray that clattered with the tea paraphernalia. Concern, however, was evident upon his handsome face.

"Miss Veronica, is everything quite well?" he asked, hurrying into the room. He slid the tray onto the top of the sideboard and approached her. Veronica held up a hand as if to shoo him away, but realised she was still shaking.

"I heard footsteps. Has Sir Maurice finished with his work?" he asked, the trepidation evident in his voice.

"No, no. All is well, Scarbright. Sir Maurice is still... otherwise engaged. Do not trouble yourself," she said, her voice quavering slightly.

"But Miss Veronica..."

"No, Scarbright. It's fine. Now pour me a tea, will you? Be a good chap."

Scarbright frowned. "Forgive me, Miss Veronica, but you're looking terribly pale. Are you sure there's nothing I can do?"

Veronica forced a smile. "No. No, I shall remain here and wait for Sir Maurice. Thank you, Scarbright." She could tell he was not convinced, but he acceded to her wishes, crossing to the sideboard and straining her cup of tea.

"Here you are, miss," he said, handing it to her.

"Thank you," she replied.

He made to leave, but turned about on the threshold. "I'll be in the kitchen, Miss Veronica, if there's anything you need." He paused, as if to add emphasis to his words. "Anything at all."

She nodded. "I'm sure I will be just fine," she said, although she knew her voice lacked conviction.

A moment later—when she was sure Scarbright's footsteps had receded—she let out a single, brief sob, which she stifled quickly with a handkerchief. Her every instinct screamed at her to leave, to snatch up her hat and coat and get as far away from Newbury's house as possible. She wanted to be anywhere but there, somewhere where she didn't have to face that man who was so different from the Newbury she had come here to visit.

Nevertheless, she had to be strong. She'd dealt with worse. He hadn't meant to be so vicious—it was simply embarrassment. She had burst in on him naked and vulnerable, and he hadn't known how to react. She had uncovered a secret, something he'd managed to keep from even his valet, and he'd felt exposed. Perhaps this was what he'd been talking about yesterday when he'd spoken of trust?

More than any of that, though, she needed to be there to help him. This was not some trifling matter that could be shelved and forgotten. For how long had he been succumbing to these episodes? Was it that, rather than the opium, that had left him so weak, so diminished?

She had a sudden, startling thought: was this how he was healing Amelia?

It was too much of a coincidence that her episodes had ceased just around the time that Newbury's had begun. Was that what was going on? Had he somehow found a way to draw off her condition, to take it upon himself? Her mind reeled with the possibility.

Veronica realised she was pacing the room. Her tea had spilled in the saucer as her hand shook. She forced herself to stop, sit in one of the chairs, and drink her tea while she considered.

That had to be it. The book, the ritual… that's what he was doing. Her heart sank.

She looked up to see Newbury stagger into the room. He was dressed now, albeit hastily—he was wearing only his trousers and shirt, the sleeves rolled back, the collar open. He was unsteady on his feet—so much so that as he came into the room he had to reach out a hand to steady himself against the wall. "I..." he looked at her, his eyes pleading.

She rushed to his side, abandoning the teacup and saucer on the floor, not caring whether its contents spilt across the carpet. She caught him in a tight embrace, and he clutched at her, holding her close. He held her tightly for a moment. He was cold to the touch and she could feel him shivering. His breath was still ragged. "I'm sorry," he said. "I didn't mean to scare you. It's only... I wish you had not seen me like that, reduced to that."

She stepped back, her hands on his shoulders, searching his face. His eyes were tired and sunken, his lips thin, his face drawn. "If I had known," she said, "that this was what you were doing..."

Newbury shook his head. "You could not know. Of course you couldn't. You would never have allowed it."

"Well," she said, glancing away, fighting back tears. "It cannot continue."

"She'll die," he said, quietly. "She'll die without it. I'm stronger than her. It must continue. There's no other way."

"But look at you! Look at what it's doing to you!" she said, her voice rising in urgency. "You're right. I would never have allowed it, and I cannot allow it now."

"It's not for you to decide," he said, solemnly.

She reeled on him. "Amelia would not want this, Maurice. You must know that. She would not inflict this curse on anyone."

Newbury sighed. He looked as if he were about to keel over.

"How long has it been going on?" she asked, pressing him further. "When did the seizures begin?"

"A few months," he said, levelly.

"A few *months*!" she exclaimed.

"Ever since the ritual began," he continued. "Ever since it proved to be a success."

She took a deep breath. "Come on. Come and sit down. I'll pour you some tea."

He nodded, shuffling towards the divan. "Now that's the best offer I've had all day," he said, grinning.

"How can you be so flippant?" she asked, shocked.

"What else would you have me do?" he replied. "There's no point in getting morose. Besides..." he trailed off, glancing out of the window, as if he didn't want to give voice to his thoughts.

"Besides what?" she prompted.

"It's fascinating," he said, refusing to look at her. "Absolutely fascinating."

"For the love of.... Don't tell me you're actually *enjoying* the experience!" Veronica fought to keep her temper. She was running the gamut of emotions, from shock, to hurt, to love, to pity, to anger. Her head was spinning.

"No," he replied. "'Enjoy' would be quite the wrong word for it. But the process... the things I've seen..."

"Maurice," she said, a warning tone in her voice. "You're dabbling with things you don't understand. It's dangerous. *Too* dangerous. You're going to kill yourself if you're not careful."

He turned to look at her, his eyes narrow. "I have to protect you," he said. "The danger is closer than you think."

Veronica tried to swallow, but her mouth was dry. "What do you mean?" she asked, although she thought she already knew.

"Amelia must have spoken to you of it? The Executioner," he said. "The Executioner is coming."

Veronica held her head high. "Yes, well, I've heard all about this so-called Executioner from Amelia. And here's what I'm going to do about it: carry on as normal. What you've seen isn't the future. It's simply a possibility."

"Veronica," said Newbury, "that might well be true, but can we really take that risk?"

"What would you have me do?" she asked, her voice strained.

He shrugged. "Go away, to somewhere safe. Take a steamship to New York, or an airship to the Continent. Anywhere but here, where you're at risk."

"And how do you know that what you're seeing in your... visions doesn't happen somewhere other than here?" she asked.

Newbury's shoulders dropped in defeat. "I don't," he admitted, softly.

"There we are, then," she said, pouring his tea. She crossedthe room, handing it to him. "There's nothing more to be said on the subject."

Newbury accepted the teacup gratefully, and drained it. He placed it on the floor beside the foot of the divan, and glanced up at the clock. "You're here early," he said, changing the subject.

"Yes. I came to discuss Sir Charles and the Secret Service," she said.

"More of that," replied Newbury, sighing. The colour was beginning to return to his cheeks. "I feared that might be the case."

"You did?" said Veronica. "Then you share my concerns?"

Newbury frowned. "Not entirely, no."

"Well, if it's not the Germans, who is behind this ghastly string of murders?" she asked.

"Isn't that the question," he replied, rubbing a hand across his face. He leaned forward, resting his elbows on his knees. He looked as if he were about to continue, but turned at the sound of a rapping on the front door. "Charles," he said.

"Already?" said Veronica, feeling her opportunity beginning to slide away.

"The sound of his cane is unmistakable," he said.

"But I thought we were meeting at two."

"As did I," he replied pointedly, raising an eyebrow. Veronica tried not to look sheepish. Voices echoed from the hallway, and then Scarbright showed Bainbridge into the drawing room.

"Here we are, Sir Charles." Scarbright caught sight of Newbury, and was unable to keep the surprise from his voice. "Oh! Sir Maurice, you're here."

Newbury smiled. "How perceptive of you, Scarbright," he said, not unkindly. "Good day to you, Charles."

"Is it?" Bainbridge replied, sullenly. He seemed more than a little flustered and was still wearing his hat and coat. He appeared to see Newbury for the first time. "Good God, man! Look at the state of you!" He glanced at Veronica, who shook her head almost imperceptibly.

Newbury didn't bother to grace him with a response.

"Well, you'll need to fetch a jacket, at the very least," said Bainbridge.

"We're going out?" enquired Newbury.

"Yes," said Bainbridge. "We're going out. There's been another murder."

# CHAPTER 18

❦

"Is this how they found him?" said Veronica, with barely concealed disgust.

"Precisely," muttered Bainbridge. "He was discovered this way in the early hours of this morning, and he hasn't been moved. The verger who found him…" He trailed off, as if trying to find a delicate way of phrasing what he wished to say. "Well, let us just say that the body has not been disturbed. I rather think it would be clear to anyone that the man was beyond help or medical assistance."

Veronica nodded, but kept her thoughts to herself.

They had rushed to the scene of the murder directly from Chelsea, Scarbright securing the services of a cab while Newbury took steps to make himself presentable. He'd done a remarkably good job, too: ten minutes later he had emerged like a new man, washed and shaved, and with a glimmer of the old sparkle in his eyes. He was dressed in his customary black suit, white shirt, and green cravat, and he'd somehow managed to muster energy from some secret reserves. Veronica wished she knew how he did it, how he was able to shake off such dreadful, debilitating weariness so easily, as if all he had to do was chide himself in the mirror and pull himself together. When Amelia had suffered from such episodes it had taken her hours, if not days, to recover. Newbury had rallied in a matter of half an hour. Clearly, he was right about one thing: He was stronger than her sister.

Veronica didn't yet know what that meant in terms of ongoing treatments for Amelia; how she felt about Newbury's insistence that he be allowed to carry on, that it was not her decision to make. She was sure of one thing, though: that she most definitely *would* have a say in what happened next.

It was clear that Bainbridge attributed Newbury's condition and general appearance of slovenliness to his propensity for opium abuse, and he made his opinions on the matter most keenly felt in the way he sighed and bustled about the place in an agitated manner, harrying Newbury and muttering curses beneath his breath. Veronica had wished that she could have disabused the man of such notions and outlined the truth of the matter for him then and there, but Newbury would not have thanked her for it. Besides, in so doing she would have had to tell him the truth about Amelia, and the Grayling Institute, and everything that had transpired since. She couldn't risk taking that chance.

Newbury, however, had ignored any such jibes or disapproving looks, and, as soon as they were in the back of the hansom rattling across town, had set about unleashing a barrage of questions regarding the circumstances of the corpse's discovery. Indeed, by the time they'd arrived at St. John's Wood, he was beginning to show signs of impatience and agitation, anxious to be getting on with his exploration of the crime scene.

Now, he was hunched over the body of the dead vicar, murmuring intently to himself as he examined the man's wounds.

Veronica tried not to look too closely, instead taking a moment to properly appraise their surroundings. It was an unusual sort of place for a murder, she decided, and didn't fit with the pattern of the other deaths, which—as far as she understood from Bainbridge—had all taken place in the victims' homes. Perhaps it was due to the man's occupation that the killer had struck here, in the church.

The building itself was ancient and crumbling, more of a small chapel of worship than a place that would house a regular congregation. Nevertheless, it was lavishly bedecked with the gilded relics and icons typical of those larger establishments and their elaborate rituals. A large stained glass window adorned the west wall, depicting Saint George standing bold and victorious over the slain dragon. The afternoon sun was slanting through it now, pooling on the floor around the corpse in bright puddles of multi-coloured light. A statue of the Virgin Mary looked down upon the gathered crowd, too: plaintive, sombre, as if sitting in judgement. She had borne silent witness to whatever had occurred in this sacred place. Veronica could see the speckles of blood spattered on her marble robes.

Bobbies milled around the entrance to the small church, talking in hushed tones, while Inspector Foulkes waited in the wings for Newbury to finish his assessment of the victim.

The vicar himself, the Reverend Josiah Carsen, had suffered wounds that were congruent with those inflicted upon the other victims, leaving little doubt in Veronica's mind—and, clearly, those of the other assembled investigators—that the same person was responsible.

He'd been run through with at least one blade. There were two ragged puncture wounds in his belly that indicated where the weapons had entered his body, and Veronica had no doubt that, when the body was eventually rolled over, the exit wounds would be pronounced and easily identifiable upon his back.

What was more, just like the other victims, his chest had been viciously hacked open and his heart removed. The resulting spillage of blood was horrendous, like a scene from an abattoir. It surrounded the body now, congealed and lumpy, still glossy in places where it had been disturbed. It was everywhere: spattered across the altar and the front row of pews, sprayed across the pulpit, drenching the vicar's robes. Veronica fought back rising bile in her throat as she took this in. Rarely had she been witness to something so ghoulish. Not since Aubrey Knox and the heap of abandoned corpses beneath the theatre had she felt quite so disgusted.

The stench, too, was near debilitating–the cloying scent of congealing blood, the acidic trace it left on the back of her tongue. Veronica glanced away, unable to stomach the sight of the butchered corpse any longer.

"Was he an agent of the Queen?" asked Newbury, glancing up at Bainbridge for a moment from his study of the corpse.

Bainbridge sighed. "We can only assume he was," he replied, bitterly. "We have no way of knowing without taking the matter to Her Majesty the Queen. And you know what she said about it...." He shook his head in frustration. "We need that list, Newbury."

Newbury nodded. "Yes, indeed," he said, distracted.

"So, black magic? Occult ritual?" asked Bainbridge. "Tell me what's going on. You said you needed to see the body in context."

Newbury stood, wiping his hands on a handkerchief. Veronica didn't wish to consider where they had been. "I don't think so, Charles, no. Ritualistic? Yes, most definitely. But occult? I can't see it. I think there must be some other significance to the missing hearts. It's as if the killer is taking trophies from his victims."

"Trophies?" echoed Veronica, in disgust. "Stealing his victims' hearts as trophies?" The very idea repelled her.

Newbury nodded. His expression was fixed and grim. "I fear so. I can see no other explanation. This is not a delicate surgical procedure. The hearts are being damaged as they're removed. I cannot imagine how they might be being put to use. My only thought is that they might represent some form of abysmal memento, or else a calling card left by the killer, letting us know who's responsible for the death. Perhaps there's some other significance, too, some message that we cannot decipher. What's clear to me, though, is that this murder was not performed as part of an occult rite. There must be another motivation behind the killings." He shrugged. "Aldous, of course, may be able to offer a different perspective."

"Have you heard from him yet?" asked Bainbridge.

"Not yet," said Newbury. "He needs time to consult his books."

"Time is one thing we don't have," said Bainbridge, testily.

"This isn't simply a matter of looking something up in the *Encyclopaedia Occultus*, you understand, Charles. Aldous may even now be poring over pages and pages of ancient manuscripts, searching for references in obscure grimoires, referring to records of forgotten lore and myth from all over the world. Hopefully, if we're lucky, he might be able to suggest some symbolic significance to what we're seeing here, some clue that might help us gain a little understanding of what we're dealing with. That's all. Aldous isn't going to give us all the answers here, and anything he does tell us might not actually prove to be of use." Newbury fixed Bainbridge with a firm stare. "You do appreciate that, Charles?"

Bainbridge's expression darkened. He looked as if he was biting back an angry retort, his face reddening, but he must have decided to give vent to it after all, as he rounded on Newbury. "Well, of course I appreciate that! What do you take me for? You can call me many things, Newbury, but I'm no imbecile. It's simply that I'm damn well *incandescent* to find myself standing here over the mangled corpse of yet another sorry bastard knowing that we're no closer—no closer—to having even the slightest idea of who is responsible." He looked away, trembling with rage.

Newbury took a deep breath. "You're right, Charles. Of course you are. I wish I had something more to give you, but there's nothing here. No clue as to the nature of the killer, or what it is that's driving him to commit such appalling acts of violence." He sighed. "Nevertheless, I'll see what I can do to hurry Aldous along."

He glanced round at the sound of footsteps echoing upon the flagstones behind them. Veronica followed his gaze. Professor Angelchrist strolled hastily towards them, flanked by two uniformed bobbies. He looked a little dishevelled, as if he hadn't managed much sleep the previous evening. He was still wearing the same clothes as the previous day. "Sorry I'm late, Sir Charles," he said, a little out of breath. He stopped beside Newbury, joining them in their makeshift crescent around the corpse of the vicar. "Good Lord!" he said, appearing somewhat taken aback by the sheer horror of the scene. "And in a house of God, too."

"The killer knows no shame," said Bainbridge, darkly.

Veronica looked from one man to the other. What the devil was Bainbridge playing at, inviting that man here? On top of what had happened at the exhibition, Newbury and Bainbridge were under definite instruction from the monarch herself to sever all ties with the Secret Service. By welcoming Angelchrist to a crime scene, Bainbridge was, effectively, colluding with the enemy—or at least Her Majesty's perception of the enemy, which amounted to much the same thing. He was putting them all in very grave danger.

"Whatever the case, Archibald here was right," said Newbury. "About the Germans, I mean." The others turned to regard him. Veronica bit her tongue. "The corpse has been here for some hours. The cold weather and the atmosphere in this frigid church have helped to preserve the remains, but I have no doubt that he died yesterday, probably late in the afternoon."

"At around the same time you were being chased by carnivorous birds at the Crystal Palace," said Angelchrist.

"Yes. And the same time your men were engaged in an unnecessary gunfight with the German agents," said Veronica, drily. "Do you know the full extent of the death toll yet?"

"Veronica, I really don't think—" started Bainbridge.

Angelchrist cut him off with a wave of his hand, but wouldn't meet her eye. "It's alright, Sir Charles. I'm only too aware of my failure." He raised his head, searching Veronica's face. His eyes were limned with dark rings. "I can only assure you, Miss Hobbes, that it was never my intention to allow the operation to descend into such violence, nor to put the lives of any civilians in danger. Nevertheless, the risk of allowing the Kaiser to arm his flotilla of airships with such a weapon was too great to ignore. If he had been successful, I might well have many, many more deaths on my conscience."

"And at least we've now discounted the Germans from our murder investigation," added Newbury.

"It might still have been Germans," said Veronica, levelly. "The incident at the exhibition could well have been a planned distraction."

"Perhaps," said Newbury, thoughtfully. "Although I find it unlikely they would draw attention to themselves in such a way if they were contemplating further, more clandestine operations throughout the city. Let's face it: It's not as if we were hot on their trail before the exhibition. Why put on such an obvious display if the real aim was to remain anonymous?"

Veronica nodded. At least this was in keeping with her thoughts on the subject. "Then perhaps the reverse was true. Perhaps they showed their hand to discredit themselves as suspects in the murders? If I were the Kaiser, I would certainly be taking steps to distance my agents from implication. Their attempt to steal the search lamp yesterday might in fact have been a statement of innocence, the Kaiser's way of declaring his real interests in London and distancing himself from the murders."

Bainbridge nodded. "I'm impressed with your reasoning, Miss Hobbes. There's most definitely a subtext here that we're missing. Someone is playing political games."

"You think that people are being killed simply to make a point?" said Angelchrist.

"I don't know," replied Bainbridge. "I don't know anything for certain. That's what's so damn infuriating. Someone is waging a campaign against the Queen's agents, and I don't have any real notion as to why."

"There's something fundamental we're missing," said Newbury, quietly.

"Why is there never a simple explanation?" said Bainbridge, his shoulders slumping.

"Oh, I have no doubt that there is, Charles. It's only that—as yet—we're unable to see it," said Newbury. "Inevitably, these things come down to rivalry and petty jealousies."

"I admire your optimism, Sir Maurice," said Angelchrist, with a weak smile. The events of the previous day had clearly taken their toll on him. He shrugged. "So, have we learned anything from this new victim?"

"Only that Newbury doesn't feel that there's any occult significance to the theft of the organs. He believes the killer to be taking trophies," said Bainbridge.

Angelchrist nodded. His expression did not give much away. "Yes, I've heard of such things," he said. "Most disturbing."

"Well, that does rule out a second possibility," said Newbury. "It means the Cabal of the Horned Beast can't be behind this," he continued.

"They're not?" said Bainbridge, looking increasingly crestfallen.

"No," said Newbury. "At least, I don't think so. None of their hallmarks are apparent here, the little touches or occult references I would have expected if they were responsible. People such as that, with those sort of fanatical beliefs, don't try to obscure their involvement in such things. They revel in them. I know you considered them a likely party in these murders, Charles, but it just doesn't appear to be the case. Besides which, I understand they have somewhat more particular plans in mind."

Veronica raised a questioning eyebrow, but Newbury shook his head, refusing to elaborate. "Something for another day," he said. "For now, we must concentrate on the matter in hand. We must think of nothing else." He glanced at Veronica, and she realised that last point was aimed directly at her. Did he mean to dismiss her concerns over Angelchrist? Or was it a reference to what she had witnessed back at Chelsea? Either way, she felt a kernel of frustration at Newbury's offhand remark.

"Professor, is there anything that your investigations have revealed that may help shed some light?" asked Veronica, careful to monitor her tone.

"Not as yet, I fear," replied Angelchrist, with an apologetic smile, "although I shall endeavour to help where I can. Rest assured, I have my best men on it. Now that the German situation is under control, we will work with you to bring an end to this reign of terror."

"My thanks to you, Archibald," said Bainbridge. "Right now I fear we need all the help we can get."

There was a moment of awkward silence that stretched almost to breaking. Finally, Bainbridge spoke. "So, what next?" he said, leaning heavily on his cane. He looked exhausted, as if he were carrying the weight of the world upon his shoulders.

"I shall return to Marlborough House to see the Prince of Wales, in the hope of obtaining the list of agents he has promised to procure for us. Following that, I shall pay a visit to Aldous and see if I can't jolly him on a little in his investigations."

"Very good," said Bainbridge. "I shall return to the Yard and try to keep the damn journalists at bay. And, of course, someone will have to talk to his family," he said, indicating the corpse with the end of his cane, and grimacing. "Cartwright?" he said, glancing around for any sign of the uniformed constable.

"Yes, sir?" said the young man, stepping forward out of the shadows. His jaw was set firm as he tried to avoid displaying any emotion at the sight of the corpse.

"Have this body removed to the morgue directly," he ordered. "Tell them to put it with the others."

"Yes, sir. Right away," said Cartwright, melting back into the shadows. His footsteps echoed in the empty space as he left the church, no doubt to despatch a messenger for a cart and litter.

Newbury turned to Veronica. "And you, Miss Hobbes?"

Veronica glanced at Angelchrist. "I fear I have a personal matter to attend to," she said. "Can we talk later?"

"Of course," said Newbury, with the slightest of frowns. "Call round when you're free." He offered her an inquisitive look, but she refused to meet his eye. *He thinks I'm going to see Amelia,* she realised. But that was not at all her intention.

"Very well," said Newbury, after a moment. "Do you need transportation?"

"No, thank you," she replied. She wanted to tell him not to worry, that she wasn't about to rush off to Malbury Cross to divulge everything to her sister, but now was not the time. In fact, it was probably for the best if he *did* imagine that to be the case, at least for the time being. He would be even less thrilled to learn what she was really planning, especially after his warning a few moments ago.

They turned and quit the church as one, leaving the eviscerated corpse of the Reverend Josiah Carsen for the singular attentions of the mortuary attendants.

Outside, the afternoon sun cast a diffuse bronze glow across the small graveyard. Uniformed policemen were milling about in small clusters. They looked up as Bainbridge and the others emerged from the grandiose doorway and quickly stood to attention.

Veronica loitered for a moment in the shadow of the doorway as their small group parted company. She smiled warmly at Newbury as he glanced at her over his shoulder, walking with Bainbridge towards the row of waiting conveyances. They bade one another farewell and climbed into separate carriages.

Then, catching sight of Professor Angelchrist, who had quietly slipped from the graveyard on foot, as if hoping not to draw too much attention to himself, she set out after him at a safe distance.

# CHAPTER 19

👑

*A man once asked her why she made a point of opening up her victims' chests and removing their hearts, and what exactly she did with the strange, misshapen organs after the event. Was there a purpose to these most personal of thefts? A significance? There was no judgement in his voice, none of the disgust she had faced during similar conversations over the years. Only interest.*

*This was years after she had fled Montmartre, some time in the 1850s, during her first excursion to the frigid city of St. Petersburg. She sat in the parlour of his opulent house, her hands still sticky with the blood of her latest kill. She had left the dead man lying in the snow close by, opened up to the freezing night like a silken purse, glossy and stark against the pure white snow. She had brought his heart with her in a tanned leather satchel, and it sat upon the table before her as she waited for her employer to fetch water and a towel.*

*He placed the steaming bowl carefully on the table beside the leather bag and took his seat opposite her, his eyes wide with fascination. He watched her intently, patiently, as she washed herself down.*

*He was a well-connected man with links to the Russian royal family, and he had paid well for her services. She had executed seven men on his behalf, each of them former officials of the Tsar's court who had known far more about his nocturnal habits—his predilection for spending his nights in the arms of other people's wives—than he was* comfortable with. He had ensured that they had all been dismissed from their posts, of course, but he nevertheless feared the hold they had over him, the constant threat of exposure, blackmail, or worse. And so he had ordered them killed, and she was only too willing to oblige.

By this time in her long, unchanging existence, her death toll measured in the thousands. She had spent years as a hired assassin, drifting from city to city, one day finding herself in the squalid slums of Berlin, another amongst the sumptuous, gleaming spires of Prague. She had seen much of the world, living hand to mouth, from moment to moment, always trapped in the perpetual twilight of her own half-life.

The man fetched her more water, and she considered her answer while she scrubbed the sticky blood from her forearms, slowly revealing the whorls and glyphs of the dark tattoos that covered her flesh.

She could not remember a time when she had made a conscious decision to begin removing the hearts of her victims. It had begun with the acrobat's lover. On that first occasion, of course, it was symbolic, a tribute to the woman whose heart he had broken. Yet she had been fascinated by the sight of the still-beating organ when she had cracked open the man's rib cage, the way it pulsated and throbbed, so full of life. When she'd reached in and touched it, felt it beating beneath her fingertips, she'd wanted to claim it for her own. That, of course, had been the root of the acrobat's entire dilemma: that the man had not pledged his heart to her. And so the Executioner had done it for him.

Three days later she had killed again. This time the act had been motivated purely by the need for money; she had fled the acrobat's caravan with nothing, and so she'd been forced to murder a lonely businessman for the contents of his wallet.

As he'd lain dying at her feet, she'd been struck once again by that interminable sense of curiosity. She'd wanted to examine his heart, to watch it beat its last, to take it for her own. It was as if, by making it hers, she could somehow—for a few moments—replace the heart she had lost.

The man had begged her to stop as she tore open his shirt. He was weak by this point and shivering with blood loss, and she'd have to work quickly if she wanted to see the heart before he died. She'd muffled his screams with a strip of ragged cloth, and hacked him open with her razor-sharp blade, revealing the glistening jewel within.

When the heart finally shuddered and ceased to beat, she had cut it out and wrapped it in the remains of his shirt like a treasure.

It was the closest she had come to feeling anything for some time.

She told her employer all of this in calm, collected tones, reciting as many details as she could remember. He listened to her intently, and if he was shocked by her curiously unemotional manner, he did not show it.

He was, however, shocked when—just as calmly—she withdrew one of her curving scimitars and thrust it through his belly, skewering him to his chair. He had shown her kindness and tolerance, fulfilled all of his obligations to her, and more. He did not understand.

But she felt no obligation to explain. She had addressed the situation in the most logical way she could. The man had fallen into the same trap he had faced at court, with his seven untrustworthy confidants: She had revealed to him something about herself; therefore, she could not allow him to live.

When she finished, she washed her hands again using the man's bowl and towel, and then she left, her leather bag bulging with the fruitful dividends of her evening.

# CHAPTER 20

✦

It was raining when the cab finally ground to a halt at Grosvenor Square, a relentless downpour that thrummed upon the thin wooden roof, drowning out the sounds of the outside world.

Veronica peered out of the window, wishing she'd had the foresight to bring an umbrella. The sky was a dark, brooding canopy of grey, a bruised smear across the rooftops of the city. Carriages churned the fast-flowing tributaries of gutter water with their wooden wheels as they raced past, the drivers huddled in thick coats against the inclement weather. The passengers inside stared blankly out of their temporary havens: pale, ghostly faces, briefly glimpsed.

Across the street, in the shadow of the towering tenement buildings, the door of the other cab opened and the figure of Professor Angelchrist emerged. He dipped his head and hunched his shoulders as if depressed by the onslaught from above. He glanced up and down the street, then hurried around to the driver and passed him up a handful of coins. The driver doffed his cap and pulled sharply on the reins, and the horses, their flanks glistening in the nimbus of a nearby streetlamp, whinnied and stamped their feet before starting off again, clopping away into the downpour. In a matter of moments the cab was completely swallowed by the shimmering curtain of rain.

Veronica watched Angelchrist withdraw a key from his jacket pocket, drop it, bend down to retrieve it, and then hurry to the door of one of the apartment buildings. He fiddled with the lock for a moment, pushed open the door with his shoulder, and then dashed inside. The heavy black door swung shut behind him. She made a mental note which building he had entered.

The rain was still drumming noisily on the roof of the cab, obscuring the view through the window. Reluctantly, she gathered her belongings. Just as she was about to reach for the door, there was another eruption of heavy drumming from above, and she realised that the driver was banging on the roof, attempting to hurry her along. No doubt he was getting soaked up there in his dickey box and wanted to make a dash for cover, or else he was intent on finding another sorry pedestrian looking to exchange their hard-won coppers for a brief respite from the rain.

She turned the handle and pushed open the door, struggling with it as a sudden gust almost blew it back in her face. Rain swept in, spattering her dress. She climbed down, cursing as she dropped into a puddle. The icy water ran into her boots, soaking through to her stockinged feet, drenching the hem of her skirts. She stepped up onto the kerb, squinting in dismay as the water lashed her face.

"Miserable day fer it," said the driver, hulking down in his box, his cap pulled low over his brow. She could barely see his face past the upturned collars of his thick woollen coat.

"It certainly is," she said, fishing around in her pocket and withdrawing a few coins. She passed them up to him.

"Thank you, ma'am," he said, his voice as thick as treacle. "Good day." He flicked the reins and the horses pulled away ponderously from the kerb.

Veronica glanced around. Behind her, the park appeared almost empty, the treetops swaying in the breeze. The street itself was nearly deserted, other than a handful of carriages trundling by in both directions. She could see the warm glow of lights through the windows of the row of tall tenement buildings.

Now that she was here, she wasn't entirely sure what she intended to do. She'd followed Angelchrist on a whim, jumping into a cab at St. John's Wood and ordering the driver to follow the professor's own conveyance at a short distance. She'd been following her instincts, anxious to know more about what the man was really up to. Should she simply knock on his door and confront him?

She dismissed that idea almost as soon as it had formed. He was hardly likely to respond well to her admission that she'd followed him from the murder scene. It would beg the obvious question of why, and then she'd be forced to admit her reservations about his motives, and most likely find herself drawn into a protracted argument. Even if he accepted her concerns and invited her in out of the rain to discuss the matter with her civilly, she wasn't likely to extract the truth. Better that she observe from the shadows, at least for a while. That way she might actually see something of use, something that might shed some light on his role in proceedings.

She was becoming slowly drenched as she stood there in the rain, and what was more, she risked being seen from one of the tenement windows.

There were precious few opportunities to take shelter. The park, she decided, represented her best chance at escaping the storm, so she pulled her overcoat tighter about her shoulders, dipped her head, and made a dash for the gates.

She passed a hooded figure hurriedly dragging a dog along on a lead. The poor creature looked sodden and downtrodden as it scurried along beside its owner, water streaming down its pugilist's face. Otherwise, the park appeared utterly abandoned, desolate. The weather had driven everyone to their homes. Everyone sensible, at least.

Veronica took shelter beneath the boughs of an ancient oak tree, close to the boundary of the park and with a good view of the row of residential buildings on the opposite side of the street. At this time of year, the denuded branches tapered to spindly fingers that provided little cover from the gusting weather, but she huddled close to the gnarled trunk, leaning up against it beneath a fat, overhanging limb. It wasn't much, but it was something.

Across the road, the building that Angelchrist had entered a few moments before was quiet and still. She saw the warm glow of a lamp being turned on in a fourth floor window, and then a shadowy figure appeared, seeming to peer out at the street below. The figure remained there for a few moments, watching, and then pulled the curtains to, blotting out the view. It might possibly have been Angelchrist, but she could not be certain from the brief glimpse of the person's build.

Another gust of wind blew stinging raindrops into her eyes. As she raised her arm to ward them off, she cursed herself for her interminable suspicion. If Angelchrist was now ensconced in his rooms for the afternoon, then she might as well strike out for Kensington and home. She'd succeeded only in allowing herself to be soaked to the skin, with perhaps the small victory of ascertaining where the professor lived. Although, in truth, that was information she might have gleaned easily from a five-minute conversation with Newbury. She'd anticipated that Angelchrist might have been heading to another rendezvous, one that had a more pertinent bearing on the investigation, or at least her understanding of the man and his motives. Reluctantly, she admitted to herself that she'd been wrong.

Nevertheless, she was here now, huddled suspiciously beneath a tree, so she decided she might as well remain there for a short while. If nothing else, there was a chance the rain might abate, and then she could duck out from under her makeshift cover and hail another cab. She'd asked to call on Newbury that evening, but she'd be forced to return home and change out of her wet clothes before even considering heading back to Chelsea. A few more minutes wouldn't make a great deal of difference either way.

As it transpired, however, her diligence bore the most unexpected fruit. Nearly half an hour after installing herself beneath the tree, her attention was drawn to a plain black carriage that rolled up outside the front door of Angelchrist's apartment building. Both horses were frothing at the bit, as if they'd made a punishing journey across the city.

She heard the door open on the other side of the carriage, accompanied by the gentle murmur of voices. She couldn't yet see the figures that climbed out, but it was clear from the glimpse she caught of their feet through the spokes of the carriage's wheels that there were two of them.

The driver barely appeared to move as one of the carriage's prior occupants spoke to him, giving instructions. No money changed hands, which told her it was a private carriage, and not one that had been hired for the occasion; the lack of a tip or fare suggested the driver was most likely salaried.

As the carriage pulled away, she got her first glimpse of the passengers. The first was a tall, thin man with a drooping moustache wearing a top hat and a grey woollen overcoat that came down to his knees. He was carrying a black leather briefcase in his left hand and clung to his hat with his right, trying desperately to prevent it from blowing away.

The second man was slightly shorter and a little wider around the waist. He, too, wore a top hat, and was dressed in a black overcoat. Veronica could see that this man sported greying hair beneath the brim of his hat, and a bushy grey moustache. He was leaning on a cane, talking urgently with the other man. Then he turned in her direction and appeared to stare straight at her. For a moment her heart stopped. Had he seen her? But after a second he turned back to the other man and continued his conversation, and she breathed a sigh of relief.

Nevertheless, she felt a flutter of excitement and trepidation. She would have recognised the man's profile from a hundred yards. It was Bainbridge, arriving here at Angelchrist's house less than an hour after leaving the scene of the Reverend Carsen's murder. What was he doing here? And who was the other, unfamiliar man?

She watched with bated occasions when Newbury had seen him recently, but then, the first time had seen him breath as Bainbridge approached the heavy black door of Angelchrist's apartment building. He rapped on it with the end of his cane, and a moment later a man appeared to usher him and his associate in.

*There's something fundamental we're missing,* Newbury had said that afternoon, as they'd stood together over the corpse of the killer's latest victim. He'd been right, in more ways than perhaps he realised. There was far more to Bainbridge's relationship with Angelchrist than the chief inspector was prepared to admit. She'd thought he'd been taking a risk when he'd allowed the professor to openly join them at the church, but now, to be seen visiting the man's home... well, either he was actively attempting to imperil his position with the Queen, or he thought whatever it was he hoped to achieve was worth the risk. Either way, Veronica knew she needed to get to the bottom of it.

She waited a few minutes longer to ensure the three men were not about to leave the apartment together, then she pushed herself away from the tree, bracing herself against the chill and the incessant rain. She considered waiting until their meeting had ended, but decided there was little more she could learn, and she was growing uncomfortable in the rain. Her clothes were plastered to her now, dragging at her skin as she moved, but she felt somewhat vindicated. She had not, after all, had a wasted trip.

Veronica set off in search of a cab, and a driver who'd be willing to take a fare that would leave his seats waterlogged for the rest of the day. She sighed. She supposed she'd just have to leave a good tip.

# CHAPTER 21

If the attitude of one's butler was in any way a representative of one's outlook on life, then Newbury had clearly gotten the Prince of Wales all wrong. Newbury considered this as he sat once again in the drawing room of Marlborough House, waiting for the Prince to grant him an audience.

The man's butler, Barclay, was an utter prig. He was, in Newbury's heartfelt opinion, an example of the worst sort of man, out to undermine and coax, to insinuate and judge. He had about him the manner of a sly dog: slippery and oily. On both occasions Newbury had visited the Prince, he had observed Barclay lurking in passageways or hovering outside doors, listening to the Prince's ostensibly private conversations, no doubt filing them away for later—probably defamatory—use. He wouldn't be surprised to discover the man was a blackguard or a blackmailer, although he had to admit he'd met more genial examples of both.

Whatever the case, Newbury was thankful that he didn't have to deal with Barclay for more than a few moments at a time, although he imagined the butler was most likely loitering in the hallway at that very moment, listening intently on the other side of the door.

He heard a cough in the distance, and stood as the

now familiar tapping of the Prince's cane came along the passageway, accompanied by all the bustle and grandeur he had come to expect.

"Fetch me a whisky soda, Barclay," said Albert Edward, his voice booming in the confines of the corridor. "And whatever Newbury is having, too."

"Sir Maurice declined my offer of a drink, Your Royal Highness," wheedled the butler in reply. Newbury raised an eyebrow at the blatant lie. He had done no such thing—the offer had never been made in the first place.

The Prince apparently did not deem it necessary to grant the butler a reply. A moment later he erupted through the doorway, glancing around the room until his eyes settled on Newbury.

He was dressed in a black suit with a red silk cravat and carried a large cream-coloured envelope in his left hand. He looked more relaxed than other occasions when Newbury had seen him recently, but then, the first time *had* seen him bursting in upon Newbury during an opium-induced fugue, and the other had involved Newbury interrupting him during an important business meeting.

"Please go ahead and make yourself comfortable in my presence, will you?" said Albert Edward, smiling warmly. "I think we understand each other well enough now to encourage a little informality. After all, I foresee a time in the future when you and I shall be spending a good deal of time in one another's company."

Newbury hardly knew how to take this somewhat unexpected assertion, but he did what the Prince suggested and sought out a seat. Clearly Albert Edward had already begun to consider his options for the future, and, more specifically, the people with whom he wished to surround himself when he did finally ascend to the throne. Newbury didn't know whether to feel flattered or amused. "I look forward to that time, Your Royal Highness," he said, diplomatically.

The Prince nodded sagely, as if sharing a mutual understanding. He glanced at the envelope in his hand. "Ah, yes. The information you wanted," he said, passing it over to Newbury.

"Thank you," said Newbury, opening the flap and partially withdrawing the sheaf of papers within. There were five or six pages in the bundle, and each contained a long list of names, printed in neat copperplate. Beside each was an address, or, in some instances, the name of a club at which the person could be reached. A handful of the names were struck through with a thick black line.

Newbury pushed the papers back inside the envelope. "I'm sure this will be a great help with our inquiry," he said.

The Prince nodded. He glanced behind him, took a step back and lowered himself heavily into a chair. For the first time, Newbury noticed there were dark rings beneath his eyes. "Yes. Pray tell, I am interested to hear how the investigation progresses."

Newbury glanced around for somewhere to put the envelope, but there was nowhere to hand. He decided to hold onto it instead. "The investigation has, I fear, rather stalled in its tracks."

"Stalled?" asked the Prince, his brow creasing. "I understood you were following the line of inquiry we had discussed, regarding the Kaiser's agents."

"Indeed," said Newbury, quickly. "I can assure you, Your Royal Highness, that matter has been my primary concern. However, yesterday it became clear to me that the two investigations are not linked. It seems the German spies are not in fact responsible for the deaths of Her Majesty's agents."

The Prince's frown deepened. "You're quite certain of this, Newbury?"

"As certain as I can be, Your Royal Highness," he replied, cautious not to intimate that the Prince had been wrong in any of his assertions. Newbury was not yet fully aware of the circumstances surrounding the German operation at the Crystal Palace, or what the Secret Service was planning to do with the information.

"And what has led you to this conclusion?" continued the Prince. It was clear he was not entirely enamoured with Newbury's revelation.

"Yesterday there was a bungled operation at an exhibition at the Crystal Palace," said Newbury.

"Yes, I read about it in *The Times*," interjected the Prince. "I understand one of the exhibits broke free and set out on a murderous rampage. Something to do with a new species of carnivorous bird they discovered in the Congo last year?"

Newbury couldn't help but smile. Once again, Bainbridge had worked his magic with the press, and the stories had focused on the rampant giant birds instead of the gun battle that had preceded, and indeed enabled, their escape. "I rather think *The Times* is reporting only a small portion of the truth, Your Royal Highness," he said. He measured his next words carefully. "I was in attendance with Miss Hobbes and Sir Charles Bainbridge. I saw what happened. The birds escaped because the Secret Service stepped in to foil the machinations of the Kaiser. There was a gun battle, and a stray shot damaged the bird's enclosure, providing the beasts with the opportunity to break free. The real story—the one I imagine has been kept out of the news—is that the German agents showed their hand, and the Secret Service prevented them from gaining possession of a dangerous weapon."

Albert Edward leaned back in his chair. He studied Newbury's face, chewing thoughtfully on his lip. He was about to speak when there was a polite rap on the door. They both looked round to see Barclay enter with a small silver tray bearing the Prince's drink, along with a box of cigars and a cutter.

The butler scuttled over without a word, swept up a small

occasional table with his left hand, and laid everything out neatly before the Prince. His eyes never met Newbury's as he quit the room moments later, pulling the door nearly closed–but not shut–behind him.

The Prince reached for his drink and gulped down a generous draught. He eyed Newbury over the top of the glass. "So, what you're telling me, Newbury, is that some of the Kaiser's agents were involved in a plot to steal... what? A weapon from the exhibition?" He sounded more than a little sceptical.

"An electric search lamp designed to be mounted on the underbelly of an airship. It's thought that they hoped to magnify its beam through a glass lens to turn it into a weapon. When fired from above, the concentrated beam of light would–they hoped–work to incinerate the city below," said Newbury.

"Good Lord," said Albert Edward. "This works precisely to prove my point, Newbury. The Kaiser is arming himself with a view to laying waste to London. He intends to make a play for control of the Empire."

"My contacts assure me, Your Royal Highness, that the Kaiser's operation was intended to secure the weapon only for the purposes of defence," said Newbury, cautiously.

"Balderdash!" said the Prince. "When examined in concert with the murders, there is only one logical conclusion. The Kaiser is planning war."

"But that's just it, Your Royal Highness," said Newbury, stifling his exasperation. "I do not believe that the German agents are responsible for the murders."

"On what grounds?" demanded the Prince.

Newbury took a deep breath, attempting to steady his nerves. "Firstly, I do not believe the Kaiser would show his hand so willingly at the exhibition if his real motive was to undermine Her Majesty's power by murdering her agents. Surely he would have more success in that regard if his operation remained clandestine. Secondly—and more importantly—I attended the scene of one of the deaths this very morning, and I'm convinced there is a ritualistic significance to the excision of the victims' hearts. The killer is taking them as trophies, leaving his victims heartless as some form of symbolic gesture. I have yet to ascertain what the precise significance of this macabre exercise is, but I feel I am drawing closer."

The Prince was frowning again. "I urge you not to be too hasty in your conclusions, Newbury," he said. "I fear you may miss something of fundamental importance if you pursue these concerns over a potential German plot. It would not do to leave ourselves vulnerable to attack."

"Rest assured, Your Royal Highness, I shall not allow the matter to rest. You made your feelings regarding the Secret Service very clear to me during my previous visit, but I can attest to the integrity of their agents' handling of the affair at the Crystal Palace. They, too, are independently attempting to discover the truth regarding the Kaiser's intentions. When combined with my own efforts towards the same end, I believe we can keep the matter under strict observation. In the meanwhile, I shall continue to pursue any leads I have into the murders of Her Majesty's agents, and I shall aid Scotland Yard in bringing the perpetrator to justice. I will not fail."

"No," said Albert Edward, resignedly, draining the last of his drink. "I do not doubt it."

Newbury offered him a quizzical expression, but the Prince did not elaborate any further. The moment stretched. "Did you manage, Your Royal Highness, to resolve your little problem?" asked Newbury, hoping to alleviate the tension somewhat by changing the subject.

The Prince, however, offered him the darkest of looks in reply. "My... little problem?" he said, urging Newbury to explain. Clearly, Newbury had unwittingly touched a nerve.

"Forgive me, Your Royal Highness. I meant no offense. I was merely enquiring after your success in the matter of the condemned hotel."

The Prince's frown turned almost immediately into a jovial smile. "Oh, that. Yes, I'd almost forgotten. The matter is in hand. There's very little in this world that cannot be resolved by the judicious application of money, Newbury."

Newbury laughed, but he couldn't help feeling that the Prince appeared somewhat relieved to discover Newbury was referring to his recent endeavours in the property market and not some other, undisclosed affair. Something it was clear he'd be uncomfortable discussing with Newbury.

The matter left Newbury with a rather unsavoury feeling, but he tried his best to put it out of mind. After all, he supposed there were many things of a sensitive nature that the Prince might find himself involved in. It was not Newbury's place to pry.

"Well, if that is all…" ventured the Prince. "I imagine we both have our hands rather full." The tone of the interview had changed. Gone now was the playful informality of earlier. It was clear the Prince had something on his mind, and that he wished to be left alone.

"Yes, thank you, Your Royal Highness. Once again, your support in this matter has been most appreciated," said Newbury, getting to his feet. He clutched the envelope tightly by his side. He looked round to see the door to the hall already open, and Barclay waiting for him on the threshold, a tight smile on his lips.

"Good day, Newbury," said the Prince. "And let me just say how much I admire your tenacity. Observing you at work is a lesson for us all."

"Thank you, Your Royal Highness," said Newbury. He gave a short bow, then left the room, refusing to acknowledge the sneering butler on his way out.

# CHAPTER 22

It had been months since Newbury had last visited Aldous Renwick at his unusual bookshop off Tottenham Court Road. As he approached unannounced at this late hour in the afternoon, he couldn't help but feel a stirring of guilt. Renwick was a friend as much as he was a source of information and rare, specialist books, and Newbury had ignored him of late, just as he'd ignored so much of import in his life in recent months. Or, more truthfully, he'd ignored Renwick until he'd needed something, at which point he'd sent the man an apologetic note, requesting his urgent help. No wonder he was feeling guilty, he chided himself. It was no way to treat a friend.

Renwick would understand. The man was not the sort to judge. Nevertheless, Newbury reprimanded himself for his ignoble behaviour, and decided he would make an effort to remain in touch. He had few enough real friends, and he recognised that he abused them terribly.

The small emporium was still open, so Newbury stopped for a moment to examine the cluttered, leaning piles in the window. Renwick had long ago given up on using the space for any sort of cohesive display, and had taken to using it as room to pile more of the musty old books that burst from the heaving shelves inside.

How the man ever made a sale, Newbury didn't know. He adored the shop, however; the almost-vanilla scent of the ancient, dusty books, the sight of so much knowledge, adventure, and opinion huddled together in that small space; the sense of triumph at finding something unexpected printed on a gilded, leaning spine. He could have spent hours in there losing himself amongst the maze-like stacks. Indeed, every time he visited the shop he promised himself he'd make time to return during more leisurely hours to do just that. There were few finer things in life, in Newbury's humble opinion, than spending time perusing the shelves of a good bookshop.

Newbury's particular interest in the premises, however, lay out of sight, in Renwick's private back room. That was where he kept his real treasures: the books that weren't for sale.

Renwick had one of the most extensive—if not *the* most extensive—libraries of obscure occult writing in the world. It was unrivalled, in Newbury's experience, containing riches from all the many corners of the globe. On numerous occasions he had found reason to peruse the rare tomes in Renwick's possession, and on nearly as many Renwick had been able to help him to ascertain the nature of a particular problem or the meaning of some esoteric symbolism. His hope now was that his friend had been successful in identifying the meaning behind the missing hearts, and whether there truly was a ritualistic significance behind them.

Newbury, steeling himself for some well-deserved jibing, pushed open the door to the shop and stepped inside.

Renwick was—for once—standing behind the counter, but if he'd noticed the door open and close, or the jingling of the tiny bell instigated by the action, he showed no sign of it such as looking up from his work.

He was perhaps one of the most eccentric men Newbury had ever met, and his appearance mirrored perfectly his chaotic attitude to life. He was scruffy and shambolic, with untidy grey hair that defied taming. It burst from his head in wild tufts, matted and wiry. He wore a stained white shirt—or rather, a shirt that had *once* been white, but was now more of a dirty pale brown—and a worn leather smock around his waist. The fingers of his right hand were stained yellow from the excessive smoking of cigarettes, and his teeth had a similar, dirty hue, although Newbury hesitated to assume it was for the same reasons. He had a plethora of unusual—and somewhat antisocial—habits, including the brewing of his own disgusting beverages, which he consumed with hearty abandon.

Most interestingly, Renwick's left eye had at some point been damaged beyond the bounds of normal medical repair, and had been replaced by a primitive viewing device reminiscent of a jeweller's eyepiece. This small machine had been wholly embedded into Renwick's skull, wired directly into the visual centre of his brain.

Renwick had claimed on more than one occasion that the unseemly device had actually improved the quality of his vision, and that he felt no regret at the loss of its biological predecessor—other than, perhaps, the effect it had on customers, who would at times enter his emporium bursting with enthusiasm, but leave again hastily when they caught sight of the owner.

Newbury had grown used to it by now, of course, but still found it mildly disconcerting when the eye appeared to move of its own accord, shifting the lenses around with tiny gears to refocus Renwick's vision and compensate for any changes in the quality of the light.

It wasn't, perhaps, the most aesthetically pleasing of mechanical enhancements, but it clearly worked, and Renwick himself seemed more than satisfied with its performance.

Newbury wove a path through the heaped stacks of books towards the counter, narrowly avoiding sending some of them toppling over in his wake. He peered over at what

Renwick was doing. He appeared to be engaged in repairing the binding of a rather tatty old book, carefully stitching the printed sections into a new leather spine.

"I'll be with you in a minute, Newbury," he mumbled, his head down. "Tricky operation, this."

"What is it?" asked Newbury, showing no surprise that Renwick had already established the identity of his visitor.

"A first edition of *A Key to Physic and the Occult Sciences*," said Renwick, slowly, as he threaded through the final stitch and tied off the thread with a flourish. "Very rare." He placed the needle on the counter beside the book and stepped back, admiring his handiwork. "There. A bit of tidying up to do, but much more satisfactory."

He glanced up. "You look terrible, Newbury," said Renwick.

"Oh, so we're skipping the pleasantries?" said Newbury, jovially.

Renwick leaned closer, bringing his face disconcertingly close to Newbury's own. His warm breath smelled of alcohol. His mechanical eye turned in its socket with a metallic grating as it refocused. "It's not the opiates, is it?" he said, his voice level. It was a rhetorical question.

Newbury shook his head. There was no point in lying to this man, or attempting to make light of his words. Renwick could see through Newbury's bluster like a hawk spying a scurrying rodent amongst the mulch and twigs of a forest floor.

"You'd better come through," said Renwick, pushing open the dividing door to his back room. A waft of something foul smelling gusted out of the door, but Renwick did not seem to notice. Smiling, Newbury stepped inside.

There was a warm familiarity to the room, and Newbury felt himself relax. It was like stepping into a vault of ancient treasures, and he hardly knew where to look first. Row upon row of mahogany bookcases lined the deceptively small space, each of them crammed full with some of the most valuable books outside the Vatican library. At the back, a pan sat steaming on a small stove. Closer, on his right, was a large still, set up with numerous rods and bottles. Strange coloured fluids bubbled and fizzed, some of them being slowly siphoned off into small jars, others emptying into a large plastic bucket on the floor. Most surprisingly, the brass skeleton of a large bird was laid out on the floor, components spilled haphazardly around it; cogs of all sizes, levers and keys, trailing wires.

"You're building something, then?" asked Newbury, indicating the slurry of parts.

Renwick nodded. "I *was*. I've been rather busy with something else for the last few days." He patted a small stack of books on a stool by the door.

Newbury looked a little sheepish. "Yes. I apologise for calling on you, once again, out of the blue."

Renwick shrugged. "So, tell me what's going on. First I hear nothing from you for months, and then I receive a note asking some *very* interesting questions. Then you happen to turn up here at the shop, looking like that," he motioned up and down with his hands, as if appraising Newbury's appearance.

Newbury sighed. He could see he wasn't going to get away without explaining himself. He dropped into a fusty-looking armchair, sending a huge plume of dust into the air. He waved his hand before his face, coughing. "Well, first of all, the two things are not related," he said, once the choking had abated. "The contents of the note and my... appearance, I mean."

Renwick reached for one of the flasks on the still and raised it to his lips, taking a swig of the bubbling liquid. He grimaced, glanced at the contents of the flask, and put it back on the still with a shrug. He eyed Newbury, but didn't say anything in response.

Newbury grinned. "I managed to obtain a copy of the book," he said, knowing this would provoke a reaction.

Renwick frowned, his mechanical eye whirring—always a giveaway that Newbury had captured his attention. "*The* book?"

"Yes, *the* book," replied Newbury.

"Have you got it with you?" said Renwick, with an urgency that surprised Newbury.

He shook his head. "No. It's back at Cleveland Avenue."

Renwick shook his head in mock offense. "So you've managed to obtain a copy of one of the rarest, most sought after books of ritualistic magick in the world, and you *haven't* brought it to show me. Now I'm *really* hurt."

Newbury laughed, but there was truth in what Renwick said. "Give me a week, Aldous, and you can come to Chelsea to visit. There are things I have to do first."

Renwick nodded. "You've been using it, haven't you? That's why you look like such a damn mess. I've told you, Newbury, that's a dangerous book. The things you're dabbling with… you'll end up getting yourself killed."

"I have my reasons, Aldous. I'm trying to help someone," said Newbury, softly, seriously.

"And I'm trying to help *you*!" said Renwick, evidently trying to contain his outrage. "Where did you get it from, anyway?" he asked. "There are only two known copies in existence."

Newbury remained silent.

"Oh, no. You didn't. You stole it from the Cabal, didn't you?" said Renwick, with a heartfelt sigh.

"The only other copy is in Constantinople, under guard by a hundred clockwork warriors. This one was a mile across town, in the vaults of a band of devil-worshipping imbeciles. Of course I took their copy," said Newbury, exasperated. "They didn't even understand the significance of what they had."

"It hardly matters," said Renwick, "whether they understand or not. You might think them imbeciles, Newbury, but that makes them all the more dangerous. They won't rest until they get it back. Their entire belief system is centred around the ritualistic practices in that book." His good eye twitched erratically. "Have they sent you any threatening parcels yet? That's their usual method."

Newbury nodded. "Yes. A most unpleasant assortment of oddities it contained, too."

"Newbury..." said Renwick, his voice strained. "You need to take this very seriously indeed. Get away for a while. They're a dangerous enemy. You mustn't underestimate them. Throw them off the trail. Head to the Continent for a few weeks."

"What, and leave the book with you in the meanwhile?" said Newbury, laughing.

"*I* don't want it!" said Renwick. "I want to see it... but I don't want it here. I don't want them sending one of their ghastly creations after me. I don't have your nerve, Newbury, or your resources. I don't want the Cabal as an enemy."

Newbury shrugged. "They've already tried to get it back once, but even in that they failed miserably. They couldn't even hold me prisoner for more than a day or two. They're nothing but credible fools, Aldous."

"*Newbury...*" stressed Renwick.

Newbury nodded. "Very well. I'll heed your advice. Once I've dealt with this miserable affair of the missing hearts, I'll give the Cabal my full and proper attention."

"Make sure that you do," said Renwick. "And I suppose if that's what's holding you up, I'd better get on and tell you what I've found out about your missing organs." He reached for the stack of books on the stool and withdrew a volume bound in black leather from approximately halfway down the pile. "Although, I warn you, you're not going to like it."

"I didn't imagine for a second I would," said Newbury, sitting forward in the armchair and disturbing further clouds of billowing dust. He glanced down at the light layer of dust that covered his black jacket and trousers, and decided it wasn't worth worrying about until he was home.

"In your note you described three corpses. Each of the victims were stabbed, their chests cracked open, and their hearts removed," said Renwick. "The missing organs were not found at the scene, and have not been recovered as yet?"

"Yes," said Newbury. "That's correct. Except that there are now five victims."

Renwick nodded. "You asked if there was any occult or ritual significance to the removal of the hearts. I presume this was because you're hoping any such significance will help you to divine a motive."

"Precisely," said Newbury, beginning to wonder where this was leading. "I could think of no significance other than the sacrificial practices found in the Aztec civilisations, but the murders did not bear any other hallmarks that suggested this might be the case. We're at a loss. I need ideas that might lead us to the killer. Anything at all is useful."

Renwick shook his head. "There's no need for ideas. I've already identified your killer."

"You've *what*?" said Newbury, taken aback.

Renwick grinned, evidently pleased with himself. His left eye let out a grating whirr. Newbury could see the winking red light at the heart of the mechanism, deep inside Renwick's skull.

"Allow me to tell you a story," said Renwick, dragging out another stool and lowering himself onto it, "about 'the Scourge of Paris.'"

Newbury sat back, making a steeple with his hands. "The Scourge of Paris?"

Renwick nodded. "In the early 1820s there was a spate of vicious murders in the streets of Montmartre. The victims came from all walks of life: nobles, peasants, soldiers, maids. Their bodies were found in a variety of despicable conditions, some of them with their throats cut, others disembowelled, others still with their limbs lopped off or garrotted. The locations varied, too. Some were killed in their homes; others down darkened alleyways, left amongst the detritus of the slums. Only one thing connected them: the fact that they'd all been brutally killed within the space of a couple of weeks. The authorities claimed it was the work of a single, insane killer, although no witnesses came forward. At least, not officially."

"Like the Ripper," said Newbury.

Renwick nodded. "Similar," he said. "The newspapers of the time called this killer 'the Executioner.'"

"The Executioner?" said Newbury, his voice cracking. He felt a sudden palpitation in his chest. *The Executioner.* The resonance of the word was like a physical blow.

Renwick frowned. "Does that mean something to you?" he asked.

"Possibly," said Newbury, waving his hand and urging Renwick to continue. His mind continued to race, but he tried to focus on the rest of Renwick's tale.

"Soon after, the final victim was discovered. He was an inventor named Monsieur Gilles Dubois. He had been dead for nearly two weeks, found stabbed to death in his drawing room. His adoptive daughter—an orphan he had taken in when his wife had died of a wasting disease ten years earlier—was missing. The girl had recently been diagnosed with a weak heart. They eventually gathered that Dubois had been carrying out unusual experiments on her."

"What kind of experiments?" asked Newbury.

"They found a workshop full of drawings and mechanical components. It seemed he'd been constructing a primitive clockwork heart to replace her failing organ. What's more, they found evidence of occult practices, of rituals and spells conducted in the cellars of the house," continued Renwick. "He'd been desperately trying to keep her alive, and it seems he was prepared to try anything."

"And she killed him for it," said Newbury. "She killed all of those people and disappeared."

"Yes," said Renwick. "It's thought that's where she started."

"Started?" said Newbury, surprised. "It sounds like quite the career already."

Renwick smiled knowingly. "She was next seen in Prussia, almost five years later," said Renwick. "It's not known what happened to her in the intervening time, but by the time she surfaced in Berlin, she'd adopted the moniker given to her by the French newspapers. She was selling her services as a murderess for hire under the name The Executioner. And she had a trademark now, too. She always stabbed her victims with a curved blade, then opened up their chests and claimed their hearts."

Newbury sat forward again in his chair. "You can't seriously be telling me it's the same woman. Is that what you're suggesting?"

Renwick laughed, but otherwise ignored the question. "Throughout the course of the nineteenth century she is seen again and again, popping up all over the Continent. St. Petersburg, Constantinople, Leipzig, Venice, London, Madrid, Bruges. Always she is known as the Executioner, and always, without fail, she removes her victims' hearts. It's thought that her death toll is in the thousands."

"But how can that be?" said Newbury, sceptically. "Surely she'd be dead by now."

"There are very few descriptions of her, as most who meet her do not live to tell the tale. But those few that I *have* found," he indicated the pile of books on the stool, "all describe her in the same way. Slim, around twenty years of age, her pallid flesh completely covered in elaborate tattoos, said to describe ancient rites and pacts with the very devil himself. It's claimed she has precious metals inlaid into her cheeks, highlighting particular runes or symbols. She wears a metal brace across her left shoulder which contains the clockwork mechanism that long ago replaced her heart. It bears a porthole in its outer casing, through which her own, decaying organ is still visible, now just a blackened, shrivelled lump. She is ruthless and unfeeling, and will stop at nothing to accomplish her goal—to kill the person she has been charged with executing—and claim their heart for her own unspecified purposes."

Renwick leaned over and passed Newbury the black book he'd been holding throughout his tale. His thumb marked a specific page. Newbury took it and scanned the contents. The text was in Flemish, but the etching that filled the entire right edge of the page was of a woman, just as Renwick had described. She was dressed in a form-fitting black suit, and what flesh was visible—her hands, forearms, and face—was covered in intricate tattoos. She was wearing what looked like a sword guard on her left shoulder, and she carried twin scimitars, one in each fist.

Newbury took a deep breath. "You still haven't answered my question," he said. "How can it be the same woman?"

Renwick shrugged. "Whatever Dubois did to her, it worked. Whether it's the machine he built to replace her heart, or whether he really did make a pact with the devil… I don't know. Whatever the case, there's no denying the truth. She exists. Her presence is felt on the sidelines of history throughout all the great nations. Everywhere you look, she's there in the background, and she's always the same, always killing to order and stealing people's hearts."

"Why has no one stopped her?" asked Newbury. "In all that time?"

"She chooses her clients well. Lords, ladies, governments… the sort of people who know how to suppress information," replied Renwick.

"But if it is her…" said Newbury, gauging the immensity of what he'd just said.

"Then you have two problems," finished Renwick. "The Executioner herself, and whoever is pulling her strings. She doesn't kill for pleasure, and she is not aligned to any particular regime. She is a mercenary. If she's here in London, she's here because someone has contracted her services."

Newbury glanced again at the image on the page before him. "It sounds like pure fantasy," he said. "A fable. A myth. It's utterly preposterous. And yet..." He trailed off again, deep in thought.

"I know," said Renwick. "I know. It's hard to stomach. But I've spent days looking into this, Newbury, and it's all here in these books. Once you piece it together, her life story is right there, as old as the last century. If you have any doubt, think of the Queen. Life can be sustained beyond its natural span. Inevitably, however, something is lost in the process."

Newbury nodded absently. *The Executioner*. The name he had heard in his dreams. The name he had scrawled upon ream after ream of paper in a clairvoyant frenzy; had screamed in terror and rage as he'd scratched it into the floorboards with his bloodied fingernails, back in his study in Chelsea. The name Amelia had warned him of, once he'd disclosed his secret to her.

The woman who would kill Veronica.

Renwick was right. Despite everything, it made sense. What he'd seen in his hallucinations had been real. The corpses told their own tale.

"It's remarkable, isn't it?" said Renwick, flexing his shoulders and reaching for the flask on the still once again. He took another swig, shuddered, and put it back.

Newbury stood, placing the book back on the pile. "I'm sorry, Aldous. I have to go."

Renwick frowned, suddenly concerned. "What is it?"

"It's Veronica. She's in great danger," he said.

"So you agree? These deaths, they're the work of the

Executioner?" said Renwick—surprised, perhaps, at how readily Newbury had accepted his report.

"Yes," said Newbury. "Yes, I agree. It's her. And I have reason to believe that Veronica is likely to become one of her targets. I need to find out who's directing this woman. I need to get to them before she gets to Veronica."

Renwick stood, clasping Newbury's shoulder. "Go, then, go. And be careful. With the Executioner on one side and the Cabal on the other, you need to watch your own back, too."

Newbury smiled, but it was mirthless. "Thank you, Aldous. For everything."

"Thank me by keeping yourself alive," said Renwick as he held the door open for Newbury to exit.

"I'll do my best," said Newbury over his shoulder as he left.

# CHAPTER 23

*This man was the same as all the other desperate souls who had sought out her most particular of services over the years. He, like them, had deceived himself that what he was doing—hiring a murderess to despatch those who might oppose him—was ultimately altruistic. He believed he sponsored these terrible deeds because they contributed to the greater good, and that by using her as an instrument to carry out such distasteful and necessary measures he remained one step removed from the responsibility. In other words, he wished to ensure that his hands remained clean and his conscience unblemished. He used phrases such as "a necessary evil" and "if I had any other choice"… but, truthfully, he was fooling only himself.*

*She had seen men—and women—struggle with such rationales a hundred times before, and she knew this behaviour for what it was. Their fragile minds were unable to cope with the truth: that they shared equally in the responsibility; that they, in effect, were guiding her hand as she hacked apart her victims' chests and relieved them of their hearts. Men like this (for it was, predominantly, men) entered into the arrangements willingly, enthusiastically even. Afterwards, when she returned to describe the target's death and show them the leather satchel containing the stolen, bloody organ, they wished to distance themselves from the results almost without fail.*

*She found this amusing, if, perhaps, a little tiresome. Only the*

*Russian had remained impervious to such things, all those years ago in St. Petersburg. But he had paid for his inquisitiveness with his life.*

*Of course, she did not really care to understand the motivations of her clients, nor the means by which they made peace with themselves after the event. Hers was not to question, but to act. She understood, however, that in accepting a commission from a man such as this, she also accepted a role in a political game.*

*This time, though, something was different. The demeanour of the man had changed. Whereas before he had adopted a business-like approach to their encounters, had refused to look her directly in the eye, now he sat staring at her across the table as if imploring her to understand.*

*He looked tired, with dark rings beneath his eyes, and she wondered if he, too, was plagued by demons. This thought piqued her insatiable curiosity. Was that what it was to feel? It had been so many years, she could no longer remember.*

*He took another sip of his whisky and cleared his throat, but did not speak. The room was silent, other than the steady ticking of a grandfather clock. It stood in the far corner monotonously checking off the minutes: a steady, mechanical heartbeat, measuring each second.*

*She found the sound of a clock deeply reassuring. To her it was as if the constant tick-tocking was an echo of the heartbeat at the centre of the universe. It reminded her that she was still alive, despite her inability to appreciate the joy that such a thing should inspire. Indeed, she surrounded herself with clocks wherever she went. Her own heartbeat had died long ago, but in the tiny mechanisms of stolen clocks—often removed from the homes of her victims—she found peace.*

*The man was ready to speak. She could sense his need to divest himself of his burden. She would listen with ambivalence, and then ask for her instructions. She had no interest in his reasons, or how he felt about them. She wished only to know the name of the person he wanted her to kill.*

*The man placed both of his palms upon the table, exhaling. When he spoke, it was with great gravitas and solemnity. "I have* another task for you," he said. "There has been an alteration in our circumstances."

She nodded, but did not reply.

The man reached for a sheaf of papers that he had laid out on the desk earlier in preparation for their meeting. He withdrew a single sheet from amongst the others, cast his eye over it, and then, with a sigh, slid it across to her. She noticed his hand was trembling.

She glanced down at the name and address written on the page:

### SIR MAURICE NEWBURY, 10 CLEVELAND AVENUE, CHELSEA

She took the piece of paper, folded it twice, and slipped it carefully into a concealed pocket.

"It is with great reluctance that I ask you to do this," he said. "I had, until recently, hoped to spare this particular agent from the fate which awaits his colleagues. However, his tenacity is such that he puts us at risk of exposure." He paused, looking her directly in the eye. "I ask that you end things swiftly and efficiently, and that you do not, under any circumstances, deprive the body of its heart."

This was new. He was asking her to alter her modus operandi, to break the habit of almost a century. She had not killed without opening a victim's chest since she'd fled Montmartre in the 1820s, aside from an incident in Bruges almost twenty years ago, when she had been interrupted in the process of cracking a man's breastbone and was forced to flee to avoid capture.

She thought she should be outraged by the man's impertinence, but she looked inside herself and could find no spark of anger, no consternation. Only the perpetual void where her heart had once been.

Outwardly, she shrugged her agreement, and the man nodded, clearly relieved.

Inwardly, however, she decided that she would make her decision after the deed, when the man lay dead before her on the floorboards of his Chelsea home. Only then would she know if she were truly *prepared to do it, if she could leave empty-handed, knowing that she was granting the dead man a privilege she had willingly granted no one since her father: allowing him to keep his heart.*

*"So—you will do it this evening?" asked the man.*

*"Yes," she replied, pushing back her chair and standing. "I shall end his life before the night is out."*

# CHAPTER 24

Veronica was relieved to discover, upon arrival at Newbury's house, that Angelchrist had not been invited to join the evening's conference. She'd half expected to discover the three men—Newbury, Bainbridge, and Angelchrist—already ensconced in the drawing room, deep in conversation. Instead, she found the two old friends hunkered down over a brandy, and couldn't help but smile as she was instantly reminded of old times.

She stood in the doorway for a moment, leaning against the jamb. The two men looked dour and serious, yet it was the first time she had seen either of them so comfortable in each other's presence for quite a while. Gone was Bainbridge's blatant frustration over Newbury's opium use, replaced by a shared concern that had rendered all other issues between them insubstantial. The way they sat together, brooding and silent, was reminiscent of the way they had acted when she'd first taken her post as Newbury's assistant, just a year and a half earlier. So much had changed in the intervening months.

Newbury looked healthier than he had for some months, with colour in his cheeks and a gleam in his eyes, though his expression was dark and worrisome. She tried not to recall the sight of him curled up on the rug in the upstairs room, twitching and seizing as he suffered the repercussions from his treatment of her sister.

He must have sensed her standing there, for he looked up, smiling with evident relief. He placed his drink on the coffee table and stood to greet her.

Bainbridge followed suit, crossing the room to take her hand. "Good evening, Miss Hobbes," he said.

"Good evening, Sir Charles," she replied. She glanced at Newbury. "Sir Maurice."

"We must talk," said Newbury, hurriedly. He looked concerned, distracted.

"Yes, yes, Newbury. Let the woman get through the door," said Bainbridge. He raised an eyebrow at Veronica, and she smiled. "Would you care for a drink, Miss Hobbes?" he continued.

"No, thank you," she said, looking for a place to sit down. The sofa was still piled high with precarious towers of books. She decided she'd be better off perching on the footstool between the two armchairs than risk shifting anything. She'd only end up sending something priceless crashing to the floor. She settled herself on the low stool, enjoying the warmth of the fire at her back. "I take it, then, that you've had some success in obtaining the list of agents from the Prince?" she asked, searching Newbury's face for any clue as to the nature of what was troubling him.

"Indeed," he said, returning to his seat and producing an envelope from beneath his chair. He held it out to her. She took it and opened it, withdrawing the thin sheaf of papers from inside. As she'd anticipated, it was a long list of names and addresses, written in small print on around eight sheets of paper. "There are more names here than I'd anticipated," she said. She passed half of them to Bainbridge, who took them and glanced through them eagerly.

"Quite," said Newbury. "I doubt any one of us were aware

of the extent of Her Majesty's network of agents and spies."

"Some of them have been struck through in black," said Bainbridge, pointedly.

"I gather they are all deceased. Killed in the line of duty, presumably," replied Newbury. He glanced at Veronica, his expression dark. Clearly, he thought there were other, more sinister reasons behind some of those deaths. It was entirely possible that the Queen had removed them to suit her own obscure whims. "The recent murder victims are all present on the list, but not struck through."

"We're all named," said Veronica, scanning the list. She pointed to Newbury's name, holding the page up for him to see.

He nodded. "Remember, it's a list of agents, not a list of targets."

"Which might yet amount to the same thing," said Bainbridge, bitterly.

"Well, yes. I suppose you have a point," Newbury conceded. "All the same, we must look for patterns. Were the dead agents all part of a single investigation, for example? There are annotations in the margins denoting key operations. Do they have something in common that might point to a motivation? Revenge, perhaps, from a villain they thwarted? Any or all of these things might point to a reason for their deaths."

"I can hardly conceive of understanding the motivations of a killer who removes his victims' hearts as trophies," said Bainbridge, balefully.

"Ah," said Newbury, "but it is not the motivations of the killer herself that we're interested in, but the person who is pulling her strings."

"Her?" said Veronica, surprised. "You have some notion of the killer's identity, then?"

Newbury nodded. "There's more. I've been to see Aldous."

Bainbridge glanced up from the pages on his lap. "He's found something, hasn't he? Well, give it up, Newbury!"

"Aldous believes he has identified our murderer," said Newbury. "A hired killer from Paris, brought over by some enterprising person—or, perhaps, a faction or organisation—with the express purpose of eradicating the Queen's operatives in London. It has all the hallmarks of a certain individual. A woman."

"A woman!" echoed Bainbridge, shaking his head. "Did Renwick give you a name?"

"Not a name," said Newbury, his jaw tightening. "A moniker. She's known as the Executioner." He glanced pointedly at Veronica, who felt herself growing suddenly pale.

*The Executioner.* Was it true, then? Everything that Newbury and Amelia had seen, had told her? That this woman, this killer-for-hire, was to come after her? Was she the next target on the list? She had dreaded this moment since the first time Amelia had uttered that name.

Veronica swallowed, but her mouth was dry. She suppressed her urge to bombard Newbury with questions. She had made her decision, and she would stick to it. She would not flee. The future was not fixed and settled, despite this alarming revelation.

"Is that all?" asked Bainbridge, frowning now over his empty brandy glass. He had evidently downed the contents while she'd been distracted, as he assimilated the new information. "What about the missing hearts? Is there any relevance?"

"That's her hallmark," said Newbury. "That's what led Aldous to the conclusion it was her. It's said that she never leaves a corpse without first removing its heart. And, as we suspected, they mean something to her. They are symbols of a life she cannot have."

He glanced from Bainbridge to Veronica. "This is the difficult bit to stomach. According to Aldous, the Executioner is nearly a century old. She's almost mythical. She appears in the footnotes of history, all across the Continent. Aldous showed me the stories, drawn from esoteric books and papers, woodcuts and etchings. She looms large in the shadows of all the important events that have shaped the world for the last eighty years. She's always there, in the background, operating on behalf of the highest bidder."

Bainbridge sighed, placing his empty glass upon the table. "This is ridiculous, Newbury. Utterly ridiculous."

Newbury held up his hand, staying Bainbridge's objections. "Hear me out, Charles. I have every reason to believe that Aldous is correct in his assertion." He took a swig of his own brandy. "The story goes that this woman, who appears as if she's in her early twenties, wears a substantial metal construction on her left shoulder, and is covered from head to toe in elaborate tattoos"—Veronica raised an eyebrow at the bizarre description—"is actually as much a machine as a human being. Just like the Queen herself, she is part mechanical. The Executioner's heart has been replaced by a clockwork mechanism that feeds her blood through her veins. Occult enchantments and runic rituals have prevented her flesh from withering, leaving her locked in a sort of permanent stasis. But she has lost something in the process. By becoming something more than human, she has somehow given up her humanity. So now she walks throughout history, massacring people for money and removing their hearts as a reminder of the one thing she can no longer have: a real life of her own."

Bainbridge was frowning. "Say this is true, that this woman actually exists and is responsible for the deaths. Who is pulling her strings? Who's this enterprising person you spoke of?"

Newbury shook his head. "I don't know. That's what we need to find out. It's one thing to stop the Executioner herself—and at the moment, I'm no clearer on how we might achieve that; it's another entirely to identify her employer."

"Well, let's consider the facts," said Veronica. "We have a string of deaths, apparently related only by the fact that the victims are all agents of the Queen. If we assume that's why they're being murdered—reasonable enough under the circumstances—then we're looking for someone who has access to that sort of information." She held up the sheaf of papers in her hand. "After that, it's a case of identifying any further links between the victims, just as you suggested. If they were all part of the same operation, for example, that in itself might suggest a potential perpetrator. Otherwise, we may be looking at a person or organisation that has something to be gained by undermining the Queen's position. In that case, the targets may in fact be chosen at random, and we're back to the beginning again. Who else besides the Queen and the Prince of Wales might have access to this list of names? A servant? No one would suspect someone such as Sandford, for example. He might be swayed by untoward pressure from a third party."

"I cannot believe that of Sandford," said Newbury, frowning. "But you may have a point, nonetheless."

"Astute as always, Miss Hobbes," said Bainbridge, passing her the rest of the papers. She shuffled them together and returned them to the envelope. "I think it best, under the circumstances, for me to take possession of the list. As you've both established, we can go no further until we've ruled out whether there are any significant patterns to the choice of victims. I will spend some time this evening analysing the list and applying what I know of Her Majesty's prior operations. Clearly, I am not aware of everything," he said, with a shrug, "but I may be able to glean some insight from my years of service."

Newbury nodded. "Good idea." He glanced at Veronica. She passed the cream-coloured envelope across to Bainbridge, who accepted it with a weary smile. "There's one other matter we need to address," said Newbury, shifting uncomfortably in his seat. "I have reason to believe that Miss Hobbes may be in danger."

"From the killer? This Executioner character?" asked Bainbridge. "Whatever gives you that idea, Newbury? If you know something more, you should spit it out. Now's the time."

"It's just… a feeling I have." He looked at Veronica as he spoke. "A concern."

"And what do you propose we do, Sir Maurice?" she asked.

"I know you will not be persuaded to leave London, but I suggest that you temporarily move into the spare room here, at Cleveland Avenue. That way, I can protect you if my fears prove to be justified," he replied.

Bainbridge frowned. "It's hardly proper, Newbury! You don't wish to sully the woman's good reputation, surely?"

"Not at all, Charles. But I do wish to protect her from a murderous assassin who may be hell-bent on eradicating us all. Is it really worth the risk, just to protect a reputation?" said Newbury, firmly.

Veronica felt herself going red in the face. "I am here, you know, gentlemen! I rather think this decision should be made by me!"

Newbury sighed. "Quite so, Veronica. Of course. I apologise if I seem forward. It's simply that I'm concerned for your well-being."

"I understand your concern, Sir Maurice, and I rather think of it as an opportunity for us to look out for each other. I am, as you are only too aware, no shrinking violet, but I see the sense in your suggestion of strength in numbers." She glanced over at Bainbridge, whose expression was one of scandalised amazement. "I shall take you up on your kind offer, on the understanding that I shall return to Kensington just as soon as the matter has been resolved." She felt no small measure of relief at the chance to share her burden with Newbury. And, besides, it would give her an opportunity to judge precisely how frequent his recent spate of precognitive seizures had become.

"Of course," said Newbury, smiling. "I suggest you go immediately back to Kensington and collect an overnight bag. We can send Scarbright for the rest of your belongings in the morning."

"Very well," said Veronica.

"In that case, I urge you both to take precautions," said Bainbridge. "This matter is far from over, and as we find ourselves drawn deeper into the affair, we risk making ourselves more pressing targets. Perhaps you're right, Newbury, after all."

"I usually am," replied Newbury, with a wry grin.

Bainbridge pushed himself up from his chair and went to reclaim his coat and cane. Veronica stood, too, smoothing her skirts. She turned to Newbury. "We can talk later?" she asked, in hushed tones.

"Indeed, we must," he said. "I'll be here when you return. I need some time to think. Perhaps Scarbright should come with you?"

She shook her head. "No. It's only a short journey, and I don't wish to alarm Mrs. Grant."

"Very well," said Newbury. He seemed distracted. She decided to leave him to his thoughts, and joined Bainbridge in the doorway as he returned bearing her coat.

"Forgive me, Sir Charles, but have you seen any more of Professor Angelchrist since we left the church?" she asked, trying to make it seem as if she weren't interrogating him. She slipped her arms into her coat.

Bainbridge frowned. "Why, is everything quite well?"

"Oh, yes," said Veronica, smiling. "It's just that there was something I'd hoped to discuss with him."

Bainbridge smiled. "I'm glad to hear you're finally warming to the fellow, Miss Hobbes. He's a good man. One of us." He tugged at the corner of his moustache as if in thought. "Alas, I haven't seen him since we met at the church. I've taken your advice, Miss Hobbes, and I've been observing a distance. Wouldn't do to get Her Majesty all worked up. The professor and I have an understanding."

"You haven't seen him since the church?" echoed Veronica, stifling her incredulity. She considered calling him out on his blatant lie right then and there, but decided against it. She needed to establish what he was up to, why he should wish to lie to her about his discreet visit to Angelchrist's apartment. If she confronted him now, in front of Newbury, she risked being shot down. Not only that, but she'd be admitting outright that she'd been spying on the professor. "Well, I think you're wise to take precautions, Sir Charles," she said, diplomatically.

She glanced at Newbury, who was still sitting in his armchair, staring vacantly into the crackling fire.

"I think it's best we give him some time to think," said Bainbridge, under his breath.

Veronica nodded. Newbury withdrew a tarnished silver cigarette tin from his jacket pocket and popped it open. He extracted one of the thin white sticks, balanced the end of it loosely between his moist lips, and slipped the tin back into his pocket, close to his heart.

Bainbridge sighed. "Come along. I'll help you find a hansom." They pulled the door to the drawing room shut as they left.

Outside, fortune favoured them with two horse-drawn cabs almost as soon as they stepped through the door. Bainbridge helped her up into the first, then bid her good night, assuring her that he would see her the following day with any further information or findings.

"Where to, miss?" came the gruff voice of the driver, leaning down so he could hear her through the open window.

"Kensington High Street," she said, leaning back in her seat and watching as Bainbridge's hansom pulled away from the kerbside, trundling off into the evening. She frowned, then made a snap decision. She leaned out of the window and caught the driver's attention. "On second thought," she said, "follow that cab."

As the hansom trundled down the familiar streets, spraying dirty gutter water in its wake, it dawned on Veronica that Bainbridge was, in fact, heading directly for his own home.

She couldn't see the other cab from where she was sitting in the back of her own conveyance, but she'd promised the driver a half crown if he could follow behind at a respectful distance, no questions asked.

Now, however, she was feeling somewhat conflicted about the whole endeavour. What would Newbury think if he knew that, instead of returning directly to Kensington as they'd agreed, she'd set off in pursuit of Bainbridge, with the express intention of spying on the man? He'd certainly have disapproved, claiming it was a gross betrayal of trust. She supposed, in many ways, it was.

She considered for a moment telling the driver to stop and turn around, but the uncertainty continued to gnaw at her. She couldn't bear not knowing the truth, and she'd be unable to face Bainbridge the following day with that incertitude unresolved. More than that, if he *were* involved in something underhanded, it would be best to get to the bottom of it. Steeling herself, she decided she had to see it through.

Nevertheless, her nagging doubts continued unabated as they raced down the rain-slicked street. It was the deep sense of disappointment, she realised, that a man she had until recently viewed as incorruptible might, in fact, be quite the opposite. That unease was coupled with the fear that if she *did* uncover something untoward, she'd feel compelled to tell Newbury about it, or possibly confront Bainbridge about it herself. The idea did not fill her with glee. She'd considered–

she *still* considered—Bainbridge a good friend, a man she could rely on and who would go out of his way to protect the people he cared for, but all of that had been thrust into doubt in recent weeks. Now she felt as if she didn't know him properly at all.

She sighed, trying to suppress a feeling of nausea. There was a part of her that would rather have buried her head in the sand and ignored her suspicions. It would certainly have been easier.

Still, however she felt about it, Bainbridge had clearly lied to her back at Newbury's house. That fact in itself gave her cause for concern. He was continuing to work with Professor Angelchrist despite claiming he was not, which implied that he was actively and knowingly engaging in something suspicious. Why else would he choose not to divulge the truth to her and Newbury?

With a sigh, Veronica leaned back in her seat and watched through the window as the amber-lit streets flitted by in a hazy blur.

Presently, she heard the driver barking commands to the horses and felt the hansom slowly draw to a halt. She leaned forward, sliding the window open and peering out.

They were, as she'd anticipated, close to Bainbridge's house. The rain had abated, although water dripped from the roof of the cab, spotting Veronica's cheek and trickling down her collar like icy fingers as she strained to see through the semi-darkness.

They'd come to a stop a little way up the street from Bainbridge's cab. She watched as he flung open the door and hurried down the steps of the cab, fished around in his pocket, withdrew some coins, and paid the driver in a hurry. Then, turning his back on the street, he walked abruptly to his front door and opened it. He stepped inside and the door swung shut behind him.

Why was he in such a rush? Clearly, it wasn't to get out of the rain. Was he late for an appointment? It was close to ten o'clock, and the night was closing in. Who would he be seeing at this hour?

Veronica opened the door of her cab and stepped out into the cold night. She shivered as the damp breeze brushed her cheek. Once again, she fought an urge to simply get back into the cab and tell the driver to take her home.

"Oi, miss?" said the driver. She turned to see him leaning over from his dickey box, rubbing his thumb and index finger together suggestively. "'alf a crown, you said."

She nodded. "I'll throw in another shilling if you wait there for me," she said, passing him up the promised coin.

He nodded enthusiastically. "Spying on the old fella, are we?" he said, conspiratorially.

"I said, no questions," replied Veronica, firmly, turning her back on him and walking slowly up the street towards Bainbridge's house.

The light was on in the living room, and the curtains had not yet been drawn. She hesitated on the pavement, straining to catch a sight of what was going on in Bainbridge's house. She almost gasped aloud as she saw Professor Angelchrist stand and turn around. He must have been waiting for Bainbridge to arrive home. She watched as Bainbridge opened the inner door from the hallway and strode in, still wearing his hat and coat. The two men shook hands and exchanged a few words. Then Bainbridge reached inside his coat and withdrew a large cream-coloured envelope, which he handed to Angelchrist. They both laughed. Angelchrist clapped Bainbridge on the back, then they turned and left the room together, Angelchrist still holding the envelope.

Veronica barely knew what to do. She felt as if she wanted to retch. Had she really just witnessed Bainbridge handing the list of agents directly to the professor? Her own words echoed loudly in her mind: *who else beside the Queen and the Prince of Wales might have access to this information?*

Clearly, the Secret Service was now privy to the list. What else had Bainbridge given them? Enough to lead them to their first handful of victims?

Almost without thinking, she turned and staggered back to the cab. She didn't even glance at the driver as she clambered up the steps and slumped inside. Her mind was racing. She would have to tell Newbury. Of course she would. Then, together, they would work out what to do. Bainbridge, it seemed, had betrayed them both.

"Kensington High Street?" called the driver, merrily.

"Yes," she said, giving an automatic reply. She closed her eyes as the cab lurched into motion, and wished that everything could just go back to the way it had been, before the Executioner and the Grayling Institute, before the Prince of Wales, Dodsworth House, and *The Lady Armitage.* Just for a moment, she wanted a simple life, but this was now something forever out of her reach.

# CHAPTER 25

Newbury stirred.

He rubbed his neck and arched his back, realising that he must have drifted off in his armchair in the drawing room once again. His head was thick with the residue of too much brandy quaffed with Bainbridge, as well as the opium cigarettes he had imbibed upon his guests' departure. His neck and shoulders ached from where he had lolled insensible in the chair.

He opened his eyes. It was dark, but not yet the witching hour. Pale moonlight slanted in through the window, its silvery fingers probing inquisitively into the room. Everything was quiet, other than the distant rumble of traffic through the fog-shrouded streets.

Veronica had not yet returned. He cursed himself for falling asleep. She was probably even now flaunting his advice, electing to sleep in her own bed rather than under the safety of his roof. He'd have to speak with her again in the morning.

Newbury rubbed a hand across his face and leaned forward, blinking blearily. He had the sense that something had disturbed his sleep. He thought he sensed movement by the door and turned to look, but there were only shadows, gloomy and impenetrable. The moonlight and the dying embers of the evening's fire were not enough to illuminate the far corners of the room.

"Scarbright?" he said, his voice hoarse. It echoed loudly in the empty house. "Are you there?"

There was no response.

Newbury laughed quietly to himself. Perhaps it was just his mind playing tricks on him, another spectre resulting from the drugs he'd consumed. It wouldn't be the first time he'd imagined people in the room who weren't really there.

He stood, a little unsteadily, and crossed to the wall-mounted gas lamp to the left of the fireplace. He turned up the tap and the bulb blossomed with a soft, steady glow. Still, he had the sense that he was not alone. The hairs on the back of his neck prickled with unease.

He turned and caught sight of something shifting in the shadows. His heartbeat quickened, sending a sudden rush of blood to his head. He felt his dulled senses sharpen with fear. There was a dark figure standing in the doorway; the silhouette of a woman, her face obscured in the low light.

She was about five foot two, of athletic build, and dressed in a revealing black bodysuit that clung to the shape of her body, accentuating her curves. Her hair was a ragged bob, hacked short around the base of her neck, and in her hands, hanging loosely by her sides, were the curving blades of twin scimitars.

*The Executioner.* Newbury had no doubt. This was the woman Aldous had told him of. She was the instrument of death, the killer of the Queen's agents, the stealer of hearts.

She came at him, a sudden, startling whirlwind of motion, her blades scissoring through the air towards him. His reflexes kicked in and his hand shot out, snatching one of the pokers from the coal scuttle on the hearth. He swung it around in a wide arc so that it clattered against the two crossed blades, parrying her attack and sending painful reverberations along his forearm.

She stepped back, lowering her blades. He could see now that her face was set in a hard, unforgiving expression. It might have been beautiful, if it wasn't for the cold intensity, the emptiness in her dull, blue eyes.

The bleached flesh of her cheeks and forehead were tattooed with an elaborate sequence of patterns, arcane designs that even he did not recognise. Hints of silver and gold glinted in the reflected light, describing whorls and accents where it had been intricately inlaid into her skin. The effect was entrancing, drawing his eyes so compellingly that he was almost caught off guard when she pressed her attack.

The assassin grunted and came at him again, this time thrusting the blade in her right hand forward whilst the one in her left parried his poker as he raised it in defence, leaving him open and exposed. He stepped back, pivoting on one foot, narrowing her target.

He blocked the blade on the left while the one on the right missed, skewering his belly by less than an inch. He saw his opportunity and lashed out in response, but the window was narrow and the poker struck her left shoulder and rebounded with the dull clang of metal upon metal. He had struck her sword guard—or, in fact, what he had taken to be a sword guard, but was actually the housing of a form of primitive machine.

As she circled, not taking her eyes from him, he was granted a better view of the porthole in the machine's surface, and was surprised to realise that the shrivelled black mass at the centre of it was, in fact, the remnant of her heart. This, then, was the machine that was keeping her alive, working in concert with the occult ritual that preserved her flesh. He could hear the mechanism whirring faintly now, the clockwork components inside it turning as it channelled her blood, feeding it through her veins.

The machine had fulfilled this duty for over eighty years. It was remarkable, and utterly fascinating. She looked no older than a twenty-year-old woman: striking and unique.

"Beautiful," said Newbury, breathless, as he raised the poker again, battering away her advances. She cocked her head slightly to one side, as if confused by his comment, but did not slow, did not alter the pattern of her attack.

He could not go on like this for long. She was fast and would overbear him, particular in the semi-coherent state in which she had found him.

"Who sent you?" he said, between thrusts of the poker and ragged, gasping breaths. He fell back, lashed out with his makeshift weapon, and stepped away from the hearth, attempting to give himself some more room to manoeuvre.

Her face remained impassive. She struck out again, but he danced to the side—just a little too slow, so that the edge of the blade slashed his shirt and jacket and opened a thin, painful gash across the side of his belly. He felt warm blood ooze to the surface and grimaced in pain, but knew it was only a flesh wound.

He stared into the woman's face, and she looked back with cold, dead eyes. She was a strange, mesmerising creature, trapped somewhere in the interstitial space between life and death, an unrelenting, inescapable limbo. She must have witnessed so much of history, so much of life, but seeing her here, now, seeing the coldness and indifference in her eyes, he wondered if she even understood how lucky she was. He could hardly conceive that this was the woman Aldous had described to him: almost a century old, bound by an ancient rite and powered by a clockwork engine devised long before his time.

She feinted to the left, came hard at him from the right. He misread her intention and lurched backwards to avoid the tip of a piercing scimitar. His foot caught on a stack of books and he went down, tumbling onto his back. He threw his hands out to break his fall, sending the poker skidding away across the carpet.

He cursed himself for his ineptitude. He was unprotected now. The Executioner saw her opportunity and her other blade fell, stabbing down towards his chest.

Newbury rolled and the weapon struck the floor. The second blade followed. His scrabbling fingers found purchase, grabbing hold of a thick, leather-bound book. He swung it around, grasping it with both hands and wielding it as if it were a shield.

The Executioner's blade struck the hefty tome and bit deep, skewering the binding and the precious pages within. The tip erupted from the other side, only inches from Newbury's face. She fell back, the book still stuck upon the end of her sword, wrenching it from his grasp.

"Be careful with that," quipped Newbury. "It's a rare first edition." He scrambled to his feet as the woman wedged the book between the floor and the sole of her boot and yanked her sword free. "You still haven't answered my question," he continued, his flippant tone masking his fear. "I'm most interested to discover who sent you to visit."

Still the Executioner did not speak, or even show a glimmer of interest in what he had to say. She was relentless, like a machine, intent only upon her goal: to end his life—and, no doubt, to claim his heart for her own. The notion did not appeal to him.

Newbury glanced around for anything he could use as a weapon, making a mental note that—should he survive this encounter—he should make a point of secreting more weapons around his house. His eyes settled on his prize automaton, the owl. There was little else to hand. "Sorry, old chap," he said, scooping it up off its perch. It trilled mechanically, its brass wings twitching.

The Executioner twisted her lithe body, coiling like a

snake about to strike. Newbury hefted the owl in his hand like a rugby ball, and then, turning to face the woman as she launched into a charge across the room towards him, he hurled it into her face.

She tried to duck, to alter her path, but the owl struck her hard in the chest, exploding in a flurry of metallic wings. She stumbled back, dropping one of her swords and sending a chair careening across the room. The owl tumbled to the floor with a heavy thud, and was still.

It didn't stop her for long, however. She stooped to reclaim her dropped blade, and then leapt forward, planting her foot on the coffee table and launching herself through the air, sending empty glasses and papers careening across the floor.

Her momentum carried her towards him and she brought her right fist down across his face. He didn't have time to get his hands up in defence, and the pommel of her sword smashed into his nose, causing blood to erupt in a fine spray. He stumbled and coughed, tasting it on the back of his tongue.

She pressed in for the attack, kicking him hard in the stomach and sending him sprawling once more onto the floor. She moved with the grace of a cat: taut, wiry, and powerful. Newbury couldn't help but be impressed, despite the dire circumstances under which he was being granted this remarkable demonstration of prowess.

The Executioner swung her swords around in a flurry, and he swept out with his leg, trying to catch her by surprise, to unbalance her. She anticipated his movement, however, and pirouetted out of the way, slicing down with her left scimitar.

He flicked his wrist out in defence and deflected the thrust, but opened a painful gash in his forearm as a result. She shifted, raising one foot and slamming her heel down hard into his shoulder, pinning him to the ground.

She was standing over him now, looking down upon him, her swords poised. There was no gleam of triumph in her eyes, however; no wicked smile. Her face remained cold and impassive, as if she were simply going through the well-trod motions of another kill, untouched by the enormity of what she was doing.

The realisation of this terrified Newbury. He'd faced death before, on numerous occasions. Each and every time, without fail, the person or beast he had stood against had showed some measure of emotion—anger, hunger, some level of investment in the kill. There was always a *reason*. The Executioner, however, demonstrated none of this. She might as well have been an automaton, inhuman and unfeeling.

She brought her fists together, her twin blades side by side, and raised her hands above her head. The tips of her blades were pointed at his chest. Panicked, he tried walking back on his hands, dragging himself away from her. But she simply pressed down harder with her foot, crushing his shoulder, keeping him pinned to the ground. Besides, he was close to the wall, and there was nowhere left to go. He raised his arms in desperation, as if he might fend off the weapons for a moment longer—and then he heard the thud of running footsteps. He saw the Executioner hesitate. His eyes flicked to the door. And then Scarbright was there, slamming into the woman with his shoulder and sending them both crashing to the floor.

She cried out in frustration as she careened into the coffee table, causing an eruption of loose papers to billow into the air all around her. Scarbright thudded to the floor at Newbury's feet, but sprang up again instantly, snatching up the poker that Newbury had dropped a few moments earlier and circling the woman.

Newbury leapt to his feet. The Executioner was backing away, her swords raised. Clearly, she wasn't keen on the change of odds. Scarbright thrust forward with the poker and she battered it away with the end of a sword.

Newbury saw her eyes flick to the door. He started towards it, intent on slamming it shut, but she made her decision and bolted, throwing herself towards the opening before Newbury could make it there himself.

She disappeared into the darkened hallway.

"No! Stop her. Don't let her get away!" bellowed Newbury, stumbling as he lurched towards the door. He swung himself around the door frame, almost losing his footing in the hall, and charged after her, Scarbright at his heels. He hurtled for the front door, which was swinging back and forth on its hinges in the darkness.

He burst out into the freezing night, skidding to a halt on the top step, glancing both ways along the street as he tried to establish which way she had run. He heard her footsteps and turned to follow, but when he finally caught sight of her, he knew he was too late. He'd never catch her. Not now. She was too fast and he was injured and weary.

He hung his head, panting for breath. Blood was streaming freely from his burst nose, soaking into his collar and down the front of his torn shirt. His hand was sticky where the gash in his forearm was weeping in time with the rapid beating of his heart.

Newbury watched as the Executioner charged into the foggy, frozen night. All he could see was the back of her head receding into the distance. It was somehow familiar, dragging at a memory somewhere in the back of his mind.

And then it struck him where he'd seen it before. "It's the Prince!" he exclaimed, suddenly.

"The Prince?" echoed Scarbright from behind him, confused, concerned. "He's here?"

Newbury turned, hanging onto the door for support. "No. He's not here. But he sent her," he said, solemnly. "He sent her to kill me."

The look on Scarbright's face was a mix of incredulity and

horror. "No. I can't believe it. It can't be…"

Newbury shook his head and spat blood into the flowerbed. "There's no time to explain now," he said, firmly. He clapped Scarbright on the shoulder, inadvertently smearing blood on the man's dressing gown. "I owe you my life, Scarbright. If it wasn't for your timely intervention.…" He trailed off.

"Think nothing of it, Sir Maurice. Anyone would have done the same," said Scarbright, drawing himself up, perhaps a little uncomfortable with the praise, and with Newbury's assertion of who was behind the attack.

"No, they wouldn't," said Newbury, quietly. He coughed back on the blood that was still streaming down his throat. "Come on," he said, pinching the bridge of his nose. "Help me clean up this mess. I need to speak to Charles as a matter of urgency."

# CHAPTER 26

♛

"I'm not sure you quite grasp the gravity of what you're saying, Archibald," said Bainbridge, reaching for his cigar, which lay smouldering on the lip of the ashtray.

"Oh, I assure you I do, Sir Charles. That's precisely my point. If Her Majesty the Queen continues to take us down this path—" He stopped short at the sound of a resounding thump on the front door, which set it rattling momentarily in its frame.

Bainbridge glanced at the clock. It was approaching midnight. Who could be calling at this hour? Clarkson was long retired for the evening. He rose slowly to his feet. There was another thump at the door, followed by a series of rapping thuds. "Open the door, Charles!" came the muffled shout from outside.

"Newbury?" said Bainbridge, hurrying into the hall. "Newbury, is that you?"

"It's me, Charles," confirmed Newbury. "Let me in, for goodness' sake!"

Bainbridge unlocked the door and unthreaded the chain. He snatched the handle and pulled it open. "Whatever is the…" He trailed off when he saw the state of his friend. "Good Lord," he said, shaken. "Get inside, now. Archibald's in the sitting room."

Newbury, gasping, nodded in acknowledgement and staggered into the hallway. He was smeared in blood and was clearly in pain. His suit was slashed open across his left arm and his right side, exposing the bloodstained flesh beneath. Bandages were expertly wrapped around his forearm, but blood continued to ooze out through the gauze.

"What the devil happened, man?" asked Bainbridge, urgently. "Who did this to you?"

"The Executioner," said Newbury, between ragged breaths. "She came for me at Chelsea. With Scarbright's help I managed to fend her off."

"She got away?" prompted Bainbridge, as Newbury fell back against the wall, propping himself up. He'd evidently hurried across town directly from the scene of the attack.

He nodded. "Yes, she got away. But not before I worked out who's behind all of this," he said, wincing in pain. "That's why I'm here."

Bainbridge studied him for a moment, surprised. "Let's get you a brandy and then you can explain," he said, patting Newbury on the arm and urging him on into the sitting room.

For a moment he found himself considering what Isobel would think about the inevitable bloodstains on the carpet, then smiled sadly as he remembered she was no longer there to raise such concerns. It was about time he laid her ghost to rest.

Angelchrist was on his feet, pacing the room as he waited for them. "I overheard," he said, hastily. "Are you sure you're well enough, Sir Maurice? Perhaps we should get you to a hospital?"

"I'm fine," said Newbury, resolute. "I'm fine." Bainbridge thought it sounded as if Newbury were trying to convince himself as much as Angelchrist.

Newbury crossed the room and dropped heavily into a chair. He was still gasping for breath. Bainbridge went to the silver tray atop the sideboard and sloshed out a generous measure of brandy. He handed it to Newbury, who took a long, deep draw.

"You didn't run all the way here, I take it?" said Bainbridge.

Newbury shook his head. "No. Although it was a struggle to get a cab to stop for me at this hour, in this condition," he said. "So I set out, and managed to pick one up about halfway here."

"I admire your determination," said Angelchrist, sincerely.

"It's my determination that almost got me killed," replied Newbury, laughing.

"Go on," prompted Bainbridge. "Tell us. What happened?"

"I'll spare you the details," said Newbury, "other than to say our murderess must have broken into my house after I'd fallen asleep in my chair. I woke to find her in the room. I'm lucky I did—a couple more minutes and I'd have been run through in my sleep."

"Good Lord," said Bainbridge, again. "And was she just as you described, half-mechanical, with all those dreadful tattoos?"

Newbury nodded. "Although 'half-mechanical' is something of an exaggeration. She has a mechanical heart, but it's old and clumsy and she wears it on her shoulder, rather than carrying it inside her chest."

"You said you'd determined who sent her?" said Angelchrist, leaning forward in his chair, his hands folded on his lap. He was wearing small reading spectacles that were perched neatly on the end of his nose. He peered over the top of them at Newbury.

"This is going to sound outlandish," said Newbury, frowning in obvious discomfort at his wounds.

"More outlandish than a century-old killer with a clockwork heart?" said Bainbridge, with a grin.

"Perhaps," said Newbury, resisting Bainbridge's attempt to make light of the situation. "It's the Prince of Wales."

Bainbridge, who was still standing in the centre of the room, nearly dropped his own brandy glass in astonishment. "The Prince of Wales!" he barked. "Are you listening to yourself, Newbury?"

Angelchrist motioned for Bainbridge to calm himself. "Let the man speak, Sir Charles."

Bainbridge nodded, feeling slightly aggrieved to be dismissed in such a way.

"It all makes sense," said Newbury. "We agreed earlier this evening that the person behind the Executioner had to be someone with access to the list of agents. The Prince had that access. He's the one who provided me with the list. He's had it all along."

"That's hardly enough to incriminate the man," said Bainbridge.

"Except there's more. That first time I called on him at Marlborough House, he wasn't expecting me, and I saw something I shouldn't have. He was in the library when I arrived, talking in hushed tones with a woman. I only saw the back of her head, but it was distinctive enough for me to know it was the Executioner, now that I've encountered her in the flesh," said Newbury, encouraged now by Angelchrist's attention.

"But why would he send her after you, Newbury?" asked Bainbridge. "You, to whom he recently granted privileges of an unparalleled nature. I mean, he even went to the effort of calling on you himself, at Chelsea!"

"That's precisely the point, Charles! He was attempting to throw me off the trail, sending me after the Germans so that I'd be distracted and wouldn't look to where the real problem might be. He wanted me close, in order to manipulate me. When Archibald proved to us that the Germans weren't, after all, involved in the murders, I swore to the Prince that I would see the real perpetrator brought to justice. At that point I—how did you put it?—I made myself a more pressing target."

"But why? What has he possibly got to gain? You're talking about him undermining his own mother!" said Bainbridge, although he could clearly see the merit in what Newbury was saying. It did make a horrible sort of sense.

"The throne! That's what he has to gain. He made his feelings towards the Queen quite clear to me when he came to Chelsea. He feels that she has lost her way, and that the Empire needs a firmer hand to guide it—his hand. He believes there's a war brewing on the Continent and that, if we're not careful, it will spill over onto our shores. Most of all, he's grown tired of waiting for his mother to die, and now that she's strapped into that diabolical machine, there's no end in sight for the man. He sees his time slipping away, and it's driven him mad."

Bainbridge glanced at Angelchrist, who nodded slightly.

"I don't doubt it for a minute," said Angelchrist. "I believe the Prince is perfectly capable of such a political manoeuvre. He claims to care for the good of the people. While that may be true in part, in reality, he cares more for himself. He's worried he'll miss his opportunity to rule. Something must have tipped him over the edge, persuaded him to act."

"I think it's time we told you a little more of what's been going on, Newbury," said Bainbridge, with a dour expression. He dropped into a seat. "The Secret Service has had the Royal family under observation for some months."

Newbury frowned. "To protect them?" he said.

"No," said Angelchrist, levelly. "To judge their intentions. It is our belief that the Queen has lost her way."

"You're not trying to tell me that you *are* mixed up in this business with the Executioner, are you?" said Newbury, his face creasing in concern.

"Indeed not!" said Bainbridge. "Nothing like that. Nevertheless, the parliament has begun to question the real motivations of the monarch, and whether she truly has the best interests of the nation at heart." He looked Newbury straight in the eye. "To be honest, Newbury, I've begun to doubt her intentions, too. Archibald, of course, feels the same.

That's why he's here tonight. He came to collect a dossier I've assembled, containing observations of the Queen and her immediate family."

"All of this subterfuge!" said Newbury, hotly. "Why didn't you say something?"

"Because I didn't want to put you at risk, Newbury!" said Bainbridge.

"Well, it hardly worked, did it?" replied Newbury, shaking his head. "Quite the opposite. And besides, have you never considered that I might feel the same way? I'm only too aware of the Queen's dubious, self-absorbed nature."

"And Miss Hobbes?" asked Angelchrist.

"I assure you, Veronica has more reason to doubt the monarch than most. The Queen has woefully wronged her in recent months. We are forced to maintain a charade of servitude, to avoid exacerbating the situation," said Newbury, wincing. Bainbridge noticed that he was nursing the wound on his forearm.

"What has the Queen done to so affront Miss Hobbes?" asked Bainbridge, concerned. He wondered why Newbury, in turn, had not spoken of the matter, but decided not to press him on that for the time being. He was still reeling from the shock of realising that Newbury shared his concerns regarding the monarch.

"It can wait," countered Newbury. "Right now, my concern is to put a stop to the Prince's plans. We can worry about the Queen later. We need to prevent any more people from dying."

"You're right," said Bainbridge. He grabbed the brandy bottle off the sideboard and sloshed another measure into Newbury's glass, which Newbury drank thirstily. Bainbridge hoped it would help to numb the pain. "Where might the Prince be harbouring her, this 'Executioner'? We can hardly go storming up to Marlborough House and ask him."

Newbury looked thoughtful. "He won't be keeping her at

Marlborough House. He wouldn't want her under his roof any longer than is necessary, to avoid associations such as the one I made after my unexpected visit. He clearly doesn't realise that I saw her in the library, or, if he does, he believes I won't make the connection, at least until it's too late." He raised his hand, suddenly, as if an urgent idea had just come into his head. "Yes! That's it!"

"What is?" asked Bainbridge, perplexed by Newbury's sudden outburst.

"The Prince told me he was involving himself in the property market, purchasing an old, abandoned hotel with a view to restoring it to its former glory. I thought it odd at the time, but now I can see that there must have been an ulterior motive. I'll wager that's where we'll find her," replied Newbury, animated now.

"Where is this hotel?" asked Angelchrist.

Newbury shrugged. "I don't know. It has to be fairly central. The murder scenes appear to have been spread evenly throughout the city."

"We can find out," said Bainbridge. "We have files on the Prince, observations gathered over the course of the last few months. Surely there must be something in there? If he's purchased a property, it must be a case of public record."

Angelchrist nodded enthusiastically. "The files are held in my safe, back at Grosvenor Square."

Bainbridge stood. "Then we should go there immediately. We must strike while the iron is hot. If we're correct and she's hiding at this abandoned hotel, we may be in a position to catch her before the night is out. Once we have the Executioner, we'll also have the Prince."

Newbury stood, too. "Veronica didn't return, Charles. She's not at Chelsea. I need to go to her, to ensure she is safe. What if the Executioner goes after her while we're busy looking for an address?"

Bainbridge nodded. "Yes, of course. Go to her. Get her back to Chelsea. We'll send for you there once we have the address."

Newbury nodded. "Excellent. We'll await word, then meet you at the hotel before the night is out.

"Shall I send for reinforcements from the Yard?" asked Bainbridge.

"No," replied Newbury. "If there're too many of us, we'll frighten her off. But for all of that, remember: there's strength in numbers. Do not attempt to tackle this woman without us. I've seen what she's capable of. If it wasn't for Scarbright, I'd be dead now, and she'd have walked away with my heart."

Bainbridge nodded. "I knew I'd let a good one go in Scarbright, Newbury. Not only is he the best chef I've ever known, it seems he's pretty handy in a fistfight, too." He grinned, trying to make light of the situation. In truth, he was deeply concerned for Newbury. He didn't look at all well, and his clothes were stained with blood. "Get some rest, if you can. You're going to need your strength."

Newbury nodded. "Until later, then," he said, clasping Bainbridge on the shoulder and shaking Angelchrist's hand. "Good hunting, gentlemen."

"Until later," said Bainbridge. He watched Newbury go, a little unsteady on his feet, then turned to Angelchrist. "Come on," he said. "You heard the man. There's a murderer to catch."

Angelchrist grinned. "Two, in fact," he said, rising to his feet. "Don't forget the Prince of Wales."

Bainbridge sighed. "Not likely," he said, with feeling. He downed the last dregs of his brandy. "That's one conversation with the Queen I'm truly dreading."

Angelchrist laughed. "Makes me glad I only have to answer to the Home Secretary," he said.

"Come on, you damn republican," said Bainbridge, gruffly. "There's work to be done." He opened the door to the hall and ushered Angelchrist out.

# CHAPTER 27

### ♛

Veronica paced before the window of her drawing room, looking out across a damp, dimly lit stretch of Kensington High Street. It was mostly deserted now, with only the occasional hansom steaming past, funnels belching soot-coloured smoke into the grey night. Most of the horse-drawn cabs had retired for the evening, with only the hardy steam-powered variety still buzzing around the city, their drivers warmed by the proximity of their miniature furnaces and tanks of boiling water.

Try as she might, she still couldn't believe what she had seen through the window of Bainbridge's sitting room. She kept attempting to rationalise it, to explain away what she had witnessed.

However hard she tried, though, she could not find an alternative explanation. Bainbridge had lied to her, brazenly, about seeing Angelchrist, and almost immediately afterwards had returned home to find the other man waiting for him. It had not been an unexpected call, either: the manner in which Bainbridge hurried to greet him and hand over the envelope suggested it was a prearranged appointment. Angelchrist had been waiting for him to return with the list. No wonder Bainbridge had been so keen to take possession of it back at Chelsea.

Could it be that the Queen was correct about the Secret

Service? It certainly appeared as if they were involved in something covert having to do with the Crown agents. And Bainbridge had clearly thrown his lot in with them. Could they really be the ones behind the Executioner? She didn't want to believe it, but the facts were beginning to mount up.

Veronica decided it was time to tell Newbury the truth: that she had been spying on Angelchrist and Bainbridge, and that her worst fears had been confirmed. She could put it off no longer.

She glanced at the overnight bag she had placed by the door in readiness. Mrs. Grant had been in bed for hours, and she was used to Veronica coming and going at unsociable hours. She'd barely stir, if she even heard anything at all.

It was probably for the best. Veronica didn't really want to have to explain that she was planning to spend the night– or, indeed, the next few nights–at Newbury's house. Despite everything she had said to Newbury, she did fear for her reputation, if only in the eyes of her housekeeper, who would not approve. Newbury was, after all, ostensibly her employer, and the affection between them was hardly a secret.

Nevertheless, if she left now and hailed one of those dreadful steam-powered cabs, she could be at Newbury's house within half an hour, then tomorrow she would make her excuses to Mrs. Grant and explain that she was staying with a friend for a few days.

In the meanwhile, she and Newbury could decide together how they might tackle Bainbridge and the professor. Assuming, of course, that Newbury could be persuaded to take her at her word. She still feared he would react badly to the news, and refuse to see ill of his friend.

Veronica grabbed her still-damp coat from where she'd left it flung over the back of a chair, and collected her bag. Quietly, she slipped out of the house, careful to lock the door behind her.

* * *

The house was shrouded in darkness, and no lamps appeared to be burning in the upper windows. The front door was still locked, however, and there was no sign that anyone had forced entry.

Newbury's assumption, then, had been correct. Once home, Veronica must have changed her mind about spending the night at Chelsea, and instead taken to her own bed for the night. He admired her for her courage and independence, but wished, on this one occasion, that she'd adhered to the agreed plan.

Nevertheless, he'd have to wake her now. She'd want to be by his side as they stormed the abandoned hotel in a few hours' time. More pertinently, it provided him with the chance to keep a watchful eye on her. Renwick's revelations regarding the Executioner had terrified him, particularly when coupled with the horrifying things he had seen in his feverish dreams. Veronica was in danger, and it was up to him to protect her.

He stood for a moment in the front garden, catching his breath. The rain was a constant mizzle, soaking his clothes. They were already ruined, though, and he could change as soon as they'd returned to Chelsea. He'd need to prepare himself for another possible encounter with the Executioner, too. He'd seen what she was capable of, and fully intended to go into the situation armed with his pistol and sword.

He glanced behind him to see the driver of the steam-powered hansom he had flagged down waiting patiently for him at the roadside, huddled against the rain, a cigarette dripping from his lips.

Deciding there was no way to approach the matter with any degree of subtlety, he walked up to Veronica's front door and rapped loudly with the brass knocker.

After a moment, a lamp flared in one of the upstairs rooms.

He waited patiently on the doorstep, trying to ignore the rain. Shuffling footsteps sounded in the hall.

"Who is it?" came a suspicious voice from the other side of the door. It was Mrs. Grant, Veronica's housekeeper.

"It's Sir Maurice Newbury, Mrs. Grant. I need to speak with Miss Hobbes as a matter of urgency," he replied, trying to keep his tone level. He didn't wish to worry her unduly.

He heard the bolt scrape in the lock and the jangle of keys, and then the door yawned open. Inside, the hallway was dark. Mrs. Grant stood there in a heavy quilted dressing gown, her greying hair scraped back beneath a net. "What sort of time is this to be calling on a young lady?" she said, briskly. She gave him a severe look.

"I'm sorry to rouse you from your bed, Mrs. Grant, but this really is a matter of urgency," he said, pressing her. "I do need to speak with Miss Hobbes. It cannot wait."

"Very well," she conceded, with a sigh. "I suppose you'd better step in out of the rain." She held the door open for him and he ducked into the hall, thanking her.

She looked him up and down. "Oh…" she exclaimed, as she fully appreciated the condition of his torn and blood-spattered clothes for the first time. "You appear to have been in the wars, Sir Maurice. Are you quite well?"

Newbury nodded. "Yes, thank you, Mrs. Grant."

She shook her head, in what Newbury took to be a gesture of exasperation. "Right. Well, if you'd be kind enough to wait there for a moment, I'll see if Miss Hobbes is prepared to see you."

"Thank you," he said. She ascended the stairs to the next floor. Everything was quiet in the house other than the creak of her footfalls on the treads and the rattle of his own breath.

She reappeared a moment later, wearing a frown, and hurried back down to join him in the hallway. "I'm afraid Miss Hobbes is not here," she said, the concern evident in her voice. "Her bed is undisturbed, and she is not in the drawing room."

Newbury smiled reassuringly, but his heart was hammering in his chest. Where was she? Perhaps he'd missed her, and she had returned to Chelsea as planned after all. If so, she'd be sitting with Scarbright now, awaiting his return. The alternative was almost unfathomable. "I'm sure it's nothing to trouble yourself with, Mrs. Grant. I had, in fact, arranged to meet with Miss Hobbes at my house, but found myself otherwise engaged. I'd assumed she would return home for the evening, but I must have been mistaken. I imagine that she is awaiting me at Chelsea even now."

"Hmmm," said Mrs. Grant, a note of disapproval in her tone. "At this hour. You may be a gentleman, Sir Maurice, and I do not doubt your intentions, but you must think of Miss Hobbes's reputation and well-being."

"I understand," said Newbury, patiently, "and your concern does you credit, Mrs. Grant. I assure you, I have only Miss Hobbes's best interests at heart." He smiled. "Now, I apologise profusely for waking you unnecessarily. If Miss Hobbes does happen to return before I've had chance to speak with her at Chelsea, I'd ask that you please explain to her that I called, and that I will call again first thing in the morning."

"Very well," said Mrs. Grant, with a heavy sigh. "Good night to you, Sir Maurice."

"Good night," he replied, taking his leave. He signalled to the driver as he hurried down the garden path to the waiting cab. "Cleveland Avenue, Chelsea," he said. "As quickly as you can."

Newbury willed the cab to go faster, despite the fact that it was already churning through the wet streets at an undeniable pace. He desperately hoped that he'd return to Chelsea to find Veronica waiting for him there. It was late, and by his reckoning she'd been missing for some hours. Rationally, he knew there must be an explanation for her absence, but given his encounter with the Executioner earlier that evening and his epiphany regarding the Prince of Wales, he couldn't deny that she was an obvious target. She was close to both Newbury and Bainbridge, for a start, and she was involved in the investigation into the Executioner's murders. If the Prince wanted to tidy up after himself, she would be the next logical target after Newbury himself.

He stared out of the window, but could discern little of their location from the misty smear of houses as they rushed by in the darkness. He glanced at his pocket watch. They had to be halfway there by now.

He started at the sound of a heavy thud on the roof of the cab. The vehicle jolted slightly, as if the driver was struggling to keep it under control. Newbury leaned forward to open the window and call up to the man when the cab swerved suddenly to the left. He was thrown across the seat, banging his head painfully against the wooden frame. He righted himself, smarting, but the entire vehicle was rocking violently now as it continued to pelt along the cobbled lanes. He struggled to maintain his balance.

He heard a man cry out, followed by a piercing, inhuman shriek, an animalistic wail that caused his hackles to rise. The cab shuddered again as it struck the kerb and careened away, still barrelling along at speed, but clearly out of control.

Newbury grasped the handrail by the left-hand door and steadied himself. Then, with a huge effort, fighting against the momentum of the bouncing vehicle, he pulled himself upright and slid the window open. The cold night wafted in, blasting his face with rainwater. He could see now that the cab was describing a zigzag pattern up the street, thudding against the kerb on one side, then careening into the other and bouncing back again, over and over.

He twisted, glancing up at the dickey box, and recoiled in

horror at the sight. The driver swayed back and forth with the movement of the vehicle, but only the lower half of the man's torso was visible. His head, one arm, and most of his chest were missing. What remained was still propped up in the driver's box, blood spurting from the ragged wound. The man had literally been torn in half. Whatever had done that to him was capable of immense strength.

Newbury felt something shift on the roof, and slid back into the main compartment of the cab. He had to get out there and take charge of the vehicle's controls before they careened into the side of a building or another oncoming vehicle. He considered jumping out, but at this speed he'd be dashed across the cobbles, or at the very least would sustain numerous shattered bones, leaving him injured and prey to whatever was up there on the roof.

Could it be the Executioner? He didn't think so. The manner in which the driver had been killed was far too feral—primal, even—and lacked the finesse of her previous kills. What, then?

His question was answered a second later when a fist slammed down through the wooden roof in a hail of splinters. Newbury covered his eyes with the crook of his elbow as the fragments rained down upon his face and shoulders, stinging where they punctured his flesh.

He staggered back as a clawed hand thrashed about in the cab for a moment, before withdrawing and punching through the roof again, widening the aperture. Newbury ducked from side to side to avoid the creature's curving black talons as they swept back and forth, searching for him. He dropped into the footwell, out of reach, and peered up through the hole, trying to get a sense of what it was that had set upon the cab.

His first thought was of a revenant—the pale, ragged flesh, the unnatural strength, the elongated black talons—but when he saw the thing lower its face into the hole and peer through

252

at him, everything suddenly became clear.

The creature had, indeed, once been a man, but unlike a revenant it was not the victim of an unpredictable microscopic plague, but the result of an appalling experiment in surgical augmentation. This man had been afflicted by design, not by an accident of nature. His lower jaw had been replaced with a brace of enamel tusks, and one eye had been entirely excised, a strange, mechanical lens affixed in its place. Black tubing erupted in a knot from its throat, then curled away over its shoulders and out of sight. The remaining human eye was jaundiced and watery, and was fixed on Newbury, radiating hatred.

This was the work of the Cabal. He had seen these minions before, half-transformed into monsters through their unwavering devotion to their insane masters. Aldous was right. The Cabal *did* want their book back, and enough to send one of their abominations to kill him for it. Clearly, they'd decided he'd had long enough to accept their invitation to commit ritual suicide, and had decided to take matters into their own hands.

The man-thing screeched, working its false jaw up and down in a gnashing motion. It began scrabbling at the sides of the hole, ripping free large chunks of wood and casting them away into the road. It was as if the creature were peeling away the layers of an onion, with Newbury trapped inside, awaiting the inevitable.

All the while, the cab continued to veer out of control, the dead driver's foot still pressed firmly upon the accelerator.

If he remained where he was, Newbury was going to die. He wasn't strong enough to take on the creature unarmed in such a cramped space, and if he didn't deal with the out-of-control cab in the next few moments, it would all be over regardless.

He glanced at the door. He could force it open and climb out onto the footplate. From there he'd have a chance to leap up onto the roof and scrabble across to the dickey box, provided the cab didn't hit something in the meantime and throw him off completely. It was a chance he'd have to take.

The creature was on the roof, though, between him and the dickey box. He didn't fancy his chances against it up there.

He needed to swap places with it. If he could trap it inside the cab, even if just for a moment, he'd have a chance to get to the controls. After that, he had no idea.

He watched it gouging away more of the wooden roof and shuddered. It was more animal than man. It would rip him apart within moments if he gave it the opportunity, just as it had the driver. He had to strike first, to take the initiative and catch it unawares. It was his only chance. It didn't feel like much of a plan, but it was all he had.

Newbury crept forward, keeping low.

The scrabbling stopped, and the man-thing returned to swiping for him, its glossy black talons—each about three inches long, formed from spears of iron—only inches from his head. It grunted as it leaned forward, shifting its weight, and the shattered wood around the hole creaked in protest, threatening to cave in. Newbury was breathing hard, trying to pick his time.

The cab lurched again, suddenly, and he fell back, the creature splaying its hands across the roof to help it hold on. It recovered faster than Newbury, and its next swipe caught the back of his collar, shredding the fabric and drawing large welts across the nape of Newbury's neck. He howled in pain and dropped low, rolling out of its reach. He drew to his knees just as the man-thing was straining forward with its arm extended. Then he saw his chance. He leapt up, grabbing it firmly by the wrist and yanking down, hard, throwing all of his weight behind the motion.

Newbury fell backwards towards the door, and the creature, unable to slow its momentum, came crashing forward through the hole in the roof, tumbling face down onto the floor of the cab.

Newbury didn't wait to see if it had survived the fall. Instead he twisted around, grabbed the handle of the door, and leaned against it. It opened and he fell through.

For a moment he hung dangerously from the door, his feet trailing inside the main compartment of the cab. Rain lashed his face, and the shuddering of the cab as it bounced unattended over the cobbled road threatened to shake him free.

He saw the creature shifting inside, and swung his legs out, mercifully finding purchase on the footplate. He pulled himself up so that he was once again vertical, clinging to the side of the cab, and shuffled to the edge of the footplate, giving him room enough to slam the door shut on the creature inside. He didn't imagine it would offer him much extra time, but he was unsure if the man-thing would be able to work the handle in its rabid frenzy.

He glanced along the street. They were approaching a junction. He had only moments to get to the controls before the cab careened into the side of an office building, or was struck by traffic coming from another direction.

The remains of the driver's body were still rocking back and forth with the motion of the cab, moving spasmodically like a suffocating fish in the last of its death throes.

Gritting his teeth, Newbury reached up and felt for the rim that ran around the edge of the cab's roof. He could hear the creature shifting about inside, prowling in circles as it tried to work out how to get to him.

He took the strain in his fingers and heaved himself up, crying out in pain as he bloodied his fingertips in the process. His damaged forearm protested, but he clung on for dear life as the cab swayed and shook, threatening to overbalance. He got the tip of his shoe on the window frame and finally managed to push himself the last few inches up, until his chest was over the lip. He scrabbled up and wound up spreadeagled on the roof, close to the ragged edge of the hole. His breath was coming in short, shallow gasps.

He was close, now. He had no idea how to operate the contraption, of course, but hoped he'd be able to work it out when he got there. He heaved himself up onto his knees, his palms still pressed flat to the roof. He started forward, but felt his trousers catch on something. He tugged, but there was no give. He glanced back, and realised in horror that it wasn't his trousers at all, but that the man-thing's left hand was wrapped tightly around his ankle.

Newbury growled in frustration and lashed out with his other foot, kicking at the creature's forearm. It refused to let go, pulling down sharply on his leg, dragging him inexorably back towards the lip of the hole.

Newbury thrashed around, trying to find something to grab onto, but there was nothing there. He felt himself slide back, heard the creature howl in triumph. His legs were over the hole now, and he allowed himself to be pulled further back, slipping deeper into the nightmare maw of the cab. Then, at the last moment, he stamped down blindly with his right foot, hammering again and again with his heel. He felt something crunch as he connected with the creature's face. It screeched in pain, releasing its grip on his ankle.

Swiftly, Newbury hauled himself up out of the hole again and scrambled across the roof towards the controls. He spun around and dropped feet first into the driver's box, nudging the flapping remains of the driver to one side.

The controls consisted of two pedals, a lever, and a small, round steering wheel. He grabbed the wheel first, fighting the bucking vehicle as they careened towards the office building. He leaned to the left and pulled the wheel around hard, causing the vehicle to bank sharply. The cab veered out of the path of the building but tipped wildly in the process, two wheels lifting entirely off the ground.

For a moment Newbury thought the thing was going to overbalance, but he spun the wheel back the other way and the vehicle shifted, the two right-hand wheels dropping back down to the ground heavily. The driver's body slumped towards him with the motion, and Newbury fought to steady himself as the contents of its lacerated belly spilled out across the floor. A moment later, when the direction of the cab was somewhat under control, he grabbed the corpse by the belt and, with both hands, heaved it over the side of the box. It tumbled to the cobbles with a wet, dull thud, trailing sticky blood and entrails.

Newbury wiped the rainwater from his eyes with his sleeve. He heard a scraping noise from behind him and glanced over his shoulder. The creature was pulling itself up out of the hole in the roof. It must have clambered up on the seats to gain enough height to get leverage. Perhaps it wasn't as dim-witted as he'd imagined.

His choices, however, remained limited. He could hardly maintain control of the vehicle and fight the creature at the same time. He decided his only hope was to shake it off. If he could strand it in the road while he still had control of the vehicle, he could get away.

He glanced at the road ahead, then looked back at the creature, which had just about hauled itself onto the roof. He braced himself, then yanked the steering wheel sharply to the right, and then hard to the left, causing the cab to veer wildly. It pitched and rocked as the wheels shifted beneath it, barely able to compensate for the exaggerated gestures. The man-thing slid across the roof, scrabbling for purchase, its legs dangling over the side. It didn't, however, go over.

Newbury tried again, swinging the cab across the road, but realised that the creature had managed to dig its talons into the fabric of the cab, pinning itself in place. It clung on while the vehicle weaved from side to side, biding its time. He'd have to try a different approach.

Mercifully, the road ahead remained silent and empty. The rain and the late hour had driven the civilians home to their beds. Newbury found himself longing for the tranquillity of his drawing room, the peace of a book and a cigarette. He'd had his fill of being attacked by half-mechanical assailants for one night.

The man-thing issued a keening wail as it dragged itself up from where it was hanging off the side of the cab and thumped across the shattered roof towards him. Newbury didn't look back, but could feel its presence only feet away. His every instinct told him to try to get away, but he held a firm grasp on the wheel.

He stabbed at the accelerator with his foot and the vehicle lurched forward, the engine roaring with power. They sped along the cobbled road, bouncing and juddering, gaining momentum with every passing inch. Newbury could practically feel the creature's rancid breath on the nape of his neck, but still he did not turn.

He counted to five beneath his breath. It was now or never. He lifted his foot from the accelerator and slammed it hard upon the brake, releasing the steering wheel and ducking down into the driver's box, covering his head with his arms.

The next few moments passed in slow motion. All Newbury could hear was the rush of blood in his ears, his heart thumping against his ribs. He was thrown heavily forward with the momentum, bashing his hip against the steering wheel.

The rear of the vehicle bucked like an angry horse as the front brakes fully engaged, flipping the man-thing forward and up into the air, sending it careening along the road. It hit the cobbles with a sickening thud and lay still, broken bones jutting through torn flesh and clothes.

The hansom shook as the rear end slammed back onto the road, venting hissing jets of steam. Another section of the roof collapsed into the passenger compartment.

Newbury stood, hesitantly, as the shuddering finally abated. He peered along the road.

The creature was nearly twenty feet in front of him, sprawled upon the cobbles. It was moving, its legs scrabbling ineffectually, its head lifting slightly, pathetically. Newbury could see that one of its arms was completely smashed, its torso was twisted out of shape, and half of its enamel jaw had been shattered. It was, without a doubt, dying.

Newbury felt a moment of deep sorrow for this thing that had once been a man. The Cabal had transformed him into a monster, removed all but the smallest traces of his humanity. And for what? So that they might construct their own army of patchwork soldiers? They would have to be stopped. But that didn't mean he would let this one live.

Newbury grabbed the steering wheel and stamped on the accelerator again. He could not leave the thing to die in misery and pain, whatever it had done to him. He gripped the wheel firmly and held his course as the cab barrelled along, gaining speed. He closed his eyes and held on as the cab smashed into the prone man-thing, thundering over the top of its shattered body, crushing it utterly beneath its rumbling bulk.

He did not look back as he drove on down the street. The creature was dead, and he did not wish to dwell on the results of his decision.

Veronica would—he hoped—be waiting for him back at Chelsea, and he was desperately in need of a drink.

The front door was hanging off one broken hinge when Veronica arrived at Newbury's house a short while later.

She stood at the bottom of the short flight of red stone

steps, and felt utterly overcome by a dawning sense of dread. Was she already too late? Had Newbury been betrayed by his supposed friends? She wished that she hadn't spent so long at Kensington considering her options.

She rushed up the steps two at a time and burst into the hallway, steeling herself against whatever she might find.

In this case, it was only Scarbright, who turned to regard her, a screwdriver in his hand. "Ah, Miss Hobbes. I fear you'll find the place in a rather dreadful state, but please do come in."

She offered him a quizzical look.

"A brief incident this evening involving an intruder," said Scarbright, reading her expression. He moved to the door as he spoke and began tightening screws.

Veronica watched him work. "An intruder?" she said, unsure whether to be concerned or relieved, given the valet's calm and understated manner.

"I fear I am not fully apprised of the circumstances, Miss Hobbes, and I'm sure it would be best explained by Sir Maurice himself, but in his absence I shall do my best to give as full an account as possible." Scarbright cleared his throat. "It seems a woman, armed with two scimitars, managed to break into the building while we were both asleep and set upon Sir Maurice in the drawing room. He fought her off–most valiantly, I might add–but she managed to get away before we could entrap her."

"The Executioner!" said Veronica. "Was he hurt?"

"He suffered a number of minor injuries from her blades, but I can assure you, he is quite well," said Scarbright. He stood back from the door, admiring his handiwork. He swung it shut, and nodded as the latch gave a satisfying click.

"Where is he now?" demanded Veronica, feeling increasingly frustrated and helpless. She needed to be by his side.

"He went to call on Sir Charles," said Scarbright.

*Bainbridge.* Veronica's heart hammered in her chest. Their

paths had practically crossed. And now he was there, with Bainbridge and Angelchrist.

"I gather from the late hour and the presence of your overnight case that Sir Maurice has invited you to spend the night in the spare room," said Scarbright. "I'm sure he will return soon—he's been gone for some time. Please, allow me to take your coat."

Veronica shook her head. Her eyes alighted upon an envelope on the hall table, Newbury's address written in Bainbridge's familiar hand. "It looks to me as if you already have your hands full, Scarbright. I'll make myself comfortable, thank you."

"Very well, Miss Hobbes. Then perhaps you would care for a pot of tea?" replied Scarbright.

"Yes. Thank you. That would be lovely," she said.

Scarbright smiled, and set off in the direction of the kitchen with a nod.

Veronica waited until his footsteps had receded down the hall, and then picked up the letter. She turned it over. It was sealed.

She placed it back on the table, just as she'd found it. She shouldn't pry. This was Newbury's personal correspondence. But then... what if it gave her insight into what was going on? Newbury had gone directly to see Bainbridge after the attack. Did he know something? Would the letter reveal it? Might Bainbridge even be attempting to involve Newbury in whatever he was plotting with Angelchrist?

Taking a deep breath and biting her bottom lip, she snatched the envelope up again and tore it open. Inside there was a small slip of cream-coloured paper. She quickly extracted it and glanced at the note inside:

**THE FORTESCUE HOTEL, CHANCERY LANE,
TWO O'CLOCK.**

                                                    **CB**

She frowned, and then glanced at the ancient grandfather clock that stood like an attentive sentry in Newbury's hallway. It was just after one. What was going on? Could Bainbridge be leading Newbury into a trap? Surely not... but why else would they meet at a hotel at such an unsociable hour? She reminded herself of what she had seen through Bainbridge's window. Whatever it was, there was something going on that she did not understand, and all she could think about was preventing Newbury from unwittingly putting himself in harm's way. He trusted Bainbridge completely. She wondered now if that trust was gravely misplaced.

Veronica stuffed the letter back into its envelope and returned it to the table. Her mind made up, she stooped to her bag and rifled around inside it until her fingers closed around the handle of her pistol. She withdrew it and tucked it safely into her belt, covering it with her coat, then she opened the front door and slipped out, quietly pulling the door to behind her.

Newbury drew the hansom to a jerking, erratic stop outside of his home.

He'd considered abandoning the vehicle in an alleyway a few streets away, but decided it might yet prove useful before the night was out. A bobby or passer by had probably discovered the corpses of the driver and the man-thing by now, and Newbury would need to explain the whole incident to Bainbridge later that day. He could turn the hansom over to the police at the same time.

For now, however, he had some temporary transportation at his disposal—assuming, of course, that he didn't inadvertently run it into a wall. It wasn't the simplest of contraptions to drive, and the journey across town was plagued by hazards and near misses. Newbury was forced to rely on his instincts, and wrestled with the machine until he managed to get it under some modicum of control.

He disengaged the engine, but the rear funnel continued to belch thick, black smoke into the damp night air.

Still smarting from his wounds, he swung himself down from the dickey box, dropping awkwardly to the ground. The rain had now abated to a gentle drizzle that matted his hair and beaded on the lapels of his jacket. His shoes were slicked with the driver's blood, and he was chilled to the very core of his being. He hoped he'd have time to change and warm himself beside the fire before heading out to meet Bainbridge and Angelchrist, and that Veronica would be waiting for him within.

He left the cab parked by the kerb and hurried up the garden path to the front door. Scarbright had evidently reattached it in Newbury's absence. He was still unsure precisely how the Executioner had managed to tear it from its hinges without waking him, but he was impressed all the same by her stealth. It would serve him well, in future, to pay more attention to his personal safety. For a start, Aldous was correct about the Cabal. They were clearly more dangerous than Newbury had given them credit for. He would have to deal with them as soon as the situation with the Prince was successfully resolved.

He searched his pockets for his key and realised he hadn't stopped to claim it as he'd rushed out to see Bainbridge, so he rapped loudly with the knocker instead.

Scarbright was at the door within moments, wearing a concerned expression. "Sir Maurice…" he said, as Newbury staggered up the steps and into the lobby.

"I'm fine, Scarbright," he said, leaning against the wall with his left hand, catching his breath. "Just another little altercation on the way home. Nothing to trouble yourself with." He spotted Veronica's overnight bag in the hallway, beside the narrow table, and sighed with relief.

"No, it's not that," said Scarbright. "It's Miss Hobbes."

"She's here, then?" said Newbury. "I'm sorry I didn't have chance to explain. She's going to be staying in the spare room for a few days."

Scarbright shook his head, and Newbury frowned. "She was here, Sir Maurice, but now she's... well, she's gone."

"Gone?" said Newbury, perplexed. "But her bag is just there...." He searched Scarbright's face for an answer. The man was clearly embarrassed.

"Well? Where is she?" asked Newbury, exasperated.

"That's just it, sir. I don't know. Miss Hobbes arrived about thirty minutes ago. I showed her into the hall. She was most dismayed to learn of your encounter with that dreadful woman this evening, but she said she would make herself comfortable while I fetched a cup of tea, so I left her here in the hall while she removed her coat and gloves. When I returned a few minutes later, she was gone." He looked shamefaced. "I'm terribly sorry, sir."

Newbury sighed and shook his head in defeat. "I fear Miss Hobbes and I have unwittingly found ourselves engaged in a rather fruitless game of cat and mouse this evening, Scarbright. I don't imagine there was anything you could have done."

"Thank you, sir," said Scarbright. "I shall, of course, remain alert for any sign of her return."

"When exactly did she leave?" said Newbury.

"It can't have been more than twenty minutes ago," replied Scarbright.

Newbury nodded. "Very well." He couldn't see what else he could do. Hopefully, she'd simply popped out for a walk and would return shortly. "Anything else?" he asked.

"A letter, sir. It arrived shortly before Miss Hobbes, delivered by a cabbie. I left it on the table there." Scarbright turned, retrieving the small cream envelope. As he turned it over, his face fell.

"What is it?" said Newbury, when he saw Scarbright's brow crease in a deep frown.

"The letter has been opened, sir. When I placed it on the table it was sealed," said Scarbright, perplexed.

Newbury took the envelope from him and slid the slip of paper out from inside. On it were printed the words:

**THE FORTESCUE HOTEL, CHANCERY LANE, TWO O'CLOCK.**

**CB**

"Oh, no…" said Newbury, his heart sinking. "Oh, Veronica…"

"What is it, sir?" said Scarbright, alarmed.

"She's gone to the hotel. She's gone looking for me there." He could hear the panic in his own voice. This was it. This was what he'd seen in his dreams. Veronica and the Executioner.

"The hotel, sir?" said Scarbright.

"It's where the Executioner is hiding," said Newbury, making a snap decision. "If she's gone there alone…" He discarded the note on the floor. "I must go after her."

"I'll accompany you, sir," said Scarbright, resolutely.

"No, I need you to stay here. If I'm wrong and she returns, you must keep her here. Keep her safe, Scarbright. Miss Hobbes is in grave danger."

"Yes, Sir Maurice. You can count on me, sir," said Scarbright, stoically.

"I know I can, Scarbright," replied Newbury.

He turned and hurtled back out of the door towards the waiting hansom. If Veronica had gone to the hotel alone, he might already be too late.

He only hoped—beyond all hope—that he was wrong.

# CHAPTER 28

👑

The Fortescue Hotel, it transpired, was a building in a dire state of repair. Where once the corner of the structure had met the pavement, there was now a gaping hole, ragged-edged and open to the elements. Wooden scaffolds had been erected all around it, clambering over the damaged building like a coterie of bizarre, angular insects swarming to their nest.

In better days the hotel had been grand and opulent. That much was clear to Veronica as she approached from the opposite side of the road, searching for any signs of habitation. There were none. Not even the glimmer of a lamp in a window. The place had simply been abandoned. She could see that there were still decorations in the front windows, which themselves were framed by heavy velvet drapes, pulled back as if the receptionist had forgotten to draw them for the evening. It was as if the proprietors had simply up and left in the middle of the day; leaving everything perfect and *in situ*, save for the enormous hole in the wall.

Veronica recalled reading a newspaper report of an accident in the area, almost two years earlier. A runaway ground train had thundered into the side of a hotel, demolishing a large section of the wall and killing five people in the lobby, along with the train's driver. The engine's boiler had burst, badly injuring scores of passengers in the ensuing explosion, and the local hospitals had been flooded with burn victims, causing widespread panic and calls from politicians for the public to boycott the ground train services.

The proposed boycotts had never come to pass, of course, as Londoners proved far more concerned with their own ability to get to and from their homes than with making a statement to the train operators regarding public safety.

The Fortescue Hotel, then, must have been the site of the accident. The wreckage of the train had been removed, but the wound in the building remained, bleeding shadows. She wondered why nobody had made an effort to restore or secure the premises. Perhaps there was an ongoing legal dispute, or perhaps the owners had simply run out of money.

Veronica shuddered at the thought of entering such a place, and hugged herself unconsciously inside her coat. Even from the other side of the road, it felt strangely as if the place were repelling her, urging her to carry on walking in the opposite direction. She didn't truly believe in ghosts, but she could swear that the Fortescue had something of a haunted air about it.

What business might Bainbridge and Newbury have at such a place, particularly in the dead of night? She could think only that it was some sort of trap—that Newbury was being coerced unknowingly into a situation from which he may not return. Although worrying away at the back of her mind was the poisonous notion that Newbury, too, might somehow be involved, that this meeting had been planned surreptitiously between the three men. She did not want to acknowledge even the possibility of such a thing.

Veronica could see no sign that the others had arrived. She checked her watch. It was approaching two in the morning. She sighed, feeling the energy seeping from her weary bones. However tired she was, she had to carry on. She had to protect

Newbury, or at least get to the bottom of whatever Bainbridge was up to.

All she could do was wait.

She crossed the road, approaching the chasm-like hole in the wall. She hadn't realised quite how large it was until she was standing before it, but the aperture was more than twice her height and half as wide again. Inside, she could see only darkness.

Bracing herself, she stepped gingerly over the heap of shattered bricks, picking through the rubble until she was standing in the gloomy lobby. There was a thick layer of dust on the marble floor, which swirled around her feet as she walked. She could see little in the gloom, other than an overturned potted plant, the vase shattered, the plant now dead and withered like a shrivelled hand.

She stood for a moment, listening intently for any sounds that might betray the presence of others in the ruins of the hotel. She became aware of the faint sound of ticking clocks, somewhere off in the darkness. Unsure what else to do, she followed it, her feet scuffing on the dusty floor.


Newbury leapt from the driver's box of his temporarily commandeered hansom, dropping awkwardly to the pavement. The engine was still running, grinding noisily in protest. He'd put the vehicle through its paces, hurtling at speed through the quiet city streets, and now, after being damaged and abused, it sounded as if it was almost ready to give up the ghost.

He stretched. His limbs felt leaden and weary after the two sudden, explosive bolts of energy he'd been forced to expend that night. Nevertheless, he was spurred on by the thought that Veronica might be in danger. He had promised to be there for her if she needed him, and he would make good on that promise, no matter what it took.

He surveyed the building. He could see now why it had been abandoned; the shattered structure and gaping hole spoke volumes. He'd seen properties such as this before—damaged in an accident and forever after mired in legal disagreements over whose responsibility it was to pay for repairs. It was clear to him why the Prince should choose such a place to squirrel away a dirty secret like the Executioner. No one had been near the building for months, it seemed, and even now there was no sign of any activity from within.

He turned at the sound of footsteps behind him.

"A most unconventional entrance, Newbury," said Bainbridge, his moustache twitching as he indicated the ruined shell of the cab. He was holding a lantern in his left hand, which cast his face in a warm orange glow. "What the devil's going on?"

"Not now, Charles," said Newbury, dismissively. He would explain everything later. For now, his only priority was Veronica.

Bainbridge furrowed his brow. "What is it, Newbury? What's the matter?"

"Veronica," said Newbury. "Have you seen her?"

"No," replied Bainbridge, perplexed.

Angelchrist, who was standing to one side appraising the damaged hansom, looked over. "We've only just arrived," he said. "Moments before you."

"I thought she was back at Chelsea, with you?" said Bainbridge.

Newbury shook his head. "I fear she came here alone," he said. "She was missing when I arrived home, and she'd discovered your note. Scarbright said she up and left without a word." He started towards the hole in the side of the building. "If she's in there, Charles…" he said, trailing off. The implication was obvious.

"We'd damn well better get in there after her, then," said

Bainbridge, determined, hefting his lantern and cane.

Angelchrist slid his revolver from his jacket pocket. "Lead on," he said, quietly. But Newbury had already raced into the ruins and been enveloped by the darkness within.

*She lay in the gloom upon a bed of scarlet cushions, listening to the clocks.*

*To her they were the heart of the building, beating out their weary, cacophonous rhythm. She had scavenged them from the homes of her victims and repurposed them, given them new life here in the ruins of this ancient hotel. The clocks were trophies; much like the organs she had ripped from her victims' corpses, cracking open their chests to get to the soft, beating muscles inside. But they were something more, too. They bestowed life on a once-dead building, arousing it from its deathly slumber. The clocks imbued her with power, much like her weapons: with her scimitars she ended life, with the clocks she began it anew.*

*Tonight, for the first time in decades, she had failed to terminate the life of her target. It mattered little to her—she would make another attempt in the coming hours, and this time she would prove successful. She felt no sense of disappointment or ill ease at this recognition of her own failure, simply curiosity that a man should prove capable of defending himself so successfully. She had, of course, made an error of judgement; she had not expected to be interrupted by another. Next time she would kill them both.*

*She glanced over at her leather satchel, which rested on a chair a few feet away, empty. By dawn it would contain another heart.*

*She started at the scuff of a shoe, distinct amongst the undulating tick-tock of her clocks. Her head turned.*

*There was someone in the room.*

*She stood, slowly and silently, lifting her swords. She eased into the shadows, trying to get a look at the newcomer. Had someone come searching for her, or had they stumbled unwittingly into her lair? Either way, they would have to die.*

*She stilled her breathing, pursed her lips. She listened to the many clocks, meting out the seconds.*

*She caught a glimpse of movement.*

*The intruder was a woman. She was young and pretty, and scared. She did not appear to be armed.*

*The Executioner watched as the woman approached the shielded lantern on the table and took it in her hands, unsheathing the light.*

*Dazzling beams lanced through the gloom, and the Executioner moved swiftly to avoid being seen. Dust swirled in the air behind her, picked out by the light.*

*The woman watched, fascinated, attempting to decipher the secrets of the room. Had she sensed that she was not alone? Had she noticed the whirling trail of dust?*

*The Executioner circled the intruder, intrigued. The woman seemed to radiate life. Her panic and desperation were somehow vital, energising.*

*She touched the flat of her blade playfully against the woman's cheek, and then danced away into the shadows. This was her domain: the dead of night, the darkness, the ghosting hours. The woman seemed to recognise this, and it terrified her. She trembled, and the lantern in her hand cast quivering shadows upon the walls and floor, illuminating the myriad clock faces that loomed out from the walls like grinning lunatics.*

*It was clear the woman had not come here looking for a murderess. There was something else, something she had lost. It did not matter what it was, but the irony of the situation would not be lost on the woman in the moments before she died. She had blundered into a trap of her own devising, walking blindly into the Executioner's sanctuary. And now the Executioner would take her heart, so full of life, and feel it beat its last in her tightly clenched fist before excising it and adding it to the heap of rotting organs in the corner.*

*The woman moved suddenly, unexpectedly, flinging the lamp across the room and brandishing her pistol. She squeezed off a couple of shots, which barked and flared in the semi-darkness. The Executioner moved easily, fluidly, and the bullets sailed past, thudding into the furniture close by.*

*She stepped forward, raising her sword, and plunged it swiftly into the chest of the woman, feeling it slide through soft flesh and snapping bone, exiting through the woman's back with a spray of dark blood.*

*The woman emitted a muffled wail as she recognised what had happened, and then crumpled to the floor, the Executioner's blade still jutting proudly from her chest.*

*The Executioner knelt, tearing away the woman's blouse. She ran her finger between the woman's breasts, measuring her breastbone.*

*"Veronica?"*

*She heard the familiar voice echoing from the passageway on the other side of the door.*

*"Veronica?"*

*She would have to work quickly. She would not give up this heart.*

*She set about opening the woman's chest with her blade, working by the feeble light of the near-extinguished lantern on the floor.*

The ticking of the clocks was a discordant cacophony that echoed throughout the bowels of the ruined hotel, not unlike a flock of birds, each of them chattering at once. Newbury, Bainbridge, and Angelchrist crept on towards it, cautious and alert.

"Veronica?" called Newbury, more concerned with finding her than alerting the Executioner—if the murderess was, in fact, there in the hotel—to their presence.

"Veronica?"

He listened for a response, but there was none, only the constant ticking of the clocks.

"What was that?" said Angelchrist from behind him, startled.

"What?" said Newbury.

"I heard a—" He stopped suddenly, and Newbury heard it too: the breathless wail of a woman in pain.

"Charles, your cane," said Newbury urgently, holding out his hand.

"My cane?" said Bainbridge, frowning.

"Your *cane*, Charles!" snapped Newbury, and Bainbridge reluctantly handed it over.

Newbury hefted it in his right hand, and then dashed in the direction of the sound, the others following in hot pursuit.

The source of the wail was not difficult to ascertain; a moment later Newbury burst into a darkened room, only to be assaulted by the riotous noise of a hundred clocks, each of them holding their own incongruous time.

He took in the scene as a series of snapshots—images that would be forever emblazoned in his mind.

The walls and surfaces were covered in timepieces of myriad shapes and sizes, every available space littered with them. Decrepit furniture was heaped in the corners of the room, and the stench of rotten meat was nearly overwhelming.

At the heart of this, the dark figure of the Executioner was hunched over the still form of Veronica, who was spread out upon the filthy floor, unmoving. The Executioner's hands were steeped in dark blood, and in one of them she still clutched the pommel of a curving scimitar. The other was buried deep inside Veronica's chest.

For a moment Newbury hesitated in the doorway, unable to comprehend the sight he was witnessing. Then, overcome by a rage of a ferocity he had never before encountered, he charged at the hunched figure of the Executioner, swinging Bainbridge's club violently at her head, bellowing in primal fury.

The Executioner shifted, but not in time, and the heavy silver head of the cane connected with her temple, sending her sprawling across the floor. Newbury pressed his advantage, whipping the cane up and around and striking again, this time shattering a rib as he brought it down upon the right side of her chest. He kicked at her, too, but she recovered and she rolled, avoiding his shoe.

The Executioner flipped up onto her knees, swinging her scimitar above her head to fend off another swipe with the cane. He heard Bainbridge and Angelchrist talking in urgent tones behind him, but shut it out. They would see to Veronica while he took care of this woman, this abomination.

He raised the cane and she reacted with terrifying speed, twisting her arm and stabbing at him with her blade. The move was designed to make him fall back, and he was forced to do just that, providing the Executioner with the opportunity to scramble to her feet.

He swung again, and then kicked, causing her to parry on one side and take a blow to the hip on the other. He stepped in, punching out with his left fist, striking her hard across the jaw, and then following through with his elbow.

She grunted in frustration and brought her knee up, narrowly missing his groin, but driving him back again.

Once again she jabbed at him with her sword, then swung it out in a wide arc, as if about to bring it down upon his head. He raised the cane in defence, but she changed the angle of the attack with a sudden twist of her wrist. He was forced to parry with his wounded left forearm, knocking the blade away but crying out in pain simultaneously as the wound was reopened.

He fell back and they circled, sizing each other up.

The Executioner had a feral look in her eyes, and her face was spattered with blood. Veronica's blood. Newbury growled in animosity. He would end this here and now.

Newbury grasped the handle of Bainbridge's cane and gave it a sharp twist.

The four thin panels on its shaft levered open, revealing the reinforced glass chamber within. With a whirr, the mechanism began to revolve and a spark of blue lightning flared inside the glass rod.

The Executioner came at him again, and he raised the

device, parrying her attack and hoping that her blade would not damage the mechanism as it spun around the generator core. The weapon sparked and crackled as the charge continued to build. Newbury remained on defensive footing, biding his time. He stepped back, circling again, judging each cut and thrust, sidestepping, parrying, waiting. The Executioner was toying with him, waiting for him to make a move, hoping he would overcommit himself and leave himself open to a fatal reply.

He could use that to his advantage.

The electrical hum reached a feverish crescendo, and Newbury saw his opening. He feinted right as if he was overreaching, leaving his left side open, but then twisted suddenly to the left and jabbed the tip of the cane towards the metal brace on the Executioner's shoulder.

The Executioner, who had by then committed to an attack on the left, had no chance to alter her momentum, and stepped forward into the thrust.

If the cane had been a sword it would have glanced harmlessly off her shoulder. But Newbury had not been searching for an opportunity to bury the cane in her flesh, but to discharge it into the clockwork mechanism embedded in her shoulder.

Crackling blue light burst from the end of the cane as the metal tip made contact with the shoulder guard. The Executioner shuddered and dropped her weapon as the electricity discharged into her body. She staggered back, but Newbury pressed forward, watching the fizzing light crawl all over her flesh, sparking as it sought out the precious metals inlaid in her cheeks, arcing between her teeth as she opened her mouth to scream.

He held the lightning cane in position, waiting for the woman to die.

* * *

*She staggered back, her vision swimming. Ethereal light bloomed all around her as the crackling energy crawled over her flesh.*

*And then she felt it: a lancing, stabbing pain in her chest, so sharp that for a moment she thought he had punctured her chest cavity with the end of his weapon. It blossomed until it consumed her, a white-hot agony that almost made her swoon.*

*It came again, and then again, and she screamed, clutching at her chest as the electricity coursed through her body. She fell to her knees, wailing, dying.*

*The detached part of her mind was attempting to establish the nature of the injury that was causing her so much pain. It came relentlessly in waves, drumming in her ears, pounding inside of her. The pressure in her chest made it feel as if she were going to explode.*

*And then—fascinated and appalled in equal measure—she realised what it was. Despite her agony, she was overcome by a strange sense of calm.*

*Her heart was beating.*

*The black, shrivelled remnant of her original organ was shuddering inside of her, thumping like a pounding drum. The electricity was causing the decayed muscle to contract, again and again, over and over.*

*She was filled with an immense sense of sadness, and joy, and relief—the first things she had felt in nearly a century. This man, this Newbury, had come here not simply to kill her, but to set her free. This, she knew with a sudden clarity, was what she had been searching for all along. All of those long years, wandering the streets of a hundred nations, taking life after petty life... all she had wanted was release.*

*She slumped forward onto the floor. The pain in her chest was excruciating, and yet beautiful, peaceful. Her lips creased into a smile.*

*With a gasp, Élodie Séverin died.*

"Newbury!" bellowed Bainbridge. "Get over here!"

Newbury dropped the discharged lightning cane atop the body of the Executioner and staggered over to where

Bainbridge and Angelchrist crouched over Veronica's prone form. He couldn't see her through the jumble of limbs as both men tried desperately to attend to her injuries.

Bainbridge looked up at Newbury, his expression grave. He shook his head, lowered his eyes.

"Let me through!" barked Newbury, pushing them out of the way, dropping to his knees before her. He almost choked at the sight of Veronica, lying there on the filthy floor, her head lolled to one side in the dirt, her chest ripped open, blood gushing from the yawning wound. Bainbridge and Angelchrist were trying to stem the tide with bundles of rags and handkerchiefs, but they were not enough.

"No! No, no, no, no…" He trailed off, unable to find words. He could barely register what he was seeing. Her clothes had been ripped asunder, and he could see the fingers of her rib cage, broken and splintered, jutting out of her pale flesh. The skin was pulled back like a pair of bloody curtains to reveal the precious cavity beneath. Inside of her, her heart was pulsing, glossy and alive.

Angelchrist put a hand on his shoulder. "I'm sorry," he said.

"The Fixer," said Newbury, his voice cracking. "We have to get her to the Fixer." He shrugged Angelchrist away, then reached down and scooped Veronica up, cradling her in his arms. Within moments he was covered in her blood. He staggered to his feet.

"It's too late, Newbury," said Bainbridge, his voice filled with infinite sadness. "She's dying."

"No!" bellowed Newbury. "No! If you won't help me, Charles, I'll get her there myself." He rushed towards the door, his eyes stinging. He would not let her die. He could not let her die.

Bainbridge ran after him, the lantern swaying wildly in his hand. "I have a carriage waiting outside, Newbury. We'll get her there in that."

Newbury nodded, running as fast as he dared in the dim light.

"Archibald—secure the scene," he heard Bainbridge call behind them as they rushed out into the rain-soaked morning. The frigid air was like a slap in the face.

"Over here!" cried Bainbridge, struggling for breath. They rounded the corner to find the police carriage waiting for them, the driver looking on in confusion. Bainbridge opened the door and Newbury hastily bundled Veronica inside, clutching her close. "Get us to the Fixer, now!" shouted Bainbridge, hopping up onto the footplate.

The engines roared, and the carriage shot away into the night.

# CHAPTER 29

"Can't this damn thing go any faster?" snapped Newbury, as the driver stepped on the brakes to prevent the carriage from rolling over as they took a sharp bend in the road.

He was cradling Veronica in his arms, her head lolling against his chest, mercifully insensible. Her breath was shallow, like the fluttering of a tiny bird, and she felt lighter than he remembered. He felt tears pricking his eyes but fought them back. He needed to be strong now, to see her through it.

"He's going as fast as he can, Newbury," said Bainbridge, sullenly. He was pale and he wouldn't meet Newbury's eye. He looked as if he were already grieving.

"Don't you dare give up on her, Charles!" barked Newbury. "Don't you dare." Bainbridge looked up, and his eyes were so full of sadness and compassion that Newbury almost faltered. His anger dissipated. "She can't die, Charles. She simply can't die," he said.

Bainbridge nodded, and looked away again, peering out of the window. Newbury could see that his friend understood his desperation, was making allowances for it, and in many ways it made matters worse. Newbury refused to admit that it was too late.

"We're almost there," said Bainbridge, after a moment. "This is Bloomsbury."

Newbury bundled Veronica even tighter in his arms, as if attempting to hold her together himself. She was bleeding profusely, all over the back of the carriage, and Newbury's jacket and trousers were soaked through to the skin. He felt cold, and he wasn't sure whether it was the wet blood, or simply a form of terrible numbness creeping over him, threatening to consume him.

He looked down at Veronica. Her pale cheek was spattered with obscene streaks of scarlet and the fingerprints of the woman who had tried to kill her. Newbury wiped them away with his thumb, smearing the blood.

The carriage screeched to a halt, and Newbury planted his feet firmly in the footwell to prevent himself from rocking forward and jolting Veronica. Any sudden movements might worsen her condition or exacerbate her wounds.

Bainbridge was up and at the door before they'd even come properly to rest. "Get her around to the side entrance," he said. "I'll get Rothford and the Fixer." He ducked out into the rain-swept night, and Newbury struggled to his feet, following swiftly behind. Fat raindrops cascaded from the heavens, lashing his upturned face.

So strong was his intent to get Veronica to safety that he didn't bother to check for passers-by. Her life was like sand streaming through an hourglass, and the only man who could stem the tide was the Fixer.

Once before, Newbury had seen the man work miracles, stitching Newbury's torn shoulder back together and transfusing esoteric compounds into his bloodstream to hasten his recovery. That was some time ago, but Newbury hoped that the Fixer might be able to perform a miracle again.

The house was a three-storey end terrace in an exclusive area of Bloomsbury. Newbury saw Bainbridge running up the steps to the front entrance, where he might alert Rothford, the Fixer's manservant, to Veronica's dire circumstances. Newbury, however, would take the side entrance to the cellar, which held the Fixer's workshop, laboratory, and surgery.

He struggled down the narrow cast-iron steps towards the basement door, careful not to knock Veronica's head on the iron railings. Once there, he hammered on the wood-panelled door with his foot.

For a moment he heard nothing, no sign of movement from inside the house. He was struck by thoughts that panicked him. The house was dark and silent. What if the Fixer was not at home? What then for Veronica? He moaned in frustration and kicked the door again.

This time he heard a muffled voice from the other side. "I'm coming!"

It was too early yet to feel any sense of relief, but the familiar voice was reassuring.

Bolts slid out of their sockets and the door creaked open, revealing the Fixer, standing in the shadows of his workshop. He was a balding man in his mid-forties, with a neatly trimmed black beard and wire spectacles. He was thinner than Newbury remembered, and free of the bizarre accoutrements with which he'd been adorned during Newbury's previous visit.

He looked ruffled, as if he'd just pulled on his trousers and shirt. He was rolling up his sleeves as he appraised the situation, and his expression was harried. "Come in, come in!" he said, beckoning Newbury through the door. He rushed over to the wall and flicked a switch. The room, tiled in gleaming white porcelain, was suddenly flooded with harsh illumination that stung Newbury's eyes.

"She's in a bad way," said Newbury, brandishing Veronica's limp form.

"I can see that, Newbury," said the Fixer. "Bring her over here; put her on this table."

Newbury staggered over to a large trestle table topped with a white marble slab. It reminded him of the operating tables in the morgue so much that he almost hesitated to lay Veronica down upon it. He didn't want to let her go. What if it was the last time he would hold her? He felt short of breath, his heart hammering in his chest. He realised he was being irrational, so he placed her gently down upon the table, brushing her hair from her face.

"Hurry, man!" said the Fixer. He was scrabbling about amongst his surgical tools. He turned to Newbury, brandishing a small pair of scissors, then crossed to where Veronica lay on the slab and set about cutting away the remains of her clothes. His face told a thousand tales as he exposed the extent of the wound between her breasts. He glanced over his shoulder at Newbury. "I'll do what I can," he said. "Now go."

"I won't leave her," countered Newbury.

The Fixer glared at him. "Let me work. I can't have you harrying me. Go."

Newbury sensed movement behind him and turned to see Rothford standing on the other side of the room. He smiled warmly. He looked immaculate in his black suit, with grey, receding hair and a hooked, equine nose. "This way, sir," he said, extending his arm to indicate the way. "We have a waiting room upstairs. You may sit with Sir Charles while the master does his work."

Newbury glanced at Veronica. The Fixer was standing over her now, donning his worn leather smock and gloves. Her milky-white torso was exposed, and the gaping wound where the Executioner had cracked her chest yawned open like a sickly, smiling mouth. Inside, he could see her labouring heart, straining to maintain its rhythm. He felt as if he was going to swoon. "Yes," he said, faintly. "Yes, I'll come with you."

He felt Rothford take his arm, and realised the man had crossed the room to steady him. He allowed himself to be led away.

* * *

The waiting room was sterile and immaculate. The floor was the same gleaming white marble as the operating table in the basement, and the walls were hung with gilt-framed paintings by many of the old masters of Europe. Strangely, the room smelled of freshly cut flowers, even at this time of night.

Bainbridge perched on the edge of a Chesterfield by the crackling open fire, hunched over a large glass of brandy, his expression fixed and unreadable. Newbury paced back and forth before the bay window, jittery with nervous energy.

An hour had passed with no word. Newbury had lost track of time, but knew it must be the early hours of the morning. Rothford had appeared once to offer them tea, but both men had shaken their heads dully, preferring to take comfort from the decanter of brandy he had provided them with earlier.

Neither of them had spoken a word. Newbury kept replaying the events at the abandoned hotel, thinking that if only he'd done something differently he might have gotten to her in time.

If only she hadn't gone to that place alone. If only he'd been able to stop her, to make her listen. He knew the attack was coming. He'd seen it in his opium-fuelled dreams. Why hadn't she listened? Why hadn't he *made her*? Surely he could have prevented this if he'd been stronger.

He realised he was shaking in anguish. He moved to stare out of the window, but then turned at the sound of footsteps approaching in the hall.

The Fixer appeared in the open doorway. He was wiping blood from his forearms with a damp towel, and Newbury saw that it was spattered over his clothes and soaked into his white shirt, despite the smock he had worn. His jaw was set firm, his eyes dull and unrevealing.

Newbury didn't want to hear what the man had to say. He

couldn't bear it if she were dead. He'd almost prefer to be trapped in this perpetual twilight of uncertainty, to stretch this moment out indefinitely. At least here, now, there was hope.

"How is she?" asked Bainbridge, quietly.

"She'll live," said the Fixer. "For now."

The tension, which until that point had been nearly unbearable, seemed to snap. Newbury exhaled for what felt like the first time since he'd found Veronica at the hotel. His shoulders dropped, and relief washed over him.

"Her heart, however, was damaged beyond repair," continued the Fixer, his expression unaltered. "I was forced to remove it."

"*Remove* it!" said Newbury, realising his relief had come too soon.

"She would have died," said the Fixer. "The organ was lacerated during her attacker's attempt to extract it."

"But… with no heart? Surely…?" stammered Bainbridge.

"There's a machine," said the Fixer. "A machine that will circulate her blood for her, developed many years ago by Dr. Fabian as a prototype for the one that now supports the Queen. It is temperamental and will not serve our purpose indefinitely. We have a few weeks at most to find a more permanent solution, otherwise she will be lost."

Newbury felt his heart sinking once again. "But you healed me! You brought me back from the brink of death. Can you not find a means?"

"I stitched up your shoulder, Newbury. I cannot repair an organ as complex and fragile as a heart," said the Fixer, with resignation.

"Show me," said Newbury. "Let me see her."

The Fixer nodded. "Very well. Follow me." He led them through the house to a small door beneath the grand staircase in the main entrance hall. Behind the door, another flight of steps led down to the basement. "Down there," said the Fixer. "But

I'll warn you, it's not a sight for those of a weak disposition."

"Is she awake?" asked Newbury, hesitantly, as he led the way down the steps.

"No. I've kept her under. The pain would be excruciating. She will remain unconscious until we find a solution, one way or another," replied the Fixer.

At the bottom of the stairs, the room suddenly opened up into a vast space, familiar to Newbury from his own brief stay. This massive chamber was adjacent to the one in which he had deposited Veronica earlier, but at least three times the size. It was brightly lit by another electric arc light that spanned the vaulted ceiling, flooding everything in its clinical gleam. An array of strange and unusual machinery lined the walls: whirring clockwork engines that pumped bubbling pink fluid through glass valves and coiling tubes; devices that resembled multi-bladed weapons but were, in fact, surgical tools; an automaton assistant that scuttled around at waist height, bearing trays of spatulas and scalpels. Empty beds stood like sentries, posted at intervals amongst the machines. The room stank of carbolic and blood.

In the far right corner, a series of bellows attached to a large brass box were wheezing as they slowly inflated and deflated, over and over, as regular as the ticking of a metronome or a clock. Newbury could see more tubing snaking out of the brass box, disappearing into the chest of what looked like a pale wax dummy laid upon a bed beside it. He felt his own heart breaking at the sight. "My God," he whispered, as he drifted mechanically across the basement towards her. He had no words with which to adequately describe his thoughts.

Veronica lay there, unconscious and unmoving, much like a corpse. The place where her chest wound had been now erupted with a bundle of fat tubes, filled with dark, red blood. The flesh around them was puckered and purple.

Her head had fallen to one side on the pillow and her

lips were slightly parted, as if in a wry smile. Her hands were folded over her stomach, and a white gown—the front of which had been hastily modified to provide access to the tubing in her chest—protected her modesty. She was pale, and her skin had taken on a damp sheen. Beside her, the brass contraption gurgled as it fed hungrily on her blood, cycling it through her veins.

"She would not have wanted this," said Bainbridge, clearly appalled. "She would not want to live like this."

Newbury turned on him, but there was little fight left in him. "I'll find a way, Charles. There must be a way." He glanced at the Fixer.

"She needs a new heart," said the Fixer. "A replacement for her original organ. With Fabian dead, however…" He trailed off, but Newbury caught his meaning. He didn't know of anyone capable of such a precise feat of engineering and invention. The irony was not lost on Newbury: if he and Veronica had not allowed the Bastion Society's attack on the Grayling Institute to go ahead, Fabian would still be alive.

"There'll be others," said Newbury, defiantly. "There must be others."

"If you are to find them," said the Fixer, the doubt evident in his voice, "then you must act swiftly."

Newbury nodded. He could feel the anger swelling in his chest. Anger at himself, anger at Veronica… but most of all, anger at the Prince of Wales. This was his doing. Newbury would ensure that he paid for what he had done.

"Look, she's safe for now, Newbury. You need to get some rest. You're wounded and tired, and you can't do anything else for Miss Hobbes here. Not now. Go home, and I'll go directly to the palace to lay it all out for the Queen," said Bainbridge, putting a hand on Newbury's shoulder.

"I'll kill him, Charles," muttered Newbury. "I'll have his head for this."

"Newbury!" There was a warning note in Bainbridge's voice. "You can't even think of it. Do not go there. Let the Queen handle it. You'll get yourself killed if you try to take matters into your own hands."

Newbury looked at the Fixer, who was watching them with interest. He looked back at Bainbridge. "You're right, Charles. You must go directly to the Queen. Ensure that she understands who is responsible for this sorry mess." He turned and strode towards the door.

"Newbury? Where are you going?" Bainbridge called after him. "Newbury!"

Newbury didn't answer, didn't look back at Bainbridge, the Fixer, or Veronica. He simply carried on walking towards the door and the steps that led up to the entrance hall.

He had business to attend to.

# CHAPTER 30

✦

The sun was coming up as Newbury stalked determinedly along the gravel driveway towards the monolithic home of the Prince of Wales.

He looked dishevelled and exhausted, limned by the amber glow of the breaking day. His hair was mussed, his collar open, and his cravat long discarded. His once-black jacket was sticky with Veronica's drying blood. There was rage in his eyes, and a deep, burning desire for revenge in his belly.

Bainbridge had warned him not to come here, to leave the matter to the Queen to resolve, but Newbury could not let it rest. He needed to look the man in the eye, to understand what had driven him to commit such heinous atrocities. Even more, he needed to ensure the Prince would pay for what he had done to Veronica, one way or another.

His hands were bunched into tight fists, and he was barely aware of the sounds of the household waking as he approached, or the twittering of birds overhead, heralding the dawn. He had only one goal in mind: to get inside the building and locate the traitorous Prince of Wales. He'd work out what to do when he found him.

He approached the front entrance, his feet stirring the gravel. He reached for the bell pull and gave it a sharp tug.

The bells jangled deep inside the building, beckoning to the servants within. Newbury paced restlessly back and forth for a moment in the shadow of the awning, until the sound of footsteps in the hallway caused him to stop and look round.

The door creaked open a fraction and Barclay's pale face appeared in the opening. When he saw Newbury his expression darkened. "Sir Maurice," he said, looking him up and down, an eyebrow arched in snide amusement. "You seem a little out of sorts." He waited for a response, but Newbury was not forthcoming. "But I'm afraid your journey here has been in vain," he continued after a moment, when it became apparent that Newbury had chosen to ignore his jibe. "The Prince cannot see you at this early hour. I'd suggest making an appointment. And," he added, pushing for a reaction, "that perhaps you should consider adopting a more formal appearance."

"Let me in, Barclay," growled Newbury in response. He felt his ire rising.

"I cannot," replied the butler, tartly.

"You shall," said Newbury, stepping forward and shoving the door open with his left hand.

Barclay fell back, attempting to block his entrance. "Desist, Sir Maurice," he said, boldly, although he was clearly shaken by Newbury's unexpected intensity.

"Step aside," said Newbury, a note of warning in his voice. "I will not ask you again."

"I will not," came the response.

Newbury sighed. He would tolerate the imbecile no longer. He let his shoulders drop in apparent resignation, but then lashed out suddenly with his fist, catching the odious little man across the jaw with a right hook that rendered him almost immediately insensible. His legs buckled beneath him, his head dropping, and he slumped to the tiled floor. Newbury didn't bother to catch him as he pitched forward onto his face. "I've wanted to do that for the best part of a week," he said to the unconscious man, flexing his smarting fingers.

He stepped over the threshold, closing the door behind him. He left the butler lying in the hallway as he followed the sounds of bustling activity deeper into the house.

He began by retracing his steps from the previous day. The drawing room proved to be empty, however, and the library door was locked. He considered forcing the door in with his shoulder, but decided he would be better off searching for his quarry elsewhere in the immense house before resorting to drastic measures. It was still relatively early, although he assumed the Prince would have risen from his bed by this time on a winter's morning.

He passed a maid as he hurried along the passageway and she stared at him, her eyes wide. She looked as if she were about to speak—probably with a view to offering assistance or enquiring after his dishevelled appearance—but he silenced her with a glowering look, and she scuttled off, her head bowed.

Two further rooms—a sitting room and a music room—yielded no results, but the third, which turned out to be the dining room, proved eminently more fruitful.

The Prince of Wales sat at the large table, attired in a quilted dressing gown of imperial red, and hunched over a plate of sausage, bacon, and eggs, with a freshly pressed newspaper at his elbow. He was alone. Newbury suspected that Barclay had been in attendance up until a few moments before, when he had rung the doorbell and called the butler away.

Albert Edward glanced up as Newbury burst into the room. He looked startled, and somewhat confused. "Newbury?" he said, peering across the table to where Newbury stood in the doorway. "Well, I must say, this is something of a surprise. Most unorthodox."

Newbury stalked further into the room, his face like thunder. "I rather think you imagined me to be dead, Your

Royal Highness," he said, almost spitting the last few words.

The Prince frowned. "Why ever would you say such a thing, Newbury? Why should I consider you dead?" He paused, contemplating his breakfast. "Although, judging from the look of you, you have rather been through the wringer. Are you hurt? You appear to be covered in blood." His tone was genial and gave little away.

Newbury offered him a hard, unwavering stare. "I know it was you," he said, gravely. "I know what you are."

"Now look here, Newbury," said the Prince, placing his cutlery neatly on the side of his plate and meeting Newbury's eye. "I haven't the faintest idea what you are talking about, and I cannot say that I approve of your tone. Now, it is clear to me that you have been involved in a distressing episode, and so I shall overlook your rather inappropriate implication. It occurs to me, though, that I may have been ill advised in extending to you a certain level of informality, such that you might deem it appropriate to burst in on me like this, first thing in the morning and dressed like a common tramp."

"Cease your excuses!" bellowed Newbury, grinding his teeth in frustration.

"Good Lord! How dare you speak to me in such a manner?" The Prince, incensed, pushed his chair back and stood, slamming both palms down upon the surface of the table. "Leave now, Newbury, before I am forced to take action. Go home and take stock of whatever has occurred. You may return here to Marlborough House later this afternoon if you still have matters which you wish to discuss, and assuming you can do so with at least some sense of propriety."

Newbury shook his head. "You misunderstand," he said slowly, in an effort to control his temper. "It's over. Your hand in the matter has been exposed. Even now, Sir Charles Bainbridge is before the Queen, explaining your part in proceedings, how you commissioned the Executioner to carry out your plans, how you orchestrated the deaths of key agents to undermine your mother's power. How you even sent your pet murderess after me when I failed to engage in your carefully planned distraction and strayed too close to the truth."

"You're delusional, Newbury! Too many of those damnable cigarettes, I don't doubt. That's what it is. You're seeing things that aren't there," replied the Prince hotly. His cheeks were flushed red with anger and embarrassment.

"You know as well as I do that I am not delusional. Her Majesty the Queen is unlikely to see it that way, either, once the facts are laid out before her." Newbury was now standing only a few feet away from the Prince. "This blood," he said, indicating the stains on the front of his jacket, "belongs to Miss Hobbes. It is on your hands."

Albert Edward's shoulders dropped. He lowered his eyes, gazing at the floor. "Your trouble, Newbury, is that despite all of your dreadful habits and obsessions, despite your best attempts to kill yourself with narcotics and ridiculous occult games, you're too damn clever. Too astute. You could have stayed out of it. If Miss Hobbes found herself caught up in this dreadful business, then her blood is on your hands, Newbury. Your hands, not mine." The Prince looked up, met Newbury's gaze. His eyes were cold, hard. "You had the opportunity to save yourself. Your damn pride and relentlessness is what's landed us both in this position."

"So you admit it, then? You admit it all. You were behind the Executioner. You were feeding her targets, looking to destabilise and overturn your mother's rule so you could claim the throne for yourself," said Newbury, shaking his head. He'd known it to be true, but even now, even hearing it from the man himself, he could hardly believe it.

"I was doing it for the good of the Empire, to prevent her from passing everything to that... *abomination*," spat the Prince.

"She would have cut me out, Newbury, and installed her own little puppet on the throne. A child grown in a laboratory! She's insane. She thinks only of herself, not the people of our great nation. Surely you must see that? It's for the good of the Empire that she falls!"

The Prince's words echoed in Newbury's skull. *An abomination... a child grown in a laboratory...* Newbury had seen such things at the Grayling Institute, facsimiles of Amelia propagated in vats of amniotic fluid. Could it be that Dr. Fabian had been successful, that he had managed to smuggle one of the clones out for the Queen before the end? And a child? All of the copies he had seen were adults–if you could call the disturbed, animalistic things adults at all. Perhaps this was something different.

"Whatever the truth of your words, the manner in which you have set about achieving your goal is detestable and extreme. Innocent people have died, their hearts ripped out by a licensed madwoman, authorised by your own hand," said Newbury, bitterly.

"This is a war, Newbury! Can't you see? Their deaths could not be avoided. It was necessary for the greater good." The Prince sounded as if he were pleading now, for an understanding that Newbury could not provide.

"I don't believe measures such as that are ever necessary," replied Newbury. "The ends never justify such means."

"Then I'm afraid you leave me no choice," said the Prince, his expression hardening. "I'll just have to finish the Executioner's work myself."

He lurched back, grabbing for the pommel of a display sword that was mounted on the wall behind him. He slid it from its housing with a swift, fluid motion, causing the accompanying shield to clatter noisily to the floor. He rounded on Newbury with a flourish, the tip of the sword only a foot away from Newbury's chest, poised over his heart.

"This really is a most regrettable interlude, Newbury," said the Prince. "I had planned for you to be by my side as I ascended to the throne, to become the head of my security forces. Together, we would have achieved great things. But now, you have reduced me to this, to lowering myself to such base matters. I will not make such a mistake again." He launched himself forward, the blade humming through the air towards Newbury's chest.

Newbury fell back and his right hand shot out, snatching a large silver candlestick from the dining table beside him. He swung it around before him in a sweeping arc. It struck the Prince's épée with the dull clatter of metal upon metal, sending the Prince's attack wide. Newbury continued the motion, stepping forward and at the same time twisting the angle of his wrist so that the thin blade became entangled amongst the triad of silver stems that comprised the candlestick. With a sharp jerk, he twisted the sword out of the Prince's grasp and sent it clattering away across the floor.

The Prince cursed and stepped back, nursing his wrist. Newbury, still holding the candlestick, stepped forward again, raising the heavy decoration above his head as if to strike the other man.

The Prince cowered, raising his hands above his head in a pathetic attempt to stave off the anticipated attack. Newbury could see the fear in his eyes, could tell from the sharp intake of breath that the man was panicked. He had tried to murder Newbury, and his botched attempt at undermining the Queen had resulted in the near-death of the woman Newbury loved. Newbury would be justified in striking him down, if not, perhaps, more.

Instead, however, Newbury dropped the candlestick upon the floor and stood back, looking down upon the pathetic man whom he had once held in such high regard. "You are not worthy of my time," he said quietly, firmly. "I shall leave you for your mother to deal with."

The Prince stared up at him with confusion in his eyes. He seemed unable to grasp that Newbury was not going to see the attack through, that he was not going to end the Prince's life then and there on the parquet floor of his dining room.

Newbury turned his back on the Prince of Wales and strode defiantly from the room.

He walked along the narrow passageway until he entered the hall. The main door was hanging open, and two maids were attending to the unconscious Barclay. They looked up at Newbury in apparent fascination. He ignored them, heading directly for the door.

As he stepped over the still-prone form of the butler, he heard the Prince bellowing loudly and fretfully for the man from the bowels of the house. Newbury spared a weak, sad smile for the maids on his way out the door.

# CHAPTER 31

❦

How is she?" said Bainbridge, as he bustled through the door to Newbury's drawing room, forgoing the usual formalities.

He was anxious to hear word of Veronica, and also to check on his old friend, who was taking it very badly indeed. Two days had passed, and Bainbridge had been busy dealing with the aftermath of the whole affair: fighting off reporters, placating the Queen, informing the families of the Executioner's victims.

He didn't yet know what had happened to the Executioner's corpse, which was missing from the scene, or what had become of the Prince of Wales, who had not been seen since the morning after the events at the abandoned hotel.

Newbury, however, was sitting cross-legged on the rug before the hearth, surrounded by an impressive spread of newspaper cuttings, open books, and sheaves of notepaper covered in his spidery scrawl. He'd pushed the furniture back to create a temporary space in which to work, researching– Bainbridge gathered–potential engineers who might be able to craft a new heart for Veronica.

"Is there anything to report?" Bainbridge prompted, when no response was forthcoming.

Newbury didn't look up. "There's been no change," he said absently.

He continued to study the open book on his lap. Bainbridge could see it contained diagrammatic illustrations of the inner workings of clockwork machinery.

Bainbridge sighed heavily. At least the room, for once, did not carry the stink of opium smoke. In fact, the window was slightly ajar, and the curtains open. For the first time in weeks, there was natural light spilling in. If there was one good thing about the whole affair, it was that it may have shaken Newbury from his more detrimental habits. For a while, at least.

"She's stable, then," said Bainbridge, for lack of anything else to say.

This time, Newbury did glance up. His expression was fierce. "She's dying, Charles!" he said, angrily. "She has no heart, and she is dying." He looked away, and the anger suddenly dispersed, replaced instead by an anguished, haunted look. "What's worse is that there's very little you or I can do about it," he continued, after a short while.

The moment stretched. Bainbridge hardly knew what to say to the man. He couldn't reassure him that everything was going to be well, because he fully suspected it might not. And he couldn't tell him not to embark on some ill-fated folly to find a new heart for the girl, because all that would achieve was Newbury giving him the cold shoulder. The best thing he could do under the circumstances, he decided, was to offer his support and ensure that Newbury was at least looking after himself. "You cannot continue to blame yourself for what happened," he said, in what he hoped was a reasonable tone.

"If I'd listened to Aldous, Charles... if I'd taken the threat of the Cabal seriously, then I might have arrived back here in time to stop her. I might have saved her life." His voice cracked with emotion as he spoke.

"You *did* save her life, Newbury," replied Bainbridge, softly. He could understand that deep sense of guilt, that need Newbury felt to replay those fateful events over and over in his mind, looking for things he might have done differently. Bainbridge had gone through a similar process with Isobel.

At least he was beginning to grieve now. It might make things more bearable later, when the inevitable happened.

"Temporarily, perhaps," said Newbury. "But I will not rest, Charles. I'll scour the Continent, or farther afield if necessary. I'll find her a heart."

Bainbridge shrugged out of his heavy overcoat and laid it across the back of the divan. He balanced his cane beside it. "Well, at least allow yourself a few moments to have a drink with a friend. You need a rest."

Newbury nodded in silent acquiescence. He placed his book carefully on the floor and stood, trying to avoid disturbing the neat stacks of paper.

Bainbridge set about pouring them a drink, while Newbury pulled over two armchairs. They settled by the window, with the sound of bustling people and horses carrying through from the street outside.

"So, what *of* the Prince?" said Newbury, accepting his drink.

Bainbridge smiled. "Indeed. What of the Prince," he echoed. "I know you went there, Newbury, to Marlborough House. There's no use denying it. I heard about the butler's unfortunate 'accident.'"

"The damnable wretch deserved it," said Newbury, taking a sip of his brandy.

"He wanted to press charges," said Bainbridge.

"I'll bet he did," replied Newbury. "Although I doubt it would do him much good. I imagine there's plenty of evidence that places him squarely in the dock alongside the Prince. He knew everything that was going on in that house. I'll wager he was privy to the Prince's plans. Probably even helped them along a bit, to curry favour."

"Foulkes will be keeping an eye on him for the foreseeable future," said Bainbridge. "But that wasn't why you went there, was it? For the butler, I mean."

Newbury glanced out of the window, as if avoiding the question. When he looked back, his expression was pained. He was searching for Bainbridge's understanding. "I needed to hear him say it, Charles. I needed the Prince to admit what he'd done. I didn't go there to threaten him, or strike him, as much as it might have granted me some satisfaction. I went there to see the expression on his face as he told me what he'd done."

"To look for remorse?" asked Bainbridge, surprised.

"Perhaps," said Newbury. "I don't really know."

"Well, it's in the hands of the Queen now. It remains to be seen if she'll send him to the gallows for treason," said Bainbridge, before taking a long draught of his brandy. "Although it's a rum business to have to face your own child in such circumstances. I'm not convinced I could do it."

"The irony is," said Newbury, "I think we might have been better off if he had succeeded. He might have changed things for the better. Under the circumstances, however, I cannot forgive him. I'll never forgive him for what he's done, whatever becomes of him."

"If only he'd found another way," said Bainbridge, morosely. "If he'd asked for our help, rather than making us his enemies."

"He was consumed by his own hubris," said Newbury. "And at the end, when it was all out in the open, he spoke of an abomination, a child grown in a laboratory. It was the thing that tipped the balance. He seemed to suggest that the Queen would favour this child over him, displacing him as the rightful heir to the throne."

"He's done a darn good job of ensuring that," said Bainbridge, pointedly. "But it's the first I've heard of this child. It may, of course, have simply been the ramblings of a deluded man. He cannot have been in his right mind."

Newbury frowned. "No. I mean, you're right—he was undoubtedly suffering from grave disillusionment, to the point of inducing madness—but the child bears investigating all the same. I think it might be the product of one of Dr. Fabian's more unsavoury experiments at the Grayling Institute. I understand he was dabbling in such things."

Bainbridge nodded. "I'll brief Archibald on the matter," he said.

"The investigation continues, then?" said Newbury, his interest piqued.

"For now," replied Bainbridge, still unsure how much to say on the subject, "Archibald will continue to keep the Queen under observation."

"And what about you, Charles? Where will this all end?" said Newbury, gulping down the last of his brandy.

"Who knows, Maurice?" replied Bainbridge, with a shrug. "For now I'm just content to carry on. Someone has to."

"It's a dangerous game," said Newbury, "but when this business with Veronica is over and she's back on her feet, I'd like to help."

Bainbridge nodded. He couldn't help but smile, despite everything, at his friend's candour. "We'll get through this, Newbury. Whatever happens."

Newbury gave a fleeting smile, and stood, dusting himself off. "I must continue with my research," he said, glancing over at the book he'd left lying open on the floor.

"Oh, right. Yes. I'd better be off, then," said Bainbridge, levering himself up out of his chair.

Newbury stepped forward and put a hand on his shoulder. "You can stay, if you like. Pour yourself another drink. It'll be good to have company while I work."

Bainbridge nodded. "For a little while, then," he said. It was rare for Newbury to openly invite anyone to remain while he worked, and a signifier of precisely how much support he needed. "As long as you don't mind if I smoke."

Newbury laughed. "Of course not, you old fool. Now, go and tell Scarbright to put a kettle on the stove, will you? I've had enough of brandy and maudlin. I'm in need of a pot of tea."

"Right you are, Newbury," said Bainbridge, grinning. His friend returned to his spot by the hearth, reclaimed his book, and immediately lost himself in its pages. "Right you are."

# CHAPTER 32

"Come forward, child. Come into the light where we can see you."

Alberta did as she was commanded, shuffling forward into the soft orb of light cast by the Queen's lantern. The monarch turned to her and smiled, flashing the stumps of her blackened teeth. "Ah, there you are, Alberta," she said. She held her lantern up so that it swung back and forth on its creaking handle, scattering ghosts. "Today we must continue with your education."

Alberta gave a solitary nod. Her lips did not betray the turmoil roiling in her belly. It was not that she was scared of her adoptive mother—although, perhaps, on reflection, there was a small modicum of fear. It was more that she wished not to disappoint. The punishments for such disappointment were grave indeed. This she had discovered during the many months of rigorous preparation she had so far endured, the training lavished upon her by the Queen to equip her for her future role as monarch.

Alberta looked up at the Queen, whose demeanour remained unchanged: ever vigilant, ever waking. She looked sickly in her massive, engine-like chair: pale, with dark rings beneath her eyes. A thick bundle of cables and tubing now sprouted from the back of the device, fanning out across the tiled floor behind her and trailing off into the shadows. These were new. Another improvement devised by the odious Dr. Warrender, no doubt; another of his desperate attempts to keep the monarch—and thus, her patronage—alive.

Alberta was disgusted by these machines, the industry with which they whirred and groaned and wheezed as they fought to keep the decrepit woman alive. And yet, she could not deny the stirring of pity that she felt for her adoptive mother, nor the respect and affinity she had for the effectiveness of her rule. If there was one thing she had learned during her indoctrination, it was that the Queen, despite her circumstances and eccentricities, was an effective and dedicated ruler.

"Today, child," said the Queen, startling Alberta from her thoughts, "we shall talk of loyalty."

"Loyalty, Your Majesty?" echoed Alberta.

"Loyalty to family," said the Queen. "Loyalty to the Empire. Loyalty to what is good and proper."

Alberta nodded. "I believe I understand, Your Majesty," she said.

The Queen ignored her reply. "You shall learn of loyalty, Alberta, by looking upon the face of a traitor. One who would put his own interests above those of his country and his monarch. One whose greed became absolute and utterly consumed him."

"Of whom do you speak, Your Majesty?"

"See for yourself," replied Victoria, placing the lantern in the crease of her lap and grasping the wooden wheels on either side of her chair. She rolled herself forward, slowly and painfully.

Alberta gasped as she realised there was another person with them in the audience chamber. As the diffuse light of the lantern moved closer, she saw a man sitting in the shadows, bound to a chair, arms pinned behind his back. His legs were tied to the chair, and he was wearing a cloth gag so that he could not speak. It looked decidedly uncomfortable. He was a portly man, balding, with a large grey beard and hooded eyes that scowled at the monarch with ill-concealed rage. His grey suit was rumpled and creased, and stained with spots of what appeared to be spilled blood. She could not tell if it was his own.

Alberta recognised him at once. "Is this not..." She hesitated, unsure for a moment whether to continue. She decided it was better to go on rather than remain silent, under the circumstances. "Is this not your son, Albert Edward, the Prince of Wales, Your Majesty?" she asked, her tone level.

The Queen emitted a wet, rasping cackle. "It is a traitor," she replied, "and all traitors are as one in the eyes of the Empress. Remember that, Alberta. Blood shall count as nothing in circumstances such as these. Those who would betray us must pay dearly for their sins."

Alberta said nothing, but stared silently, curiously, at the pale face of the Prince.

Albert Edward raged in his chair at the Queen's words, struggling to break free and cursing ineffectually from behind his gag. His bonds, however, were expertly tied, and he did not have the strength to break them.

"This man," continued the Queen, "would take what is ours, Alberta. He works to undermine our power, to expose us so that he might claim our throne for his own. This insurrection will not be tolerated."

Alberta nodded. What would the Queen do, to this, her own son? Surely he would not hang like a common criminal?

"However, we are not, Alberta, wholly without mercy," said the Queen, as if reading her thoughts. "He shall not hang."

Alberta felt no relief at these words, simply a cool, collected interest. The effect on the Prince, however, was immediately visible. He slumped back in his chair and ceased his struggling. His demeanour softened. Alberta could see the relief in his eyes.

"No," went on the Queen. "For him, we have a different solution in mind." She glanced over her shoulder, into the looming shadows. "Warrender?" she called.

Alberta heard footsteps from behind her. The doctor apparently had also been lurking in the shadows. "Yes, Your Majesty," he said, his voice giving little away. Alberta shuddered.

"Have the traitor removed to a comfortable room at Bethlehem Hospital," she said. "I wish to hear of him no more. We shall suffer no mention of the man, and hear no reports of his progress."

"As you wish, Your Majesty," said Warrender, as the Prince began again to buck wildly in his chair.

The Queen, as if unprepared to witness this distasteful display, wheeled herself backwards, allowing the darkness to swallow the Prince once more. "You see now what becomes of traitors, Alberta. You must remember this moment. The time will come when you, too, will be forced to make such judgements."

"I understand, Your Majesty," she said again. Today, it seemed, she would avoid punishment. The appetite of her adoptive mother for such things had clearly been sated.

"Very good," said the Queen. "Now, run along. Return to your rooms. Your tutors will be wondering what has become of you. There is still much to be done."

"Yes, Your Majesty," said Alberta.

She turned and hurried from the audience chamber, pretending to ignore the sounds of struggling men as they fought to contain the Prince's desperate thrashing, and the sickening, vindictive cackle of his mother.

# EPILOGUE

❧

The Gare du Nord was as imposing as any of the major London railway stations, Amelia decided, as she stood on the bustling platform, jostled by the surging crowd of fellow travellers.

It was mid afternoon, and the sun was slanting in through the half-moon windows that lined the upper walls of the station, falling in great columns upon the multitudes below. Dust motes swirled and danced on eddies high above their heads.

The air was filled with the cloying scents of steam and smoke, and the clamour rang loudly in her ears: the hiss of pistons and the screech of whistles; the exhalations of the sighing engines; the chatter of a thousand or more people gathered beneath one roof.

Amelia glanced at Newbury, who looked broodingly handsome in his tailored black suit and top hat. His complexion, however, was almost as pale as his collar and cuffs, and he was thinner than she'd ever seen him. He did not wear his concern lightly. Behind him, a struggling porter fought to maintain his composure beneath the weight of their bags.

She studied the engine at rest at the platform before her. It was like nothing she could have imagined: a feat of engineering so miraculous that it might well have been born of a feverish dream, rather than designed on a drawing board by men of science. The gargantuan train snaked the entire length of the platform and beyond, its dark wooden panels and gold livery resplendent. The carriages themselves were two-storied and twice as tall as Newbury, even wearing his hat. Row upon row of gleaming windows reflected the sunlight, making it difficult to see into the cabins inside.

Earlier, she had watched in awe as the engine had arrived at the station, raging along the platform as if it were a fabulous mechanical beast at the close of a hunt, steam dribbling from the corners of its mouth. Now, even from where she was standing on the platform, she could still feel the intense heat of its furnace. She felt for the fire men who would feed such a thing as it dragged its huge payload across the Continent towards Russia.

Amelia couldn't help but feel a pang of trepidation at embarking on such a journey. Nevertheless, Veronica, in her comatose state, was relying upon them. There was little choice. "Confirm to me again, Sir Maurice, that this journey is absolutely necessary," she said, seeking reassurance.

Newbury looked over, his expression firm. He put his hand on her arm, gripping it intently, and she wondered for a moment if he wasn't clinging onto her as much for his benefit as hers. "Amelia, it is entirely necessary. If we are to help Veronica, then we must undertake this journey. Only the artisans of St. Petersburg can provide us with the intricate mechanisms we need to replace your sister's heart." Amelia nodded. "And," continued Newbury, "if I am to take such a journey, you understand that you must accompany me. It is the only way in which we can continue with your treatment. We will be gone for some weeks."

"Very well," said Amelia, forcing herself to smile. "Then we must continue as planned."

"I have booked us adjoining cabins," said Newbury, "that open into a shared living room. We should be comfortable." He smiled. "Come on, let's try to settle in whilst our fellow travellers board." He gestured to the porter, and the man, now sweating profusely, struggled across the platform towards the train. Newbury held the door open for Amelia, and together they boarded *L'Esprit du Paris* for the onward leg of their journey.

Across the platform, unseen by both Newbury and Amelia, a figure emerged from a recess by the ticket office. He was dressed in a black suit, and bore a distinguishing scar across his lower jaw, puckering his bottom lip. Within his pocket he clasped a dagger in his fist, its blade hewn from a shard of human femur, and around his throat he wore a necklace fashioned from the finger bones of the sacrificial victims he had killed with that very weapon.

He watched Newbury and Amelia as they boarded the immense train. Then slowly, purposefully, he crossed the platform, clambered up onto the shuddering vehicle, and located his own cabin.

Soon the Cabal would have their revenge against Sir Maurice Newbury, and he, the Keeper of the Blade, would reclaim for his brothers what was rightfully theirs. Not only that, but in so doing so he would be granted the honour of adding two further totems to his collection. His power, and his standing, would increase amongst his brothers.

The man's hand strayed unconsciously to the string of bones around his throat, and he smiled.

Newbury and Hobbes will return in
*The Revenant Express*

# ABOUT THE AUTHOR

George Mann was born in Darlington and is the author of over ten books, as well as numerous short stories, novellas and original audio scripts.

*The Affinity Bridge*, the first novel in his Newbury & Hobbes Victorian fantasy series, was published in 2008. Other titles in the series include *The Osiris Ritual*, *The Immorality Engine* and the forthcoming, *The Revenant Express*.

His other novels include *Ghosts of Manhattan* and *Ghosts of War*, mystery novels about a vigilante set against the backdrop of a post-steampunk 1920s New York, as well as an original *Doctor Who* novel, *Paradox Lost*, featuring the Eleventh Doctor alongside his companions, Amy and Rory.

He has edited a number of anthologies, including *The Solaris Book of New Science Fiction* and *The Solaris Book of New Fantasy*, and has written new adventures for Sherlock Holmes and the worlds of Black Library.

# GEORGE MANN
# SHERLOCK HOLMES:
## THE WILL OF THE DEAD

A young man named Peter Maugram appears at the
front door of Sherlock Holmes and Dr Watson's Baker
Street lodgings. Maugram's uncle is dead and his will
has disappeared, leaving the man afraid that he will be
left penniless. Holmes agrees to take the case and he and
Watson dig deep into the murky past of this complex
family.

A brand-new Sherlock Holmes novel from the
acclaimed author of the *Newbury & Hobbes* series.

Available November 2013

# GUY ADAMS
# SHERLOCK HOLMES:
## THE BREATH OF GOD

A body is found crushed to death in the London snow with no footprints anywhere near it. It is almost as if the man was killed by the air itself.

Sherlock Holmes and Dr Watson travel to Scotland to meet with the one person they have been told can help: Aleister Crowley. As dark powers encircle them, Holmes' rationalist beliefs begin to be questioned. The unbelievable and unholy are on their trail as they gather together the most accomplished occult minds in the country. But will they be enough? As the century draws to a close it seems London is ready to fall and the infernal abyss is growing wide enough to swallow us all.

# GUY ADAMS
# SHERLOCK HOLMES:
## THE ARMY OF DR MOREAU

Dead bodies are found on the streets of London
with wounds that can only be explained as the work of
ferocious creatures not native to the city.

Sherlock Holmes is visited by his brother, Mycroft,
who is only too aware that the bodies are the calling
card of Dr Moreau, a vivisectionist who was working
for the British Government, following in the footsteps
of Charles Darwin, before his experiments attracted
negative attention and the work was halted. Mycroft
believes that Moreau's experiments continue and he
charges his brother with tracking the rogue scientist
down before matters escalate any further.